SHIFTED

Shifted

HAVEN WYNNE

SHIFTED

HAVEN WYNNE

Perfectly Imperfect Productions

First edition

Dedication

For every victim who became a survivor.

Acknowledgements

I'm forever grateful for my supportive husband, and the unceasing encouragement he's given me as I follow my dreams. I would also like to thank the friends and coworkers who have been cheering me on as I took on the monumental task of writing my debut novel. I wish everyone had a tribe as wonderful as mine! I also want to give a shoutout to the amazing indie author community on Booktok who have shared invaluable advice all throughout this process. An extra big thanks goes out to my beta readers for their time, investment, and dedication to making "Shifted" the very best it could be!

Contents

Content Warning

"Shifted" includes several topics that may be upsetting or difficult to read. The following is a list of potential topics that may impact certain readers:

❖ Characters dealing with the aftermath of sexual assault and attempted murder.

❖ Both positive and negative character attitudes about sex work and sex workers.

❖ Explicit descriptions of consensual love scenes.

❖ Character discussions and involvement in crime and criminal activity including drug-dealing, exploitation of sex workers/human trafficking, assault, and murder.

❖ Scenes depicting violence including gun violence, physical fights/assaults, mob/mafia violence, fairytale violence, and mild gore.

Your mental health matters!

"THE CLOCK"

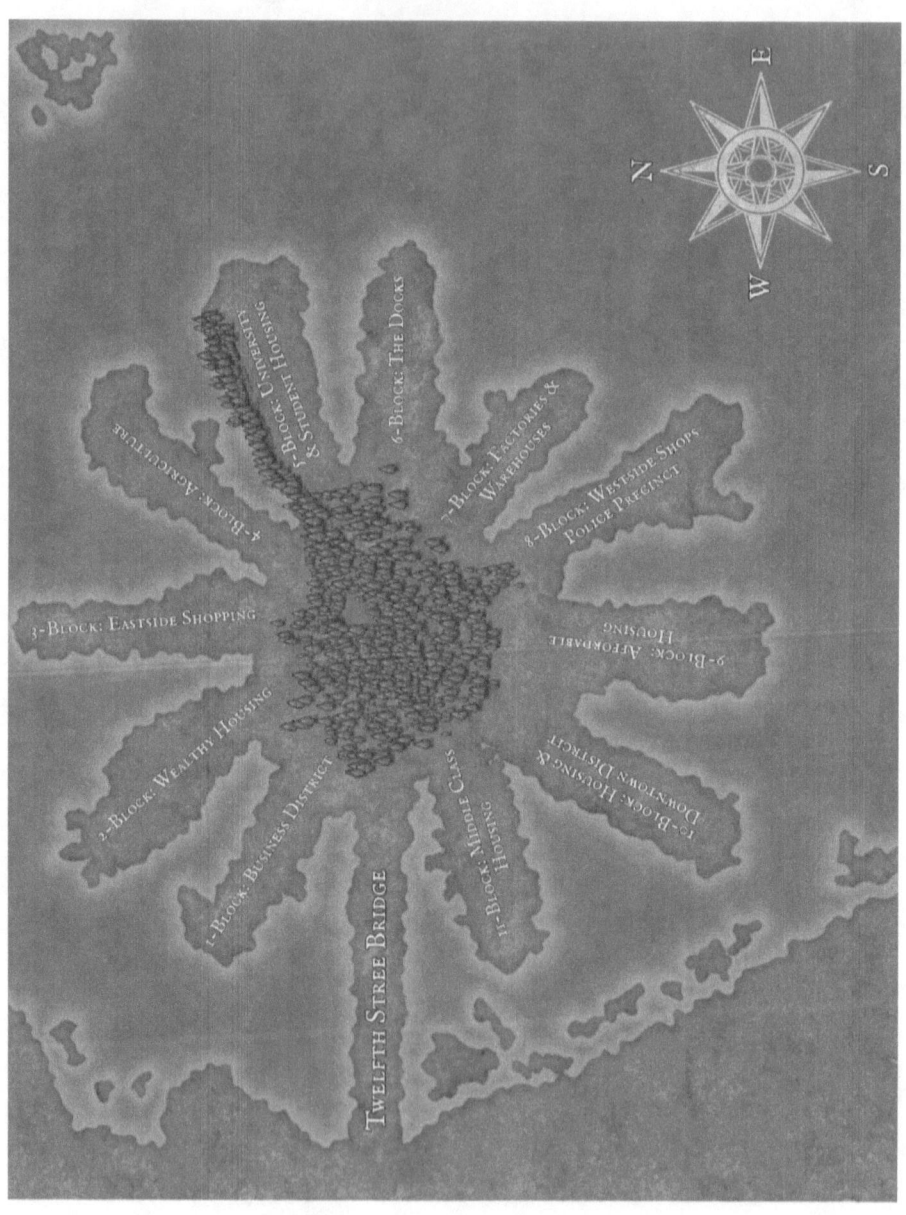

Chapter One

Alexis

I had to leave my whole life behind to save myself. The only thing I brought with me was fear.

My legs shook as I mounted the five cracked concrete steps to my new apartment building. Marshal Davis assured me he'd found the perfect placement. My call with one roommate had gone well, so I risked a tiny bit of hope. But as I looked up at the six-story red brick building, some of that hope faded.

The building loomed over me, its dusty windows casting silent judgment as I approached. It was ominous in the fading daylight. A scuff of gravel behind me tore my attention back over my shoulder. It was a motion I had become all too familiar with in the past eight months and thirteen days. But, hey, who was counting? The source of the noise that sent my heartbeat into turbo drive was an old woman taking out her trash cans. A mix of relief and exasperation washed over me. He's in prison. You're safe, I coached myself.

I took a deep, steadying breath and turned once more to face my new home. Narrow alleys separated the building from the ones on either side. All the buildings on the street stood closely spaced, well-worn brick with dark metal railings. The pockmarked asphalt road I'd come in on was a dead-end street.

I didn't like having my back to the street for long, so I tried to shake off my nerves before I pressed the buzzer on the panel next to the door with the peeling label "3A." Several nervous beats passed before a voice crackled through the intercom.

"Yeah?"

"Oh, hi…I, um, it's Alexis, your new roommate." Even though I'd practiced on the bus ride here, I couldn't hide the nervousness in my voice.

Silence hung heavy on the other end, followed by a round of fevered whispering.

"Hello?" I shifted my suitcase from one hand to the other.

"We'll buzz you in," a second voice eventually responded.

A grating buzz and a loud click sent my heart racing again as the lock disengaged, signaling that I could enter the building. I strained to open the heavy door one-handed, but was grateful for its sturdiness. Once inside on the main landing, a tight wooden staircase went down to my right and up to the left. The door to my left said "1A." Two flights up with suitcase in hand and I found myself at "3A." Before I could raise my fist to knock, the door to my new apartment flew open and a smiling woman with an olive complexion, kind face, and ample bosom greeted me.

"You must be Alexis," she beamed. She took two steps forward and wrapped me in a warm, tight embrace.

"You don't have to maul the girl, Moira," a woman standing behind her warned. This second young woman had jet black hair and more angular features, but there was a similarity between them that made me think they must be related. The second woman had her arms crossed over her chest and was frowning at the scene.

Moira pulled away and put her hands on her rosy cheeks and grinned. "Sorry, hun, I'm a hugger."

"Obviously," the second woman sighed.

"Come in, come in." Moira bustled past the woman in the doorway and motioned for me to follow. I gripped my suitcase tighter and ventured inside.

"Welcome to our little haven," Moira spread her arms wide.

The door snapped shut behind me and I jumped, looking over my shoulder to find the second woman examining me. A cold shiver ran down my spine. I took another deep breath and returned my attention to my surroundings.

We were standing in a small living room with a mustard yellow couch facing an old box television against the far wall. Just to the left was a kitchen with faded oak cabinets and a mint green refrigerator. The lights were dim and the chill in the air made me shiver.

"Your room is down this hallway," Moira waved past the kitchen, back behind my left shoulder. "It has an attached bathroom, so you don't have to worry about fighting for toilet time," she chuckled. I tried to muster a smile, but my face wouldn't quite cooperate.

"Our rooms are in the back," she pointed to a hall to the right. "Oh, I'm Moira, by the way," she gave a little wave. "...And that little storm cloud is my sister, Chloe." She rolled her eyes at the raven-haired woman behind me. "Our younger sister, Lacey, is back in her room. You'll meet her eventually; she's shy. Oh, and she's mute, so don't be offended when she doesn't speak to you. It's not because she doesn't like you."

"Okay," I squeaked out.

"We're thrilled to have you, and we'd love to show you around town to help you orient yourself as soon as you're ready." Moira's genuine warmth helped ease some of the tension that held my shoulders in a vise.

"Maybe you should let her go get settled, sister," Chloe interjected.

"Of course," Moira threw her hands up. "We'll leave you to it. Give us a holler if you need anything, Alexis."

"Thank you so much," I smiled weakly.

I headed down the hall to my room, trying not to look like I was running away from my new roommates. Closing the bedroom door behind me brought a deep sense of relief. I dropped my suitcase and scanned the room. It consisted of a full-sized bed with a metal frame, a tiny nightstand, a wooden chest of drawers, and a simple desk and chair. An empty closet with a broken sliding door was on the right and a darkened bathroom was a few feet away from that.

Suitably oriented to the space, I collapsed onto my back on the bed, arms splayed out at my sides. The sheets smelled freshly laundered, and a single red rose blossomed in a blue ceramic vase on my nightstand. Moira must have set up the room for my arrival. Chloe didn't exactly seem the type to leave a cozy touch for a stranger.

I closed my eyes and pressed my hands against my chest. Whenever my body stopped moving, my brain started sprinting. To ease the ache I felt, I took ten deep breaths, like my agency-appointed therapist had taught me. Anxiety had never been an issue for me until after it happened… but now it was my constant companion.

When the memories pressed hard against the flimsy, battered wall in my mind, I got up and opened my suitcase, busying myself once more by putting away the few outfits I'd been able to bring with me. The drawers of my dresser protested upon being opened and I couldn't close the broken door of the closet, but I felt more settled once I put my things away. The old laptop I had been given pinged to life as soon as I opened it at my new desk.

Things had been prepared for me in advance, which meant I would jump into my new life tomorrow morning. I would start the Social Work graduate program at the local university, as well as my job as a Victim's Advocate at the police precinct. It took a considerable amount of begging to convince Marshal Davis to let me continue the work I loved, but he reluctantly agreed.

He reasoned it out to his superiors that working in a police precinct would let them keep a closer eye on me and ensure my safety. Getting back to school and work were the first things I looked forward to for a long time.

With my class schedule set for the next day, I glanced over the campus map once more. Luckily, it was a small university, so I was confident I could find my way around within a few days. Maybe the familiarity of university life would help me adjust to my new surroundings.

Without much more to do, I closed the laptop and got ready for bed. I lingered in the shower, letting it ease the tension in my muscles, then slipped into the fresh smelling sheets. I screwed my eyes up tight and hoped against hope that tonight would be one of my distressingly infrequent nights of dreamless sleep.

When I woke up the next morning, I cursed the universe for its continued cruelty. The nightmares inevitably came and pulled me in and out of sleep all night. I did my best to calm myself as I dressed and went out into the kitchen. The earthy smell of brewing coffee permeated the room.

"How'd your first night go?" Moira smiled and handed me a steaming mug.

"Thank you," I sipped gratefully. "Mmm, just how I like it." I managed a small smile at Moira and her grin spread even wider.

"Then you have good taste," Moira nodded. "I figured you hadn't had time to buy any groceries, so I made you some breakfast. I hope you don't mind." She waved at a plate on the small round table by the back window of the apartment. "Do you like ham and cheese omelets?"

"Yes, I do, thank you. This was so thoughtful!" I sat on the blue cushioned chair and inhaled the warm scent of melted cheddar.

"Coming to a new place can be hard," Moira patted me on the shoulder. "We want you to feel welcome here. Chloe and Lacey already left for work, but I wanted to make sure you started your first day right."

My heart felt a little lighter as I looked into Moira's face. She radiated a genuine goodness, and I couldn't help but be pulled into her light.

"Do you need a ride somewhere?" Moira popped a piece of a muffin into her mouth. "I have a moped I use to putter around the Clock."

"The Clock?" I tilted my head to the side.

"It's a name we locals use for the city," she explained. "The city is laid out like a clock," she pulled a piece of paper off the kitchen counter and drew a clock face. "Since the 'Burg is surrounded by water, the only way you can get into town is from the Twelfth Street Bridge," she drew a line from the center of the clock straight up to the 12. "That brings you to the Face, the middle of the city. I'm sure you saw the woods in the middle of town when you came in."

I nodded.

She drew eleven more lines on the clock, each going directly to another number. "Each street matches up with another number on the clock. We live here on 10'o'block," Moira grinned at me. "Get it? It's like 10'o'clock but with…oh, you get it. We just call it 10-block. There's the business district on 1-block, mostly tech companies and rich men in suits. They all go home to their mansions on 2-block. Then 3-block is fancy shopping, 4-block is mostly agriculture, and 5-block has the University and student housing. Down on 6-block are the docks; shipping and freight and the stink of fish," she crinkled her nose.

"Then there are factories and warehouses on 7-block. Over on 8-block is a bunch of shops run by some of the 10-block locals and 9-block is mostly cheap housing. Here on 10-block we've got some more housing, a couple bars and clubs, and a bodega where we buy all our food and sundries. Last, 11-block is where the few middle-class people live, a nice park, and some mom-and-pop type restaurants. There you have it; the Clock." She set the pen down.

"Where's the police precinct?" I asked, staring at the drawing.

"It's on 8-block. You plan on bailing someone out of jail?" Moira winked at me.

"Ah, no. I'll be working at the station," I explained.

"Are you an officer?"

"No, a victim's advocate."

"Oh, that's tough work I gather."

"It is, but I love it. Do you mind if I keep this drawing? It's a lot to remember and it would help me get oriented."

"Of course!" She scribbled "precinct" onto the line by 8-block and slid it across the dining table to me. "How about that ride?"

"Um, sure." I folded up the map and stuck it in my pocket.

"Where are you headed?" Moira popped out of her seat, gathering her bag and keys.

"The University, uh, 5-block, right?"

"You're already getting the hang of it," she enthused.

"It's not too far out of your way, is it?"

"Nothing is too far out of the way in the Clock. It will only take me about 15 minutes to get to work from the University."

I grabbed my backpack and my laptop from my room, then met Moira out front. She gave me a key to the building and a second key to our apartment. I tucked them safely into the pocket of my jeans before I pulled on the helmet she'd handed me and climbed onto the back of her moped.

It was nice not having to talk on the drive since we couldn't hear each other, but I got the sense Moira was bursting to chat.

She dropped me in the middle of campus and gave me an enthusiastic wave as she drove off. I hoisted my backpack higher on my shoulders with a deep breath and blended into the bustle of campus. The buildings were Gothic-style structures that reminded me of old English estates. The wooded area around the perimeter of the grounds showcased leaves still clinging to their summer greenery.

The sun warmed the slight chill on the breeze; early autumn back home was still pretty hot. Mental note: buy warmer clothes. What block did Moira say shops were on again? I'd have to check the map in my pocket.

I went to my three classes: Social Policy, Psychopathology, and Forensic Theory & Practice. My cohort was small, with only six other students. They all seemed nice enough, but I kept to myself. The familiar rhythm of the classroom helped ease my anxiety. A part of me still resented having to start my grad studies all over again when I had been so close to graduating before this mess. But the program couldn't exactly transfer my credits when I was supposed to be a completely different person blending anonymously into a new city.

After class, I pulled out my phone to check the bus schedule. Bus number eight took me to the police precinct. 8-block looked like my new neighborhood on 10-block, but the precinct was distinctly newer than the other buildings. A blue "Beckburg Police Department" sign hung across the front of the cream brick building and some basic, well-kept landscaping around the base.

A bell above the door jingled as I entered the lobby, announcing my presence to the fair skinned, blonde receptionist with long, bubblegum pink fingernails. She glanced up from her boxy computer and raised her eyebrows at me. "Can I help you with something?"

"Yes, I'm Alexis… Alexis Henson, the new victim's advocate."

"Oh, yeah, yeah, yeah," she bent below the desk and reappeared with a manila folder. "This is your employee paperwork. You gotta fill it all out and then I'll go get the Chief for you."

My stomach dropped. There was no way I could remember all my new personal information without the cheat sheet the Marshal had given me. "The paperwork should already be done. It was emailed over last week." I hadn't done it, but Marshal Davis had.

"Nah, you gotta do it in person. It's department policy," the receptionist tapped her finger against the manila folder.

Panic was rising in my chest. I did my best to push it down. "My previous employer worked it out with Chief Whitmer after I was offered the job. He should already have all my paperwork."

The receptionist sighed heavily and rolled her eyes. "It's never been done that way, honey," she scolded. She appeared to be about my age, and I didn't take kindly to being called 'honey.' "You gotta follow procedure around here or everything goes to hell." She slid the manila folder over the desk toward me and tapped it again.

"Could you get Chief Whitmer and ask him about it? I'm sorry to be a bother, but maybe he forgot to mention it to you." I shifted from foot to foot.

"The Chief doesn't just forget things like that, and he tells me everything," she insisted. "It's you that's wrong here, sweetheart." She tapped the folder three times and glared.

"Brittney, has the new hire...oh!" A tall, heavyset man with an ashen pallor and a salt and pepper beard walked into the waiting area. "You must be Alexis." He reached out a hand to me. "Chief Whitmer."

We shook hands.

"It's a pleasure to meet you, sir."

"She hasn't filled out her new hire paperwork yet, Chief," Brittney tattled.

"It's taken care of already, Brittney," he easily dismissed her obvious annoyance.

"But, Chief," Brittney started.

"It's already taken care of. I'll take Ms. Henson from here," he waved me down the hall. I spared one last glance at Brittney as we walked away. She looked like she'd been force-fed a raw lemon.

"Let me show you around and then we'll head back to my office to get you caught up to speed. You're the first victim's advocate we've ever hired. You're a bit of a guinea pig to see if it works with our boys or not."

The Chief kept pace with me. He had a distinct air of understated confidence about him.

"Copy room is to your left, lockers to your right. Down that hall are the bathrooms, evidence lock-up, and interrogation rooms three and four." He turned a corner into a spacious room filled with desks, bustling cops, and suited detectives. "This here is the think tank. My office is back and to the left, interrogation rooms one and two to the back right, and the break room is to the right." I cataloged the directions in my mind as he spoke. "I'll give you a proper introduction to the crew when you come in tomorrow morning at round table."

We crossed over to his office. He closed the door behind us and offered me a seat before taking one across the desk from me in a worn leather rolling chair. He gazed at me with kind eyes and interlaced his fingers atop the desk.

"I just got off the phone with Marshal Davis before you got here. He wanted to be sure everything was set up for you today."

"He's a good man. He's helped me a lot," I nodded.

"I want to assure you I'm the only one here at the precinct who knows your history. We'll do check-ins every once in a while, but if you ever need anything, you let me know. What you've been through is unconscionable and we're gonna take good care of you."

"That means a lot to me, Chief Whitmer, thank you." Tears welled in my eyes, and I blinked hard to hold them at bay. It was a relief knowing at least one person here knew my history without me having to relive it.

"Today you'll be reviewing the files of the cases you'll be working. We were thinking of having you bounce around from case to case, detective to detective as needed, but I'm not gonna lie, a few of the boys weren't too keen on the idea. So, we settled on partnering you up with Detectives Alvarez and Briggs."

It was a kick to the gut knowing that the men and women I would work with had played an office-wide game of "Not It" to avoid working with me. I did my best to swallow my pride. It wasn't uncommon for outsiders like advocates and social workers to be seen as more of a pain in the ass than they're worth. It wasn't personal; at least that's what I kept telling myself.

"They're good men, solid detectives, and they make a damn good team," Chief Whitmer continued. "They work most of the violent crimes that come in, so it makes the most sense to put you on those cases. Alvarez damn near jumped for joy to have the help, but Briggs might take a little time to see what an asset you can be."

"Will I be meeting them today?" I asked, looking over my shoulder out the window overlooking the think tank.

"Nah, they're out on a case, but you'll meet them tomorrow. I'm gonna put you in interrogation one with your case files. I can't say the reading will be peaceful, but the room will be the quietest place for you to do your work."

The Chief stood from his desk, and I followed suit. "The room's all set up for you." He opened the door and walked me to a door with a metal number 1 screwed into it. "Give me a holler if you need something." He opened the door and gave me one last nod before heading back into his office.

The door to interrogation one closed heavily as I settled at the metal table surrounded by at least a dozen boxes. I shifted them to one side, skimming the labels, and organizing them alphabetically. Having a system always helped me focus. I lifted the top off the box marked "Benicio, Maria," pulled out a stack of files, and started to read.

I felt a familiar clench in the pit of my stomach as I read what this poor woman had gone through, especially knowing that I would be tasked with helping her navigate the rest of the investigation and potential court case. No matter how many cases I assisted on before my own happened, I never got used to the brutality one human being could inflict on another. Returning to this work now, after what I'd been through, I had a new, visceral understanding of the victims. For Maria's sake, and the rest of the victims represented by the stack of boxes next to me, I hoped I was still up for the challenge.

Chapter Two

Alexis

I rested my forehead against the window of the bus on my way back to my apartment. I made decent headway with the case files, but there was still so much more to go. All those stories of pain and suffering affected me deeply, especially now... But that was exactly the reason I had become a victim's advocate in the first place. Those victims deserved to have someone witness their stories—no matter how dark— and stand by their side. Someone had to make sure they got the support and protection they needed in a system that failed them spectacularly. I was more than willing to be that someone.

The bus lurched to a stop and hissed as it lowered to allow passengers to disembark. The grip I had on the kubaton in my pocket tightened. Darkness swallowed up the city hours ago. My shoulders were tight the entire walk home from the bus stop, but I made it safely.

"Surprise!" Moira squealed as I opened the door.

I almost jumped out of my skin.

"Oh God, sorry to frighten you!" She hurried over and patted my shoulder. "Surprise," she whisper-shouted. She pulled me over to the dining table where Chloe and a very petite woman with olive skin and enormous eyes sat staring back at me curiously. "We got you some dinner and made you a cake!"

My heartbeat slowed as I took in the scene. Moira was beaming, gesturing to a butter-cream yellow cake with tiny pastel pennants hanging from a suspended line. I tried to admire the cake, but it was hard to take my eyes off the glassy gray eyes of the petite woman at the table.

"Ah, this is Lacey, our younger sister," Moira added.

"It's nice to meet you, Lacey," I greeted. She gave me a timid smile and a wave.

"Come sit down and enjoy," Moira ushered me to an empty chair. "How was your first day?"

Moira had all the energy of a proud mama. She took a seat next to Chloe, giving me her full attention as she served the fried chicken and mashed potatoes onto four plates, then set one in front of each of us. Chloe watched me wordlessly. Lacey shifted her wide-eyed attention to her food.

"It went well, surprisingly," I responded.

"Why surprisingly?" Moira inquired.

"I didn't expect things to go so smoothly. Things have been anything but smooth for me lately. It helped that school and work are like what I was doing before…" I hesitated and covered the near slip by taking a bite of my mashed potatoes. They were silky and buttery on my tongue. Moira waited for me to finish.

"It's a lot like what I was doing before I moved here, you know. It made the newness of it so much easier."

"I'm glad to hear it." Moira nodded. Chloe shot Moira a look.

We lapsed into silence as we ate. The food was excellent. I thought about thanking the chef but hesitated to start another round of conversation. They all kept stealing glances at me out of the corner of their eyes. It was unnerving.

"You should come out dancing with us tonight," Moira broke the silence.

"Moira, stop pestering her," Chloe admonished.

"Oh, I'm not trying to be a pest and you know it," Moira playfully slapped Chloe's arm. "We really want you to be comfortable here, and I think it would be good for you to meet some people." She looked at me with hope sparkling in her eyes.

Going out seemed like the worst kind of torture, but Marshal Davis's voice sprang to mind. "Remember, it's important for you to blend in. Do nothing that draws attention to yourself. Fit in." I bit the inside of my lip.

"You don't have to come if you don't want to." Chloe rolled her eyes.

The disappointment forming in Moira's face was my undoing.

"I'd love to come," I stammered. Regret reared up the second the words passed my lips. "I'll need a while to get cleaned up…uh, where are we going? I don't have anything really fancy or anything." The meager contents of my closet were mostly casual jeans and t-shirts and a couple of business casual pantsuits for work.

"You don't have to get any type of fancy for where we're going," Moira started clearing plates. "The One Trick Pony is anything but fancy."

Chloe nodded in agreement.

"It's our favorite bar, just down the street. Most everyone wears regular street clothes," Chloe pushed off from the table. "If you get too dolled up, you'll stick out like an attention-seeking thumb."

"Chloe," Moira scolded.

"What? Do you want our new roommate to get a reputation, dear sister? Do you want her to be the next Milani?"

Lacey shook her head rapidly and covered her face. It was Moira's turn to roll her eyes.

"Of course not! I want her to be respected, not reviled."

"Casual it is," I interjected to break the tension. "Is thirty minutes okay? You don't have to wait for me if you want to leave sooner." I hoped they would want to leave sooner.

"It will take at least that long for Chloe to reapply her smoky eye, so no problem," Moira teased. Lacey covered her mouth while her shoulders shook.

"You think that's funny?" Chloe cracked a rare smile at Lacey's response. Lacey nodded, her dark hair bobbing. "We'll see who thinks it's funny when you want me to help with your makeup to look cute for Todd." Chloe sang the name.

Lacey's eyes grew wider, which I didn't think was possible, and she shook a finger at Chloe. She smoothed her hair back and headed back toward her room. Chloe followed suit.

"Chloe's going to find a surprise in her high heels if she's not careful," Moira laughed. "Sister stuff," she explained before heading back to get ready herself.

I took my time getting ready, washing the old makeup off my face and applied a new layer. I spent extra time on my eyeliner and eyeshadow to make my blue eyes pop, then picked my favorite blue shirt to match. My long brown hair still held onto the curls I put into it this morning, so I called it good and met the sisters out in the living room.

"To the One Trick Pony!" Moira called, raising a fist in the air.

"Woo hoo," Chloe replied sarcastically.

We took a left after leaving our building and made our way down the cracked sidewalk, Moira chatting the whole way. She pointed out apartment buildings and the people she knew who lived in them, the Hernandez Family Bodega that was open 24/7 for groceries and other necessities, and even a stray cat or two that she had named and created life stories for.

When we reached the One Trick Pony, it was exactly how I pictured a back-alley bar would look: A rearing horse sign hanging over the entrance, neon signs advertising the beer on tap hanging in the dusty windows, and thumping bass reverberating through the walls.

"Good evening, Taron," Moira inclined her head at the burly security guard at the entrance.

"Ladies," Taron replied in a deep tone. Moira made to enter, but Taron held up a hand. "Who's the spare?" he pointed to me.

"This is our new roommate, Alexis." Moira hooked her arm in mine. I waved a hello.

Taron examined me. "You vouch for her?" he asked, his gaze intense.

"She's good people," Moira replied with confidence, pulling me closer.

"She's on you," Taron shrugged. He stepped out of the way for us to pass.

"What was that about?" I asked Moira as we filtered into the bar.

"Oh, nothing," she dismissed. "Taron is just protective; it is his job, after all. We're a pretty tight-knit group around here, so a new face puts him on guard."

"Okay," I shrugged. But I still felt the discomfort of being scrutinized following me as we weaved our way through round tables, scuffed chairs, and pool tables to arrive at the bar.

"Well, if it isn't the tenacious trio of 10-block," the bartender called as we approached. He was a willowy man with the smoothest, fairest skin I had ever seen. He had a small hoop earring in one ear and a dangling feather earring in the other.

"Woah, woah, woah! Since when did the trio become a quartet?" he asked, taking me in.

"Since yesterday." Chloe tucked a strand of her raven hair behind her ear and smiled at the bartender. He gave her a million-watt smile.

"Alexis, meet Riel," Chloe introduced.

Riel stretched a long arm over the bar for a handshake.

"It's a genuine pleasure to meet you," he beamed.

"Likewise." I had to raise my voice over a round of cheering from the pool tables.

"Alright, fresh blood, what'll you have?" Riel whipped a hand towel over his shoulder.

The tightness returned to my stomach. New environment, new people, lots of unknowns… the battle to fit in pulled me from one side, but the need to stay in control pulled me from the other. My anxiety won out, so I decided to stay sober.

"Would you be less pleased to meet me if I ordered a Shirley Temple?" I forced a chuckle.

Lacey's eyebrows shot up, and she clapped her hands together. She pointed enthusiastically to herself, then to Riel.

"It's your lucky night, newbie! I just so happen to make the sweetest Shirley Temple this side of the Rio Grande, thanks to this little lady," Riel gestured to Lacey.

Lacey put her hand over her heart, licked her lips, and sighed.

"Your favorite, I'm guessing," I winked. She nodded vigorously, gave me a quick side hug, then settled onto a stool at the bar.

"The usual for you ladies?" Riel motioned to Chloe and Moira. They both nodded. "Coming right up!"

Moira pulled me onto a stool next to her, spinning me around on it to face the rest of the bustling room. "I hope you have an excellent memory, because I'm about to tell you everything you need to know about the 10-block social scene."

"You should have warned me to bring a notebook," I joked.

"Don't worry, she's always talking about it, so you'll have a hard time forgetting." Chloe leaned back and surveyed the room with us.

Moira looked at Chloe with a gleam in her eye. "You've met Riel, the object of Chloe's deepest affections…"

"Moira!" Chloe shot a look over her shoulder. Lucky for her, Riel was grabbing something down the counter.

"The gentlemen, and I use that term very loosely, over by the dartboard are the Knuckle Crew. They always get wasted right off the bat and they're more than a little slow on the uptake." Sure enough, empty tankards surrounded them, and they were right in the middle of talking a member of the group into holding the dartboard in his hands while they took aim.

"The group in the corner booth is our friend Donna and her party crew. Don't take anything they offer you or you might wake up in a treehouse with a tattoo of a mushroom on your face."

"Got it. No taking stuff from the corner booth crowd."

"The lady by the jukebox is Jukebox Hiro…"

"She's got stars in her eyes," Chloe sang. I chuckled.

"She's obsessed with music. You'll have to bring a stack of quarters and fight Hiro off if you ever want to play a song of your choosing." Moira finished.

Hiro bobbed her head to the sound of "Crazy Train," making her electric green and purple hair bounce in time with the music.

"The group at the pool tables are some more of our friends: Ricky, Grace, Taylor, and the pool sharks. They're a hell of a good time, but don't put any money on a game with them. You'll never see that green again."

She swiveled on her barstool and continued to point people out in the crowd. I should have brought a notebook because I was losing track quickly. Moira seemed to know every single person at the One Trick Pony.

"Ah! And here comes trouble," she finished, waving toward the front door.

Two men were striding our way. One had bronze skin, a fedora, and a roguish smirk. The other was tall and tanned, with dirty blonde hair and thick stubble along his chiseled jaw. They were both dressed in button up collared shirts, slacks, and loosened ties; the first in neutral browns and the second in blues and grays.

My eyebrows rose; they were both genuinely good-looking. I made eye contact with the taller one and he cocked his head to the side, studying me as much as I was studying him. His eyes were searching and skeptical.

"My beauties, my beauties," the man in the fedora raised his arms in greeting. "What a lovely surprise to see you here tonight." He hugged Lacey, got rejected for a hug by Chloe, and winked at Moira. "And who might this beautiful creature be?" He motioned to me with one hand over his heart.

"Alexis, our new roommate, you blatant ass-kiss," Chloe replied. She spun her chair back around to face the bar as Riel placed a martini on the counter next to her.

"Alexis, this is Andre…" Moira introduced.

The fedora-clad man kissed the back of my hand. "Enchantee."

"…and Finn," she motioned to the tall man still taking my measure. He nodded silently to me, then leaned against the bar.

"You get used to the strong, silent treatment," Andre patted Finn on the back. "Can I buy you a drink, Alexis?"

"Sorry, Andre, I already have the lady taken care of," Riel passed me my Shirley Temple.

"Riel knows the way to a lady's heart is through her bloodstream." Andre waggled his eyebrows.

"Thanks for the anatomy lesson," I laughed.

"I'm an anatomy expert," Andre flashed me a grin.

"God, could you be any grosser?" Chloe complained. She pushed away from the bar and took me by the arm, leading me away to the dance floor. "Sorry about Andre. He seems like the exact kind of creep you try to avoid at the bar, but he's not all that bad. He's just showing off."

"I don't mind him," I replied. "My creep radar isn't pinging yet, so he's in the clear for now." I looked back at the bar. Andre and Moira were in an animated conversation while Finn swirled his drink. Lacey was happily sipping her own Shiley Temple, seemingly oblivious to everything else around her.

"You didn't have to come out with us tonight, you know," Chloe set her martini on an empty table. "Moira can be a lot sometimes. She means well, but her enthusiasm can be a little…much."

"No, she's been wonderful. Really, I couldn't have asked for a better welcome. And she's right, I needed to get out. Meeting your friends has been nice."

"I'm kind of a bitch," Chloe blurted.

"No," I tried to reassure her, but a part of me resonated with her statement.

"No, really," she held up her hand to stop me. "I am. It's not me shitting on myself, it's a deliberate choice. There's a lot to learn about a person you don't know, and I like to keep my guard up until I see what they're made of."

"At least you're self-aware."

"Right," she chuckled.

"So, what have you decided about me?"

"So far, you're not half bad," she shrugged. "You've put up with my big sister with the patience of a saint and been kind to my little sister. You're not a drunk," she nodded at my Shirley Temple. "You didn't slap Andre for his bullshit… But there's still a lot to be seen."

"That's valid. A day and a half doesn't tell you much about a person. I'll do my best to keep showing you I'm not a bad person."

"Just as long as you remember that the bitch thing isn't personal," Chloe patted my arm and glided away.

The music shifted to a rock ballad. A few couples took the floor to dance. I sat at a table, my back pressed against the wall, and did some people watching. Jukebox Hiro was pretending to sing into an invisible microphone to my right. I sipped my drink and watched the hustle and bustle around me. The vibe was good here: joyful, cozy, and warm. It wasn't like bars back home where you constantly had to dodge grabbing hands as strangers barfed on each other's shoes.

If only I could relax and just be in the moment. But even as I watched the obvious camaraderie around me, I still felt on edge. Fear was such an omnipresent part of my life that I had become almost numb to it. The energy at the One Trick Pony made me yearn for the relief of a genuine sense of home, safety, and comfort. I wanted to let go, relax, but I couldn't make myself. It was like waiting for a charley horse to release with no end in sight.

My first full day in Beckburg had given me the tiniest amount of hope, though. As Moira's boisterous laugh echoed through the room, I smiled to myself. What if I could finally relax here, now that I was far, far away from my problems? My mind wanted to embrace the thought, but my body tensed. Even with the warm welcome so far, I was still waiting for the other shoe to drop.

My skin prickled with the familiar feeling of being watched. My nervous eyes scanned the room until they found Finn. His gaze met mine. Instead of looking away when I caught him staring, he kept staring. His gaze was searing, searching, and analytical. I narrowed my eyes at him before turning to look away.

Maybe *he* was the other shoe.

Chapter Three

Finn

The Bianchi case had been consuming me for months. We thought we'd gotten a lead on their money laundering operation down on 7-block, but by the time we arrived, someone had wiped the warehouse clean. Not a single fucking shred of paper left behind. I wanted to pull my hair out. Those assholes were damn near untouchable!

Every cop in Beckburg knew that the Bianchis's businesses on 1-block and their real estate holdings all around the Clock were fronts for their criminal enterprise, but we couldn't get enough proof to make it stick. Every time we thought we were on to something, they were ten steps ahead of us. Always. And those assholes knew that if you threw the right amount of money to the right people, you could avoid a lot of trouble. Their charitable donations alone kept them legitimate in the eyes of the powerful elite in the Clock. But we knew better.

When Andre insisted that we head to the Pony to clear our heads and drown our sorrows, it didn't take long for me to agree. I could use the distraction. Taron gave us a wordless nod as we entered, and we caught Moira's shrewd eye the second we came through the door.

"Ah, and here comes trouble," Moira called.

A woman I didn't recognize sat next to her. My guard instantly went up. I inhaled fully, deliberately, then frowned.

"What do you think of her?" Andre whispered.

"Woman in her mid- to late twenties, about five foot seven, brown hair, blue eyes…"

"You gotta learn to describe a person without treating them like a perp," Andre shook his head.

I ignored his chiding and continued assessing her. She eventually caught me staring. Perp-glasses off, she was attractive enough, intelligent eyes, but with an undercurrent of nervous energy.

"My beauties, my beauties! What a lovely surprise to see you here tonight," Andre schmoozed. "And who might this beautiful creature be?"

"Alexis, our new roommate, you blatant ass-kiss," Chloe snapped.

Hmm, the new roommate. Moira mentioned that a new person was moving into their perpetually empty back bedroom. Their last renter only lasted a few days before they'd run off on some drug bender and never came back for their stuff. I tried telling Moira that she needed to vet people more carefully, but she wouldn't listen. She never listened to things like that. She always knew better than I did.

Moira introduced us, and I gave her—Alexis—a courtesy nod.

"You get used to the strong, silent treatment," Andre slapped me on the back. "Can I buy you a drink, Alexis?"

"Sorry, Andre, I already have the lady taken care of." Riel slid a drink to her. The cherry was a dead giveaway. Non-alcoholic. A lightweight? A recovering alcoholic? A religious nut?

"Riel knows the way to a lady's heart is through her bloodstream," Andre flirted. I had to hold in an eye-roll. That man was a walking case of second-hand embarrassment around women. It was his unending confidence that made it work at all.

"Thanks for the anatomy lesson," Alexis bantered in return. She had a pleasant laugh.

"I'm an anatomy expert."

Andre was really trying to work his magic tonight. Normally I would step in as his wingman, but something held me back. I didn't know if it was my preoccupation with the case or the woman he was laying it on thick for.

"God, could you be any grosser?" Chloe pulled Alexis away, and I focused my attention on my drink. Throw enough Scotch at a problem and either you disappear, or it does.

"What's the word on the new girl?" Andre continued.

"She's just lovely," Moira gushed. "So kind and smart as a whip. Really dedicated to doing the right thing and taking care of others. She can be a little jittery, probably comes with her own set of demons, but who doesn't?"

"What kind of demons?" I asked.

"Who's to say?" Moira evaded. "A woman's story is her own, and if she wants to tell anyone about it, she'll do it in her own time."

This time I didn't hold back my eye roll. I should have known better than to ask. Lacey put her little hand on my arm and looked at me seriously.

"I know, kid. I know." I sighed. She seemed satisfied by that response and turned back to her kiddie drink. Riel was already bringing her a bowl of cherries to go with it. Her innocence always grounded me, despite my mood.

"Well, I'm always up for a good story!" Andre adjusted the brim of his hat.

"You're going to make yourself look like an ass if you keep pushing this hard, man," I warned.

"Says who, Finn?"

"She doesn't seem the type to be schmoozed," I shrugged. "Call it intuition."

Andre checked with Moira. She gave him a polite but hesitant grin. "He's not wrong," she confirmed.

"Damn, I'm off my game. I'm coming in too hot." Andre straightened his tie, and everyone laughed.

Chloe rejoined the group and tapped the bar for another drink. Riel rushed off to comply.

"I'll take it as a personal favor if you stop trying to get into our new roommate's pants," Chloe rounded on Andre.

"At least let her settle in a bit before you overwhelm her," Moira added.

"You don't want your new friend to end up with a stud like me?" Andre batted his eyelashes. "It would be fantastic."

"I have zero desire to listen to you down the hall from me attempting to reach 'fantastic,'" Chloe quipped. "Do us all a favor, Alexis especially, and set your sights on a different bed buddy for the night."

"I'm hurt, Clo, truly."

Chloe and Andre continued to squabble back and forth, but my attention was across the room on the object of their conversation. Alexis seemed deep in thought. All I could think about as I studied her were the demons Moira alluded to. I didn't enjoy being out of the loop. Sure, everybody has their demons, but I need those demons to be known to me if you're going to be around me and my people. Once I know what I'm facing, there's no fear. The demons I came across were nothing compared to the demons I possessed.

Alexis turned and caught me sizing her up. Her muscles tensed at the attention, but she didn't look away. Her social smile slipped and was replaced by thinly veiled concern. She had an expressive face, and that made her easy to read. Curiosity was already setting in. Nobody ended up in the Clock for no reason and I wanted to know hers.

"Are you buzzed enough that I can talk you onto the dance floor, sister?" Moira tugged at Chloe's arm.

Lacey jumped out of her seat and grabbed hold of Chloe's other arm. Lacey smiled, exposing a line of cherries across her teeth. Chloe burst out laughing. Moira took the opportunity to drag her to the dance floor.

"Alexis, come dance with us," Moira called.

Alexis rose from her lonely table and joined them with more than a brief hesitation. Had I made her nervous? She was avoiding my gaze as the sisters twirled her around.

"What do you think?" Andre asked.

"What do you mean? What do I think?"

"You've been staring at her since we got here. I know that look. What have you read so far?"

"She gets unnerved easily, like Moira said. Not much else to tell." Another swig of my Scotch burned my throat. I slid the empty glass to Riel. He had a second glass already waiting for me. I nodded my appreciation.

"That's it?" Andre popped one of Lacey's abandoned cherries into his mouth.

"I haven't even spoken to the woman, Andre. What else am I supposed to know?"

"Do you have a good sense about her, I mean?" Andre was serious this time. He wasn't asking his wingman whether he should take her home. He wanted to know what I wanted to know. Is she safe?

"She isn't like us," I confirmed. "But she doesn't raise the hackles on the back of my neck, either."

"That's enough for me," Andre huffed.

"Andre," a sugary voice called from across the bar.

"Milani," Andre puffed out his chest and extended his arms. He strode off toward the corner, back on the prowl. The man was an enigma with the way he could shift from serious to perfectly cool in an instant. I didn't share the same talent.

"You okay, Finn?" Riel was wiping a tankard.

"The usual, Riel."

"Work is kicking your ass and you're too obsessed to take a break?"

Ouch. The man had an eye for the truth. But he didn't need to call me out about it.

I gulped the rest of my drink and slid the second empty glass back to him. "That was low, even for you, bartender." Riel chuckled, and I pushed off the bar.

The rest of my night consisted of playing pool with the sharks. I didn't have any cash to bet, but they kept their noses clean around me and my badge. I kept an eye on the sisters and their new roommate throughout the night, and my opinion of her started to form. She smiled a lot, too much for my taste. If a person smiled that often, how did you know if they were ever sincere?

She split her attention equally between the sisters, including Lacey, which was a rarity. Most of 10-block ignored the silent sister. Her silence scared them. They knew what she was capable of, so most steered clear. But the new roommate seemed clueless. I'd have to ask Moira just how much she knew, but I suspected it was very little, if anything at all. There was no concern if she knew nothing; the sisters knew better than most how to keep a secret.

She drank nothing else the rest of the night; she finished her virgin mocktail soon after Andre and I arrived and didn't return to the bar except to rest and chat with the others. A few of the locals came over to introduce themselves to the unfamiliar face. Curiosity from the rest of the patrons of the Pony followed her wherever she went. Her body language betrayed her nervousness at the approach of each new stranger, but her smile rarely faded.

By midnight, I'd tired of playing pool and wandered back to the bar with the others. Ricky, Vikram, and Vijay had joined them, and the laughter echoed from every side. I settled wordlessly at the edge of the group.

"Then our mother demanded to know what I had done with Vikram," Vijay was recounting. "I thought for sure she was going to hear him from outside the door, but the music was so loud."

"It also helped that he'd taped my mouth shut," Vikram inserted.

The group laughed.

"Did I forget to mention that part?" Vijay stroked his chin. "Anyway, once I'd convinced Mother that he was still at the library studying, the revenge really began. Without getting into the gory details, let's just say the hot wax I stole from our sister works as well on a man's leg as a woman's, maybe better."

Uproarious laughter erupted. Vijay was wiping tears from his eyes and Vikram's cheeks were pink. I paid special attention to Alexis, continuing my investigation into the woman. She laughed along with the group, but she caught me staring once more. A determined look formed on her face, and she shifted in her chair.

"Ever had your legs waxed by a vengeful brother, Finn?" she asked.

"Excuse me?" I cocked my head to the side.

"If not forced leg waxing, any other pranks by pesky siblings?" Both her tone and expression were challenging me.

"Nope," I shrugged.

"C'mon, never?" She was clearly trying to get a rise out of me.

"I'm an only child." I crossed my arms over my chest.

We were in a stare down.

"Chloe used to pour motor oil in my shampoo when she was upset with me," Moira piped in, trying to break the sudden tension. "I could never understand why my hair always looked so greasy, no matter how many times I washed it."

A round of forced laughter went around the group, but Alexis didn't break eye contact. There was another attribute I could add to my growing list: stubbornness. It was a battle of wills between us. Who would be the first to break?

The awkward silence went on long enough that Vikram, Vijay, and Ricky excused themselves. From my periphery, I caught Andre and Milani leaving together. There went my ride. But still Alexis and I stared each other down.

"I think it's about time we called it a night," Moira fake yawned.

She looped her arm through Alexis' and gave her a gentle tug. It forced Alexis to look away to avoid falling off her barstool. When she turned back to me, I was already giving her a triumphant smirk.

"Goodnight, Finn. Goodnight, Riel," Moira called down the bar.

Chloe took Alexis' other arm and Lacey gave me a docile wave. I gave her a half smile. As they left the bar, I felt a strange mix of satisfaction and defeat.

I slapped a twenty on the bar. Riel nodded farewell. Even though I'd lost my ride, it didn't bother me a bit. Running was one of my favorite forms of transportation. It helped me clear my head. I took off through the shadows of 10-block toward home.

If there was one thing to be said for tonight, it had taken my mind of the Bianchi case. Now it was placed squarely on Alexis. If I couldn't solve my actual case, maybe I could figure *her* out.

. . . . .

"Another day, another criminal," Andre slapped me on the back in the locker room. "You look like hell, man."

"Thanks for the confidence boost." I slammed my locker closed and adjusted my holster. "You look like you got wrung out by a succubus."

"She wrung me out *real* good!"

"I don't want to know."

"My girl Milani has moves I've never seen before," Andre continued as we headed to our morning round table. I straightened the cuffs of my sleeves and kept my eyes straight ahead. "Why you haven't ever showed an interest in her is beyond me, my friend."

"You show enough interest in her for the both of us. What's last night, six or seven times you've taken her home?"

"A man's got needs."

A crowd was already forming in the center of the office. My long strides were a special gift today. I wasn't eager to listen to my partner's sexual exploits when I was in such a dry spell. A few people greeted me before I settled on the edge of my desk, waiting for round table to start.

"Alright, ladies and gentlemen," Chief Whitmer called over the crowd. "Bring it down," he waved the noisy chatter away. The Chief commanded respect without demanding it. "We've got a few cases on the board that need to be assigned. There was a robbery at Delgado's at two a.m. Yamir and Hodgkins, that's yours." A clerk handed a folder to the assigned detectives.

"We got a round of complaints from 2-block about some shady characters lurking around. Jensen and Aster, shine up your shoes and head over." A few people chuckled. "Patrol is noticing some increased drug activity on 9-block, so Olivier and Lot, that'll be on you. Last up, we had another beating down at the docks that follows a familiar pattern. Alvarez and Briggs, you know what to do."

I sighed. Not even a single cup of coffee yet, and I was already dealing with more shit from the Bianchi family. I pinched the bridge of my nose.

"That's it, back to work," Chief called. The crowd dispersed. "Alvarez and Briggs," Chief strode over to us. "I've got one more thing for you. Follow me."

"What's up, Chief?" Andre asked.

"Remember that new project we're trying out?" Chief led us to interrogation one. "I've got someone to introduce you to."

Chief opened the door, and my jaw dropped.

"Gentlemen, this is Alexis Henson, our first victim's advocate. She's going to be partnering with you on some of your cases, as we discussed."

Andre was doing a cartoon double take between Chief and Alexis. Her expression mirrored my own. She was sitting at the table surrounded by stacks of boxes… our case files. My chest tightened at the thought of someone other than my partner reading through my cases.

"We meet again," Andre managed. "Good to see you, Alexis."

"You've met?" Chief furrowed his brows.

"Just last night," I responded. "She's living with some friends of ours."

"I hope you didn't stay up too late, boys. You've got a lot to catch Alexis up on." He motioned to the organized chaos around her. "Have at it." He closed the door behind him.

The room was silent. Even Andre seemed to struggle to find something to say. That was really saying something. The man was rarely at a loss for words.

"Where do you want to start?" Alexis was the one to break the silence. "I'm only halfway through, from what I can tell, so I'd prefer to start on a case I've already reviewed."

Andre looked at me. I was the senior detective in our partnership, and he deferred to me on most things. But I was wrestling with anger and indignance. I didn't want her here; not necessarily her as a person—although the jury was still out on that—but anyone here that didn't belong. No one had wanted to be guinea pigs for Chief's new project, but he'd singled us out for some reason. Now we were stuck babysitting some random civilian.

"No matter where we start, it'll still be a waste of our time," I blurted. Her eyes widened with shock. After gaining her composure, she frowned and narrowed her eyes at me.

There, at least a frown was honest.

Chapter Four

Alexis

Finn stared at me, cold as ice, while Andre mumbled an apology for his rudeness. The Chief had warned me that the detectives hadn't been too keen on bringing in a victim's advocate. But why, for the love of God, did it have to be Finn? Andre I could manage; he was nice enough once he turned off the flirtation. But Finn's energy held a distinct air of smugness and stubbornness; my two least favorite qualities when working with a detective.

He had watched me all last night. I knew it. The hairs on the back of my neck prickled all evening. While I was trying to get to know people, attempting to make new friends and blend into my new environment, the man had stalked me with his eyes. When I asked Moira about it on the way back to our place, she'd only said he was protective. Chloe was too drunk to add anything much to the conversation and too hungover this morning for me to bring it up.

"Whatever problem you have with me or with the program is between you and Chief Whitmer." I launched into my usual reply when I got push-back. Having a zero-tolerance policy for bullshit was necessary at my last job and I wanted to set the same precedent at this new station, too. "I'm not here for you or in spite of you. I'm here to support the victims of violent crimes and help them find justice."

"They have enough support already," Finn snapped.

"If they did, I wouldn't have a job, now would I?"

His jaw clenched, muscles spasming. Had I gone too far? ...No. There is always room for what I do at every station. Detectives are usually more focused on the case, the crime, and the perpetrator. Every victim deserves to have someone to advocate for them. They are my first priority. Always.

"What cases have you already reviewed?" Andre clapped his hands and settled in across from me.

I glanced once more at Finn. He was biting his tongue hard. Good.

"I've worked my way through the L's." I pointed to my organized stacks. "That means we can start with Maria Benicio, Maude Crepley, Poppy Ferguson, Zara Hidalgo, Leticia Johnson, or Lin and Suzy Leng."

"We have a follow up scheduled with Maria later this week," Andre confirmed.

"Great, her case is pretty fresh in my mind. How has she been responding to you when she's giving her statements?"

"She holds back a lot. Her English isn't great, so I switch back and forth between English and Spanish. She lives in the rougher part of 9-block, so my best bet is that she's scared to talk. There's a code down on that side of town."

"Code of Silence," I nodded. Too often criminals continued hurting others, and it left the victims terrified of seeking help because of that fucking code. "Does she have close family? Friends she would like to bring in to help her feel more comfortable?"

"That's not how we do things." Finn hadn't moved from his position by the door.

"Are you getting what you need from Maria so you can get the bastard who sent her out to be raped and beaten?" I had to work hard to keep my composure, but I did.

He didn't answer, so Andre spoke up, "No. Poor thing's scared shitless."

"Okay, I'll sit in with her follow up," I pulled out my scheduler. "I'd like to spend some time one-on-one with her, build some trust before you question her."

"Can we bring you a side of fries while we're at it?" Finn snarked.

I ignored him. Let him pout like the petulant child he was. Andre and I would get it done.

"We can make that happen." Andre looked at Finn out of the corner of his eye. "She'll be in around one in the afternoon on Friday. That work for you?"

I checked my school calendar. There was a lecture until 12:10 on my schedule, but that would give me plenty of time to make it from the University to the station. "Yes, it works."

"How do you do it?" Andre asked.

"Do what?"

"Advocate… Help them open up to you."

"I care about them," I answered simply. "Get to know them; get to know their world, the people in it, their thoughts, feelings, opinions. It's not just about talking about the crime; in fact, that's the thing we usually talk about the least until they're ready."

"How the hell do you ever accomplish anything?" Finn rolled his eyes.

"Victims aren't a box to be checked. They're real people in genuine pain. Most of them feel helpless and out of control. Letting them pace things—not pushing harder than they're ready to move—gives them some of their power back. They've been victimized enough, and I'm here to make sure the justice system doesn't keep victimizing them even more."

A knock at the door interrupted us. Finn opened it and a cop handed him a note. He skimmed it, then gave Andre a look.

"We've gotta go," he stalked out of the room.

"I swear to God he isn't as big of a dick as he's making himself out to be today," Andre rose from his seat. "Give him some time to get used to this and I think he'll buy in."

"Don't worry about it," I waved his concern away. "I've dealt with plenty of detectives who care more about collaring the criminal than taking care of the victim. I'm used to it."

"No one cares more about the victim than Finn."

"Clearly," I agreed sarcastically.

"You'll see." Andre pulled on his suit jacket. "Work with us, be patient, hold your judgment and you'll see." He gave me a tip of his fedora and left the room.

Once they were gone, I breathed a sigh of relief. My shoulders popped as I rolled them and urged myself to relax. I pulled Maria's box back over to me and dove into the files once more. The details she had provided about her attack were scant. Then I read and reread the witness statements. I absorbed every single detail I could, committing her story to memory. Learning her story by heart would help me focus completely on her during our meeting. She deserved to feel seen.

Another few hours in interrogation one gave me time to make it through two other boxes, leaving only four more of Finn and Andre's active cases to review. I stacked the boxes over in the corner in alphabetical order and made sure I locked the door when I left. I waved to Chief Whitmer, then grabbed my backpack from the locker room.

I tried to keep my mind on my work in my Criminal Psychology class and then in Interviewing and Counseling, but my mind was still buzzing with Maria's case. Cases rarely took up so much space in my head, but I was rusty. It had been a long time since I focused on someone else's case besides my own.

After school, I made my way to the bodega on 10-block and got myself some groceries. I couldn't keep depending on Moira's surprise meals to keep me fed. The owners of the bodega were a nice older couple with matching smile lines. They pointed me to the freshest fruits, and the husband insisted on helping me carry my load of groceries back to the apartment.

My next errand for the day was to use a bit of the startup money Marshal Davis had given me to buy some new clothes. Using the crude map Moira had drawn for me, I navigated my way to the shops on 8-block. I found several new outfits that suited my taste and would be appropriate for the upcoming change in seasons. I also came across a beautiful, warm, knee-length peacoat in autumn colors that I just had to have.

On my way to find dinner, I ran into Vikram and Vijay from the bar. They acted beyond thrilled to see me. The brothers co-owned a restaurant on 8-block where they made the most sumptuous smelling Indian food. It was easy to agree to dinner with them and taking some leftovers home for my roommates to pay them back for feeding me for a couple of days. By the time I was on the bus back home, my belly was full, my closet was about to be fuller, and I relaxed a little more into this new life in the Clock.

It was hard for anything to feel like home to me. Dad died when I was little, and Mom wasn't even the least bit reliable. We bounced from place to place a lot. The only person I'd ever been able to count on was Abuelita, but she was gone, too. It had been hard to leave my life behind to come here, but it was a familiar hard. All I could hope for in any place was to at least feel comfortable. It was nice that almost everyone I met here was going out of their way to be kind, even Chloe, despite being a self-labeled bitch. Everyone, that is, except for Finn. But I would not let myself get too upset about one grump out of dozens of nice people. Those were some pretty good odds, in my experience.

Back at the apartment, the sisters and I spent the rest of the evening getting to know each other better. I showed them what I bought at the shops, and they made a fuss about everything. Lacey grew attached to a pearl headband I'd bought to accessorize one of my work outfits, so I gave it to her. She kept pushing it back into my hands until I assured her it was okay and I wouldn't miss it one bit. She spent the rest of the night admiring it until she went to bed.

The rest of the week went along similarly. I immersed myself in my studies and fell into the familiar rhythm of university life. At work, Andre and I went through each case from the pile I had been given, while Finn spent most of our meetings in silence. The sisters and I were genuinely enjoying one another's company and Chloe had warmed up to me a bit. She wasn't as effusive in her enjoyment as Moira, but there was a mutual respect growing between us. Lacey was all things light and lovely, but she would sometimes disappear into her room with no explanation for long periods of time. Apparently, she suffered from intense migraines that would strike out of nowhere.

On Friday, I caught the bus to the station at 12:25. I was both looking forward to, and nervous about, my meeting with Andre, Finn, and Maria. Finn was still sour about my role in their work. Today would be the ultimate test to see how he would handle it in action.

I was prepped and waiting in a freshly cleared interrogation one by 12:45, reviewing the case files one last time. Out of the four interrogation rooms, the first was the most comfortable, and they used most often it for interviewing victims and witnesses. The station wasn't big enough to have separate spaces for each, so they tried to reserve interrogation one unless there was an overabundance of perpetrators being interviewed at once.

The door opened, and Andre motioned for a timid-looking woman to enter the room with me. I rose from my chair and gave her my warmest smile. She glanced up quickly, then her gaze went right back down to her scuffed sandals. She was a tiny thing, barely over five feet tall, with raven hair cascading down her back. From what I read, she'd been through more in her forty-two years than most people had to suffer in a lifetime.

"Take a seat, Maria." Andre pulled out a chair across from mine. "This is the woman I've been telling you about. Her name is Alexis, and she's here to help you."

Maria barely acknowledged that he had spoken. I observed her body language. Her trauma was carved into every line of her body, every twitch, every hitched breath. My chest tightened as we prepared for the plunge into humanity's darkness.

"I'm going to step outside and round up Detective Briggs. Is that okay?" Andre asked.

The way he handled her impressed me. He asked her permission. He didn't touch her without consent. He kept his tone low and calm. It endeared me to him even more than I already had become in our work together this past week.

"Si," Maria whispered. She wrapped a red knit shawl more around her shoulders.

Andre gave me a hopeful look and left.

"Hi Maria," I started. "My name is Alexis. I'm happy to meet you."

Maria nodded in reply.

"I can't imagine how strange this situation might feel for you, sitting here with me. You've probably had to deal with so many unfamiliar faces already. Andre might have explained what my job is, but I want to reassure you I'm here to support and help you with whatever you might need."

She still didn't look up.

"Hola, Maria. Mi nombre es Alexis. Estoy feliz de conocerte," I tried again, this time in Spanish. Maria perked up and met my gaze through her eyelashes. "No sé qué te dijo Andre, pero mi trabajo es estar aquí para ayudarte y apoyarte en lo que necesites. Cada vez que tengas una pregunta, estaré aquí."

She lifted her head a little more and met my eye for the first time. It was a good sign. Spanish was obviously what she was most comfortable with. That was the goal: to help her feel comfortable.

"If it's okay with you, I'd like us to get to know each other first," I continued in Spanish. "I can ask you questions, or you can ask me questions."

"Where did you learn to speak Spanish?" Maria whispered.

"My abuelita taught me," I smiled. "My grandma died when I was five. Two years later, my grandpa remarried the most wonderful lady; my abuelita. My mom left me at their house every summer on their little farm. Abuelita insisted on only speaking Spanish to me. When I asked her why, she told me, 'Mija, a woman's wisdom is her greatest treasure. Speaking another language is a precious jewel you can add to your treasure.' That was enough for me."

Maria smiled more earnestly, and something sparked in her eyes. "My abuela taught me how to cook."

"What are some of your favorite meals she taught you to make?"

"Oh, so many: chilaquiles, cochinita pibil, caldo Azteca, gorditas de nata, torta ahogada," she ticked them off on her fingers as she listed them.

My mouth watered. "You're making me hungry!"

"What about your abuelita?"

"She tried her best, but I was such a picky kid, she usually made me arroz con pollo. I wised up in my teenage years and got a few good cooking lessons before she passed away." Just the thought of abuelita brought a tear to my eye.

"When did she pass?"

"Ten years ago."

"I'm lucky to still have my abuela. She lives with my mama in New Mexico. I miss them a lot."

"Of course you do. Your abuela sounds like a talented, special lady." I rested my arms on the table and leaned forward.

"She is." Maria's eyes glistened. Her body was more relaxed, and she was making eye contact with me more often.

"Did you grow up in New Mexico?"

"Yes, my family moved there when I was three. My father was killed the year before, so Mama and Abuela packed up all five of us kids and came to America." Maria fiddled with the small gold cross around her neck.

"That must have been hard for them."

"It was, but they were strong. We never went without because of them."

"You come from a long line of strong women, then."

"I do," Maria beamed. "When my teachers asked me what I wanted to be when I grew up, I would tell them I wanted to be Mama and Abuela."

"What brought you out here to Beckburg?"

Maria's eyes clouded over and some of the liveliness faded from her face. "Love… well, what I thought was love." She sighed and looked down at her hands. She had bitten her nails down to the skin.

"A story as old as time, huh?" I leaned back. "How many women have made that same journey in the name of our hearts?"

"Mama called me foolish when I told her I was following Ramond out here. But I was stubborn and stupid and told her she didn't get to control my life. I didn't want to be an old maid anymore. I said things I'm not proud of… Turns out she was right. But it was too hard to admit it to myself, or to her. I still can't."

"What happened with Ramond?" The conversation was naturally moving toward the present. From her case files, I knew Maria moved here a little over a year ago, and her assault happened last month.

"I don't like talking about it." Maria pulled her shawl tight again.

"Then we don't have to talk about it."

"Really?"

"Really. What do you want to talk about instead?"

"I didn't think I wanted to talk at all, but it's been nice so far." She gave me a shy smile.

"Who doesn't like talking about abuelas and gorditas de nata?"

She chuckled, but her expression changed quickly.

"When the detectives come back in, they'll want me to talk more about… about what happened to me…"

"They will," I confirmed.

"Are you going to help them find him?"

Him. Ramond. The man who had convinced Maria to leave her beloved Mama and Abuela and come to Beckburg for the promise of true love and happily ever after. The man who lulled her into a false sense of security and then forced her into sex work to support his drug habit.

"I'm not here for the detectives. I'm here for you. They're in charge of resolving the case, and I trust them to do their job without my help. My job is to be here for you, to make sure the detectives do their job while keeping you from being hurt or scared any more than you already have been. To be someone for you to talk to, even if it's just about abuelas."

The relief washed over her face. These were the moments that made all the hard stuff worth it. When a victim gave me their trust, when I could ease their suffering if only a little, and comfort them, that was worth it all. She nodded, a tear rolling down her cheek.

A soft knock sounded on the door. Andre and Finn entered. I watched Maria's shoulders tense.

"Here, Detective Alvarez, take my chair so you and Detective Briggs can sit together," I offered. "I'll go sit next to Maria if that's okay with her." Her head bobbed as she nodded her approval.

They took their seats, and I sat next to Maria. Andre pulled out a notebook and clicked his pen. Finn's body language was completely different than what I had expected. Instead of his usual tense haughtiness, he was relaxed, no tie, and his sleeves were rolled up to his elbows.

"How are you, Maria?" Finn asked.

"Okay," she replied in English. There was a slight tremor in her voice. I scooted a little closer to her.

"We have some follow-up questions for you, if that's okay," Finn continued.

Another wordless nod.

"The man you said attacked you is refusing to cooperate with us," Finn explained. Maria flinched. "He claims he didn't do it. And he won't tell us anything about his sources, how he heard about Ramond trafficking you and possibly some other women, nothing. We were hoping you could tell us what you know about the operation."

"I…" she looked between Andre and Finn a few times before shooting me a terrified look. "I don't know nothing." She dropped her head and rubbed her cross necklace.

Finn and Andre exchanged a look.

"We really need anything you can give us," Andre jumped in. "Even if you think it's not important, even the minor details can point us in the right direction."

Maria went from a slight tremor to full-blown shakes. I put a tentative hand on her shoulder. Just that simple touch made her jump. She glanced at me out of the corner of her eyes and dissolved into tears.

"I don't know nothing," she choked out.

"Please, Maria," Finn began, but I shot him a look.

"Could you get Maria a glass of ice water, Detective Briggs?" I asked.

He glared, but I could tell he wasn't going to snap back at me in front of Maria. But, boy, did he want to.

"Of course," his tone was cooler than his expression. He left the room.

"Maria," Andre was about to continue his partner's push, but another look from me and he stopped.

"Take some deep breaths for me, Maria," I urged.

She tried, but her breathing was ragged and sharp.

"Breathe with me," I coached. I took a loud, deep inhale and motioned for her to copy me. I exhaled slowly, deliberately, and inhaled again. Maria followed my lead, eyes locked on mine. After five or six breaths, her shaking subsided.

Finn reentered the room and handed her a glass of water. She wrapped her small hands around the glass and drank with fervor. Finn settled back in his seat.

"Anything you could give us, Maria, anything at all," Finn continued.

"I don't know nothing." Maria's voice was stronger this time.

"Would you feel more comfortable telling Alexis?" Andre inquired.

Maria looked at me with wide, scared eyes. I shook my head and closed my eyes. I should have prepped Andre and Finn better than this.

"You don't have to tell me anything you don't want to," I reassured.

Maria's shoulders relaxed, and she took another drink of water.

"We can protect you if that's what you're worried about," Finn pressed.

Maria gave him an incredulous look. Her hand returned to her necklace once more. She put her glass on the table and pushed it away from her.

"I don't know how many times I have to tell you... I don't know."

Finn rubbed the bridge of his nose and sighed.

"Okay, Maria," Andre relented. "Thanks for your time. We'll reach out to you in case we need to follow up on anything."

Maria stood, but hesitated.

"Will you be here again if I have to come back?" She whispered to me in Spanish.

"I'll be here every time," I assured her.

She smiled and hurried out of the room.

Finn waited a few beats before shutting the door behind her and rounding on me. "What the fuck was that?"

"What was what?" I shot back.

"I don't know what you got away with at your last station, but I will not put up with being interrupted during a line of questioning with your touchy-feely bullshit."

"Touchy-feely bullshit?" Heat was rising in my chest.

"I could have gotten something out of her if you'd stayed in your lane," Finn growled. "The longer it takes for her to talk, the further away that bastard Delgado gets from us, and you just lost us God knows how much time."

"She wasn't going to talk." I gritted my teeth.

"Yeah, because you were too busy babying her instead of pushing her to get past her fear and stand up for herself."

"Finn," Andre warned.

"Do you know anything about trauma?" I shot out of my chair, arms tight over my chest, heat rising in my cheeks.

"Trauma's a part of life, princess," Finn replied. "You don't need to throw glasses of water and handholding at it to get results. You gotta fucking face it. This is exactly why I told the Chief this was a bad idea. You and your fluffy pseudoscience could have just cost us a collar." He threw his hands in the air.

It was my turn to start shaking. Not with fear, but with rage.

"Maria was having a trauma response, Detective," I spat. "When you push a person outside their window of tolerance, you trigger their sympathetic nervous system into a fight-flight-freeze-fawn response. When the amygdala senses a threat, it shuts down the neocortex—your higher-level thinking brain—and you go into survival mode. The only way to bring a person out of that response is by stimulating the parasympathetic nervous system through things like deep breathing and drinking water. Maria can't access her memories outside of her trauma when she's in a trauma response and she sure as hell isn't going to feel safe enough to give you information on the man who caused said trauma if you don't respect that process. It's not 'fluffy pseudoscience,' you arrogant asshole, it's neuropsychology."

I grabbed my bag and stalked out of the room, leaving Finn and Andre with their mouths hanging open behind me.

Chapter Five

Finn

I downed another gulp of coffee and rubbed my forehead. Hunching over my desk, I tried to focus on the Bianchi files. But no matter how hard I tried, I just couldn't fucking focus. Big Dominic and his asshole family mocked me from the pages.

"Still licking your wounds from the verbal beat-down Alexis handed you?" Andre rolled his chair over to my desk.

"Shut up, Andre," I snapped.

"I'm just sayin', man... when I run out to grab lunch, I can pick you up some aloe vera for that wicked burn." Andre was grinning like the cat who ate the canary. It wasn't often he saw me get my ass handed to me like that, and he was obviously enjoying it.

"Yeah, yeah, keep pushing and see what other first aid supplies you'll need to pick up after I'm done with you."

I shoved the files away and leaned farther back in my chair. It groaned with the shift of my weight. As much as I hated to admit it to myself—and I sure as hell would never admit it to Andre—the dressing down Alexis had given me was pretty well-deserved. She was right; I had no idea what she was doing with Maria had a purpose. It hadn't even occurred to me, and that made me an arrogant asshole. I wanted to nail the piece of shit who had pimped Maria out and almost gotten her killed by a particularly violent John. That kind of horseshit was happening more and more often in the Clock, and we needed to figure out what was driving the uptick before it exploded out of control and more innocent women like Maria got caught in the crossfire.

Andre and I hadn't been given much of a choice when the Chief assigned us the new victim's advocate. Every other partnership curled up their lip at the idea. It felt like a violation; felt like the Chief didn't trust us to do our jobs without a babysitter. Chief had pulled us into his office a couple weeks back and told us he had a pet project he wanted to try out and we were his prime candidates. When he told us what exactly that pet project was, we protested. But he wouldn't have any of it.

The force had gotten some bad press after a couple of rookies took evidence photos out of lockup and shared them back and forth with their buddies.

The victims eventually stumbled across them on social media and went nuclear on the Chief. Chief fired them on the spot, even though they threatened a lawsuit. They tried to bully their way out of trouble and Chief didn't put up with that kind of shit.

What those immature assholes pulled meant we had a little PR problem on our hands, and my bet was this pet project of the Chief's was a way to deal with it. I tried to tell him that the victim's advocate should be paired with the detectives most likely to fuck up and do something equally stupid, not seasoned pros like us. But he insisted it be us. He told us we were the only two he trusted to get this program off the ground, and violent crime—our beat—was where the victim's advocate would be needed most. I could give him that one, but I still wasn't happy about it.

When I walked into interrogation one and discovered that our new "partner" was the sisters' new roommate, my distaste for the project only grew. Our interaction had left me unsettled at the bar, feeling both defeated and victorious after our stare down. Even my run home hadn't helped as much as it should have. She was still an unknown, and we had enough unknowns around here to add another one. Now we had one who was supposed to be a part of our investigation process. Getting her caught up to speed on a round dozen of our live victims irked me to no end. If I was honest with myself, which was a glaringly obnoxious habit of mine, I didn't like that she didn't defer to me like everyone else did.

"Briggs! Alvarez!" Chief came striding over to our desks, breaking me out of my reverie. He had that look about him. It was never good news when he wore that look.

"We've got another dead body at the docks." Chief handed me a slip of paper. "An anonymous tipster called it in. Said they saw a hand tangled in some fishing nets at the end of dock three. Uniforms just called in to confirm."

"Shit." Andre grabbed his coat and hat. "That beating earlier this week and now a body. Any ID on the vic?"

"We'll have to wait for fingerprints to come back from the lab." Chief shook his head.

"Did the uniforms recognize it as a local?" I asked, grabbing my keys.

"Impossible to say… the head's missing."

My guts clenched. It was the Bianchi family again. It had to be.

"We're on our way," I confirmed.

Andre and I hurried to my black Dodge Charger. I threw it into "Drive" and peeled out of the parking lot. My mind was already in overdrive.

"Bianchi hit," Andre threw out. It wasn't even a question. Andre knew it as well as I did.

I nodded, jaw tight, eyes on the road, siren and lights blaring.

Every cell in my body was vibrating by the time we got to the docks. A crowd of disgruntled anglers and dock workers stood behind the yellow tape. Andre and I pushed through the crowd and ducked under it. At the end of dock three, the coroner was waiting while the forensics team photographed and examined the scene.

"Catch us up, Gregor," I barked.

"In a fine mood today, I see," the old coroner bated.

"You don't want to go there," Andre warned.

"Alright, let's go here then." Gregor walked the rest of the dock to a tangle of fish nets hanging off the last post into the water. "Male victim, been in the water at least seventeen to eighteen hours by the looks of him." Gregor dug a finger into his bad ear and yawned. How a person could get so used to decomposition and decay was beyond me.

"Any personal items that could help us determine the vic's identity?" I asked.

"Not that the boys have dredged up so far," Gregor shrugged. "No clothes on the body, no visible tattoos or scars, no 'Hello, My Name Is' sticker, nothing." I rolled my eyes. "But he sure ticked somebody off. See the bruising all around the chest and torso? He took a beating before they took his head."

"What I'm seeing is similarities to just about every single body we've pulled off this dock in the past eight months." Andre scratched his chin.

"It doesn't take a rocket scientist to figure out he's the next contestant on 'Who Ran Afoul of the Local Mob,'" Gregor concurred. "I'll have the boys bag him for me and I'll get right on things back at the lab." He tipped his fisherman's hat to us and lumbered off.

Andre went to talk to the uniforms who were first on the scene as I walked the dock. My eyes scoured every surface, every board, every piece of discarded fishing equipment looking for clues. The crime scene always told me more than any witness ever could. I inhaled and tried to fight the urge to gag at the reek of fish. There was something else in the air that I couldn't quite place.

The hairs on the back of my neck were prickling. Crimes scenes were never a picnic, but there was something about this one that had me on edge. It wasn't fear…it was dread. Some instinct buried deep inside me was telling me to run, to hide, to defend. Ninety percent of the crimes that happened out here on the docks were related to the Bianchi crime syndicate. But this felt like something more.

I returned to the body and knelt next to the fishing nets while the forensics guys raised the victim out of the water. Several yellow, numbered placards had already been placed by the forensics team. I examined each one, collecting them in my mind like scattered pieces to a puzzle: a lone piece of discarded and bloodied duct tape, a clump of mousy blonde hair, red stains on the splintered wood. I breathed in once again, and my blood turned to ice.

I had only smelled something like this once before… Dublin. The lines of bodies we'd had to clean up back then made even the most hardened cop blanch.

The sense of dread I'd been nursing since we arrived went from a heavy weight to an oppressive force. Things were about to get much, much worse.

"Andre, you got what you need?" I grabbed my partner by the elbow and steered him toward the car.

"You look like you've seen a ghost, man. What's up?"

"Something real, real bad."

We nodded to the uniform guarding the perimeter and ducked under the tape once more. I propelled us forward, fighting the urge to break into a run. After we'd reached the privacy of my car, I exhaled loudly. I pounded the steering wheel and swore.

"What's gotten into you, Finn?"

"Do you remember our last case back in Dublin?"

"Dublin?" Andre's face grew serious. "That was a long, long time ago. What makes you think about the shitstorm from Dublin? We're half a world away."

"Remember when the body count skyrocketed? One body a week, then two or three, then a new one every single night for three weeks?"

"What are you getting at, Finn?" The memories swam in his eyes. The disgust, the anger, and the fear. We weren't afraid of much, but something had gone horribly wrong in Dublin. Before we could find the culprit, it had stopped as suddenly as it had started.

"That body," I pointed over my shoulder at the crime scene behind us, "Smells exactly like the ones from Dublin."

Silence.

I revved up the car and took off. Andre wasn't speaking, and I couldn't look over to gauge his reaction as I navigated the streets. But I could feel the tension rolling off him in waves. It was the same tension that was gathering in the muscles in my back.

"Are we going back to the station?" Andre finally spoke.

"No, not yet," I gritted my teeth.

"One Trick Pony?"

"You bet your ass."

Chapter Six

Alexis

My textbooks sprawled across the table and a glass of wine in my hand, I recounted Finn's tantrum to Moira and Chloe. Lacey was having another migraine day, so she locked herself away in her room. Talking through my frustrations helped me unwind. I'd been in a foul mood since I left the station. But once I unloaded on my roommates, the mood dissipated.

"Did you really call Finn an arrogant asshole?" Chloe threw her head back as she laughed.

"Yes."

"Girl, you are growing on me more and more every day." She patted me on the back.

"I can't believe he said those things to you," Moira shook her head. "You were just doing your job!"

"Apparently, it was me doing my job that was so offensive to him." I took another sip of wine.

"Typical male ego." Chloe poured herself another glass. "Nothing shakes an alpha like Finn quite like a strong, intelligent woman. God, I wish I could have seen the look on his face when you walked out."

"It was pretty epic." A smile perked up at the corner of my mouth.

"Do me a favor and record it on your phone next time." Chloe closed her eyes and smiled. "Wait…never mind, don't. It'll only spoil the image I have in my head."

"Well, I hope you never have a next time," Moira cleared her dinner plate. "The things he did and said were unacceptable. I have a mind to read him the riot act the next time I see him."

"That's something I'd like to witness." Chloe's eyes popped open. "Do you think he'll be at the Pony tonight? We should go!"

"No!" I protested. "I'd rather not spend more time with him than I absolutely have to, thank you very much. Having to deal with his grumping at work is more than enough for me."

"Oh, come on! How could you deny me this simple pleasure?" Chloe pouted. "Please, I swear I'll never be a judgy bitch to you ever again. You'll have my whole heart for life if you let me watch the look on his face when you stroll into the bar like he was no more bothersome than a fart in the wind."

"Well, when you put it that way, it sounds pretty empowering. It would be nice to visit some other people at the bar, too."

"That's my girl," Chloe slapped my knee. "I'll go get dressed. Ooo, this is going to be classic." She clapped her hands and disappeared into her room.

"Are you sure you want to go?" Moira asked.

"I don't mind. It's not like he'll cause a scene at the bar, will he?"

"Oh, not at all. That's not like Finn. He'll just sit back silently and watch."

"That works for me." I cleared up my books and put them in my backpack.

"Well, if you're sure, then… I wouldn't mind seeing his face either," Moira grinned.

"I'll try to put on my best show then." I rolled my eyes.

"Excellent!"

We got ready in record time. Thinking of seeing Finn brought up conflicting feelings. I was still so angry, but I didn't want to create more tension. We still had to work together, after all. But there was a wicked part of me that wanted to rub my victory in his face a little more. The more I thought about it, the more I wanted the first time I saw him after our argument to be in the bar surrounded by people who were fast becoming my friends. The station felt more like his territory than mine; I was far less well-received there than I was at the One Trick Pony.

Moira left a note for Lacey that we'd gone out. The walk to the Pony was one of giddy anticipation for all three of us. Taron waved us in the front door and my eyes instantly scoured the bar for Finn.

There he was, at the far end of the bar with Andre, set off from everyone else. They were deep in conversation with Riel. Finn glanced up and caught sight of us, his eyebrows drawing together. Without lingering, his eyes flicked back to Riel. Not the reaction I had been hoping for...

"That's no fun," Chloe sighed. "Let's go break up the boy's club. I demand satisfaction!"

She grabbed my hand, pulling me behind her as she headed straight for Andre and Finn. Moira tailed behind us, clucking her tongue. I waved to Vikram and Vijay as we passed, and they returned the gesture.

"Which one of you sad saps are going to buy a few beautiful women a drink?" Chloe pulled up a chair next to Finn and pulled me to her side.

Finn glanced up at me and I instantly knew something was wrong. His eyes were pinched and the muscle in his temple was tight. Andre's characteristic humor that always played across his face was gone.

"What's wrong?" I eyed them both.

"What could possibly be wrong now that you ladies are here?" Riel greeted. "I can't say no to buying a round for such beauty. What are you all having?"

Moira examined the trio and frowned. Even Chloe dropped her bravado. They shared a significant look.

"Guys?" I raised my eyebrows at Finn and Andre.

"Nothing out of the ordinary, Alexis. We caught a fresh case, and it's... troubling. Just another day in the life of a detective in Violent Crimes." Andre shrugged.

"Can I help with the victim?"

"Unfortunately not. This one didn't make it." Andre shook his head.

"Oh." Suddenly, our silly plan to ruffle Finn's feathers felt completely insignificant. "I'm sorry. Truly, I am."

I put a hand on Finn's arm. The look in his eyes took me off guard; pain and...fear? Worry? I couldn't place it exactly. It brought a lump to my throat, remembering how often Andre and Finn had to deal with this kind of human loss. All the work I did was with the people who survived; they had to take care of both the living and the dead. It must be a heavy, heavy burden.

"Can I help *you guys*, then?"

"Maybe you can help take their minds off their troubles," Riel suggested.

"How so?" Chloe eyed Riel, and he shot her a sly grin.

"Drag 'em out on the dance floor."

"Only if you come with us," Andre teased.

"I have a bar to tend but be sure to get a dance in for me. Hiro," he called. "Play something slow."

Hiro nodded, her neon hair bobbing, and pushed a few buttons on the jukebox. With a Fonzie-like thump against the glass, the song switched from an energetic pop song to a soulful rock ballad. She gave a satisfied little smile.

"Well, what do you say, Andre? Can I dance away your troubles?" Moira held out a hand to him.

"It would be my genuine pleasure." Andre took her hand and led her onto the dance floor. He twirled her in a circle and then pulled her into a loose embrace.

"I'll stay here and order drinks," Chloe offered.

I shot a look at Finn. He sighed and raised his eyebrows, then held out a hand to me. My stomach did a little backflip. This wasn't exactly how I pictured tonight going. I took his offered hand, and we joined Moira and Andre on the floor.

I wrapped my hands tentatively around Finn's neck and he placed a hand on each side of my hips. He swayed in time to the music, but the look on his face was miles away. I bit my bottom lip, not sure what to say. The energy between us had been so conflictual since I arrived last week. It felt awkward to be so close, dancing in time to an 80s hair band love song. Finn's jaw clenched, and he sighed.

"This one weighing on you?" I ventured.

"Hmm?" He looked down at me.

"Is this one bothering you?" I repeated.

"Oh, yeah. It's… a messy one."

"Do you have a lead on the perpetrator?"

"Odds are high it's related to the Bianchi crime family, but we're not sure who carried out the actual hit."

"Have you been able to contact the victim's family yet?"

"No, not yet. We don't even have an ID on them yet." His grip tightened on my hips. His face darkened, and he looked away.

"Wow, I'm terrible at this."

"Bad at what? Dancing?"

"No, I can rock back and forth from foot to foot better than any ninth grader," I teased. "I'm bad at taking your mind off the case. Isn't that supposed to be what this is?"

He chuckled lightly. I could feel the rumble reverberate through his chest. It sent a small shiver down my back.

"Yeah, I guess so."

"Then talk to me about something non-work related. No shop talk allowed."

"What do you want me to talk about?"

"How about yourself?"

"That's a long story," he hedged.

"Then tell me a small piece of it."

"Like what?"

"You're going to make this conversation thing way harder than it needs to be, Briggs," I swatted his chest playfully. "Tell me about your family."

"If I do, you'll head-shrink me," he challenged.

"God, you're impossible." I rolled my eyes. "Then tell me your favorite food."

"A hamburger."

"Just a plain piece of meat on a bun?" I prodded.

"A juicy hamburger, medium rare, thick slices of bacon, with all the fixings," he relented.

"There, that wasn't so hard!"

"It was torturous." The corner of his mouth twitched up.

"Tell me more."

"I'd rather hear about you," he countered.

"What do you want to know?"

"Where are you from?"

Shit. What seemed like such a normal, innocent question was one I absolutely could not answer honestly. I flashed to the story Marshal Davis had concocted for me, but my stomach clenched at the thought of lying to Finn. I had a distinct feeling that lying to him wouldn't help us work past the strange impasse between us.

"A lot of places," I answered. It was honest, but vague.

"What places?" He pressed. It was my turn to grin at his persistence.

"I was born in Germany," I offered.

"Germany? Really?"

"Yes, my dad was military."

"Ah, explains the moving around a lot," Finn nodded.

It explained the first few years of moves, but not the moves after Dad's death. But I didn't want to get that deep into my past. "I can't really remember all the places we lived. We moved every two years or so until he passed."

"When did he die?" Finn's face softened.

"When I was seven. Then it was just me and Mom."

"No siblings?"

"Nope. I'm an only child like you." I hadn't realized it, but the song had changed. The new song was still slow enough that we could get away with the continued slow dance, though.

"What brought you to the Clock?"

"School." It was barely a lie.

"Seems like a random school to choose. I'm sure a smart woman like you had plenty of options aside from Beckburg University."

"There are always plenty of options," I shrugged. "I got some advice from a friend…" More like a Marshal… "And it seemed like as good a choice as any. I was up for a new adventure."

"Were you getting sick of your old adventure?" Finn's eyes scanned my face.

"Why does it feel more like you're interrogating me instead of getting to know me?" I cocked my head to the side.

"Maybe it's a little of both." He spun us in a slow circle.

"Then have out with it," I offered. "What are you really asking me?"

"I want to know who you really are."

My stomach dropped. How could he know? I looked over my shoulder at the door.

"I don't like not knowing. The Clock's a small place; I know pretty much every person in it. I know their stories, their histories, and their motives. A week with you has given me a decent idea of who you are, but I'm not a patient man. I don't like to nibble; I like to swallow things whole."

"What you want is to drink from a fire hose, not a faucet," I finished for him.

"Exactly."

"That's a hell of a lot to ask of a person." I swallowed hard.

"I never said it was fair." Finn's eyes didn't leave my face. The demand was clear, not angry or frightening, just hungry. He had flecks of gold in his emerald eyes.

"Are you the type to return the favor, then? If someone opens the floodgates, do you give up your secrets in return?"

His full lips became a thin line.

"I didn't think so," I smirked.

"That's not really my style," he admitted.

"I can tell. You're not used to being on the other side of the interrogation."

"No. I may have control issues." Finn gave me a sly smile.

"Then I'll make a deal with you: I'll tell you mine if you'll tell me yours." I locked eyes with him. Finn didn't break eye contact, and neither did I. Just like the first night we met, it was another stare down, but this one felt distinctly different.

"We'll see how that goes," Finn shrugged eventually. His hands slid from my hips, and he stepped away as the second song faded into silence. "Thanks for the dance."

"I guess we will," I nodded.

He gave me a final half smile then strode away. He grabbed his jacket from the bar, tossed it over his shoulder, downed the rest of his drink, and left. I watched Andre follow suit, throwing me a wave before he disappeared out the door as well.

Finn and I weren't exactly friends, but something had shifted between us. I understood him a little better and I think the feeling was mutual. Maybe the reason we butted heads was because we were more similar than different. I had secrets and so did he. It felt a lot less personal knowing he didn't trust easily. How could he with what he did for a living?

At that moment, I realized I wanted to be a person he could trust, and I wasn't sure why.

Chapter Seven

Finn

I stripped off my shirt and threw it across the room. It landed on the edge of the laundry basket. Fuck. I was off my game. I ran my fingers through my hair as I strode into the bathroom. The handle of the shower squeaked when I turned it to just past where the blue line ended, and the red line thickened. I leaned against the counter until the steam fogged up the glass door before I stepped in.

The hot water peppered my skin. I sighed and leaned my forehead against the cool tile wall. My muscles were tighter than a damn vice and I silently begged the water to ease the tension.

Our conversation with Riel hadn't answered any of our questions; it had only created more. He didn't have much to add to our hypothesis, no insights, no direction, only deep concern. I hadn't been able to shake the scent from the docks for hours.

At least not until Alexis and the sisters came in. I chuckled to myself. The dance had been a pleasant distraction. Alexis was a firecracker, to be sure, but she was also a mystery. She answered some questions and dodged the rest. There was something in the way she inhaled right before answering a question she didn't want to answer that made me recklessly curious. She was a mystery alright. My relentless curiosity demanded to unravel it.

When I had gotten everything I could from the shower, I toweled off and headed to bed. I wanted to go for a run in the woods, but there wouldn't be enough time. We had lingered at the Pony longer than I intended and we had work to do tomorrow. Andre and I were going to rustle up some low-level stooges that ran in the wrong circles. Picking them up would be easy, but getting them to talk wouldn't.

With the heavy comforter pulled up to my chest, I sprawled across my king-sized bed. When I'd broken my ancient full-sized bed after a case went bad last year, Andre had talked me into getting a "grown-ass man" bed. It wasn't the worst idea he'd ever talked me into, I had to admit.

As I drifted off to sleep, I had two questions warring for center stage in my head: Who the hell was the new Bianchi hitman, and what was Alexis Henson hiding?

. . . . .

"We got a hit on the fingerprints of our headless corpse." Chief dropped a file onto my desk. "Gregor put a rush on it for you, and it didn't take long to get a match."

I flipped open the folder and found myself face to face with a mugshot paper clipped to the top right corner of a very long rap sheet. Our vic was a criminal, a lifelong one, according to this.

"Percy Grim," I read. "Street name: Ferret." I scanned his list of priors. "Lots of petty thievery, some drug charges, solicitation, drunk and disorderly," I flipped the page, "and lots of possession with intent to sell."

"Olivier and Lot," Chief hollered across the room. The two vice detectives came over. "You recognize this guy?"

"Yeah, that's Ferret," Olivier confirmed. He flicked the toothpick he was chewing from one side of his mouth to the other. "Why? What's he done now?"

"He's dead," Chief said.

"What? You've gotta be shittin' me." Lot's eyebrows shot up.

"Fingerprints confirm that he's our vic from the docks last night." I tapped the report on top of Ferret's file.

"God dammit!" Lot pounded his fist on my desk. I shot him a look, but he didn't catch it. "We've been working that little shit for a month. We just got him to agree to inform on the higher ups in that drug runnin' operation on the South side of town."

"That's a possible motive," Andre suggested. "If they found out he was talking to vice, his buddies might have shut him up for it."

"It wouldn't be the first time something like that's happened," Olivier agreed.

"Why go to the trouble of taking his head, though?" I asked. "A low-level pusher like him? Unless he had some kind of smoking gun information on the operation, I doubt they would go to such extremes. The Bianchis are brutal, for damn sure, but they don't act needlessly. A rat gets one quick one to the head; it's the real traitors that get special attention."

"Ferret wasn't anybody special." Olivier crossed his arms over his narrow chest. "He's a repeat offender looking at serious jail time after his last offense. Judge Crawford warned him not to show up in his courtroom again or he'd throw the book at him."

"For Crawford, that might have been literal," Lot guffawed. "The old loon was sick of Ferret's bullshit. He had him thrown out on his ass after his last hearing for mouthin' off. Olivier had to scrape him off the concrete on his way out from testifying."

"We need to find out a lot more about our boy Ferret if we wanna figure out why he went out the way he did." Andre stroked his chin. "I'll start looking into him."

"I'll get out to 9-block and start asking some questions." I grabbed my keys.

"Nobody's gonna talk to you, Briggs," Lot warned, running his hand through his slick, black hair. "I guarantee you that word's got around over there about what we found—and didn't find—out on the docks last night."

"I can be persuasive," I dismissed. My fists clenched. Lot had no idea what I was capable of.

"Watch your back," Chief advised.

I spent the rest of the day canvassing 9-block, going door to door to get somebody to talk to me. But all I ended up with was a lot of doors shut in my face. Lot had been right; word had already gotten out about Ferret's fate. All I accomplished was letting the residents and drug dealers of 9-block know who the victim was. Head shakes and denials were a dime a dozen out here.

Andre's day turned out to be much more fruitful than mine. He'd combed through Ferret's criminal history, reviewed old interrogation tapes, talked to other cops who collared him, and he came up with a mountain of information on the guy. We pored over it late into the night, trying to understand what had made Ferret run this far afoul of the Bianchis. But nothing sang out the answer. We should have known better than to get our hopes up. The mob didn't give up their secrets without a fuckin' fight. We were only scratching the surface.

Monday started off just as hopelessly. Andre and I were still combing through Ferret's history, this time his personal connections, to see if we could find the needle in the damn haystack and still nothing. By lunch time, I was seeing red.

"They were only together for a few months before he got locked up for his fifth DUI," I argued.

"You never know the loyalty that can develop in a few months," Andre shrugged. "I think if we bring her in, she'll clam up to protect his memory."

"Not if it means finding his killer. That could pull at her loyalty, too."

"They didn't leave things all that peachy, Finn," Andre popped a grape in his mouth. "She won't give a damn about his killer, but she won't squeal on him about his last months either. Not without some persuasion."

"Who needs persuading?" Alexis' voice caught me off guard.

"Afternoon, Lex." Andre tipped his hat and smiled. "You don't mind if I call you Lex, do you?"

"Just as long as you don't call me late for dinner," Alexis chuckled. I rolled my eyes. "Sorry, that was lame. My jokes are always rusty on Mondays."

"Only on Mondays?" Andre teased.

"I'm hilarious every other day of the week," she confirmed. "And who needs persuading?" The woman was like a dog with a bone.

"Don't worry about it." I closed the folder in front of me. "It's not one of your cases."

"It doesn't mean I can't still help. Especially if it's about the case that had you both so down at the bar."

"No. This case is dangerous." I shook my head. "We're not getting you wrapped into it."

"Alright, but the offer stands if you change your mind." She tucked a strand of her hair behind her ear, and I caught a whiff of her shampoo. "If you have some time, I was hoping to ask a few questions about the Ferguson case before Poppy comes in to prep for her deposition with the DA."

"I'll catch up with you guys in a second," I stalked off.

I refilled my coffee in the break room and grabbed a stale croissant. My stomach growled in protest. You take what you can get at the station. I didn't have someone to pack my damn lunches like the married guys, and I forgot more often than I remembered to grab something before I headed out the door every morning. Shitty coffee and stale pastries were the primary food groups in my diet.

When I got to interrogation one, Andre was leaving the room. I furrowed my brows at him.

"I gotta go see a man about a horse." He patted me on the back and brushed past.

Alexis gave me a quick smile. I sat off to the side against the wall and sipped my coffee. The silence was thick between us. The last time we were in this room, I'd barked at her for fucking up my interrogation and she'd kicked my proverbial ass for it. It wasn't a pleasant memory.

"Alexis." I cleared my throat.

"Yeah?" She peered up at me through her lashes.

"I owe you an apology."

"For what?"

"For being an arrogant asshole," I reminded.

"Ah, yeah, that," she nodded.

"I underestimated you and disrespected you. It was out of line. You're here to do a job, same as me. In fact, I should probably trust Chief when he says you're here to make my job easier." I scratched at the stubble on my chin.

"I'm not here to bust your balls," Alexis sighed. "When I say I'm here for the victims, that's really all there is to it. Do I want to help you and Andre? Yes, of course. But sometimes I might get in your way if it means protecting the victims from further harm. I won't ever do it on purpose, I swear, but it might happen. If you have an issue with it, then talk to me about it. We can figure something out. Just keep the decibel level down on it."

"Fair enough," I conceded.

"Nothing makes me happier than seeing the bad guys get theirs. I really want to help, if that's any consolation."

"I don't doubt it. What you need to understand is that this job has a lot of moving parts. If you say the wrong thing on the wrong day, you could blow the entire case, especially with a witness or a vic. We walk that tightrope every day. Andre and I have a system; we've been working together for a long time. So having a complete stranger sweep in and throw off that balance is…"

"An enormous pain in the ass?" Alexis ventured.

"Complicated," I corrected. "It eases my mind that you're as highly trained as you are. I wasn't aware of that at first. I thought you were some rookie college student looking to pad her resume. Now I know my assumption was wrong. You care about this work; I can see that. We just have to find a way to... get used to each other."

"If you stop dragging your feet every time we work together, I think things would be significantly easier."

"You could be right," I chuckled. I pulled my chair closer to hers as a show of willingness. "How can I help you help me?" I charmed.

"There's nothing more endearing than a man who is willing to compromise." She patted my shoulder. "I want to pick your brain. You're a good cop, Finn, I know it. The way you put pieces together, the intensity you have when you're onto an idea, it could be incredibly useful to me and to the victims if we can work as a team."

"I'm not sure if that's a conciliatory ego stroke or the truth, but I'll take it." I felt a lightness in my chest.

"I'm serious," Alexis laughed. I liked the sound of it. "It's like with the Ferguson case: You stood up to the piece of shit boyfriend of hers and convinced her to testify against him. You made her feel safe enough to take an enormous leap of faith. That takes more than a keen eye for detective work. It takes someone who cares. I read in a report that the boyfriend came into the station and threatened you. You could have blown up, puffed out your chest, and arrested the guy on the spot, but you didn't. Why not?"

"Poppy was in the interrogation room when it happened. I hadn't closed the door all the way when I left, so I knew she could hear everything we were saying in the think tank." The memory was vivid, right down to the color tie I wore that day. I'd fought back the beast inside, wanted to tear the guy's throat out for what he'd done to Poppy and the balls he had coming into my station and threatening my life.

"Detective Jensen's report said you walked right up to the guy and whispered something quietly to him, totally calm, hands in your pockets. What did you say?" Alexis' eyes were shining with curiosity.

"I told him he might be able to intimidate a woman half his size, but he didn't scare me. Then I told him he'd get his." I fudged the last part a little. I'd really told the guy I could smell the stink of fear on him, and I'd follow that stench until the ends of the earth to make sure he got what was coming to him. I didn't think that level of detail would be impressive to Alexis.

"Then you had him escorted out of the building like he was nothing," Alexis finished for me. "You treated him like the insignificant schoolyard bully he is, and Poppy saw it. Instead of his appearance intimidating her out of pressing charges like he'd intended, your response to him gave her the courage to press forward. I doubt that was an accident on your part."

"It was very deliberate," I confirmed. "She needed to witness someone stand up to him so she knew she could, too."

"It was the *right* thing at the *right* time," Alexis continued. "Without ever taking a psychology course, that means it was pure instinct on your part. I want you in my corner, Finn. Both you and Andre have a gift for this, and we could do a lot of good for the victims of Beckburg if we learn to work as a team. Tell me what I need to do to earn your trust and I'll do it." She turned her body to face me and leaned forward. Her sweet scent washed over me.

"Time," I answered. "Keep showing up like you have, kicking my ass back in line when I deserve it, and I'll get there. You're not as big of a pain in the ass as you could have been." I nudged the leg of her chair with my foot.

"I've got nothing but time." She leaned back and crossed her arms over her chest. She had a deliberate, stubborn set to her jaw. I fought back a smile.

"Then let's get some work done." I pulled the Ferguson file across the desk and flipped it open. "What do you want to know?"

She smiled at me in earnest. The tension was gone between us. I still intended to learn as much about her as I could, but that would be infinitely easier to accomplish with a good relationship instead of a sour one.

The sisters approved of her, and I held their opinions in high regard. Chloe was the hardest to win over, and it appeared as if Alexis had already done it. Maybe it was safe to let this woman in.

But only just a little.

Chapter Eight

Alexis

Work went from a tense challenge to a genuine joy once Finn and I made peace with one another. When the next victim I met, Poppy, came to prep her testimony, I had already learned a lot about her from Andre and Finn. It proved to be incredibly helpful in our first joint meeting. They told Poppy how lucky she was to have me to help her navigate the system. She opened up to me after that. She clutched my hand while she recounted her experiences to DA Vance. I told her how brave she was, and she glowed at the compliment.

I relaxed more around Finn at work and out with our friends, and he did the same. He even cracked a few jokes around me. It was refreshing to find he had a sense of humor; It made him less intimidating and more human to me. We developed a routine of ending our nights at the One Trick Pony. Instead of taking the bus home, I'd ride with Finn and Andre to the bar in Finn's sleek Charger. The rumble of the engine became a welcome and familiar comfort at the end of my days. Moira, Chloe, and Lacey would meet us there, and we'd drink, laugh, sing, and even dance occasionally. Not Finn, though. He told me he wasn't much of a dancer, and I couldn't coax him onto the floor after that dance on his bad day. Instead of getting on the floor with us, he'd sit back and watch with a drink in his hand.

Before I knew it, a full month passed. I never expected to settle into this new place so easily, but I was beginning to feel like I belonged here. I had friends, a roof over my head, and a job that gave me meaning and purpose. If someone had told me nine months ago that I would be this content, I never would have believed them. My nightmares were even becoming less frequent, which was pretty damn close to a miracle. The constant plaguing fear was slowly diminishing. It was more than I ever expected.

"Okay, Lex." Andre pulled my rolling chair over to his desk. "We just got a tip about Ramond from an inmate at the jail. It's a location where he might be holed up, but we want to run it by Maria before we follow up on it. If we don't look in the exact right place, he might see us and have plenty of time to take off. We need that slippery bastard, so we need Maria to confirm."

"Is she even willing to come in again?" I asked. The idea of seeing that piece of human refuse behind bars would feel like a personal vindication after what he'd done, but I had to keep Maria's well-being in mind.

"We already called, and she said she would come in as long as you're here with her." Finn spun around in his chair to face Andre and me. "She feels comfortable with you."

"That's good to hear. She deserves peace of mind, and I don't think she'll be able to get it until we lock Ramond up. I can imagine the fear she has to endure every day, worrying if he'll show up at her door and hurt her again." I shuddered. That fear was all too real for me, too.

"You okay?" Finn's eyes scanned my face.

I took a deep breath and nodded. "I'm thinking about how to help her feel safe enough to talk. She made it clear last time that she had no intentions of opening up about Ramond."

"What would make you feel safe if you were in her shoes?" Andre asked. He tapped his index finger against the arm of my chair; it was a nervous habit he had.

It was a question I didn't really want to consider; it would bring my fear to the surface when I was constantly working so hard to shove it down. But I needed to get into Maria's head. What would make me feel safe if my attacker was running free, and it was up to me to give evidence to put him away? Hell, I didn't have to imagine it: I'd lived it.

Goosebumps erupted all over my skin. The familiar creeping terror started in the base of my spine and crawled its way up my back. I tried to swallow, but my throat was too tight. I had to focus hard to keep my breathing even. I closed my eyes to block out the buzz of the station around me. I tried to visualize Maria, but my mind wouldn't cooperate. It kept flashing back to the darkness of my old apartment, the smell of cigarettes on his breath, the unending compression of the shoelaces cutting into my wrists.

"Alexis?" Finn's voice snapped me back to reality. "You don't look good. Are you sure you're okay?"

I locked eyes with him. Concern was etched into the lines of his face. I focused on my breathing once more, remembering what my therapist taught me. Trauma lives in the body, not just in the mind. Calm the body, calm the mind. I could almost hear Dr. Barrow's voice in my mind, coaching me through these breaths.

"He's right, Lex," Andre added. "You look like you're gonna to throw up."

"You both know how to charm a woman," I joked. But the wobble in my voice betrayed me. I sounded anything but calm, even to myself.

"I'm going to get you some water." Andre left for the break room.

"Hey." Finn laid a hand on my forearm. "What's up? Really."

"Just a few of my own demons coming out to play." I leaned back in the chair, resting my head.

"You wanna talk about it?" Finn continued assessing me.

"We've all got our shit, right?" I shrugged. He continued to stare at me, brows furrowed. "I don't really want to get into it. But I appreciate your concern. Really, I do."

"Okay." Finn pulled his hand away. My arm felt colder. "I'm here if you change your mind."

Andre came back and handed me a cone shaped paper cup. I sipped it slowly. I chuckled at the irony of them using my own tips to help me. It made me proud.

"If I was Maria, this would make me feel safe," I motioned to both of them. "Having everyone in the room more concerned with how I feel than with pushing me to get what they want. I think if we can give her a sense of control, to help her feel like she has a choice in the matter, that might help."

"That's something," Andre nodded.

"We've got to give her some peace of mind if she talks," Finn continued. "We can offer police protection, move her to a safe house, whatever she needs."

"I think those are good options to offer." I shifted in my chair and tucked my hands under my thighs. "Let's give her a voice in her own fate."

"She's coming in after lunch today. You guys want to go grab something first?" Andre hopped up from the edge of his desk.

"I could eat," I replied.

"As long as you don't make us get gyros again." Finn grabbed his coat and keys.

"What?!" Andre acted affronted. "They're so damn delicious!"

"There are so many other food groups we can introduce you to, though," I teased. "Whole new culinary experiences waiting to be had."

"What if I had something new and… wait for it… gyros?!" Andre spread his arms wide.

"If you're not careful, Andre, you're going to turn into a gyro." I rolled my eyes.

Lunch, thankfully, was not gyros; it was Finn's turn to pick, and he stuck to his guns despite Andre's protests. We got Thai food instead. The pad kra pao absolutely knocked my socks off. Finn stole a few bites off my plate and declared it one of the best things he'd ever eaten. I returned the favor and fell equally in love with his kao ka moo. Andre started off pouting but couldn't deny that his massaman curry was at the very least equal to a gyro.

By the time we got back to the station, spirits were high, and stomachs were full. I tossed my coat over the back of Finn's chair, and he snatched it right back up.

"We have a coat rack, you know," he chided.

"I know, but I don't get a rise out of you when I use the coat rack," I laughed.

"I'm going to petition the Chief to get you your own desk so I can leave my shit all over it. Give you a taste of your own medicine."

"I'll be sure he puts it right next to yours, so you'll never be able to get rid of me." I batted my eyelashes innocently at him. The corner of his mouth pulled up as he tried not to smile.

"Ms. Benicio came in a little early." Chief Whitmer came up from behind us. "You three better get in there." He pointed to interrogation one. His face was serious.

We hurried over and I knocked softly on the door before entering. Maria was sitting across the table with her head down and shoulders hunched. Before she said a word, I knew something was wrong. I could feel it in the air.

"Maria?" I ventured softly.

She raised her head. I gasped. Her face was black and blue, her right eye was swollen, and she had a cut on her cheekbone.

"Oh, my god! What happened, Maria?" I rushed to her side.

She sniffled and lowered her head again. I switched into Spanish and asked her again what happened to her.

"A message from Ramond," she answered in kind.

Andre was fluent in Spanish, but Finn wasn't. I turned to look at his face. Despite not knowing the first few words she had spoken, he had clearly heard her say Ramond's name. His face clouded over, and he looked…dangerous.

"I'm so sorry this happened." I took her hand. "What can we do for you? Do you need medical care?"

"No, no. My friend is a nurse, and she already checked me over."

"Do you know who did this?" Andre joined the conversation.

Maria paused. I could feel the tension rolling off her. This attack must have frightened her more than ever. We would never get her to open up to us after this.

Finn circled the table and knelt in front of her. "Maria?" His tone was soft, gentle. She met his eye timidly. "We're not going to force you to do or say anything if you don't want to. But we won't let you go out and get hurt like this again. No matter what happens, we want to protect you."

Andre translated what Finn said softly into Spanish. Tears spilled down Maria's cheeks. She didn't break eye contact with Finn. As I watched the exchange, the fire and conviction in Finn's eyes was clear, and I knew Maria could see it too. She took a deep breath.

"Yes," she whispered in English. "I know who did this."

"If you want to tell us, we want to help," Finn replied.

"His name is Ronaldo. He's Ramond's cousin."

Andre jotted something down in the little notebook he kept in his chest pocket.

"Do you have a last name for us?" Finn prompted.

"Vega," Maria wiped a tear. I squeezed her hand.

"Andre?" Finn turned to him.

"I'm on it," Andre nodded, and left the room.

"Is there somewhere you feel safe you can stay?" Finn continued.

Maria seemed confused. I translated his question into Spanish. Another tear slid down her cheek.

"No, not here."

"Where?" I replied.

"Mama and Abuela," she whispered.

"Then we'll take you there." I touched her face gingerly, careful of the bruises.

"We'll get him, Maria, I promise," Finn vowed.

"And Ramond, too?" Maria asked in English.

"We don't know where he is," Finn admitted.

Another silence. The air in the room felt heavy. The implied question weighed on Maria's shoulders.

"I don't know where he is either." She turned to me. I translated for Finn. "But I know of someone who might." The last few words were like molasses in her mouth. It was a clear labor for her to get them out at all. The second she closed her mouth, she shuddered and burst into tears. I wrapped my arms around her. She held me tightly in return. Finn and I locked eyes over her back. He looked at Maria and I with a surprising tenderness.

What Andre said to me the first time I'd met the two detectives emerged from my memory: "No one cares more about the victim than Finn. You'll see. Work with us, be patient, hold back your judgment and you'll see." With my biases against detectives, and Finn himself, out of the way, I could see it so clearly. My chest got tight as I held back the surge of emotion I felt. I swallowed hard.

Once Maria had cried herself out, she peeked up at Finn as he waited patiently for her. I handed her a tissue so she could dry her eyes. She blew her nose loudly, then gave a shy smile.

"Whenever you're ready to talk, Maria, I'm ready to listen." Finn poised his pencil over a blank page.

Maria took several more steadying breaths. She hesitated, so I nodded to her, encouraging her to take her time. One last nose blow, then she was talking. She knew Ramond left the city after her initial assault. He had met up with a cousin in the Washington D.C. area, then had gone west from there. Ramond had sent her a menacing postcard from Tennessee, but she hadn't heard directly from him since. She remembered he had an aunt named Tia Marco who lived in a little blue house on the South side of a city called Morristown.

"That is the last person I know of who saw him," Maria finished. "He would only trust family to know where he is. He would trust Tia Marco to know where he was going. That is really all I know."

I had translated her entire story to Finn as she told it. She waited patiently for Finn to take notes between breaths. Finn's face was screwed up in concentration. I knew him well enough now to know that once he heard all the details, he wouldn't need the notes. He'd lock that in his mind until Ramond was in cuffs. The notes were a formality.

"That's plenty for us to go on, Maria," Finn finished. "Thank you. I appreciate the courage that took."

"I kept thinking of my abuela," she explained. "When she taught me to cook, she would always tell me not to be afraid of the fire. 'It can burn you, but it can protect you, too,' she said. It cooks the bad things out, the fire. 'Don't be afraid, mija,'" Maria sighed. "I don't want to be afraid anymore."

"It's hard to face your fears," I agreed. "But today you did exactly that. Your abuela would be so proud of you."

A knock drew our attention to the door. Andre had returned. "Detective Briggs, we have an arrest to make." His tone was triumphant.

"You found him?" Maria gasped.

"I have two squad cars heading over to Ronaldo's job right now. I just got off the phone with his boss and he confirmed he's there," Andre assured.

"I'm going to have an officer escort you home so you can pack what you need," Finn told Maria. "After I see Ronaldo behind steel, I'll take you to the airport myself."

"Are you serious?" She brightened.

"If that's alright with you," he nodded.

"Will you come, too?" Maria asked me.

"Of course. I'm here for whatever you need, remember? That's a promise." I rubbed her back.

"Thank you." Maria kissed the back of my hand three times. "Thank you!"

Andre signaled a uniform into the room and introduced him to Maria. The uniformed officer offered Maria his arm, and she took it. He led her from the room with Andre on his heels.

I wrapped my arms around myself, feeling a thousand things at once.

"Nice work, little rookie." Finn put his hand on my shoulder.

"No, that was all you, Finn," I turned to him. "Seriously, you were spectacular!"

"I have an excellent teacher." He beamed at me. "You should head to your place and grab what you need. It's going to be a nine-hour round trip to the airport. I'll come get you before we pick up Maria. But first I've got a shitbag to go arrest."

He left the room, and I was left with a satisfied smirk.

Chapter Nine

Finn

Ronaldo Vega almost shit himself when he saw me, Andre, and six uniforms storm the warehouse he worked in. It was one of the most satisfying busts I ever made. I kept the image of Maria's bruised and battered face in the forefront of my mind as I tightened the handcuffs behind Ronaldo's back. The piece of filth had the nerve to complain that the cuffs were too tight. He whined about it the entire way to the station for booking. Andre usually checked the cuffs if perps complained, but my stalwart partner feigned ignorance with a placid smile.

I stayed with Ronaldo while Andre went to deliver the good news to Maria. My Spanish comprised about six words, half of them not fit for polite company, and we both wanted her to ask questions if she had them. Ronaldo continued his bitching through booking, tried to pull the tough guy act, and threatened the man who took his fingerprints. He was clearly easy to rile; interrogating him would be a breeze with a little button pushing. I'd have to pass that info along to Andre. As much as I wanted to watch him squirm, I had a promise to keep to Maria.

I smiled to myself as I left Ronaldo in his four-by-four station cell and it lingered as I caught Andre up on my insights for interrogation. Half of the smile was for a job well done, but the other half, I was surprised to realize, was because I was looking forward to spending time with Alexis. With my pride set aside, she was easy to like. We had built an easy friendship despite our rough start. Time with her would move faster, so I was glad she agreed to come along for the drive to the airport.

When I got to her place, her apartment on 10-block was surrendering to the twilight. Its windows were lighting up one by one as the residents guarded against the growing darkness. I pressed the buzzer for 3A and waited, hands in my pockets.

"I saw you coming a mile away," Moira's voice crackled through the intercom.

"You see everything coming from a mile away."

"Alexis is on her way down. Don't do anything Chloe would do, okay?"

"Hey!" Chloe's indignant voice echoed in the background.

"I'll be on my best behavior," I chuckled.

Alexis came around the last turn of the staircase and gave me a wave. She opened the door, and I reached for the backpack she was carrying. She smelled like honeysuckle; the scent magnifying with every swish of her hair.

"You didn't have a chance to change into something more comfortable?" She pulled at the lapels of my suit coat.

"The sooner we get Maria on a plane home to her mom and grandma, the better."

"Hmph. I thought you were going to say you couldn't wait to see me again," she teased.

"That was a close second."

I opened the passenger door for her, and she slid in, murmuring something about 'chivalry' that I didn't quite catch. The second I was belted into the driver's seat, her eyes were on me. I could feel the question before it came.

"Did you get him?"

"Do you even need to ask?" I gloated.

"I guess not. I never doubted you for a second."

"Andre's probably grilling the little fish as we speak." The engine purred as we sped through the streets. "He'll be easy to crack, mark my word."

"Consider it marked. Was Maria relieved?"

"Andre said she cried some more, but yeah, she seemed relieved."

"Let's not talk about it once she's in the car unless she brings it up herself. I think keeping a future focus will get her on the right track emotionally before she gets on a plane." Alexis pulled chapstick out of her backpack and applied it liberally. It smelled like the vanilla frosting I put on my toaster pastries.

"You're the boss," I agreed.

"Since when?"

"Since you owned my ass that day in interrogation. You know your shit, Allie." I tapped my fingers against the steering wheel and turned the heat down to a more comfortable level.

"Glad to know you finally see reason." She patted my hand on the gearshift.

We pulled up to Maria's tiny trailer house on 9-block. The marked car was still sitting outside, as instructed. I gave a small salute to the uniform behind the wheel, and he returned the gesture. Maria hurried out the front door, struggling with the two battered suitcases she pulled behind her. I took over suitcase duty while she settled in the back of my car.

The four and a half hours to the airport passed in a mixed of gentle silence and Spanish conversation. Alexis and Maria chatted easily, Alexis translating for me occasionally. I mostly kept to myself, which is my natural way. I had little to add in most conversations in English, so it was easy to hold my silence while the two women carried on in Spanish.

At the airport, Alexis and I escorted Maria through the terminal until we got to the security checkpoint. Maria gave us both a tight hug and thanked us repeatedly in both English and Spanish. She kissed Alexis once on each cheek before hurrying to the scanner. Once she met up with her plain-clothes police escort on the other side, we gave her one last wave before heading back to the car.

The late-night air had a sharper bite to it than usual for this time of year. Alexis pulled a sweatshirt out of her backpack and pulled it on before buckling her seatbelt. Then she pulled out a bag of chips and some peanut butter M&M's, setting it on the console between us.

"You're not seriously considering eating in my car, are you?" I scrutinized the bags.

"Oh, come on! What's a road trip without snacks" She opened the chip bag with a pop. I cringed. "I promise to vacuum your precious car if crumbs dare besmirch her beauty."

She held a chip up in front of my mouth, tempting me. It smelled like sour cream and onion. My favorite.

"I promise," she reiterated.

"Fine," I huffed. She popped the chip into my watering mouth, and I crunched down on it.

"Something salty and something sweet." She tossed a few M&M's in her mouth. "The perfect combination!"

"Okay," she turned sideways in her seat toward me. "Now you have to tell me something no one else knows. The next rule of road trips is secret telling and deep emotional bonding."

"What kind of road trips are you taking?" I asked incredulously.

"Very few with dudes," she admitted. "But what else are we going to talk about? We both hate sports. There's only so much shop talk I can stomach after a day like this. And we've got over four hours of clock to burn."

"You're not going to stop bugging me until I play along, are you?" I pretended to be annoyed, but I wasn't at all. This was just another part of what made Alexis so endearing to me; she called a spade a spade and when she wanted to say something, she did it straight forward. I liked that she didn't waste time beating around the bush.

"You are correct, sir." She popped another chip into my waiting mouth.

"Then ask me something," I mumbled as I chewed. "Give me something to work with."

"Tell me a secret about your dating life."

"We're going straight to it, huh?"

"Mm-hmm," she confirmed.

I thought for a second, picking the remnants of the chip out of my teeth with my tongue. What secrets was I willing to share? Without her saying it aloud, I knew whatever I shared with her on this ride would stay between us. She wasn't one to tell other people's secrets. If only she knew the secrets we kept from her for her own good...

"Hmm," I sighed. "Okay, here's something. I once had a girlfriend who was deep into BDSM." I felt a little heat burning in my cheeks.

"And?"

"And she liked to make me dress up in her underwear before she shackled me to the bed," I finished with a nervous laugh.

"Granny panties or thongs," she snickered.

"Thongs." My cheeks were burning now.

"I'm trying to picture your tough-guy man-ass in a thong!" She fed me another chip.

"Please don't," I warned.

"Why? You self-conscious?"

"Not a bit. I looked like a fucking Greek God in pink silk and lace," I bragged. "But I've got your number now, Henson. If you go too far down that mental pathway, every time you see me at work, you'll be picturing me in a thong, not a suit."

"You've got me there."

"Your turn. Now you have to tell me a secret about your love life."

"I'm into BDSM and I used to make my ex wear pink lacy thongs in bed."

"Ha ha. Really though."

"Okay, okay... How's this? I've had a couple of serious boyfriends in my day, but I don't think I've ever really been in love."

"You haven't?" It surprised me at how casually she made the declaration.

"I cared about them, sure, but there was always something missing," she shrugged.

"What was missing?" I grabbed a handful of M&M's.

"It's hard to say. They were good guys, but we never really clicked in all the ways I always imagined I would when I was in love. The emotional connections were shallow at best, the passion was dull or missing altogether, and I never felt prioritized. Maybe my expectations are too high, but I want to be in passionate love with someone; someone I could enjoy forever. I want the kind of love you don't have to question; you know it's love without a doubt. Does that make me sound like a stupid little girl?"

"No. It makes you sound like you have appropriately high standards. You deserve nothing less than that."

"Have you ever been in love?" She leaned her head against the headrest, eyes still on me.

"I was once. It didn't end well for me, though. I got my still-beating heart ripped out of my chest. I haven't made a go of it since." The memories of Brie threatened to burst through the steel wall I'd locked them behind. I fought them off with gritted teeth.

"Was that recently?"

"A few years ago, before I moved to the Clock."

"Do you hate her?"

"Do I what?" The question surprised me.

"I'm curious, seriously; no judgment if you do or don't. But I've always wondered if you end up hating a person you once loved after something like that. Like, does love turn into something that burns you instead of warms you?" Alexis' face was thoughtful.

I considered her question. Did I hate Brie? There were definitely times I felt like I did. When I found out what she had done, I wanted to crawl out of my skin and hide for the rest of my fucking life. Then my self-loathing turned into loathing her.

"You don't have to answer if you're uncomfortable." Alexis put her hand on my arm.

"No, it's not like that. I'm just thinking about it." I frowned. "I hated her, at the beginning. But the longer I've been away, dedicated myself to other things, the less I even think about her. I guess I'm less angry and more apathetic. If things had ended differently, who the hell knows?"

"Does any part of you still love her?"

"No," I answered quickly. She raised her eyebrows at me. "There's no better way to kill love than to find out your partner never really loved you back. I was more a convenient amusement for her; she used me, got what she needed, then ditched me when someone else came along when she got bored."

"God, that sucks," Alexis sighed. "I'm sorry she did that to you. You didn't deserve it."

"Maybe I did," I shrugged.

"What would make a person deserve to be treated that way?" She sounded incredulous.

"I'm not a saint, Allie. I've done some awful shit in my life. Maybe what happened was karma catching up with me."

"Bullshit," she spat.

"You don't believe in karma?"

"I believe there are forces around us we can't control or explain, but I don't believe you're a bad person."

"You don't know me all that well," I reminded. If she only knew who I was, what I was, she'd throw the door open and tuck and roll out onto the freeway.

"Well, I haven't known you very long, but I've got a pretty good sense for people."

"Your people sensor is off then." I grabbed another chip and bit into it hard.

"Doubt it," she argued.

"You shouldn't."

"Prove me wrong then. What have you done that makes you such a bad person?"

She laid the challenge out in front of me, and I was itching to take it. The streetlights that lined both sides of the road made the insides of the car strobe as we sped in and out of their reach. I glanced at Alexis, and she was looking at me with anticipation, one eyebrow raised. In this moment, I wanted to tell her everything. I wanted to spill my guts in the dim light of the car.

But I had sworn an oath a long time ago. That oath wrapped around my will and forced it to submit. I gritted my teeth and shook my head.

"That must mean I'm right, then," she gloated.

The urge to argue with her rose in my chest, but I suppressed it. She was wrong. If an otherworldly entity exists that counts my sins, they would far outweigh the good. I wanted her to be right, so I let her think she was.

Chapter Ten

Alexis

Finn was quiet for a long time. Had I pushed too much? Probably. Who likes to recite their failures and fuck ups? God knows I had secrets of my own that I wasn't keen to spill.

"I'm sorry if it feels like we're in an interrogation. I want to get to know you better. Sometimes being friends with me can feel like deep-sea diving with a snorkel. I like it deep."

Finn chuckled. A wicked grin spread across his face.

"You might as well say it," I rolled my eyes. "Since Andre's not here, someone has to."

"That's what she said," he laughed.

"When we first met, I never would have pegged you as the guy who liked 'that's what she said' jokes."

"Why not?" He grabbed another handful of M&M's and popped them all into his mouth.

"You were so damn serious; like some stupid, brooding, romance novel vampire."

"A vampire, huh?" He ran his tongue across the front of his teeth. "I have sharp teeth, but I'm not a fan of drinking blood. Try again."

"Try what again? Assign you a romcom stereotype?"

"No," he continued to grin. "Try to figure out what kind of monster I am."

"Is there an ass-pain monster?"

"No, try again." He nudged me with his elbow.

"Fine... no to the vampire." I looked him up and down. "You're too attractive to be a Frankenstein monster... not wrapped in toilet paper, so not a mummy..."

"Wait, wait, wait," he waved a hand. "Let's go back to the part where you tell me how attractive I am."

"You're definitely solid," I grabbed his arm and shook it, "so not a ghost..." He moved his hand from the gearshift to my leg and squeezed. It gave me a tiny shiver. "It's a full moon and you're not completely covered in hair, so not a werewolf."

"Not hair you can see," he winked.

"No magic wand," I ignored his innuendo, "so not a warlock. You haven't tried to eat my brains once, so not a zombie… Damn, I'm stumped."

"You'll never guess."

"I've got it! You're a dragon."

"A dragon?!" He laughed.

"Yep, that's gotta be it. You're grumpy, you horde things, and you breathe fire when you're angry. Nailed it!" I gave myself a satisfied nod.

"What do I horde?"

"Criminals," I answered simply.

He barked a laugh.

"Fine, I'm a dragon. You caught me." Finn held his hands up for a split second, then put one back on the steering wheel and the other back on my leg. "You're running a big risk getting this close to me."

"Lucky for us, I'm a magnificent dragon tamer." An impulse seized me, and I followed it. I wrapped my arms around his arm and rested my head on his shoulder.

"I guess I have to give you that one," he rubbed my knee.

"Now you have to guess what kind of monster I am," I demanded.

"Oh, that one's easy," he replied. "You're a siren."

"What makes me a siren?"

"You can persuade and charm just by opening up that mouth of yours. If you can sing, we're all fucked."

"Are you afraid I'm going to lure you to your utter demise if I do?"

"Without a doubt."

My stomach did a backflip. What the hell was I flirting with him for? I was *so* not going there with one of my partners. Nothing would make work more awkward than any type of romance. Finn was my friend. That was it. We were only friends getting comfortable with one another.

We sat in silence for a few minutes, me still resting my head on his shoulder and him mindlessly rubbing my knee with his thumb. I inhaled the subtle scent of his cologne. It was rich, warm, and woody.

"Traditionally, the passenger on a road trip isn't allowed to fall asleep." Finn shook my leg gently.

"I'm not sleeping," I protested.

"I figured you had to be. You never stop talking otherwise."

"Untrue!"

"You can sleep if you need to. I'm just shitting you," Finn assured.

"I don't want to sleep."

"What *do* you want?" The question felt loaded.

I hesitated. I wasn't sure what I wanted. Not totally.

"I want to keep talking to my friend," I answered.

"Then talk away."

That's exactly what we did for the next four hours. We talked about everything and nothing all at once. He told me stories about his life; he had lived all around the world in tons of different countries and cultures. I told him stories about my childhood, and we connected about being only children. He told me what prompted him to become a detective, and I told him what made me want to go into social work. He briefly told me about his parents, and I skimmed over the story of mine before we pulled up in front of my apartment.

Finn walked me inside and up the stairs to my apartment. He insisted on carrying my backpack for me, which was now empty of all the snacks I had packed and was now filled with wrappers and empty water bottles.

"I'll bring Chloe's hand-held vacuum to work tomorrow and clean out the Charger like I promised." I held my hand over my heart.

"Don't worry about it." He waved the suggestion away.

"You're going to vacuum it the second you get home, aren't you?"

"Damn straight."

"Impossible man." I shook my head.

"I'm not a man. I'm a dragon." He puffed out his chest.

"And I'm a siren," I curtseyed. I stumbled, and Finn grabbed my elbow to steady me. "Thanks. I'm tired-drunk, I guess."

"Thanks for being my wingman tonight. That drive would have been a nightmare on my own. You made it so much more bearable."

"One of my many talents is to be just tolerable enough to entertain."

Finn hesitated at the door. Something flashed across his face, but it was gone before I could figure out what it was. His eyes were far away.

"You okay?" I asked.

Finn's eyes focused on me, and he smiled. "Yeah, I'm thinking about something."

"Care to share with the class?"

"Another time, maybe." He gave me a one-armed hug. "Go get some sleep."

"Yes sir," I saluted him. I gave him one last grin before shutting the door behind me. Before I could slide all the locks into place, I heard a rustle behind me. I jumped and spun around, heart pounding in my chest.

"I'm so sorry, Alexis! I didn't mean to scare you," Moira soothed. "I wanted to make sure you got home safe before I went to bed." She was tucked under a blanket on the couch.

"Oh, Moira, you didn't have to do that! It's late. Go get in your own bed." I crossed the room to the kitchen and emptied my backpack into the garbage and recycling bins.

"How was the drive? Everything go okay?" Moira asked, gathering her stuff.

"It went great. Our victim is on a flight home as we speak, safe and sound."

"And Finn was okay?" Moira cocked her head to the side. She had a strange glint in her eye. Her eyes went unfocused for a few seconds before she looked at me again with a serene smile.

"Uh, yeah. He was Finn," I shrugged.

"Good. I'm glad you two are getting along. It's nice you could move past bad first impressions and give each other a second chance. You're both so wonderful."

"You're sweet. I'm gonna head to bed." I jerked my head back toward my room.

"Okay, goodnight!"

When I was back in my bedroom, I tossed my backpack onto the back of my desk chair. What had Moira been trying to get at? Did she think there was something going on between me and Finn? I blushed at the thought. Finn and I were just friends.

Just friends, I chanted to myself as I drifted off to sleep.

I got a call from Andre early the next morning that the detective in New Mexico confirmed Maria's safe arrival and tearful reunion with her mama and Abuela. She was safe at home with the family who loved her, right where she belonged. It made going to school this morning so much easier. It was a relief to know Maria had made it okay.

The air on campus was brisk as I got off the bus. A lovely woman with long blond waves that cascaded down her back was waiting next to the bench. She might be around my age, but her face was troubled. A brief tug in my chest made me slow as I passed her. She kept her head down to avoid meeting my gaze. I slowed my walk, waiting to see if she got on the bus.

Something felt... off. I couldn't put my finger on it, but I trusted my intuition. It had literally saved my life once before.

When she didn't board the bus, I turned back to her. I felt a little foolish, but I approached her slowly. She still stared down at her feet, arms wrapped around herself, rubbing the bare skin of her arms. Tear tracks stained both of her cheeks. The outfit she wore was much too thin for the cooling weather.

"I'm probably being a total creep, but are you okay?" I asked.

Her head bobbed up, and she peered at me with large green eyes. "Are you talking to me?" She looked back and forth, but no one else was around.

"Yeah, I... Again, I'm sorry if I'm bothering you, but you seem like you're having a rough day. Can I help in any way?" I pulled my backpack higher on my shoulders.

"Oh, uh..." She checked around us again. The movement was sharp and jittery. I recognized the vigilance. "That's nice, but I... um, I'm fine."

A flash of light drew my attention down to her ankle. She wore a silver anklet with a red cherry charm. Then it hit me. She was a sex worker. Leticia, one of the victims I was working with at the station, had that same anklet.

I met Leticia two weeks ago. A John had drugged her and left in an alley. When she made it to the hospital, an officer had gotten her to talk about what happened before she had sobered all the way up. She refused to give us any information about the John after that point. She was still adamant about not pursuing a case when Finn, Andre, and I met with her, but she had agreed to start counseling. It was the same damn code of silence that kept so many others from talking. It was probably that same damn code that kept this woman silent, too.

"I'm Alexis." I held out my hand to her.

She peeked up at me again. She looked from my face to my outstretched hand and back again. I knew that fear in her eyes. It made me angry and sad at the same time. I took a deep breath and smiled gently.

"Selsha." She reached out a shy hand to me. I took it between both of my own and shook it.

"It's so nice to meet you." She nodded to me and pulled her hand back. "Are you sure there isn't anything I can do for you? You seem sad." I pointed to her cheeks. "I would hate to leave you here alone without at least asking."

"That transparent, huh?" She sunk onto the bench behind her.

"It's tough to hide sorrow like that from someone who's familiar with it themselves," I pointed to myself. "Do you want to talk about it?"

"God, no!" She shook her head.

"Do you want to talk about something else?"

"Don't you have somewhere to be?" She stared at me with those big eyes again.

"It can wait."

Her third nervous look around triggered a clench in my gut. I knew that look, too. She was checking to see if anybody was coming. But was she looking for someone in particular?

"Do you have something to eat, by chance?" She pointed to my backpack.

"Always," I laughed. I pulled a few granola bars out and passed them to her.

"I... uh... stayed with a friend last night and didn't get breakfast before I left." She ripped the wrappers off and dug in.

"Happens all the time."

By the way she ate, she had missed more than one meal. I dug around in my backpack and found some cheese crackers and an apple. I passed them to her, too. She took them and smiled, a couple of crumbs of granola slipping from her mouth as she did.

"Thank you." She held up the food to me.

"My pleasure. Are you waiting for the next bus?"

"No, my boss is picking me up. It's easier to meet him here than any other place." She took a bite of the apple. "He's just running late. He gets...busy."

"I'm happy to wait with you until he gets here," I offered.

"Oh, that's nice, but I don't think that's a good idea." Selsha looked back over her shoulder again. "I'm sure you have class." She motioned toward campus.

"Okay, I'll leave you to it then. I hope your day gets better." I pulled my backpack back on. "I hope to see you again. I'm on campus a few days a week if you're around. I always have extra snacks."

"Yeah, maybe I'll see you around." She gave me a genuine smile.

"Actually, let me give you my phone number. I get bored in between classes and I'm always happy to have a breakfast buddy." I pulled out my notebook and scribbled my number on a corner of paper, then ripped it off and handed it to Selsha. She took it and stuck it in her bra.

"I'm happy you stopped," Selsha said.

"Me too. Bye, Selsha." I waved and walked toward my class.

I thought about giving her my card, but I worried she might think I was trying to bust her. The Beckburg Police logo next to my picture probably wouldn't be super welcoming. I hoped she would reach out to me, though. She had a tough life from what I knew of the Clock's underbelly.

Class rushed by and before I knew it, I was heading back to the bus stop. Selsha was long gone, but I couldn't help thinking about her. When I boarded the bus to the police station, I decided to ask Finn to look her up in the system. I couldn't shake the feeling that she needed help.

My cell phone buzzed in my pocket. I pulled it out, hopeful that it was Selsha already. But that was wishful thinking.

"Hey Chloe, what's up?" I answered.

"Lex, Moira came up with the best idea! The weather is going to turn bitchy soon, and we want to get out into the woods for one last camp-out before it's too cold."

"I've never been camping before, so you'll have to teach me how to rough it," I replied.

"You've never been before? Impossible. That settles it. We're definitely going. You just have to convince Andre and Finn to come with us. I'm already walking over to the Pony to get Riel to come, then I'm calling a few others."

"I'll do my best," I laughed.

"Good, see you later!"

Camping. I remember asking my mom about going once when I was little. She told me that sleeping on the ground at her friend's place while we were trying to get into low-income housing was camping enough for a lifetime. Mom was pragmatic and not the least bit adventurous.

Finn and Andre were chatting with a couple detectives from vice when I walked into the station. I filled up my water bottle before plopping down at Finn's desk to wait for them. We were meeting with the Chief to update him on the cases we'd been working. He seemed eager to talk about how the pilot program was working out.

The guys didn't seem to be in much of a rush, so I picked up a notebook and started doodling. I thought about all the things Finn and I had talked about on our drive back from the airport. With little artistic skill, I sketched out a dragon and a singing siren. I wasn't an expert on mythological creatures, so I made do with my imagination. Next came an airplane with a smiling woman in the window, handcuffs on a shocked bad guy, and a black car on a long, winding road.

"Whatcha doin'?" The sudden whisper made me jump.

Andre laughed as he backed away from my ear. I had gotten so lost in trying to perfect the tiny campsite I was drawing that I didn't hear Andre and Finn approach. Finn was scrutinizing my drawings.

"Did you really have to deface my notebook like that? I actually use that thing to take important notes."

"This is a very important note from one of your cases," I argued. "See, there's Maria, and there's Ronaldo." I pointed to the smiling woman on the plane and the shocked criminal. "Then there's you and me and the Charger."

"Where am I?" Andre scrutinized the paper. "And why are you two a bat and a mermaid?"

"It's not a bat, it's a dragon!"

"It looks like a bat, Lex." Andre squinted his eyes.

"Ah, the mermaid is supposed to be a siren. I get it," Finn grinned.

"I don't get it at all. Now you guys have inside jokes that I don't understand. It's unacceptable," Andre mock pouted. "And I demand to be poorly drawn into that document."

"Keep insulting my artwork and I'll show you 'poorly drawn,'" I grumbled. "Here…"

I drew a stick figure sitting on a log next to a campfire in my campground doodle. I gave him a roasting stick with a marshmallow on the end and a big smile. Then I gave him a tiny fedora.

"There's Andre," I beamed.

"Adequate." Andre seemed slightly mollified. "But when did camping figure into this case?"

"It didn't. That's a drawing of your future," I answered.

"According to who?"

"According to Chloe and Moira."

Finn and Andre exchanged shocked looks before quickly turning back to me. When they looked at me again, their expressions were normal. What the hell had that been?

"Did they say that was my future?" Andre asked casually.

"Not exactly…" I arched an eyebrow at them. "Chloe called me on my way here and said that they want to go camping and it's my job to convince you guys to come with us."

"Oh," Andre nodded. He looked oddly relieved. Finn had relaxed his shoulders. "Okay, that makes sense."

"Did I miss something?" I asked.

"Miss what?" Andre replied a little too innocently.

"You guys are acting weird. Is there something up with Moira and Chloe that I don't know about?"

"No, we're good," Finn assured. "We were confused how we went from airplanes and dragons to campfires and…" he squinted at the drawing, "…roasting hot dogs."

"It's a marshmallow," I chided.

I still wasn't convinced. Every once in a while, Andre and Finn would share looks just like that. It usually happened when I asked them about their history as partners, their friendships with people from the One Trick Pony, or what brought them both out here to the Clock.

"We should get going. It's almost 2:00 and we don't want to keep the Chief waiting," Finn broke the awkward silence. "Come on, Doodles, let's not quit your day job."

He pulled me up out of his chair. We made our way to the Chief's office and knocked on the door. He beckoned for us to enter, but held up a finger to silence us while he finished a phone call. Once he hung up, he rubbed the bridge of his nose and sighed.

"Everything okay, Chief?" Andre inquired.

"Just fine, Alvarez," Chief replied. "Doing my least favorite part of the job."

"Kissing bureaucratic ass?" Finn guessed.

"You got it," Chief nodded. "Take a seat."

We settled into the worn wooden chairs with ripped leather cushions. The air whooshed its escape from the tear in my seat as my weight settled into it. The Chief's office always smelled like pine tree air fresheners and black coffee.

"How are things going with the victim's advocate program?" Chief leaned far back in his chair and put his hands behind his head. His back popped.

"It's turning out better than we expected," Finn answered.

"That's not a hard thing to accomplish, is it? You boys thought it was going to be a disaster from the start. Now you three are out there thick as thieves every day." He motioned to the think tank with his chin. "What does 'better than expected' mean?"

"Alexis has been an incredible addition to our cases," Andre enthused. "She gets these vics in ways we don't; it's like she's in their heads."

Little did he know…

"She's been an irreplaceable asset," Finn affirmed. "We wouldn't have been able to make the break on the Benicio case without her. And the Ferguson case has momentum again for the same reason."

I couldn't help but blush. I had hoped I was making a difference, had thought Andre and Finn were seeing the benefit of my work, but hearing them say it out loud was incredibly satisfying. The three men all turned to me.

"I'm so glad you both feel that way," I piped up. "We had a few kinks that needed ironing out, but once we got on the same page, we've been able to make quite a difference."

"What kind of kinks?" Chief asked.

"Just some misunderstandings," I explained. I didn't want to get into the argument Finn and I had, but I didn't want to lie to the Chief either. "We probably need to fine tune the orientation process for detectives before pairing them with an advocate. I don't think there was a very clear understanding of what my job was, how that looks in the room with a victim, and how we can integrate as detectives and advocates."

"That's good feedback," Chief jotted something down. "What else? What's working? What's not working? How can we improve the process? Where else can we focus on getting the most out of Ms. Henson here?"

We spent the next hour workshopping the victim's advocate program. Andre and Finn had excellent suggestions about how to help detectives be more comfortable having someone like me join in on their cases. They even suggested expanding my responsibilities into the investigative process to help them and other detectives get into the minds of both victims and perpetrators. I added my perspective about how advocates could integrate into other units, not only violent crimes.

"That gives me a lot to think about." Chief set down his pen. "I'm glad you three found a way to work together. This is exactly what I'd hoped for. I made the right choice with you two, Briggs and Alvarez. I expected nothing less."

"Thank you, Chief." Finn rose and shook Chief's hand, and Andre did the same.

"And you, Alexis, are a real treasure. These two are tough to please and please them you have. Keep up the great work." Chief shook my hand as well.

"Will do," I smiled.

"Get back to work," Chief dismissed.

When we got back to Finn and Andre's desks, Finn pulled an extra chair over for me. We didn't have any victim interviews for the rest of the week, so it was back to digging through files. Andre mentioned wanting to follow up with the DA about charges against Ronaldo and looking into the lead Maria had given us about Ramond's aunt in Tennessee. We spent the rest of our day working on Maria's case.

On the drive home, I remembered the task Chloe had given me.

"So, are you two in for the camping trip?"

They both hesitated.

"What? Not into camping?"

"No, we love to camp," Andre replied. "The weather's getting… a little chilly already."

"I can look up the forecast. I don't think it's going to be that bad." I pulled out my phone. They were being squirrely about this. I chuckled to myself at the unintended pun.

"Who else is coming?" Finn asked.

"The sisters, of course. Chloe was going to invite Riel and a few other friends from the Pony. She didn't mention anyone by name, though."

"Okay…"

"Come on, you guys have to come," I urged. "I've never been before, and you need to be present to witness the hilarity of my camping newbie mishaps."

They exchanged looks again. It was pissing me off. What was it they kept secretly, silently communicating with each other that I was too delicate to hear?

"Is everyone planning to take me into the woods and sacrifice me to some ancient gods or something? You guys are being so weird about it."

"No, ritual sacrifice isn't usually on the agenda for our camping trips." Andre tried to lighten the mood in the car.

"There's a lot of drunken…shenanigans," Finn explained. "It can get a little… weird."

"Weirder than this?" I motioned between the two of them.

"Loads weirder," Andre nodded.

"Okay… Should I stay home then? I don't want to be a buzzkill while you all strip naked and dance around the fire. I get that I'm the new kid, so I don't want to make it awkward," I offered.

"No, that's not it at all." Andre turned to look at me.

"Yeah, no," Finn joined in. "Look, we're in. Camping it is."

We pulled up in front of my apartment. I slowly got out of the car, keeping my eyes out for any significant glances between the two. But I was wasting my time; they were both looking at me with serene smiles. I guess the significant glances would be unnecessary after I was inside and the two of them were alone in the car.

"Okay, I'll let Chloe and Moira know. See you later at the Pony?"

"Yeah, we'll be there." Finn gave me a nod, and the two of them drove off.

"Weirdos," I mumbled.

Chapter Eleven

Finn

"What are the sisters thinking, inviting Alexis to come camping with us?" I growled.

"She *is* their roommate," Andre reasoned. "It would be rude to disappear on her for a long weekend with all our mutual friends and leave her behind. At least from Lex's perspective."

"This isn't like hanging out at the Pony," I argued. "This is the woods, Andre. You know how that changes things… how that changes us."

"I know, I know. Definitely not saying it was the smart thing to do. I'm trying to understand it from the sisters' point of view."

"They could have picked anything else, literally anything else, but they chose camping in the woods." I shook my head.

"The damage is already done, man, just let it…"

"The damage hasn't even started," I interrupted. "We all took an oath to protect ourselves and protect everyone around us. How are we supposed to keep that oath if we bring an outsider to where we're most likely to drop our guard… for days? Not an hour or two; days, Andre."

"I don't know why you're coming at me for this! It wasn't my idea." Andre held up his hands.

I sighed. "I know. I'm taking the bullshit out on you…"

"As usual…"

"…when I should talk to the sisters about it." I rolled my eyes and continued. "This is their shitshow after all."

"Call them up," Andre suggested.

"No, I'll pull them aside at the Pony tonight. It's harder to weasel their way out of an ass-chewing in person than it is on the phone."

"Moira's going to see you coming a mile away." Andre shook his head.

"I fucking know that," I sighed again. "But it's not going to stop me."

When Andre and I got to the One Trick Pony a couple hours later, the sisters and Alexis were already on the dance floor with Vijay and Vikram. Lacey was twirling like a ballerina, completely out of time with the music. Chloe and Alexis were dancing with the guys and Moira was eyeing me warily as I strode through the crowd.

Andre was right; a mile away…

"What can I get you tonight, fellas?" Riel called.

"I'll just have a beer," I answered. "Pick me a good one."

"I'll have the same," Andre echoed.

Riel grabbed two bottles from behind the bar and set them in front of us.

"You have something on your mind," Riel guessed. "You have a terrible poker face."

"Did Chloe rope you into a camping trip this weekend?" I asked.

"Ah, that. Yes, yes, she did," Riel replied.

"You know she's bringing Alexis, right?"

"It was…implied… that she would also be attending."

"And you still agreed to go?"

"I have to head out that direction soon anyway, Finn, you know that. It's not odd for us to venture out together," Riel hedged.

"But it is strange to go out there with an outsider." I gritted my teeth and stole a glance at Alexis over my shoulder. She was laughing raucously while she danced with Vijay.

"We haven't attempted it before, but I trust everyone to be on their best behavior. Besides, Alexis has proven herself to be trustworthy, has she not?"

"That's beside the point and you know it," I argued.

"Do you trust her?" Riel's eyes x-rayed me.

"As a coworker, absolutely. As a friend, sure. But with my, our most important and dangerous secret? I don't know if I trust any outsider with that."

"Would it be so bad if she knew?" Andre considered.

"What the hell are you talking about? Both of you?" I was incredulous. They were talking about it as if it were a parking ticket or an embarrassing mole on their ass. Had the years really made them so complacent?

"I'm not saying we run over and tell her this second, Finn," Andre continued. "But if she's going to be sticking around, isn't she bound to find out one way or the other?"

"What is the damn point of swearing an oath of secrecy if you don't intend on keeping it?"

"We are keeping it, Finn," Riel soothed. "But if it were to happen, Alexis wouldn't be the first outsider to put two and two together."

"And when that's happened in the past, someone has always gotten hurt. One of us, or one of them. Is that what you want to happen here? Is that what you want to happen to her?" I pointed to a smiling Alexis as she hugged Lacey and twirled with her.

"You know I don't want that." Riel frowned.

"Then is camping really such a good idea?"

"I already made a commitment," Riel doubled down. "But I will promise you I'll be sober and mindful of the oath we took for the duration. I'll also speak to the others to ensure they do the same. Would that ease your mind?"

"Hardly," I answered.

"You're fighting a losing battle, man." Andre nudged me and pointed at Chloe.

I turned on the barstool and caught her glaring back at me. She knew exactly what we were talking about and how I felt about it. I didn't drop my gaze from hers. The phrase, "If looks could kill," came to mind. She stalked towards me, and I braced for impact.

"We're going camping and you're not going to stop us," Chloe declared, sticking her finger in my face.

"What do you plan to do with Alexis?"

"I plan to have fun with my friends, Alexis included," she replied.

"And if something or someone gets out of control?"

"That's not going to happen. We're not teenagers, Finn. We can control ourselves." She crossed her arms over her chest. "If you're so worried about it, maybe you're projecting your own insecurities onto the rest of us. You tend to be the one who gets the most 'out of control' on our camping trips."

The accusation stung. My jaw clenched as I bit back a retort. But I didn't need to voice it for Chloe to read it all over my face. She opened her mouth to unleash on me, but Alexis stepped in between us.

"No bar fights tonight," Alexis declared. She sat down on my lap, clearly a little tipsy, and smiled up at Chloe. I put my hands on her hips to steady her, feeling her body heat all over my skin.

Alexis reached her hands up and patted Chloe's cheeks affectionately. "Please, Chloe."

"Fine." Chloe took a step back. "But tell your attack dog to pull the stick out of his ass." Chloe stomped away in her black high heels. I bristled at her word choice.

"Why are you guys always at each other's throats?" Alexis turned to look at me.

Her face was close enough to mine that I could smell the strawberry daiquiri on her breath. My mouth watered. I swallowed hard and cleared my throat.

"Chloe and I don't always see eye to eye," I dodged.

"Clearly," she sighed. "Do me a favor and play nice this week. If we're all going out into the woods together, I don't want to end up being a witness to a murder."

I held back a shudder.

"Promise me?" Her eyes were wide and pleading.

She looked so much more vulnerable when she drank. It triggered something feral and protective inside me. My grip on her hips tightened a little.

"I promise," I sighed. Shit. When did I become such a damn pushover?

"Thank you, grumpy dragon," she whispered. She kissed me on the cheek and hopped off my lap. She gave Andre a cheerful grin, then hurried over to Chloe, probably to have the same conversation with her.

"Wh-pish!" Andre mimed cracking a whip.

"Shut up," I mumbled.

"So, we're going camping." Andre raised both eyebrows at me.

"We're going camping," I folded. "But I'm going to be on everyone's ass the entire time. Don't expect to have any fun."

"Scout's honor," Andre vowed. "Not a single ounce of fun will be had."

By the look on his face, I doubted it.

. . . . .

"I refuse to do the damsel-in-distress act," Alexis huffed.

She had borrowed an extra tent from Riel and was staring at the unassembled mass like it was a rubix cube. The others were already setting up their tents in the clearing in the heart of the woods, right in the center of the Clock. But Alexis' novice status was showing already.

"How is it being a damsel if I tell you what to do and you follow my instructions?" I argued.

"Because I can figure this out. I just need to sit with it for a few minutes."

"God, you're stubborn." I grabbed a pole off the ground and started assembling it for her. "If you don't let me help, you'll be sleeping under the stars and getting eaten by bugs."

"Can you at least show me so I can do it on my own next time?" She grabbed a second pole and copied my movements.

"I wouldn't have it any other way."

I talked her through assembling the poles, then showed her which poles went through which sleeves. Her hair kept falling in her face until she grumbled and pulled it up into a ponytail. After twenty minutes, we had the tent erected and staked into the ground.

"Okay, that was easier than I thought." Alexis stood back, admiring our work.

"Come help me with mine. You'll get some more practice and mine's the only one not up at this point." I motioned around the clearing to the other seven assembled tents.

"God, Milani's tent is like a mini cabin," Alexis's mouth popped open.

"Yeah, she hauls most of her condo with her, so she needs a lot of space to put it all. She calls it 'glamping,' like camping only glamorous." I rolled my eyes. "She has a mini stove to heat the place and a couple of mattresses, so her precious goose down comforter never touches the ground."

Alexis laughed. I kicked a few rocks away from where we were setting up my tent. She took a long drink from her water bottle. It was mid-afternoon, and the sun was directly above us, making the clearing a lot warmer than it would be later tonight.

"How often do you guys come out here?"

"Every couple of weeks during the Summer, then a few times in the Fall before it gets too cold," I answered, passing her one of my tent poles.

"Wow, you're dedicated campers. I wouldn't have guessed."

"We like it out here," I shrugged.

"Clearly." She motioned to Andre as he sprawled on top of the picnic table, his fedora over his face to block the sun.

"Hand me the gray pole with the red dot," I pointed.

"You got it. What do you like about it?"

"It's nice to get away from all the demands of regular life, get back to simple things, a slower pace. We put all our phones away for the entire trip, too. No distractions."

"Except Milani's glamour tent?" Alexis raised an eyebrow as Milani carried an armful of electronic devices and portable changers into her tent.

"My God. Yeah, Milani doesn't think the rules apply to her. It's easier to let her hole up in her tent and pretend she's sitting in her loft on 2-block than it is to argue with her."

"You know, because you've tried."

"Until I was blue in the face."

"God, what does she do for a living that she can afford all that?"

"Hell if I know," I shrugged.

"Why does she even come camping then if it's only loft-living 2.0?"

"I hate this term, but it applies, so what the hell: FOMO."

"She's so afraid of missing out that she hauls half her stuff out into the woods a dozen times a year, then sits in her tent the whole time and misses out, anyway? Did I get that right?"

"Just about."

"Okay… Well, what's *your* favorite part of camping?"

"Do you ever run out of questions?" I grabbed the last pole and slid it into place.

"Never."

"I feel more myself out here than anywhere else." It was honest without being too forthcoming.

"Hmm, I look forward to meeting the real Finn, then."

There was no way I could let her see the real me. Not all of me. In fact, I would do everything in my power to make sure she never saw it.

We stood back and admired our handiwork once more. I hadn't realized how close we'd spaced our two tents until they were both fully assembled. Alexis noticed the same thing.

"You don't snore, do you?"

"Like a chainsaw." I shook my head.

"Liar," she nudged me with her elbow.

"Hey, you two," Moira yelled from the center of camp. "When you're done, we're going for a swim down at the pond."

"I think I missed the memo about swimming," Alexis frowned. "I didn't bring a bathing suit."

"Neither did I."

"You don't plan on swimming?"

"I don't plan on wearing a suit," I corrected.

"So, it's that kind of camping trip."

"Come sit by the pond. You don't have to swim if you're not feeling it."

"You're just trying to get me naked." She put her hands on her hips, but the playful smile around her lips told me she was enjoying the banter.

"Absolutely not. Then we'd have to fill out a bunch of paperwork with HR. It would be a crazy hassle." I gave her an impish grin.

"Your loss!" She tossed the empty tent bag at me and ran off to join the sisters.

I shook my head as I watched her go. That sass... She didn't miss a beat.

"Wake up, Sandman." I flipped Andre's fedora off his face. "We're heading to the pond."

"Careful with the lid, man," Andre objected. "You know that's my favorite hat." He dusted it off.

"It's your only hat."

"It's a classic."

"C'mon, the water is waiting."

I strode off toward where the others had disappeared through the woods. Andre was hot on my heels. Now that he'd had a few seconds to wake up, his enthusiasm returned. Before long, he was making plans to start a water fight, then see if he could persuade Milani to come out of hiding and join us in the water.

"Cowabunga," Donna yelled in the distance. I heard running feet, a whoosh, and then a loud splash.

"Uh oh," Andre warned, face solemn.

"What?"

"It sounds like they're...*having fun*." He gave me a look of mock horror.

"That's not the kind of fun I was talking about, and you know it." I punched his arm.

"Don't worry, I'm a man of my word." Andre crossed his finger over his heart, then took off running toward the noise.

By the time I made it to the pond, most of the crew had stripped down to their bathing suits or underwear. Andre threw his shirt right to Alexis, then did some muscle flexing and winking to make her laugh. She threw his shirt back in his face, but he caught it before it could make contact. Moira was in her classic one piece, Chloe in a black bikini, and Lacey was in her body suit plucked straight from the 1920s.

"Come on, guys, the water is perfect." Grace and Taylor were waving us into the pond.

I made eye contact with Alexis, and a wicked impulse took hold of me. I grabbed the hem of my shirt and made a show of slowly stripping the fabric off my body and over my head. My body was a well-muscled machine, and I worked hard to keep it that way. She raised an eyebrow at me. It could have just been my ego, but she seemed impressed.

The pants were next, and I matched the slow speed I'd used for my shirt as I unbuttoned my jeans and stripped them off as well, tossing them to a large boulder behind me. That left me in nothing but my maroon boxer-briefs. I strolled to the edge of the pond and swan dived into the water. I shook my wet hair out of my eyes once I surfaced.

"Showoff," Alexis hollered. I chuckled.

"You got something better?" I yelled back.

She shook her head, laughing. "No suit, remember." She pointed to her clothes.

"No suit, remember?" I motioned to my body. "C'mon, Henson. Show us what you've got."

"C'mon Alexis," Vikram yelled from the water.

Several others joined in, cheering her on. Lacey's eyes sparkled as she waved her arms at Alexis, beckoning her into the water. That seemed to be what did her in.

"Fine, I'll give the people what they want," she waved us down.

Alexis unbuttoned her shirt. There was a shy hesitation to the way her fingers loosened the buttons. I watched every torturous movement. When she slipped her shirt off, my stomach tightened. She was wearing a red lace bra, and it contrasted beautifully with her ivory skin. She shimmied off her pants to reveal matching panties. My cock hardened at the sight of her. I dropped my gaze and scolded myself. This reaction to seeing her in her underwear was anything but friendly.

"I'll have you know I used to dive in high school," she taunted from the rocks above me. "I'm about to show you up."

"You already have, girl," Donna wolf whistled.

Alexis stood at the very edge of the rocks, body straight as a board, and raised her arms elegantly over her head. I watched her muscles tense across her body as she prepared for her dive. She jumped. But instead of a graceful dive, she tucked her knees up into her chest.

"Cannonball," she yelled.

The splash she created doused all of us. She came up out of the water, already laughing at the trick. Her brown hair was now dark and glistening. She sliced expertly through the water over to where the sisters were waiting to congratulate her. I had to turn away again as I tried to ease the ache in my loins.

"Damn," Andre whispered to my right. "Girl's fine." He nodded appreciatively, then gave me a knowing wink before swimming off.

The wild inside me was pulling at my weakened barriers. I took a deep breath and all it accomplished was getting a deep whiff of Alexis's familiar scent. *Think of something totally unappealing,* I coached myself. I pulled an image of a pair of tattered, greying granny panties to mind and winced. Fish guts at the dock, Andre's bunion, mushrooms in my food, the smell of sick in the bar bathroom…

A pair of arms slipped around my shoulders, and I felt the warmth of someone's skin against my back. Her scent gave her away before her voice did. That and the scratch of the lace on my shoulder blades.

"Don't be embarrassed, Finn. You were up against a professional."

All the work I did to think of something gross went out the window. My erection strained against my boxer briefs. I was grateful for the coverage the water allowed me. The beast inside me growled to be released. Her scent was overpowering.

The woods were already lacing themselves through my senses, heightening everything to where my nerves felt like they were vibrating. An image of me pulling Alexis around to my front and pressing my hungry mouth against hers invaded my mind. The urge to bury myself inside her was intense.

One look at Chloe's smug face from across the pond was all I needed to snap myself out of it. I took a deep, steadying breath and swallowed hard. Keep it under control. Keep the secret.

"Speechless, huh?" Alexis continued in my ear. "I get that a lot. Very few people can get the form right while still maximizing the splash radius."

The familiar, casual banter helped pull me back to my iron-fisted self-control. I slipped underwater, out from under Alexis's arms, then surfaced a couple feet away.

"I'd say your form still needs work," I shot.

She tried to splash me, but I was too quick. I had already submerged and was swimming as fast as I could in the opposite direction. Distance was a necessity if I was going to regain my composure.

I wish I could say I didn't know what had gotten into me, but I knew exactly what was in me. And I desperately needed to keep it there.

Chapter Twelve

Alexis

I was glad I'd given in to peer pressure and gotten into the pond with everyone else. We spent the entire afternoon into the early evening playing in the water: chicken fights, splash wars, Marco Polo, and cool trick contests abounded. Finn stayed curiously off to the side for a while but was eventually persuaded to come back and join in on the fun. His cool trick was an underwater front flip.

Moira let me borrow one of her towels to dry off before I pulled my clothes back on. I deliberately kept my back turned to Finn, suddenly feeling self-conscious to be so exposed in front of him. I felt heat rise in my cheeks as I thought about watching him undress before diving into the water. He'd been putting on a show to tease me, but what a show it turned out to be. I had to admit he was ridiculously attractive in just his underwear. Someone might as well have chiseled him out of marble with the way his skin stretched over his lean muscles.

When we got back to camp, Vijay and Vikram got to work making dinner and someone started a fire. As the temperature dropped, I pulled on my sweater and sat close to the campfire. The smoke kept flowing into my face, so I had to move several times until I found a spot around the circle that was consistently upwind.

Taylor and Grace were the first to sit down with me. We talked about the day and then about the woods. Taylor especially seemed entranced with them. She could barely talk about anything else. The reverence in her voice as she told me the names of the plants and trees around us, the delicate balance of the ecosystem, and the benefits of spending time in nature gave me a new understanding of how much my friends loved it here.

Vijay and Vikram served dinner, and we sat around the fire eating, talking, and laughing. The food was rich and warm, and the conversation was easy. My contented sigh drew Chloe's attention.

"Are you having a good time?" she asked.

"I'm having a blast!"

"I'm glad. It's fun to have you out here with us. And it's nice to have someone around who knows how to keep Finn humble."

I caught Finn watching Chloe and I's exchange from across the fire. He looked away quickly and started talking to Riel. Weird. Maybe I'd been a little too friendly at the pond and made him feel uncomfortable.

"Humility isn't really his strong suit, is it?" I turned my attention back to Chloe.

"Never has been, never will be." Chloe took a sip of her beer. "But, as much as I hate to admit it, he's a good man. Just an enormous pain in the ass sometimes." She looked from me to Finn, then back again. "You could do worse, you know."

"What?" I could feel the instant heat in my cheeks.

"I'm only saying," she shrugged. "I don't know what's going on between the two of you, but it wouldn't be terrible if it turned out to be romantic."

"Yeah, there's no romance," I insisted. "He's a friend, just a good friend."

"Okay, I'll take your word for it. No romance."

She examined Finn from across the circle. A strange look crossed her face, and her eyes went unfocused. She sat that way for a few moments until her eyes fluttered and refocused.

"You okay, Chloe?"

"Perfectly fine," she answered with a broad grin. "A few beers in and getting tipsy."

"I've seen you drunk before, Chloe, but I've never seen you make that weird face." I surveyed her features.

"Huh," Chloe shrugged. "Must be fantastic beer."

Chloe smirked at Finn. He glared at her, then glanced at me. His expression softened and hardened all at once; I wasn't sure what to make of it. They had some kind of communication going on between the two of them across the fiery expanse. I squirmed in my seat, pulling my hands into the sleeves of my sweatshirt.

The strumming of a guitar distracted me from my discomfort. Hiro was playing a song; a slow, sad ballad I didn't recognize. When she sang, the pure, crystalline tone of her voice surprised me. She sang in a language I was unfamiliar with, but it sounded like Japanese. All the side conversations stopped.

I was suddenly intensely aware of the silence of the surrounding woods. It was like the woods themselves were listening to Hiro sing. A sense of peace and calm weaved through my body from the outside in as Hiro's voice rose and fell. I closed my eyes and visions of a far-off lake with a lone cherry tree developed in my mind. The tree was laden with pink blossoms that smelled overwhelmingly sweet. A single blossom fell from the tree and floated ever-so gently down onto the surface of the lake below. Small ripples emanated from the fallen blossom until the ripples dispersed into stillness once more. A nostalgic ache, a yearning to return to a place I'd never even been, grew in my heart. But how could I miss something I'd never experienced?

The last few notes of Hiro's song echoed around the clearing, and the vision dissolved. I opened my eyes. My friends' faces were serene and relaxed. I wondered if they had seen peaceful visions of their own. Finn examined me with keen eyes, like he was trying to read my mind. I smiled and blinked lazily at him. He frowned and glanced at Hiro as she put her guitar back in the case.

"Hiro, you are a magician," Donna enthused. Her words were a little slurred, and she looked happily intoxicated.

"You get better every year," Grace agreed. "I don't know how it's possible, but you do." She popped a grape into her mouth from the bowl perched on her tiny lap.

My head continued to feel light and woozy for a few more minutes after the last notes faded into the trees. Once I regained my faculties, I frowned. I understand getting lost in the music, but that was something else altogether. The images were too vivid, and they were certainly not something I would conjure up on my own. It was like I'd been under a spell. I shook my head. What a stupid thought. Maybe the beer was getting to me, too.

"Riel," Chloe called. "Why don't you tell us a story?"

"Oh, I'm sure you don't want me to bore you." Riel waved the suggestion away.

Everyone broke into pleas for a story. Riel glanced at Finn. Finn shook his head ever so slightly, so subtly, that I wasn't sure if I had imagined it or not.

"It's getting late," Riel replied.

More pleas from the group.

Riel appeared conflicted.

"Just a short one," Andre piped up. "One short one won't hurt." He elbowed Finn.

"A short one," Riel agreed.

Finn stood and moved outside the light of the fire. I couldn't see his expression, but I could read the tension in his posture. I felt the urge to go to him, but I didn't want to feed into the appearance of romance Chloe had hinted at. For the time being, she was staring at Riel with rapt attention, but her keen eyes would see me if I left.

"Long ago," Riel began. "There was a small village beside a river. And in that village, there was a man. He was no ordinary man. No, not ordinary at all. This man could speak with the wind. The wind was his near-constant companion; he treasured the wind. And after centuries of no one understanding it, the wind was pleased to have someone to listen to its stories."

"One day, a group of soldiers came to the man's village. They told the townsfolk they were simply in need of a place to rest and food for their bellies, then they would be on their way once more. They were headed to the coast, they said. The man stood back from the rest. *Lies*, the wind whispered to him. *Foes.*"

I leaned forward with my elbows on my knees. Riel's voice was low and compelling. He had a far off look in his eyes.

"The villagers were a kind folk, so they obliged the soldiers' requests. The soldiers made themselves comfortable at the home of the farmer and his wife. They were a gentle, elderly couple with no children. The man visited the couple regularly to help lighten their load. But one day turned to two; then two to more, until the villagers stopped counting the days, wondering when the soldiers would move on. Their resources were scare, and the kindly villagers gave more of themselves than they could afford to give."

"With the soldiers staying on the farm, the man visited more often, the wind always accompanying him. The farmer and his wife were growing weary. Their home was hardly their own anymore, and the soldiers were rowdy and demanding. The man encouraged his elderly friends in moving their guests along, but to no avail. They stayed on. Whispers began in the village; worries were planted and fertilized with fear."

My heart gave a squeeze. My pulse quickened, and I pulled my sweatshirt tighter around me. Chloe was anxiously chewing her lower lip next to me. Riel told the story with a low intensity that gave me chills.

"When two full moons had waxed and waned, the man and the wind came to visit the farmer and his wife. *Danger*, the wind warned as they approached the door. The man gripped the ax at his belt. His knocks went unanswered, and his anxiety grew. *The barn*, the wind urged."

The wind rustled around us in the trees, and I jumped. I shook my head and rolled my eyes at my ridiculousness. I was a sucker for a good story.

"With quiet steps, the man approached the barn, ax unsheathed. He heard raucous voices within, followed by cries of fear. The man and the wind hurried forward. The man peeked in the windows and the wind rushed ahead through the cracks in the wooden slats of the walls. *Hurry*, the wind called to his friend. Through the window, the man saw the soldiers surrounding the farmer and his wife. The elderly couple was bloodied and bruised. Fire burned in the man's chest. Without a thought for himself, he burst through the doors. The soldiers rushed him, but the man swung his ax with deadly aim."

Lacey slipped her petite hand into mine. I gave it a squeeze. Her breath was quick and shallow.

"But the soldiers outnumbered the man," Riel continued. "He cried out for the wind to help him. The soldiers mocked him and the wind. 'What can the wind do against our might?' They taunted. The farmer struggled to his feet and tried to help, but was knocked back, his wife rushing to his side. The leader of the soldiers, the greediest of them all, advanced on the man, sword raised. 'We take what we want, and no one will stop us. Not you. And not your wind,' the soldier spat in the man's face."

"But the man knew the wind. His friend was slipping in through more cracks, gathering its strength. He could feel the pressure building in the corner near the hay. His friend did not like to be mocked. The man smirked at the soldiers, and they laughed cruelly in return. 'Our regards to the wind,' the soldier raised his sword for a death blow. Suddenly the fierce wind burst forth from the corner."

Riel's hands shot forward and a blast of wind rushed into our circle, the campfire nearly blown out, prompting startled shrieks from us all. My heart was pounding, and Lacey's grip was vice-like. The shrieks dissolved into nervous laughter.

Riel grinned and continued, "The wind blew out the lanterns and plunged the barn into darkness. It blew the soldiers off their feet and lifted the man back up to his. It guided the man's ax blows. The farmer and his wife cried out in fear. Then... silence."

The wind blew gently around our feet, our own silence only broken by the crackling and popping of the fire.

"The farmer and his wife heard the scratch of a match and smelled the acrid scent of the light catching at its head. Looking toward the smell, they saw the man lighting a lantern. His face was covered in red stains, but his expression was gentle. The man ushered his elderly friends out of the barn and back to their home. The wind escorted them proudly. Once the man had seen them safely home, he disappeared and did not return until morning was in full bloom. His face and hands were clean, their barn emptied of the events of the night before, and their curious neighbors left, unaware of the reason for the sudden disappearance of the soldiers."

"From that day on, however, the farmer and his wife spoke of both the man and the wind with reverent whispers. That reverence spread and the villagers gave thanks to the man and the wind for ridding them of the soldiers. To this day, the descendants of the villagers pay homage to the wind for its protection. The man has long since passed, but his descendants are said to speak to the wind still. And the wind listens."

Riel leaned back, and we burst into applause.

"Oh my God, Riel! That was incredible," I enthused. "How did you time that thing with the wind?"

"I guess I got lucky," Riel laughed. "But it added a little extra something to the story, eh?"

My friends exchanged knowing glances with each other. I couldn't help but feel like I was missing some kind of inside joke. I looked from person to person, but no one was meeting my eye. A little alarm was going off in the back of my head; I felt unsettled, but I couldn't put a finger on why.

Several conversations erupted around the circle at once as everyone discussed Riel's story. Chloe was beaming at Riel. He gave her a half smile. I pushed aside the weirdness of the evening. I could roll things around in my head later, but I could do some friendly encouragement of the sparks happening between Chloe and Riel now.

"Talk about romance," I whispered to Chloe.

"He is so… virile," she growled.

"Wow, I've never heard that one before, but okay," I laughed. "Go over there and get your man," I urged.

Chloe scrambled to her feet. I steadied her as she wavered, then she hurried over and sat right in Riel's lap. His eyes popped open in surprise, but he didn't look displeased. I smiled to myself. Those two orbited around one another anytime they were together. This was the first time I'd actually seen one of them do something about their obvious feelings for each other. I held up my beer and narrowed my eyes at it. What kind of beer was this? I chuckled.

My thoughts wandered back to Finn. He hadn't returned to the campfire. I searched the line of the trees just outside the light of the circle and saw his shadowy figure leaning against a tree. Lacey had let go of my hand and was leaning against Moira's shoulder sleepily. The others were in conversations of their own, so it gave me a chance to move into the darkness without drawing attention to myself.

"What are you doing lurking out here?" I asked as I approached Finn.

"Cooling off." He had an edge to his voice.

"Are you mad at me?"

"What?"

Finn finally looked at me. My eyes were still adjusting to the darkness, so I couldn't read his expression. A mixture of embarrassment and irritation warred in my chest.

"You've been acting weird since we got back from the pond. Did I develop a contagious illness, or did I piss you off or something?"

"No, it's not…" he sighed. "You didn't do anything Allie. It's a me thing."

"Care to share with the class?"

"Not particularly."

"Are we really going back to this, Finn?"

"This what?"

"This strained awkwardness I thought we'd worked past. Listen…" I rubbed the back of my neck and shifted from foot to foot. "I'm sorry if I made you uncomfortable at the pond. Next time, I'll kept my hands to myself. I didn't mean anything by it, I swear on Andre's gyros."

"No, Allie… it's… I didn't mind… I just…." He took a step toward me, reached out a hand, and placed it on my hip. "I'm an asshole. It's just… I'm up in my head about some things. I didn't mean to make you feel like you did something wrong… and for the record, I didn't mind what happened at the pond."

I could see him clearer now that my eyes had adjusted to the dark. His expression was soft but serious, flustered even. His hand gripped my hip, and a chill ran through me.

"You took me by surprise at the pond, but you always surprise me. I should be used to it by now," he continued, brushing a loose strand of my hair back from my face.

"I don't want things to be weird, you know," I explained. He nodded. "It's probably not every day you see your partner in their underwear."

"The number of times I've seen Andre in his underwear." Finn rolled his eyes. "I'm used to it."

This felt more comfortable, more familiar. The tension I'd been holding in my back and shoulders eased. Despite our warming friendship, there was always a fear in the back of my mind that I could lose anyone at any time. People in my life had a history of bailing when things got uncomfortable.

The wind whipped around us, creating a tiny leaf tornado to my left. I shivered. Finn checked over his shoulder with a raised eyebrow, then back to me again.

"Cold?"

"It's getting a little chilly," I admitted.

Finn pulled me into his chest, wrapping his arms around me. His heart was beating strong and fast. He was incredibly warm despite the biting breeze. I sighed contentedly.

"Better?" I could feel his voice rumble in his chest. It was close to a growl.

"Much better, thank you."

"I'm sorry if I upset you, little siren," he whispered into my hair.

"I told you I was a dragon tamer," I bragged.

He chuckled. It tickled.

We stood like that for a long time. The mumbled conversations and bursts of laughter from our friends continued around the fire in the background. But I focused on the warmth I felt nestled in Finn's arms. The wind whipped around us every once in a while, and Finn would pull me in a little tighter each time.

Moira and Lacey rose and headed toward their tent. Finn sighed. I felt him kiss the top of my head. Tingles erupted and ran down my neck and back. He pulled away, and the cold returned.

"Come on, I'll walk you to your tent," he offered.

"Thank you, kind sir." I looped my arm through his.

"Get some rest," he said once we got to the tent.

"You're not going to bed yet?"

"Nah, I think I'll stay up a little longer."

"Restless?"

"I have some stuff on my mind. The fresh air will help me clear it out so I can sleep."

"Okay, goodnight, Finn." I unzipped the door of my tent.

"Goodnight, Allie," he nodded.

I stepped into my borrowed tent, and he zipped it up behind me. His footsteps faded as he walked away. I sat on my sleeping bag with a rush of emotion. Something was sparking inside me, but I tried to smother it before it lit a flame. *No romance*, I scolded. *Finn was a friend, just a good friend*, I chanted. *We work together. Just a friend.*

The chill in the air prompted me into my pajamas, then deep into my sleeping bag and pile of blankets. The sounds of the woods came alive around me; chirping crickets, rustling leaves, and the trickle of the stream that fed into the pond. They were my lullaby. As I drifted into a peaceful sleep, a howl echoed in the distance.

Chapter Thirteen

Finn

My heart pounded as I ran. My breath was heavy but measured as my legs pumped into an easy rhythm. I needed this. I needed the clarity I could only ever find from a run through the woods. I swerved past low-hanging branches, jumped over fallen logs, and inhaled the sweet, familiar scent of the trees.

Alexis was a distraction. A damn good one, to be sure, but a distraction, nonetheless. The woods always forced my guard down. Usually, I enjoyed the freedom of it, but having Alexis here made it unsettling. I couldn't relax with my friends the way I usually did, as I worked so damn hard to guard their words and actions. They slipped, like I knew they would, but in ways I hoped Alexis wouldn't notice. I couldn't think of a nonchalant way to ask her about the slips without raising alarm bells in that brilliant mind of hers.

Stop, I scolded myself. *Stop thinking about her and run.* I wanted to stop and didn't want to stop at the same time. My stomach clenched as I thought about holding her under that tree. The wild was clawing at my chest the whole time she pressed her warm body against mine, growling to be let loose; to be let loose on her. I could barely move while I held her as I worked to hold it back. The contented sighs that slipped past her lips were almost my undoing. I had wanted her in that moment. The wild wanted to claim her.

I had to protect her from it.

So, I ran. And I ran. In my running, I could fully give myself over to the beast within; to feel the freedom of full release. It was pure relief to be at one with myself in the darkness of the woods. I skidded to a halt beneath a familiar pine. I filled my lungs, both to catch my breath and to search for familiar and unfamiliar smells. Both were present. I let myself sit for a long time until weariness crept in.

I walked back to camp at a leisurely pace. The sight of Alexis's tent next to mine made the wild leap up, but it was tired now, easier to contain. I slipped quietly into my tent, trying not to wake her. I stripped down to my underwear and climbed into my sleeping bag. The soft stillness told me that the others were long since asleep. As I calmed my breathing, I focused on the soft sounds of Alexis sleeping. Her breathing was even. I wondered what she was dreaming about.

I could smell her familiar scent from here. My groin ached again. I rubbed at the annoyance and tried to shift my thoughts away. But when I slept, I dreamt of her. I dreamt of her in her red lace underwear, my lips on her neck, our bodies tangled together waist-deep in the pond. I dreamt of the slippery velvet feel of her wet skin as I ran my fingers down her stomach to the top of her panties. Her contented moans in my ear as I slipped my fingers beneath the fabric were the soundtrack to her pleasure.

But before I could claim her, the dream ended, and I woke to the sun shining through my tent. My cock ached with hard fullness. I tried to readjust it in my underwear, but it was so sensitive that the light touch shot anticipatory pleasure through me. The wild returned, fighting against the drowsy hold I held over it. It whined to be released, begged me to slip into Alexis's tent next door and finish my dream in waking moments of ecstasy. I rubbed myself as I imagined it, biting my lip to quiet the sounds of my pleasure. I pulled the image of her at the pond into my mind and mentally undressed her. I replayed her sighs at the tree as I held her.

My completion came quick and intense on the floor of my tent. I collapsed back into my sleeping bag, breathing hard. The beast inside me was slightly mollified, but hardly satisfied. I listened in the quiet stillness of the morning. Alexis was moving in the noisy borrowed sleeping bag that didn't smell like her. I ached to pull her into my arms, feel her nestled into my chest, feel her sleepy breaths play across my skin.

This camping trip was going to end me.

I pulled myself together, got dressed, and joined the bustle of breakfast preparation. It was impossible to get Vijay and Vikram to let anyone help them cook; it was in their nature. So, I hung back and watched the others emerge from their tents a few at a time while I ate an apple. I couldn't help but look at Alexis's tent more often than the others, anticipation building in my chest as I waited to see her again.

What the fuck was wrong with me? There had been absolutely zero attraction to her before we came out here. At least that's what I told myself as I inhaled the savory smell of cooking bacon. She was a friend, a talented coworker, but now she was the object of the beast's desire.

This had to be the woods. There was no other explanation for it. All I had to do was make it through the rest of this weekend, then get back to real life, and the sudden desire pulsing through me would be gone. Then I could get back to normal with her.

The zipper on Alexis's tent started moving, and my pulse quickened. A war broke out inside me; do I look away or watch? Watching won. She ducked through the door, and I stifled a moan. Her hair was in a messy pile on top of her head, sweater covering the tips of her fingers, and she wore a form fitting pair of leggings. Her face was fresh and natural.

She seemed small and vulnerable, undone like that. I turned away as she leaned, arching her back, in a long stretch. Fuck.

"Good morning, sunshine!" Andre bounded over to me.

"You're such a prick." I shook my head at him.

"What are you talking about?"

"You know exactly what I mean. Why'd you do that to me last night?"

"I have no idea what you're talking about," Andre answered, a little too innocently.

He flashed me a mischievous grin. I glared at him, tempted to throw my apple core at his stupid, meddling face.

"Oh, come on." Andre grabbed an orange and peeled it. "You can't pretend like you didn't enjoy it. You think we're all completely blind or something?"

"Do you think I want to deal with shit like that when we get back to work?"

"Fine, killjoy. I'll lay off," Andre caved.

"Thank you."

"For the record, you're not the only one who got a show."

Andre took off across the clearing before I could process what he meant. But when it sunk in, I groaned and smacked my forehead. Now I definitely couldn't turn around and face Alexis.

I ate breakfast as quickly as possible, keeping my eyes down. Luckily for me, Alexis went off with the rest of the women to rinse off in the pond before they got ready for the hike we had planned this morning. Before they got back, I had to figure out a way to act as normal as possible today. Andre's message was clear: the others were noticing the vibes. I also didn't want Alexis to think that I was upset with her again. Finding a balance between keeping my distance to hold my desires at bay and acting like my normal self was going to be a challenge.

But it turned out to be easier than I thought, mostly because Alexis spent most of the day with other members of the group. I couldn't tell if she was avoiding me or naturally gravitating to others during the hike. I hung back with Riel and Andre as we walked the trail, and she stayed near the front with Grace, Taylor, and Chloe. The further away she was, the easier it was for me to keep my focus.

Milani brushed past me. She gave me a seductive look and continued on. She made a show of walking with her ass swaying and kept looking back over her shoulder at me. Andre whimpered at the sight.

"She knows exactly what she's doing, man," Andre moaned.

"Of course she does," Riel agreed. "But I don't think this show is for you, Andre."

"I don't care who it's for so long as I can enjoy it." Andre licked his lips.

"She's all yours." I rolled my eyes.

"She doesn't want me right now, Finn. She's got her sight set on you. That woman can smell it on you." Andre patted me on the back.

"Pass." I ignored Milani's repeated glances. Maybe it would've tempted me in the past, but thinking about being with her made my stomach turn today. I took a swig from my water bottle and hiked on.

We had lunch on a hilltop at the end of the hike. Again, Alexis kept her distance; this time sitting with Lacey, Hiro, Moira, and Donna under the shade of a tree. Chloe came back to sit with Riel, Andre, and I. She kept shooting me knowing glances. I wanted to crawl out of my skin knowing what she knew.

The trip back was uneventful. I felt a sense of relief. But it was fleeting. Back at the campsite, Alexis plopped down beside me at the picnic table.

"Hey there, stranger." The tiny beads of sweat at her hairline glistened in the afternoon sun.

"Hey back," I replied, swallowing hard.

"It's strange…" She cocked her head to the side.

My stomach dropped. What had she seen? Who had slipped?

"…where I come from, hiking involves mountains. But here," she motioned around us, "it's just a stroll through the woods."

The relief washed over me like a wave down my back.

"It's hard to hike up a mountain that isn't there." I tried to sound normal. "The Clock is fresh out of mountains, unfortunately."

"Yeah, I noticed. But it was a pleasant stroll either way." She opened a bag of trail mix and started popping handfuls into her mouth. "I'm understanding why you guys love it out here so much. Grace and Taylor practically worship the woods. It's amazing."

"What did they say?" I tried to suppress the worry in my voice.

"It was like hiking with my personal trail guides. They know everything about the woods! I had no idea there were so many kinds of trees, bushes, flowers… God, it's overwhelming how much they know."

"I'm sure they were happy to have an audience. The rest of us have gotten pretty bored with it." I grabbed a handful of her trail mix and picked out the raisins before eating it.

"Then Donna told me all about her party days in New York City," Alexis continued.

"Dear God," I groaned.

"No, it was entertaining, I swear."

"Every day Donna lives is a party day. Next, I guarantee she'll tell you about her party days in LA, then London, then Barcelona…" I spun my hand in a bunch of circles.

"Well, as someone who has never had party days, I'll have to live vicariously through her." Alexis tossed a peanut at me, and I caught it in my mouth. She raised her arms in victory.

"How was your man-chat?"

"The usual," I shrugged.

"Lip gloss, butterflies, and the time you got your first period?"

"You got it." I stole another handful of trail mix.

"What are you two talking about?" Milani sat down on my other side. My chest tightened.

"The glories of nature and friendship," Alexis replied. "I'm glad you joined us today, Milani."

"Why wouldn't I?" Milani arched her perfectly shaped eyebrow at Alexis. The venom dripped from her voice.

"We just missed you yesterday at the pond and the campfire." Alexis smiled.

"I don't swim in muck." Milani looked down her nose at Alexis. I bristled.

"To each their own," Alexis kept her tone light.

"Finn, I need someone to put sunscreen on my back. Will you come help me?" The purr in Milani's voice was unmistakable. She ran her index finger down the length of my arm. Alexis shifted in her seat.

"I'm sure Andre would be happy to help you." I pulled my arm slyly out of reach. I didn't want to be used by her, but I didn't want to piss her off either. Milani was a vengeful enemy to people who crossed her.

"But I want you to help me." Milani stuck out her botoxed lower lip.

She slid her hand onto the top of my leg and trailed it down my inner thigh. Alexis raised her eyebrows and looked away from us. I wanted to shove Milani off me and pull Alexis closer, but I held back.

"I'll catch you guys later." Alexis stood and walked off, casting one last look at me as she did.

"I know you want something," Milani whispered in my ear. "I can give it to you." Her eyes darkened. "I want to give it to you. Unlike her." She glared at Alexis's retreating back. "She's a plain, unenlightened…"

"That's enough, Milani," I pulled away and glared at her. "I'm not into someone who shit talks my friends." I stalked off.

"You'll be back," she called.

"Like hell," I mumbled to myself.

That night around the campfire, I sat next to Alexis and Moira. The conversation came easy. The tension I had felt off and on was mostly under control. The smell of the burning wood helped cancel out her scent, and that was helpful in keeping my thoughts platonic. But then she rested her head on my shoulder as the night wore on and Hiro sang again. Before I could control it, my arm wrapped itself around her waist and pulled her close to me. The thoughts returned with a vengeance. I excused myself back to my tent early and rubbed one off again to relieve the pressure.

My sleep that night was fitful, but it was my own. I woke up with the sun and Alexis's sleeping bag was rustling. I inhaled deeply and had to bite my lower lip to stifle a groan. I could smell her sweetness intensified times ten. That, paired with the rhythmic way the sleeping bag moved, had me hard once more. The beast roared inside me, and I was on my feet with my fingers on the zipper of my tent before I regained control. I could almost taste what she was doing, and I wanted in. Instead, I forced myself to my knees and gripped my sleeping bag, teeth gritted. It was taking superhuman strength to listen to her quickened breaths and pillow-muffled sighs and not slash through my tent into hers.

Good thing I was superhuman.

Chapter Fourteen

Alexis

For the second night in a row, I had dreams about Finn. Maybe it was his proximity to me in the next tent, or just the amount of time we were spending together. Both nights, my dreams were steamy to say the least. The first night, we were going at it in the pond. The second night, I dreamt of him slinking into my tent and sliding into my sleeping bag. He pulled fur blankets over us as he undressed me and kissed every inch of my body. The way he touched me, explored me, and claimed me had me waking up wet and disappointed that I had to take care of myself to get a release. I tried to be as quiet as possible, but the swish of the sleeping bag advertised my every move. I could only hope that it sounded like I was getting restless sleep instead of pleasuring myself. I craved the pleasure enough to run the risk.

I took my time getting ready before emerging. Most of my friends had already eaten breakfast and were off doing their own thing. Vikram handed me a plate piled with eggs, bacon, and potatoes. It was scrumptious, as usual. We chatted about how to cook in the wilderness without the conveniences of their professional kitchen back at their restaurant. Hiro came back for seconds, and I asked her all about her love of music. She answered my questions shyly but willingly.

The hair on the back of my neck prickled suddenly. I turned to look over my shoulder and Finn was leaving his tent. His eyes were dark and intense. He gave me a terse nod and walked off into the trees. Heat crept into my cheeks. This was beyond ridiculous. I needed to put this weird blip behind me, not continue to entertain it in deliciously private moments. Coming camping together had opened up an unexpected door in our relationship and I wasn't sure it was one I wanted to leave open when we returned. Things like this had a tendency to end badly, and I needed to make things work in the Clock. This was a vital fresh start, and I couldn't mess it up.

"Sweet dreams?" Andre winked as he walked past me.

My stomach dropped and eyes popped wide. There was no way he knew, right? I mean, how could he? That weird feeling I'd had around the campfire crept into the forefront of my mind again. There were a lot of strange happenings from this trip that seemed coincidental, but my gut was telling me that something was off. Was this some kind of hazing thing they all did to new people in the group? Take them out to the woods and make them think they're going subtly insane?

After I had some time to calm down, I joined in with the others relaxing around the campsite, enjoying each other's company before we had to pack things up to go. Finn kept his distance again, but I was okay with it this time. He had taken down both my tent and his own while I was helping Moira, Lacey, and Chloe carry bags to their Jeep. It was a relief that we didn't have to be in close proximity; I couldn't look him in the face without blushing. A little time away from each other after we got home would be good for me.

We said our goodbyes, and all headed home, as the afternoon was at its peak. After unpacking the Jeep, I went straight to the shower to wash off the dirt and sweat I'd accumulated on the trip. I let it be a cleansing ritual of sorts. Clean the body, clear the mind, and get back into the right head space. Focus on school, on helping victims at my job, and on fitting in and not sticking out too much. Those were my only priorities in the Clock, and I renewed the promise to myself that I would do just that.

A good night of dreamless sleep that night helped me reset my internal clock. I woke on Monday feeling better, ready to face the day. I grabbed a cup of coffee from the bodega and rode the bus to campus while catching up on some reading for a quiz. When I stepped off the bus, a newly familiar face greeted me.

"Selsha!" I greeted. "I'm so happy to see you again!"

"Oh, hi." Selsha gave me a shy smile.

"Waiting for your ride again?"

"Yeah." She wrapped her arms around herself.

I pulled my backpack off my back.

"Snacks?" I asked brightly.

"If you have some."

"When I say 'always,' I mean always," I laughed. "If I get low blood sugar, my brain basically ceases functioning. Not a good look for me as a grad student."

I passed her an orange, a muffin, and a bottle of water. Ever since I'd met her, I had been mindful about packing extra food each day in hopes I'd see her again.

"Grad school, huh?" Selsha bit into the muffin.

"Yeah, I'm studying social work."

"What's that like?"

"Oh, it's amazing! I really love the work. There are so many tracks you can take with it, so many careers you can do. Are you doing any school or thinking about it for later?"

"I don't think school is for me," she mumbled through a mouthful.

"Why not?"

"I kind of have to focus on my... uh... job a lot. I'm working to earn enough to go back home." Selsha's eyes darted from side to side.

"What about once you get home?"

"We don't really do formal schooling where I come from. It's more like informal training stuff. It's hard to describe."

"That kind of work is just as valuable. You can learn things from apprenticeships and on-the-job training that you might not learn in a classroom. Not everything requires a college degree. Don't tell yourself you're not cut out for it if you want to keep your options open. You would be great."

"You really think so?" Selsha's green eyes were piercing.

"Without a doubt. You're capable, I know it. I have a good sense for people," I smiled.

"That's really nice of you, Alexis."

"I mean it. I have to head to class now, but I realized I packed extra food for lunch if you want it for later. Just in case."

"Yeah, thanks." She held out a hand, and I passed her the food.

"Do you still have my number?"

"I think so." She rifled around in the little purse she was carrying and pulled out a scrap of paper. "I have it."

"The offer still stands for a breakfast buddy or a random chat, okay?" I put my backpack back on.

"I might take you up on that." Selsha tucked the scrap back into her purse.

"I really hope so. Bye, Selsha!" I waved and headed off to my first class.

I saw Selsha more and more around campus over the next few weeks. She insisted at first that she was staying with a friend who lived in the area, but she eventually felt comfortable enough to confide in me she was indeed a sex worker. The more trust we developed, the more she opened up. She hated the life and desperately wanted out. But her "boss" had something of hers that was incredibly precious to her, and he refused to give it back until she worked off what it was worth.

The more I got to know her, the more I adored her. She spoke longingly of home with an ardent intensity. She was incredibly quick-witted, smart as a whip, and one of the gentlest people I knew. Sometimes she would sit with me while I studied in the library, especially as the weather got colder, and I would read my textbooks aloud to her. It thrilled her that my studies in social systems were so in line with her culture's belief in unity and working for the collective wellbeing. I tried encouraging her to consider school, but her sole focus was on getting back her treasured belonging and going home.

During those passing weeks, Finn and I slowly got back to a comfortable normal after the strange glitch that was the camping trip. The first day back at work was strained and awkward, but getting lost in work was a balm for both of us. I think we both tried to avoid being alone together at first, but we'd silently worked past it. We seemed to have an implicit agreement between us not to discuss what had happened, and that was fine with me.

Finn and Andre were still trying to track Ramond down and work the murder at the docks from months ago. Both cases were going cold, and it frustrated the hell out of them. But their big fish was the Bianchi family. I warned Finn that he was going to die an untimely death if he stressed out about that case so much. He just shook his head and assured me he was going to live forever.

More time passed; Thanksgiving rolled around, and we celebrated at the Pony with our friends and a bunch of other locals. Vijay and Vikram made an amazing spread with food from seven different cultures. It was the best food I had ever tasted. Donna convinced Lacey to try a sip of wine, and the poor thing nearly vomited at the tiny taste. She waved it away and Riel brought over her customary Shirley Temple and a bowl of cherries soon after. The sisters and I stayed after everyone left to help Riel clean up. Chloe and Riel were officially dating after breaking the friend-barrier during the camping trip.

Snow flurries fell as I wrapped up my semester. The day after my finals were over, Moira skidded into my room with an excited grin on her face.

"We're hosting a Christmas party," she declared.

"Are we now?" I had grown accustomed to Moira's perpetual party planning.

"We have to have it at the Pony, of course," she jabbered. "There's no way everyone could fit in our apartment."

"Define 'everyone,'" I lifted an eyebrow.

"Well, all our friends, naturally, but I was thinking we could invite the entire community. Just in case people don't have a place to go for Christmas, you know?"

"That's really thoughtful, Moira. How can I help?"

"Oh, I don't want to burden you too much," she dismissed.

"No, really, I want to help. I don't have school for a while, so that clears up my schedule considerably. What can I do?"

"Okay, um… oh! You can help me with flyers and invitations. You have such a good eye for things like that. The cooking is taken care of." She ticked things off her fingers.

"I wonder who's cooking," I joked.

"Chloe and Riel are coming up with a signature cocktail. Hiro is doing the music, as usual. Ricky, Grace, and Taylor are making little party favors. I think that's it so far."

"You are so on top of things, Moira. It's amazing!" I patted her arm.

"You're too sweet, thank you. Let's put our heads together for those designs later this weekend."

"Deal." A sudden idea popped into my head. "Moira, would you mind if I invited a friend I met on campus? She's far away from home and I think a Christmas party with kind people would do her some good. I'm not sure if she'll be able to come, but I'd like to invite her, anyway."

"Of course! The more the merrier," she beamed. "Alright, I'm off." She sped out of the room.

Work stalled out during the holidays, so with little more to do, I ended up helping Moira with a lot more of the planning than just the invitations. It turned out to be a lot of fun. Christmas was never a huge deal in my family, but the sisters were zealous about their love of the holiday. They spared no expense, no hall was left undecked, and we gave every little detail painstaking care.

The day of the party came, and people showed up from all over 10-block and 9-block. Moira wore a bright red knit dress and braided holly berries into her hair. She greeted every person at the door by name as they came in and directed them around the room to food, music, games, and drinks. My heart almost leapt through my chest when Selsha walked through the door. I hurried over to give her a hug and introduced her to my friends. They were all welcoming and enthusiastic. I had never seen her smile so much.

I made my way around the party once everyone had arrived, mixing and mingling with people I knew and ones I didn't. I met a lot of new people who lived on 9-block; they all seemed nice but more reserved than what I was used to with our 10-block crew. My familiar friends were the life of the party in every aspect, maybe because we were all hosts.

After making my rounds, I went over to the bar to relax and recharge. Riel slid me one of the signature cocktails he and Chloe created. It was in an hourglass shaped glass, red, slushy, with whipped cream and a cherry in the center and sugar around the rim.

"What do you think, Lex?" Riel asked.

"It's almost too pretty to drink!"

"It would be a shame to let something so delicious go to waste, though," he winked.

I slipped a straw into the cocktail and took a slow sip, letting the slushy drink coat my tongue. Hmm... strawberry or cherry base with a hint of orange. The coolness prickled across my tastebuds. Then came the familiar kick of rum.

"Good?" Riel raised his eyebrows.

"Phenomenal," I replied. He beamed at the praise. "You and Chloe make a great team."

"We do, don't we?" He picked up on my sly smile and returned the gesture with one of his own before taking off to tend to other partygoers.

"Hey, Lex!" Andre plopped down on the chair next to me. He had a sprig of mistletoe hanging from the front of his fedora.

"Your subtlety knows no bounds." I pointed to the mistletoe.

"Subtlety doesn't get the ladies." He leaned forward, strategically hovering the mistletoe over my head.

"It's tradition," he insisted innocently.

"You're shameless." I shook my head at him before planting a firm kiss on his cheek. "That's the most you're getting from me."

"I'll just have to wait until you get a few more of those in you," he pointed to my drink. "Then, I'll be back."

"Give it a rest, man," Finn joined us at the bar. "Did you really think this cheap bid would work?"

"You miss 100% of the shots you don't take, my friend!" Andre patted Finn on the back. "I'm off to try my luck elsewhere. You two get wasted and we'll see how stupid you think my idea is, then."

"If we have to be drunk to appreciate it, it's automatically a stupid idea," Finn called after him. I laughed. Finn sat on the stool Andre had vacated. "Having a good time?"

"I am," I tipped my glass to him. "Riel's getting my liquored up, the gang's all here, and my new friend from campus actually came!"

"What new friend from campus?" Finn examined the crowd with shrewd eyes.

"She's not a student. I met her at the bus stop, and we've gotten to know each other."

"Would I know her?"

"I'm not sure. She's a working girl, so she might be on the department's radar, but she's so sweet. That's her there." I pointed to Selsha, who was sitting with Lacey and Moira on the other side of the room.

Finn followed my gaze. "Hmm, I don't recognize her." He took a breath and paused. For a millisecond, recognition flickered in his eyes. Then it was gone as quickly as it came.

"Are you sure you don't recognize her?" I pressed.

"Yeah, I'm sure." Finn raised his finger to Riel, calling for a drink.

My suspicion deepened. With all the time I spent sitting in on interviews at the station with him, I'd gotten pretty good at detecting when Finn was being less than honest. What was he hiding? If he knew Selsha, why keep it from me?

A sinking feeling pulled at my stomach as a thought occurred to me: What if he had used her services at some point? Would that be reason enough to pretend not to know her? It might be. A detective using the services of a sex worker wasn't unheard of, but it certainly wasn't approved of.

I wanted to ask about it, but I bit my tongue. This was a Christmas party, not an interrogation. And if he knew her for that reason, it was certainly none of my business. I focused on downing my drink while Finn did the same. I was halfway through my second when someone pushed me from behind so hard that my chest rammed into the bar.

"Hey, watch it, asshole," Finn barked, jumping up from his seat.

He grabbed my arm and helped pull me back onto my stool. I turned to find out who had pushed me. It was a member of the Knuckle Crew; I didn't know his name. I recognized him as one of the overgrown frat boys who got wasted by the dart boards nearly every night.

"I tripped," the man grunted. His voice was an impossibly low bass tone.

"Bullshit," Finn challenged. "I saw you fall into her on purpose."

"Whatcha gonna do about it, pig?" the man slurred. He wobbled to the left.

"If you don't apologize and then get the fuck out of here, I'll beat your ass into the next century." Finn rose to his full height.

"How you think that's gonna end for you?" the Knuckle mocked. He motioned behind him to his equally drunk buddies.

"I like my chances." Finn's voice was a chesty growl.

"Maybe you boys have had enough to drink for tonight." Riel appeared behind the bar. "Why don't you go take a walk?"

"We ain't done yet," the Neanderthal snapped back.

"I'm sorry to inform you that this is my bar, and I'm the one who gets to decide who's done," Riel countered. His tone wasn't angry, but serious and powerful. It gave me the chills.

"You wanna join in on the fight, barkeep?" The drunk man stumbled to his left a few steps until one of his friends steadied him.

"No," Riel replied. "I have zero tolerance for fights in my establishment. So you can calm down and finish your night, or you can leave."

"You gonna let your daddy fight your battles, dog breath," another Knuckle challenged.

Finn took a step forward. I put my hand on his shoulder to hold him back. I could feel the tension in his back and shoulder as I restrained him.

"Apologize," Finn demanded.

"I told you, I tripped," the first man sneered.

Finn cracked his knuckles. He was shaking with anger. I wrapped my second hand around his arm to solidify my grasp. I looked around the room for some extra backup, but most everyone else was preoccupied with their merrymaking.

"If you can't behave, you're not welcome in my bar. Get out," Riel ordered.

"You're not as big and bad as you think you are, old man. Not compared to who we've got in our corner. The tides are changing around here and you're too fuckin' stupid to see it."

"Out, NOW," Riel commanded. He pointed to the door, and it flew open with a crash. I startled so much I would have fallen out of my seat if not for my iron grasp on Finn.

"You really wanna start something like this between our people?" The second Knuckle glowered. "All because Kudge tripped into your stupid human pet?"

Finn yanked his arm from my grasp. Before I could reach for it again, his hand was around the man's throat and the man's feet were dangling in the air. My mouth popped open in shock. The other members of the Knuckle Crew leapt into action. I reached for the kubaton I kept on my keychain, but before I could use it, backup arrived.

Andre ripped one man out of the circle and threw him to the ground. Donna jumped on another man's back and slipped her arm around his neck in a chokehold. Ricky dropped into a crouch and tackled a third around the knees. Finn was alternating between raining punches on the man who shoved me and the one who called me their human pet.

Chloe pulled me away from the flying fists. Riel whistled for the bouncer who came charging over to break up the fight. The rest of the attendees scattered; a large portion of them heading straight for the open door. I watched Selsha get swept up in the mass exodus and felt guilty.

"Finn," I yelled. But he couldn't hear me over the shouts.

"Riel, stop this," Chloe cried out.

Riel gave her a worried look. Chloe pulled me back further and turned me away from the fight, shielding me with her body. A loud boom radiated through my chest and the bar shuddered. I cringed. Voices cried out, but the sounds of fighting stopped. I wiggled out of Chloe's grasped, worried that someone had brought a gun and wounded one of our friends.

Everyone involved in the fight was lying on the floor, even the poor bouncer. They all looked stunned. Riel hauled the bouncer to his feet, dust him off, and motioned toward the door. The bouncer grabbed the arms of two of the Knuckle Crew and literally dragged them out of the bar, depositing them on the curb outside. He repeated the trip twice more to collect the rest of the Knuckle Crew before slamming and dead bolting the door after them. He dusted off his hands, then gave Riel a nod.

Riel held out a hand to Finn, who reluctantly took it, and hauled him off the floor. Andre lay flat on his back, his fedora halfway across the room. Donna was tenderly touching her eye while Ricky sat on the floor with an impishly pleased grin on his face.

"Was that really necessary?" Riel scolded.

"They started it," Donna replied.

"But none of you had to react to it that way." Riel had his arms crossed over his chest as he surveyed the scene.

Tables and chairs were overturned, food and drinks coated the floor, and the Christmas decorations had been torn and scattered. Watching Riel address the others reminded me forcefully of a teacher scolding a room full of misbehaved children. Finn and the others hung their heads.

"You heard what he said," Finn mumbled.

"I did," Riel glanced at me. "He was trying to provoke you, and it worked."

Finn didn't respond.

"I think it's time we call it an evening," Riel declared. The few guests left in the bar that didn't escape during the fight filtered out.

"Do you want us to stay and help clean up?" Moira squeaked. I could hear the suppressed tears in her voice.

Over my shoulder, Moira was holding Lacey. The poor thing wore a pained expression as she stared at a gutted poinsettia. A small tear rolled out of the corner of Moira's eye. My gut dropped to my feet. She had worked so hard on this party, only to have it ruined by a couple of unbearable assholes.

"No, I can manage," Riel's lips pressed into a thin line. "I'd prefer to do it alone."

Moira nodded wordlessly. She urged Lacey forward through the mess to the front door. It was out of character for her to leave without Chloe and I, but with the way Lacey was shaking, I couldn't blame her for hurrying Lacey out as quickly as possible. Our other friends followed close behind.

Chloe released her grip on me and went to Riel. He held up a hand to her as she reached out to embrace him. Her face fell, and she took a step back. Finn pulled Andre off the floor and Andre slumped out the door. Soon, Riel, Chloe, Finn, and I were the only ones left in the bar.

"I expected more from you, Finn," Riel said sadly before retreating into the back room.

"You couldn't help yourself, could you, Finn?" Chloe snapped.

"He shoved Alexis on purpose, Chloe," Finn shot back. "What did you expect me to do? Just sit there and thank him for his bullshit?"

"No, of course not. But you didn't have to start a damn bar fight over it. Look at the damage you caused."

"It's always my fault in your eyes, isn't it?" Finn glared at Chloe.

I could feel myself shaking. The shock of the situation was wearing off and my trauma was creeping up from the shadows, threatening to overtake me.

"I want to go home," I whispered.

Despite their loud argument, both Finn and Chloe heard it.

"I'm going to stay back with Riel whether or not he likes it," Chloe insisted.

"I'll walk you home." Finn grabbed his jacket from the coat rack and beckoned to me.

"You okay?" Chloe whispered.

I shook my head. It was honest, but she had enough to worry about right now. I didn't want to burden her with what was about to boil over inside of me.

"We'll talk later," she promised. She went into the back room to find Riel.

I took my trusty coat off the rack and pulled it on, hoping the familiarity of it would soothe me. My nerves were vibrating. Finn put his hand on my back and walked me outside. The Knuckle Crew was long gone, thank God. But looking at the curb sparked a question. If we talked, maybe I could keep the demons at bay.

"What did they mean when they called me your human pet, Finn?"

"How am I supposed to know?" Finn shrugged, but he wouldn't look at me.

My internal alarm was going off again. It was the same alarm that had gone off several times during our camping trip. Something was telling me it was all connected.

"Why would he call me that?" I pressed.

"Because he's a drunk asshole with a limited vocabulary."

Human pet, he'd said. *Human.* Why that word?

"Are you bullshitting me right now?" I demanded.

"Look, I don't know what the fucker meant when he called you that," Finn snapped. I widened my eyes at him.

"Then why did it push you over the edge, Finn?" I challenged.

His face dropped.

"That insult meant something to you; why won't you fucking tell me?" I threw my hands in the air.

Conflict was clear in his eyes, but it only lasted a moment. That moment was all I needed to confirm that he knew exactly what the Knuckle had meant. The proving ground would be whether he would be honest with me about it.

We were almost at my apartment. The muscle tightened in his jaw. I waited. But he continued to hold his silence.

"What did he mean by calling me your human pet?" I repeated.

"I don't know," Finn replied coldly.

There it was. Whatever the illusions I had about Finn and I being close friends were shattered. He was lying straight to my face. With all the deception I had dealt with in my life, I was completely over it. I could feel myself shutting down.

"Fine," I answered just as coldly. "You don't know." The last three words were dripping with sarcasm.

I turned my back on him and strode the rest of the way to my building several paces ahead of him. I didn't look back as I opened the door to the building and let it close behind me. If he didn't want to talk to me, I wasn't going to force him to. Real friends didn't keep each other in the dark.

Chapter Fifteen

Finn

I cursed myself the entire way home. How had I let myself get so out of control? The stupid fucking Knuckle Crew wasn't worth what I put everyone through tonight. And they certainly weren't worth violating my oath. They might choose to be traitors to their kind, but my word meant something. Even with Alexis practically begging me to tell her, I kept my tongue. But staying silent had been so hard it was physically painful.

Part of me wanted to tell her. It had started off as a tiny part, but it was growing a little bigger each day she was in my life. The intense attraction I felt towards her during our camping trip had faded within days of leaving the woods, but the deep sense of connection and the urge to protect her were stronger than ever. I cared about her. Seeing the betrayal on her face as I lied to her was a knife in the gut. It hurt worse than any of the blows I had taken in the fight.

But very little mattered to me more than my word. All the years I spent all over the world, I ran into cheats and liars around every corner. In my youth, I had even been one of them. But after becoming a man, I changed my life and held to my integrity when I couldn't trust others. Here in the Clock, the only thing that keeps us safe is the promise we made. I had nightmares about what could happen if someone broke that promise to the wrong person.

Sleep did not come easy to me once I fell into bed. I thought about calling Andre, but it was already late. I didn't want to disturb him unless it was necessary. Alexis's face was there every time I closed my eyes: the hurt, the betrayal, the loss of trust. I was stupid to think she hadn't picked up on the slip-ups at camp. How could I believe she could spend every day surrounded by us and not eventually pick up on it?

The other outsiders weren't nearly as perceptive as she was. We tried to keep a cordial distance between ourselves and people who weren't members of our community. But Alexis lived with the sisters, and the sisters adored her. She was bound to find herself right in the center of our people because the sisters were so central to us.

I kicked the blankets off me and punched my pillow back into shape. Fuck! Was I fighting a losing battle, then? Was Alexis destined to find out, and I was trying to patch the tiny holes in a dam that was riddled with cracks? I punched my pillow again, this time out of frustration. Sleep finally took me, but it was anything but restful.

I went into work in a foul mood. The second I sat down at my desk, my frown deepened. A yellow sticky note was stuck to my phone with a phone number written on it followed by the words, "Called in. Thinks they have info on dock murder."

Normally, I would be thrilled to get a tip on a case that made it past our screeners. Especially one as frustrating as Ferret's murder. We hit a dead end on it months ago, so we needed something to breathe life back into the case. But I knew the phone number. I had called that number hundreds of times in another lifetime. I hadn't called it in years and never wanted to call it again.

I picked up the phone, anyway. My personal life was a hell of a lot less important than hunting a killer. Especially one so brutal as the person who tore off a man's head. I dialed the number, my fingers keying in the familiar pattern, more out of muscle memory than conscious thought. My chest tightened as it rang. *Please, just go to voicemail...*

"Long time no talk, Finn Briggs," the voice on the other end greeted.

"Long time," I gritted my teeth.

"I wasn't sure if you'd call me back or not." Her voice hadn't changed a bit.

"You told our tip line you had information on one of my murder cases. How'd you even hear about it?"

"People talk, I listen. You know we're worse gossips than a bunch of old ladies at a hair salon."

"Brie, could you get to the point?"

"No," Brie answered simply. "It's not something I can talk about over the phone, no matter how secure you think the connection is. You'll have to come here."

The phone slipped a little in my hand. Every cell inside me resisted the idea of going back there and seeing Brie face-to-face. She was the reason I left.

"I'm sure it's not as sensitive as you're making it out to be."

"You don't think a man's head being ripped from his body is a sensitive topic?" she snarked. "My, your standards have changed."

Only a few seconds into the call, and she was already trying to make me feel small. It used to work on me, but it didn't anymore. I didn't give a flying fuck what she thought of me.

"No more bullshit, Brie. I'm bogged down with a lot of serious cases. I can't go running off because you snapped your fingers. I'm not yours to command anymore." I leaned back in my chair and crossed my arms.

"It's not bullshit, but if you don't want it, you don't want it. I was just trying to do you a favor for old time's sake. I thought you'd like to know that you'll be bogged down with more bodies than you can manage if this bad, bad bitch continues her nighttime forays."

I could imagine her expression so clearly. If manipulation was a sport, Brie would be a world champion. She knew exactly what buttons to push to get what she wanted. My job was everything to me, and she knew it.

"I'm the lead detective in homicide. I can't run off at the drop of a hat. Let me see if the chief will let me send Andre instead. He knows as much about the case as I do. He can help."

I was soothed by the idea of sending Andre in my place; he wouldn't mind seeing an old frenemy in the name of a good cause. Before she could get out the full sentence, the answer was obvious in her tone. She would not pass this along to anyone but me.

"Fine. God!" I gave in after the fourth time she insisted I needed to get on a plane and fly out to her place to get the information I needed. If it had been any other case aside from the Bianchis, I would have told her to eat shit.

"Smart man," Brie practically crowed her victory. "I'll pick you up from the airport myself. Send me your flight info as soon as you have it. Then you'll get the answers you're looking for."

The other end of the line clicked and went silent.

At that moment, Andre and Alexis entered the think tank, caught up in an animated conversation. I didn't know how either of them would take the news of what I'd just agreed to. So instead of facing their questions and possible judgment, I decided to talk to the chief about it first.

I knocked on the chief's door, and he called out for me to enter. I sat across from him while I explained that an anonymous tipster had information about Ferret's murder, but insisted that they give me the information in person. He furrowed his brow when I told him the caller wasn't willing to cooperate with our normal procedures. But after an hour-long discussion about the pros and cons, Chief granted the request and called up front to have Brittney book my flights. He agreed to give me two days to get what I needed and get back. Otherwise, I would have to pay for my ticket home.

Before leaving the chief's office, I checked for any sign of Andre and Alexis. They weren't anywhere in sight. Slipping out undetected would be my best option. I didn't want to tell either of them where I was going, especially not Andre, because he knew my history with Brie.

I snuck on my coat and hurried out of the office. My trusty Charger cut through the small amount of morning traffic. I packed a bag and headed for the airport. The drive was solemn and heavy. It reminded me of the night Alexis and I took Maria to the airport. The trip was a lot lonelier, and a lot longer than I remembered. I ran through memories of my time with Alexis to keep myself occupied.

The airport was as easy as an airport can be in this day and age. My flight was average, and I didn't hear a single infant cry the whole way to Chicago. I sent my information to that viciously familiar phone number and, sure enough, Brie was waiting for me at baggage claim.

"Don't look so happy to see me," she smirked.

"I'm not happy to see you. I'm here for the information you said you had."

"Not here," she whispered.

She led me out into the parking lot to a car I didn't recognize. She had traded up. Ironic. She had a knack for that.

The drive back to her place was awkward to say the least; the very least. She kept trying to spark up conversation and all I could think about was walking in on her, riding some other guy's dick and ruining my whole fucking life. I shuddered at the memories.

Once we got to the house, Brie took me inside and offered me food, which I declined. I was in Chicago for one reason and one reason only. I made that clear to her. But the woman never listened.

"Now that you've gotten your way and I'm here away from prying ears, what information do you have?" I crossed my arms and leaned against the wall nearest the front door.

"Don't be like that, Finny," Brie crooned.

She sat at her chipped dining table—that used to be *my* chipped dining table—and tapped her long fingernails on the surface. She motioned for me to join her, but I didn't move. God, I hated being in this place again.

"Tell me what you know, or I'm gone," I threatened.

"You won't leave." Brie took a swig of her beer. "You want this collar so bad you can taste it. And I know something you and your precious little pals on the island of misfit toys don't know." She twirled her raven hair around her finger with a victorious smirk. She had me by the balls and she knew it. Fuck.

"Take a seat," she offered again. But it wasn't an offer, it was an order dressed up as one.

I sat on the familiar chair and gritted my teeth. Brie was a sadist. Every breath I took in this house made me want to gag. Each scent was a memory tainted by the selfish, self-centered harpy across from me.

"How's your boyfriend?" Brie taunted.

"Andre is my partner."

"Same difference," she swigged her beer. "Does he miss me?"

"He hasn't mentioned you."

"I'm sure he still dreams about me, though."

"Doubtful."

"How about your other little cronies? They still think the sun shines out of your pompous ass?"

"My friends are none of your concern." I could feel the tension clawing up my back.

"I'm worried about an old flame, that's all," she winked at me. "Someone's gotta have your back." She leaned across the table toward me, her strategically low-cut shirt exposing her breasts.

"The only thing you ever had in my back was a knife, and you damn well know it."

"So tense," Brie tutted. "When's the last time you got laid?"

"What information do you have?"

"That long, huh? Pity. Despite the eventual boredom, you were a great lay." Brie leaned back in her chair.

"My case," I spat.

"I heard a rumor," Brie continued, ignoring my request. "A little birdy told me you have a new friend. A female friend…"

She eyed me, but I kept my face passive.

"Not that I care where you put your dick these days when I have dick for *days*," she waved a hand. "But the birdy told me the most delicious little tale about your new human conquest."

My eyes widened, and my gut sank. How the hell did she know about Alexis? Who was the damn bird she kept referring to and how quickly could I get my hands on it and wring its neck?

"Your poker face needs work," she cackled. "It's true then! You're fucking a human!"

She threw her head back and laughed hard. I gripped the edge of the table, my jaw so tight it felt like it might break. The beast inside me wanted to lash out at her, strike at her exposed throat, and rip out her mocking vocal cords.

"My, my, how the mighty have fallen. 'Humans are filth, Brie. They don't deserve to breathe the same air as us. Anyone who would degrade themselves by laying with a human deserves what they have coming to them.'" Brie mocked.

Decades ago, I had spoken those words. I was a narcissistic little shit back then, and she reveled in rubbing it in my face. What the hell had I ever seen in this woman aside from a piece of ass?

I worked hard to subdue my rage. Brie knew me, but I knew her, too. She was begging for a reaction, dying to get a rise out of me. I wouldn't give her the pleasure.

"If this is the reason you dragged my ass all the way out here, I'll have you brought up on charges for wasting police resources." My voice sounded calmer than I felt.

"Does she know about you?" Brie pressed. "I mean really know?" She licked her lips. "When you're fucking her and you growl her name, is she afraid and doesn't quite know why? Do you tuck her away in the dark with doubts hanging over her head, taking what you want from her and never really giving anything back?"

I swallowed hard, but kept my face impassive. Years and years of interrogating mocking perps was my best defense here. But my treacherous mind pulled up the memory of holding Alexis in the dark outreaches of the light of the campfire. I had drawn her close, then zipped her up in that borrowed tent before running off to surrender to myself. Tucked her away in the dark...

"No, she doesn't know," Brie continued victoriously. "You're tugging her around like a toy duck on a string, showing her off to your little friends, boasting about the benevolent man you've become. She's a shiny little badge to add to your uniform. You lie to her and use her to convince yourself that you're the man you want to be instead of the one you've always been. That's the only explanation for why the magnanimous Finn Briggs would slum it with a human."

Brie had no way of knowing what had happened between Alexis and I after the Christmas party fiasco. But the insult cut deep. The disappointment and betrayal on Alexis's face before she turned her back on me last night haunted me. Was I using her?

She's a pleasant distraction... My own thoughts from the dance that first month. Then again, on the camping trip, joined the mental barrage. The way I had objectified her on those unrestrained nights... How I had pushed her back to arms-length when we'd returned. Was I really the monster Brie was making me out to be? My chest ached. Brie's face was triumphant.

But as I stared into the face of my malicious ex, shame rising like bile in my throat, new thoughts came to my rescue. Watching Alexis work with our victims, her dancing in circles with Lacey at the Pony, locking eyes with her over Maria's back as she embraced her, hours of talking and laughing together in the Charger as she popped chips into my waiting mouth, the feral need to protect her as she sat tipsily in my lap and called me a grumpy dragon. No, that wasn't using. I genuinely, deeply cared about Alexis, even if I couldn't be fully honest with her. Maybe some part of that equation needed to change, but I wasn't the man Brie was making me out to be.

That final thought snapped me out of my stupor.

"My case," I snarled.

Brie's face went from triumphant to disdainful in an instant.

"What if I've forgotten the information?" she pouted.

"Then there's nothing else keeping me here." I pushed back from the table and strode to the door.

"Wait," Brie called as I reached for the doorknob. "If you tell me her name, I'll give you what you want."

I turned to sneer at her. "You don't have a single fucking thing I want. This was a mistake."

"The smell!" Brie yelled desperately. "You smelled something at your crime scene, didn't you?"

I stopped. She grinned.

"You've smelled it before... in Dublin. I remember." She sauntered over to me.

"And…"

"Her name?" Brie pressed.

"Fuck you, Brie." I walked out the front door and down the sidewalk to my rental car.

"Penanggalan," she yelled.

I whipped around to stare at her. "What the hell are you talking about?"

"You heard me." She tossed her hair.

"What kind of information is that supposed to be? A name?"

"You are so woefully ignorant of your own kind." She shook her head and went to close the door.

"What am I supposed to do with that bullshit?" I yelled in frustration.

"Ask the elf," she snapped and slammed the door behind her.

Chapter Sixteen

Alexis

"He's out on assignment." Chief took a swig of his coffee.

"Where?" Andre asked.

"He'll be back tonight," Chief dodged.

"Why wasn't I brought in on this?" Andre insisted. His normally cheerful face was drawn tight. "He goes out on assignment without telling either of his partners?"

"It's a need-to-know assignment for the Bianchi case," Chief's lips were a thin line. He was a fair man, but he clearly didn't appreciate being questioned about his decisions. "Alexis doesn't need to know, since it's not a victim's advocate case." He tipped his head in my direction. "There wasn't enough time to brief you before he had to get on a plane, Alvarez."

"Can I at least know where he went?" Andre pressed.

"Chicago."

Andre's face fell.

"If the interrogation is over, you're dismissed." Chief motioned toward the door.

When we got back to Andre's desk, I pulled Finn's chair over to sit close. Andre was still frowning.

"What's in Chicago?" I asked.

"The past," Andre sighed.

"Could you be less cryptic, maybe? We got enough of that from the Chief."

"Sorry, Lex." Andre flipped his notebook angrily across his desk. "Finn and I came to the Clock from Chicago. There's some… terrible memories back that direction."

"What kind of terrible memories?"

"Some nasty shit went down in the precinct we were in. Finn stumbled across evidence of some dirty cops, and it went bad when he tried to turn them in to the higher ups. The department covered everything up and Finn was the one that got ousted."

"What about you?"

"I followed my partner, naturally," Andre motioned to Finn's empty desk. "It didn't end up too hot for me either, since I was more loyal to him than I was to the department. And to add insult to injury, Finn came home that day to his girlfriend in bed with another guy. Well, technically not the bed, the dining table…"

"Damn…I can't imagine what that must have been like for you guys."

"I wish Finn would have said something to me before he left. It's like walking back into the remnants of a bad dream." He pulled out his phone and checked the screen for the hundredth time since we noticed Finn's absence yesterday afternoon.

"Why do you think he left without telling you? I can understand him not wanting to talk to me, but why not you?"

"I don't know." Andre threw up his hands. "It's not like him." He stood and paced over to Finn's desk.

I watched him as he combed over what was left of Finn's files on the desktop, flipped through his desk calendar, and rifled through the notepad I had doodled in months ago. The doodle was still there.

Just as he was about to give up, a yellow sticky note fell off the side of Finn's desk and fluttered to the ground. Andre bent over and picked it up, flipping it over to read what was written on it. His face fell.

"Andre?"

His eyes zoomed over the message a second time. He was mouthing soundlessly as he read. He glanced up at me, then back at the sticky note.

"What does it say?"

He handed the note over to me. A number was scrawled across the top with the message, "Called in. Thinks they have info on dock murder," written below it. I cocked my head to the side and stared at Andre. This wasn't anything new. The Chief had told us it was related to the Bianchi case and, from what I had gathered around the station, they were confident the Bianchis had a serious hand in the dock murder.

"Am I missing something?"

"I know that number," Andre frowned.

"And?"

"It's Finn's ex, Brie."

"The one that tore out his still-beating heart and stomped on it," I growled.

The thought of someone doing that to Finn pissed me off. I was still furious with Finn's bullshit, but this was basic friend code; you fuck with someone I care about; I fuck you up. I didn't know this Brie, but I hated her.

"You think this is why he didn't tell you?" I tossed the note away in disgust.

"It has to be." Andre returned to his chair. "He probably thought I would have stopped him. Maybe he didn't want me to have to go back to Chicago myself. I don't know."

The hurt in Andre's eyes was clear. Finn and Andre were two halves of one whole when it came to the job. It was like watching the two hemispheres of one brain work together. Getting left behind and left in the dark on their biggest case stung bad.

I did my best to distract Andre for the rest of the day. We continued working on some of the newer cases I had been assigned, most of them crimes against women. Andre did his best to commit his full attention, but I could feel the distance every time he went quiet. By the end of the evening, he even seemed to doze off a couple of times.

"I think it's time to call it a night," I nudged him with my elbow.

Andre startled and shook his head. His eyes were strangely glazed over, his normally brown irises a milky white. I pulled back involuntarily, my heart leaping in my chest. It reminded me forcefully of the strange look Chloe had gotten at the campfire a few months ago. Andre blinked a few times, then his eyes went back to normal as he focused on me.

"Did you just have a stroke?" I gasped.

"Huh?"

"Your eyes." I pointed at him. "What was that with your eyes?"

Andre looked guilty. Without Finn here to shield him, he was off his game. He bit his lower lip and stared down at the ground. I could almost see the wheels turning in his head. One of Finn's many lessons echoed in my ears: *When a perp goes quiet like that, he's fighting an internal battle, Allie. You're on to something he doesn't want you to know. Keep pushing.*

"Why did Finn get so upset at the Christmas party, Andre?" I asked.

Why hadn't I thought to ask Andre in the first place? He knew Finn better than anyone else.

"Because that asshole shoved you." Andre was instantly defensive.

"Yeah, that's what pissed him off at the beginning, but then the Knuckle said something that pushed him over the edge."

"I didn't hear what led up to that," Andre shrugged casually. But his averted gaze told another story. So, I continued.

"The Knuckle called me Finn's 'stupid human pet.'" I watched Andre closely. "And Finn snapped." Andre didn't react at all. Too casual. "Why would a dumb, drunken taunt like that prompt Finn to choke a guy and beat the shit out of him?"

"I don't know. Why don't you ask Finn about it?" Andre stood up and grabbed his suit coat.

"I did, and he lied."

"How do you know he was lying?"

"You and Finn taught me how to spot the signs." I moved to block the door. "He lied to me that night, and you're lying to me now. Why won't either of you tell me what's going on?"

Andre's shoulders fell. "Look, Lex, I want to tell you. I really do. But it's not my place to say anything. I made a promise, and I won't go back on it."

"A promise to who? Finn?" Finally, I was getting somewhere.

"Yes, and to other people who are really important to me. Please don't make me choose between my friendship with you and that promise. I don't want to break either." Andre's shoulders slumped.

My stomach dropped. That was a tough blow. As eager as I was to get answers, I was putting Andre in a bad position.

"I'm sorry." I stepped away from the door. "You've already had a shitty day, and I shouldn't be on your ass about this. I would never want you to feel like you have to break a promise to someone else to appease me."

"I really am sorry, Lex," Andre patted my arm.

"I know you are. You're not lying about that part."

"Are we cool?" His brown eyes were pleading.

"Yeah, we're fine. Go home."

"Do you want a ride?"

"Nah, I'll just catch the bus." I grabbed my coat off the rack.

"You sure?"

"It's kind of peaceful at night. But thanks. I'll see you tomorrow."

Before he could argue with me, I left the think tank and headed out into the cold evening. The light near the bus bench flickered overhead as I took a seat. The sharp breeze made me shiver. I wrapped my coat tighter around me and sighed. Things had sure taken a hard right turn from what they had been a few days ago.

The Clock had become my home in ways no other place had ever been. I came here out of necessity, but I had fallen in love with the place by choice. My friends had embraced me fully. I loved my job and school was more than I expected from a small-town university. Fear was my constant companion before my move. My neck was always sore from looking over my shoulder. But I felt safe here. It was almost strange how quickly the fear abated. Otherworldly even...

Stupid human pet. Human. Why that word?

The bus creaked to a halt and hissed as it lowered to admit me. The fluorescent lights were blinding compared to the dark of the bus stop. I held the pole to steady myself as I sat, the bus already in motion.

Strange things happened when I was in the presence of the 10-block crew. It started as little things that I hardly noticed or dismissed, but it had grown to bigger things I couldn't ignore. A good detective doesn't discard any evidence until he's sure it's unrelated. Finn was a good detective, and he was teaching me well. What evidence had I discarded to fit in and go with the flow?

The camping trip came to mind. I started counting instances on my fingers. The strange vision of the cherry tree during Hiro's song. Chloe's vacant stare as she looked at Finn across the campfire. The rush of perfectly timed wind during Riel's story. The intense dreams about Finn that seemed too real to just be dreams.

Then the happenings at the Christmas party; Finn's hedging about not knowing Selsha when he seemed to know her. The fight with the Knuckle crew. The booming sound I thought had been a weapon discharging that ended the fight. Finn's evasive half-answers while he walked me home. And now Andre's milky white eyes that he admits are related to a promise to keep some secret.

Human pet… For the Knuckle to call me human would be an implication that they weren't human. But that was ridiculous! What could they be if not human? The skeptic in me fought against the notion. But another part of me wondered if there wasn't something to the idea.

"Miss?" The bus driver called to me, and it startled me. "Isn't this your stop?"

Outside the dirty window was my bus stop. I had been so lost in thought that I hadn't been paying attention. I was in luck that the same four drivers drove this route each day and recognized me.

"Thank you," I nodded as I disembarked. He tipped his hat to me.

My mind was still racing as I entered my apartment. Moira greeted me with a smile. She had been so disappointed about the way the Christmas party ended that she hadn't been her usual cheerful self. The vestiges of that disappointment still lived in the crease between her eyebrows.

Moira knew everyone in 10-block. She had known Finn and Andre for a long time. She had to know what the secret was. Should I ask her? I wrestled with myself. If I asked her, I'd likely be putting her in the same position Andre had lamented: my friendship or the secret. But how else was I supposed to find out what the hell was going on around here? The more I considered things, the more I was convinced something was happening outside my awareness. My mind still fought against the idea that something was inhuman or superhuman or whatever, but my instincts told me I was being left in the dark. And the darkness had always scared me.

In the darkness, everything fell apart. Robbed of the ability to see, the darkness made me blind to potential harm. That night, the darkness betrayed me so fully, so completely, that I doubt I would ever feel safe in it again, literally or metaphorically. A shiver raced down my spine.

I shook my head, trying to veer off the track this line of thinking was headed down. But it was too late. My body was already shaking. I escaped to my room before Moira could ask me about my day. After shutting the door and locking it, I leaned my forehead against the splintered wood. The familiar creeping terror started at the base of my torso, working its way up.

The face of the embodiment of my terror lashed out from the corners of my mind. Why couldn't I leave the damn past behind? Why did his face have to haunt me still? He was in jail. I was in the program. Marshal Davis had assured me that Beckburg was far, far off the map; a tiny pseudo island connected with the mainland by a narrow peninsula. Hell, I was pretty good with geography, and it took me some serious Googling to find out anything about it before I was relocated here. My mind knew the facts, but my body was alive with dread.

I sank to the floor and wrapped my arms around my knees. *Deep breaths, Alexis, take deep breaths.* The oxygen expanded my chest with each inhale, but it made my chest feel more constricted. I reached for my phone, but the second it was in my hands, I regretted the reach. I was halfway through dialing Finn's number before I registered what I was doing.

We hadn't even spoken since our fight after the Christmas party. Now he was in Chicago, getting information from his cheating ex about his biggest and most frustrating case. He probably wouldn't give a damn about my panic attack. Did I even want to bother him with my baggage?

Yes. I sighed. Yes, I wanted to talk to him, baggage or not. At some point in all of this, Finn Briggs had become my best friend.

I threw my phone on my bed and crawled into my bathroom. Instead of calling Finn, I'd settle for my rescue meds. It had been months since I'd had to take one, but I had no other way to fight the pressure threatening to explode out of my chest tonight. I took the pill with a gulp of water and sat on the floor of the bathroom until it kicked in. Once it did, I checked the lock on my door one more time before climbing into bed.

My nightmares came back in full force. I woke up in a full sweat, screaming. I pulled my pillow over my face to muffle the screams. But it was too late. Scuffling in the hallway followed by a rapid knocking at my door told me I'd already woken up my roommates.

"Alexis, are you okay?" Chloe's voice called.

I took a shuddering breath before answering. "Yeah, sorry. Just a nightmare." The terror still clung to the surrounding air like humidity.

"Are you sure, hun?" Moira joined.

"Yeah, I'm sure. I'm so sorry. Go back to bed," I called.

They whispered back and forth to each other. I clutched my blankets and took deep breaths, trying to shake the last remnants of the nightmare from my mind. His face, his reek, the pain...

"Okay, if you're sure," Moira called through the door. "Promise you'll come get us if you need anything."

"I will," I lied. "Sorry again."

Their footsteps faded down the hall.

I sat up and pulled my covers tightly around my waist. My phone blinked innocently at me from the end of my bed where I'd left it. I picked it up and Finn's profile was already up, ready to be dialed. It was four in the morning here, so definitely the middle of the night in Chicago, too. If he was even still there.

I wanted to hear his voice; that warm, deep baritone that had become so familiar and comforting. I cursed myself. He lied to me. I should never want to hear his voice again. But I wanted to hear it. As my body shivered with anxious energy, I wanted to be wrapped up in his arms like he'd held me in the chill outside the warmth of the campfire.

Want. Don't want. I battled myself. Despite the divide, the two sides of me settled on a middle ground.

"Any chance you're up?" I typed. My finger hovered over the Send button. I closed my eyes and touched the screen, a lump building in my chest.

I shivered as I waited.

Ping.

"Oddly enough, I am. You okay?" Finn replied.

"No. 4 a.m. isn't my best hour, ironically."

Now that I'd texted him, I didn't know what to say, so I settled for sarcasm. I wanted to bare my soul and hide it deep inside all at the same time.

"What's up? Are you safe?"

"I'm safe. Just upset."

"About what?"

I tapped my finger against the side of my phone. Did I expect him not to ask? Of course, he would want to know. But was I ready to tell him?

"You know those demons I told you about before our second interview with Maria?" I typed. "They came back for another visit." It was all I could force myself to write.

"What do the demons want with you?"

"To destroy me, devour me, chew me up and leave me a lifeless husk. Shit, that sounds dramatic, doesn't it?"

"Demons don't play nice. I have a fair share of my own. So no, not dramatic. I had to face a few of my own the past couple of days, too."

"I'm sorry. Are you okay?" I pulled my covers closer.

"We're not talking about me. We're talking about you. Are you okay?"

"I'm the least amount of okay I've been in a long time." A tear slid down my cheek.

"What can I do?"

"Probably nothing, but thanks for being awake, at least."

The three little dots that showed me Finn was typing a response appeared and disappeared several times. A minute passed and nothing else came through. Then my phone lit up with the picture I had taken of Finn and Andre, laughing at one of our many lunches.

"Hey," I answered the phone.

"Hey," he replied. He sounded beat. "This seemed a little beyond texting."

"Maybe a little," my voice cracked.

"What can I do, Allie?" His voice was gentle and worried.

"I don't even know, Finn. I just wanted to talk to you." I admitted.

"Then talk to me, little Siren," he crooned. "What has you so upset?"

"Some terrible shit happened to me last year, and it came up with a vengeance tonight. I don't really want to get into details, not over the phone, maybe not even in person." I took a deep breath. "I needed to talk to you. It sounds stupid now that I say it out loud."

"It's not stupid, Allie. Whatever the awful shit is, I want to be here for you. I'm glad you texted. I thought you were still pissed at me."

"Oh, I am," I chuckled through the lump in my throat. "But you're still the first person I thought of, you stubborn bastard."

Finn laughed. The familiarity of it soothed some of the tension in my chest.

"I guess I'll take it. …I'm sorry. For all of it. For the Christmas party. For not being honest with you. I'm sorry that your demons are being assholes tonight. I'm just sorry."

"I don't like being lied to, Finn."

"I know. But can you trust that the only reason I would hold anything back from you is for your own good?"

I considered the idea. It wasn't impossible. But it was still frustrating.

"Alexis?"

"It's not only you, is it? Pretty much everyone else is in on it, too." The thought had been plaguing me since talking to Andre.

Finn was silent on the other end. Throughout his silence, an engine hummed.

"It's not just me," he confirmed. "Did someone say something?"

"No," I assured. "I got on Andre's ass about it at work, but he didn't say anything, I promise."

"Okay…"

"Am I some kind of joke to everyone?" My eyes welled up.

"No! God, no! Alexis…" Finn assured.

"It feels like I'm an outsider, Finn. I'm the newbie, stumbling around in the dark while everyone watches me make a fool out of myself. I get that you guys have this secret between all of you, but it feels shitty to find out that everyone I thought I could trust has been lying to me the whole time."

"I get that, Allie, but it's not like that. There are things that existed before you moved here, and we can't change that. We all care about you, seriously, but there are things you're better off not knowing."

The demons from my past clawed at me from inside my chest. I swallowed hard to keep from throwing up. Could I trust what he said?

"You have your secrets, too, Allie," Finn reminded. "Those demons that you won't talk about. They're yours. And I'm never going to push you to talk about them if you don't want to. All I'm asking is that you show me and the others the same respect."

Ouch. That one cut deep. I started to cry, hard.

"Allie?"

I couldn't answer him.

He was quiet for a long time. The only sound coming through the line was the hum of an engine. Then that sound stopped. A car door opening and closing.

"Come let me in," Finn requested.

"What?"

"I'm on your front porch. Buzz me in," he repeated.

I slipped out of bed and padded to the front door on my bare feet. I pressed the button that would let him into the building. It took less than thirty seconds for him to knock on the door. I was suddenly self-conscious about how I must look, panicked and covered in sweat, but I opened the door, anyway.

Finn filled up my doorway dressed in a black t-shirt and jeans. His hair was tousled, and his eyes were red with exhaustion. He gave me a half smile before pulling me into his arms and closing the door behind him. The tears continued to leak down my face.

Finn shifted my weight and lifted me into his arms, cradling me. I buried my face in his shoulder as he carried me back to my room. He kicked off his shoes and got into my bed, pulling the blankets up over the both of us. I continued to cry, clutching his shirt, as he ran his fingers through my hair, soothing me. We sat that way for a long time; wrapped up together, his warmth and gentle touch chasing the demons away.

I don't know when, but I eventually fell asleep. The nightmares didn't return. Even in my sleep, I could feel Finn's warmth. At some point, either in my dreams or in a moment of waking, he whispered to me.

"I'll always keep you safe, little siren."

Chapter Seventeen

Finn

When Alexis's breathing became deep and rhythmic, I pulled her deeper under the covers of her bed. I cradled her against my chest, unable to let go. After the disgust that churned in my stomach in Brie's presence, Alexis was a balm to my entire being. Even shattered, betrayed, and unsure, she was all softness and serenity to me. I held her closer, breathing in her sweet scent, surrendering to it, allowing it to clear my senses of what had happened in Chicago. I still needed to talk to Andre and Riel, but that could wait until morning. Alexis sighed in her sleep, and something awakened inside me.

It was the beast but wasn't the beast at the same time. My wolf growled territorially as I stroked Alexis's hair but curled itself up in a ball around her. It didn't try to attack, to consume, to destroy. It only wanted to protect. I brushed my lips against the top of her head and the beast glowed with pride. As I held Alexis in bed in her crummy apartment in 10-block, I couldn't blame any of my current feelings on the power of the woods. I felt something. It was deep and wide, bigger than me, and it scared me.

When dawn broke its hazy rays on the street outside the window, I slipped silently out of Alexis's bed, pulling her covers up to her chin to keep her warm in my absence. I took one last look at her peaceful face before hurrying out of her room. I passed Chloe in the living room and averted my gaze. I had no desire to discuss what I was feeling right now, least of all to Chloe. But she would know it, anyway.

I left my Charger where I'd parked it a few hours ago and jogged to the One Trick Pony instead. It was too early for the bar to be open, but Riel lived in the apartment above the bar, and he was expecting me. Andre would meet us there, too. We had some serious business to discuss. We needed to figure things out before we went to work today. Chief would expect an update, and I didn't know what to tell him.

For hours, Andre, Riel, and I talked about the implications of what Brie had told me. The name she shouted was meaningless to me until I did an Internet search on the plane ride home. I was shocked. Was Brie lying just to fuck with me, or was she telling the truth for once? Andre wondered the same.

My long-time partner was upset that I'd snuck out of town without telling him, but all of that was forgotten as we talked things over with Riel. None of us wanted to believe what Brie said, but the clues all added up to her information being right on the money. Shit. This was a hell of a lot bigger than we could have ever imagined. What were we going to tell the Chief...?

I was already leery of walking into the station. The muscles in my back tightened as the Chief strode toward us as soon as we entered the think tank. I was going to have to lie to my boss. But something spared us any immediate questions.

"We've got some good news, boys," Chief grinned. "We were able to pin down the place Ramond's aunt in Tennessee is hiding. A black and white spotted a woman who looks like the picture we sent out in the BOLO in a nearby town called Bull's Gap. I got off the phone with the Sheriff there. They pulled her in on a traffic violation and she's waiting in a cell, ripe for the questioning."

"Did they get anything out of her?" Andre asked.

"Nope, clammed up real tight. The Sheriff offered to let one of us to take a crack at her before they have to let her go. Andre, pack a bag and get your ass to the airport asap. The clock is already ticking on their 48-hour hold."

"Finn's not coming?" Andre looked at me. I was a little surprised, too.

"We need a Spanish-speaker, so Finn's catching desk duty while you fly to exotic Bull's Gap, Tennessee. He's got Ferret's case to crack. Speaking of which, how did that tip pan out?"

"The tipster was vague. Nothing that's going to break the case wide open, but some of what they said might give me a new direction to check out," I hedged.

"Get right on it then," Chief clapped me on the back. "Andre, get to gettin'."

Andre gave me one last look, then hurried out of the station, stopping only long enough to give Alexis a grin as she entered the think tank. My chest constricted. Her eyes were a little puffy from her night of crying, but I doubted anyone else would notice. No one else was looking close enough.

"Did Andre's back pocket catch on fire or something?" she joked, sitting on the edge of my desk. She seemed in pretty good spirits.

"Cops in Tennessee found Ramond's aunt. Andre is headed out there to question her. See if we can get what we finally need to catch her son-of-a-bitch nephew." I raised my brows at her.

"You're kidding me!" Alexis gave me a genuine smile. "Oh my God, that's fantastic news. Are we going to tell Maria?"

"Nah, let's hold off until we have something concrete to tell her. We don't know if the aunt will even talk yet. I don't want to get Maria's hopes up."

"You're probably right." Her shoulders fell a little. "What's on the docket for today, detective?" She pulled Andre's chair over to sit next to me.

"You okay?" I dropped my voice.

"Better this morning, thanks to you," her cheeks turned pink. I suppressed a smile.

"Glad I could help." I patted her leg.

"Hey, Briggs!" Someone called out to me from across the room.

Olivier was strolling over. His signature toothpick flicked back and forth from one side of his mouth to the other. It was supposed to help him stop smoking, but it just turned into a second habit in between cigarettes.

"Lot called in from an active crime scene. He made a drug bust at the sleazy motel on 9-block and he's got someone there you might know."

"Who?" I didn't cross paths with vice often, so I wasn't sure who it could be.

"The broad gave us a fake name at first, but when we ran the name on the ID in her purse, it came up as a frequent pro. File says she's got an open case in violent crimes, so I thought I'd let you know. Name's Leticia something. Looks like the John mighta got rough with her."

"Is she okay?" Alexis asked, her tone anxious.

"She's a prostitute," Olivier shrugged and rolled his eyes at the question.

"She's a person," Alexis snapped back at him. "What she does to keep food on the table for her family doesn't make her any less deserving of dignity and respect."

"You bleeding-heart liberals are all the same," Olivier shook his head.

I could practically see the steam coming off Alexis. She took a breath, and I knew whatever was about to come out of her mouth would not win her any popularity contests in the department, so I laid a hand on her arm to stop her. She glanced at me with annoyance.

"Don't be a dick, Olivier," I warned. "Just have dispatch text me the details and we'll take care of it."

"Looks like your little shrink friend here has you by the balls, Briggs," Olivier mocked.

"I'm going to give you one last chance to shut your fucking mouth, Olivier, before I shut it for you."

"Big talker," he sneered. "Let's see how that turns out for you." He flicked his toothpick at us before striding away. It was Alexis's turn to put a restraining hand on my arm.

"We have to go make sure Leticia is okay," Alexis said. "Karma will take care of that asshole. Vice obviously doesn't give a shit about her, but we do."

"Okay, I'll go check on her," I stood.

"I'm coming with you," Alexis rose, too.

"You think I'm taking you to an active crime scene?" I chuckled. "No way."

"Chief has been talking about making me a more active part of your work. What better way to do that than to take me where a victim needs me the most? If another John beat up Leticia, I need to be there for her. Please, Finn."

I couldn't ignore the pleading look in her eyes. I didn't want to give in, prove Olivier right she had me by the balls, but the denial I wanted to deliver wouldn't come out of my mouth. My mind flashed to holding her in her bed this morning and I had to shake my head to push the memory out of the way. Feelings made it harder to think.

"I'll go run it by the Chief right now," Alexis offered.

She had me there. If she asked, he would surely say yes. The scene was already under control, and he wanted to expand her role as a victim's advocate. Shit.

"Get your damn coat, then."

Alexis grinned and ran off to grab the coat she wore every day. Andre had given her shit about only having the one, and she gave him shit back about his one and only fedora. But she said the coat was her favorite. I didn't mind it; it accentuated the curves of her full hips. ...Fuck. Where was my head at?

The drive to 9-block was quieter than usual between us. The weight of last night hung in the air, unspoken, but still intense. My curiosity raged about the demons that turned such a strong and fiercely independent woman into a shaking mess. Whatever she'd faced must have been rough. I wanted to know every single detail about it.

I glanced at her face; it was lined with worry. I couldn't ask more about her demons now. I told her I would respect her secrets if she would respect mine. How could I possibly ask her for what I was so unwilling to give in return? I wish we didn't have to have secrets between us at all.

Yellow crime scene tape already cordoned the motel off. I flashed my badge to the uniform guarding the perimeter and Alexis showed her laminated ID, marking her as an employee of the force. He let us pass with a nod. I scanned the scene, mentally cataloging and gathering evidence. It wasn't my crime scene, but it was second nature.

Alexis caught sight of Leticia before I did, automatically breaking into a jog to get to her side. I lengthened my stride to catch up to her without running myself. Leticia was sitting on the bottom step of the dilapidated metal staircase, arguing with a medic.

"I told you eight times that I'm fine, for the love of God, leave me alone," Leticia snarled at the medic.

"She doesn't want you to touch her," Alexis huffed, a bit winded. "If she says she's fine, she's fine."

Alexis flashed her ID at the medic and waved him away. The medic rolled his eyes, threw his hands in the air, and stomped away. It was almost comical.

"Leticia, are you alright?" Alexis knelt down in front of her.

"What are you two doing here?" Leticia looked between Alexis and I.

"Another detective told us you'd been hurt. We wanted to check on you." Alexis put a soft finger under Leticia's chin and lifted her face toward the light.

She had fresh bruises on her face, a cut on her left jawline, and her lip was swollen and split. My blood boiled. Someone had used her as a punching bag. I clenched my fist and glanced around the scene, searching for a potential perp.

"Oh Leticia," Alexis sighed.

Leticia's eyes watered. She pulled her face out of Alexis's grip and turned away. She wrapped her arms around herself. It was freezing today, and she was only wearing a thin tank top and a miniskirt. I left Alexis to do her work and went to find the medic. He was still sulking about being turned away, but I could get a couple of blankets from him. When I got back to Alexis and Leticia, Leticia was crying in Alexis's arms. Alexis was damn good at what she did.

"It's cold this morning," I said. "Let's get you warmed up."

Alexis had already wrapped Leticia in her own coat. I handed the blankets to Alexis, and she wrapped them around Leticia's shoulders and across her lap. Leticia wiped at her nose and eyes, smearing mascara across her cheekbones. Dark marks were already purpling under the skin.

"We're not going to force you to do or say anything, Leticia, you know that. But we can't keep you safe if we don't know what we're working with," Alexis soothed.

"We can take you in, get you looked at by an actual doctor, not the pouty man-child in the EMT coat."

Leticia gave a brief chuckle. She touched the spot under her right eye gingerly and winced. She was hurting, no doubt about it.

"If I go in, you're not going to make me say nothin'?" Leticia asked.

"Of course not. Whatever all this is," Alexis motioned to the crime scene surrounding us, "it's far less important than your safety and wellbeing."

"You'll keep your watchdog on a leash," Leticia lifted her chin toward me. I bristled internally but kept my cool.

"A tight one, I swear," Alexis smiled at me.

"I'll be on my best behavior," I held my hand to the square.

Leticia stood, clutching the blanket around her shoulders. The one on her lap slipped and Alexis bent to pick it up for her. Then several things happened all at once.

A loud pop broke the morning calm, and I felt a searing pain rip through my right shoulder. An engine revved and tires squealed against the pavement. Leticia screamed and dropped to the ground. Every nerve in my body shouted 'danger,' so I took three long strides over to Alexis and yanked her down to the ground. I used my body weight to pin her to the sidewalk, covering her in case the perps got another shot off, while I drew my sidearm with my uninjured left arm. I felt a sudden pressure on my shoulder and grunted in pain but did my best to steady my aim with my non-dominant hand, scanning the scene for further threats.

The other cops on the scene were in an uproar. Some had taken cover, while a few others were running toward their cruisers. My grip on my gun was slipping and my eyes blurred. I could smell the tang of burnt gunpowder in the air. Detective Lot was screaming at the remaining cops on the scene, demanding to know how his crime scene had been compromised. Blood was pumping loudly in my ears.

"Are we clear?" Lot hollered.

"They took off that way in a brown Cadillac, sir," a uniform yelled back.

"I think we're clear," someone else added.

A few more tense moments passed as dozens of trained eyes scanned the scene. Pain was shooting down my arm and back. I could feel Alexis's shaky breaths puff along my neck.

"Clear," Lot called.

With that one word, my body slumped, my gun clattering as it hit the sidewalk. My shoulder felt like it was on fire. Leticia was sobbing somewhere behind me.

"Finn," Alexis whispered beneath me.

I couldn't answer. Every ounce of energy left me. The only thing I could focus on was the pain.

Alexis rolled me over onto my back, freeing herself from my weight. She clamped her hand on my shoulder. I tried to push her hand away, but she swatted my free hand like it was a fly. She had tears streaming down both her cheeks, but she was in complete control of herself.

"Medic," Alexis commanded. "Detective Briggs has been shot."

Is that what this was? My vision blurred once more. I fought to bring Alexis's face back into focus. Her eyes were locked on mine.

Scuffling on the pavement.

Shadows blocking out the sun.

The pouty EMT.

Someone tried to pull Alexis away, but I grabbed onto her arm with all the strength I had left. She touched my face. Then she was gone.

The world went dark.

. . . . .

The beeping was driving me crazy, but I couldn't wake up enough to turn off the alarm. It felt like I was swimming in molasses. My limbs wouldn't obey me, but I had to stop the beeping. I fought to open my eyes. The light coming through my eyelids was bright. I must have slept in.

"He's coming around," a deep, familiar voice mumbled.

"Oh, thank God," a sweet, higher one sighed.

I wanted to reach out to that voice. It sounded like home. I wanted to pull it toward me, wrap myself in it. Drink it, bathe in it. I needed it.

"Finn?" There it was again. "Finn, can you hear me?"

"Open your eyes for us, son," the deeper voice again.

A feather light touch along my cheek. I tried to talk back, but my mouth was filled with molasses, too. Someone lifted my hand and wrapped it in theirs. I responded with what strength I could.

"He just squeezed my hand."

"Alexis?" I mumbled.

"I'm here, Finn." She sounded sad in a happy way. Or happy in a sad way. I couldn't tell.

She squeezed my hand and rubbed my arm. I was regaining control; the molasses melting away at her touch. I pried my eyelids apart and blinked at the brightness of the surrounding room.

"There you are." It was Chief's voice. "Welcome back, kid."

I blinked several more times and Chief's face came into focus. He was smiling, but his eyes were drawn and worried. My eyes flicked back and forth and realized I was in a hospital room. I gasped and tried to sit up, but pressure on both sides restrained me.

"You're going to rip open your stitches if you do that," Alexis scolded.

My eyes found her face, and I stopped fighting.

"Are you hurt?" The words were thick across my tongue.

"No, I'm fine," she assured. "The blood's all yours," she motioned to her clothes.

I nearly gagged at the sight of her covered in blood. Whether it was mine or hers, it didn't matter. Alexis was covered in blood. Everything inside me recoiled at the idea.

"You're lucky that's all you lost, Briggs," Chief said. "Alexis stemmed the bleeding right away and the medic on the scene got to you quick. Bullet nicked the thoro-something artery. It could have been much worse."

His words were taking a long time to process. Someone had shot me. I covered Alexis with blood. I was lucky.

"You came out of surgery a couple hours ago," Alexis continued. "They got a couple bullet fragments out and patched you up. But you're going to have to take it easy for a while until you're healed up."

"Which means you're on leave, so enjoy your paid vacation," Chief chuckled. "I'm going to go update the boys. You've got him?"

"I've got him," Alexis confirmed.

Chief patted my leg and left. My gaze returned to Alexis. Her eyes glistened.

"You've got a little something on your shirt," I joked.

She laughed, and several tears escaped. I pulled her down onto the hospital bed next to me. She wrapped an arm around my waist and gripped my left hand with the other. I kissed her forehead as she nuzzled into my uninjured shoulder.

"You got shot," she accused.

"It wasn't on purpose," I defended.

"You're supposed to be indestructible."

"Says who?"

"Says me."

"Well, it takes a lot more than a single bullet to slay a dragon."

"I don't even want to think about it."

"You don't have to, I'm fine." I tried to move my right arm, but it hurt like a motherfucker. It was in a sling, but even the attempt to flex those muscles was like getting stabbed by an icepick. I moaned.

"You're in pain," Alexis sat up. "I'll go get the nurse."

"Don't go." The words slipped out.

"I'm not going far, I promise," she smiled. She slipped out of the room.

Holy shit. I got shot. I rubbed my forehead, trying to let the gravity of what happened sink into my brain. It was too surreal. The damn beeping continued in the background.

Alexis and a redheaded nurse reentered my room. Alexis hung back by the door. I wanted to pull her back to me, but I resisted the urge to call her over.

"Well, if it isn't the man of the hour?" The nurse rounded my bedside. She wore perfectly pressed green scrubs and her lips were painted a shade of red that matched her hair.

"Rate your pain for me." She motioned to a chart on the wall with varying degrees of pain with matching faces.

"Constipated face level." I motioned to the eight.

"Constipated face it is." She typed something into a computer and swiped her ID card. "We gave you pain meds through your IV post-op, but now we're going to have you take these orally. That means you're going to have to eat something, or they'll wreak havoc on your stomach, and I think you've had your fair share of havoc for the day."

I nodded in agreement. She handed me two chunky, white pills. I popped them in my mouth and took a swig of water from the giant hospital water bottle she held out for me. She slid me a packet of saltine crackers and a dry-looking sandwich.

"Eat up," she commanded. I obeyed. "The doctor wants you to get plenty of rest, so no big movements. We've got you hooked up to a catheter for now, but we'll take that out soon and try to get you up and going to the bathroom on your own."

The pain spiked as I tried to eat, and a wave of nausea overcame me. Without those distractions, the idea of a catheter would have been a lot more embarrassing than it felt at the moment. I laid back against the pillows and closed my eyes until the nausea abated.

"I'll get you a clean pair of scrubs to borrow, honey," the nurse continued. "You can clean yourself up in the bathroom. It's no fun being covered in blood; trust me, I've been there."

"Thank you," Alexis said from across the room.

I opened my eyes again. The nurse looked between Alexis and I with a smile.

"Your girlfriend is welcome to stay for a little longer, but visiting hours are over in about half an hour. We're sticklers, regardless of the relationship, especially post-op."

"Oh, I'm not…" Alexis began.

"It's okay, babe. I'll be fine after that. You'll have to go home to feed Whiskers, anyway."

Alexis gave me a puzzled look. I winked at her, and she cracked a grin. She rolled her eyes at me. I didn't know if they would let her stay if she was just a friend and I wanted her here with me for as long as I could keep her.

"Okay, you're set for now. I'll be right back with those scrubs." The nurse bustled out of the room.

"Whiskers?" Alexis crossed to my side again. "You hate cats."

"Who said Whiskers was a cat? I was thinking more like a husky."

"A husky named Whiskers? You are officially never allowed to name any pets, henceforth and forevermore."

We shared a smile.

"You need to keep eating," she prompted.

"It makes me nauseous."

"Strangely enough, the less you eat, the more nauseous you'll be. Eat."

"You're as bossy as the nurse," I huffed.

"Since when have I not been bossy?"

"Excellent point, Henson," I conceded.

A soft tap on the door and the nurse re-entered.

"Here are some scrubs for you, darlin'." She set a pair of dark blue scrubs on the counter. "You'll feel loads better after a wash."

"Thank you." Alexis grabbed the scrubs and gave me one last look before disappearing into the bathroom.

"You've got a good one." The nurse motioned to the bathroom door. "She helped save your life, I hear. The ER nurses had to peel her away from you to get you back to surgery and she hasn't left your side since we brought you in here."

"She's one of a kind," I agreed. I stared at the bathroom door, grateful beyond words.

The rushing fall of water from the shower drew my full attention. That deep, wide feeling stirred in the pit of my stomach again. I wanted to be in that shower with her so much it ached. I wanted to be the one to wash the blood off her body. I wanted to hold her, kiss her, and touch her as the water returned her skin to its fair pinkish color. My cock hardened at the thought. I shifted a pillow over it to hide it from the nurse. Shot or not, I was still a man.

"Press that button if you need anything and I'll be here lickity-split," the nurse instructed. "Finish up your sandwich then get some rest."

She left the room. I closed my eyes and focused on the sounds of falling water in the next room. My hand strayed down to my cock, and I stroked myself absently as I imagined Alexis's naked body just a room away. The beast inside woke from our sedated slumber and growled its displeasure. I couldn't have let it out even if I wanted to. And, God, did I want to.

My cell phone rang and snapped me out of my fantasy. I groaned at the interruption and reached out to see who was disrupting me. Andre's goofy face popped up on my screen. This was the only person in the world who I'd choose to answer the phone for in this moment. He was probably freaking the fuck out.

"How's Tennessee?" I answered the call.

"Son of a bitch, Finn!" Andre snapped. "I'm gone for less than an hour and you get yourself shot!"

"Everyone's acting like that's my fault," I rolled my eyes. The relief was clear in my partner's voice.

"When Alexis called me from the hospital, I thought I was having a lucid nightmare, man! What the fuck?"

"It's okay, Andre. I'm still in one piece."

"Dude, the only reason I still got on that fucking plane here was because Alexis vowed to drag you back from hell herself if you tried dying on me."

My heart swelled.

"The devil would have his hands full with her," I grinned.

"Damn straight. Shit," Andre took a deep breath. "You sure you're okay?"

"I heal quick," I assured.

"Lucky for you," Andre sighed. "Damn, man. Don't ever scare me like that again."

"I'm not planning on it. Anything from the aunt yet?"

"Sitting in a damn hospital bed, ass cheeks hanging out of a gown, and this fool asks me about the case," Andre groaned. "No, I just got settled in my hotel room and I'm heading to meet the Sheriff at the jail in about forty-five minutes."

"Make sure you…" I started.

"…I'll handle the case, you handle that gunshot wound," Andre demanded.

"Fine," I chuckled.

"How's Lex?"

"I'm not sure," I bit my lip. "I haven't been awake for long. She's...uh...cleaning the blood off her right now." Saying the words made the nausea return.

"Shit. She sounded like she was barely holding off a breakdown when she called to tell me what happened. No matter how strong she is, watching someone she cares about get shot right in front of her must have done a number on her."

"That's what I'm worried about," I shifted my weight and winced as pain shot through my shoulder and down my arm. "She's going to be reliving that in her sleep, no doubt."

"I got you both covered. Don't worry about it. And I already called the sisters and they're gonna keep an eye on Lex so you can focus on healing," Andre reassured. "They're thinking about dropping by the hospital tomorrow if you're up for visitors."

"Sounds good," I replied.

But the thought of visitors barely clocked. The sound of the water in the bathroom stopped, and it pulled my attention right back to Alexis. Here I had been wrapped up in thoughts of her in the shower when I should have been more concerned with her wellbeing. She had been through a huge amount of trauma. I was ashamed of myself for not thinking about it until Andre brought it up.

"I'm gonna let you go, man. Get some rest. And no more getting shot until I get back."

"You got it. See you in a few," I replied.

I hung up the phone and put it back on the rolling bed tray. A few more bites of my sandwich chased with swigs of water helped settle my stomach. The pain medication was kicking in when Alexis came out of the bathroom dressed in the borrowed blue scrubs. Her familiar scent mingled with a citrus tang from the hospital-supplied soap.

"How are you feeling?" We asked in unison.

We both laughed at the synchronicity.

"You first," she prompted, sitting on the chair next to my bed. I wanted to pull her closer, but I didn't.

"The meds here are spectacular."

"Glad to hear it," she chuckled. "Any nausea?"

"Nope, just good vibes here." I waved to my now empty plate.

"Good boy." She patted my uninjured arm.

"Now you. How are you?"

"I'm holding up okay," she fake-smiled.

"Bullshit."

"Really, I don't think it's all hit me fully yet. It's too surreal."

"Tell me about it."

"I'm glad you're okay." She put her hand on top of mine and squeezed. "Everything else I can process when it hits me. I've already got a therapist on speed dial."

"I hope it's a damn good one." I laced my fingers with hers.

My eyes were drooping. I blinked slowly a few times, trying to fight off the effects of the meds. There was more I wanted to ask Alexis, but my thoughts were jumbled.

"Time for some more sleep." Her soft voice was like a lullaby.

Alexis pulled her hand out of my grasp and pulled the blankets up to my chest. I couldn't remember the last time someone had tucked me in.

"I'm flyin'… I mean fine," I argued.

"Flyin' indeed. Go to sleep," she insisted.

The door to my room opened, and the nurse popped her head in. "Visiting time is over. Give your gal a kiss and send her on her way."

"I'll be back first thing tomorrow morning," Alexis smiled down at me. The light above her made it look like she had a halo.

"You're not a siren," I mumbled. "You're an angel."

She kissed my forehead, lips lingering on my skin. "Sleep."

Alexis nodded to the nurse and left. The nurse gave me a wink, turned the lights off in my room before she left, too. Fighting sleep was a losing battle. But my dreams were spectacular: The best moments from camping with my friends, driving my Charger through the mountains, and lots of appearances of Alexis, smiling and happy. It made me happy, too. The only thing that could have made me happier would have been having her here in reality, not just in my dreams.

Chapter Eighteen

Alexis

I was terrified of going to bed, but the shock had completely exhausted me. Thankfully, my bed still smelled a little like Finn, so I could talk myself into trying. Thank God my dreams were pleasant and calm. Finn played a major role in every dream that wound its way through my subconscious that night. Not him getting shot, but just us talking like normal at the Pony, him joking with me and Andre out to lunch, and stolen moments that had never really happened that were filled with tender touches.

Moira, Chloe, Lacey, and I gathered early the next morning in the kitchen. They were as eager to check in on Finn as I was. Moira had spent most of the day yesterday stress-baking, so we packed a bag full of Finn's favorite treats.

"Riel said he would meet us at the hospital." Chloe put the bag in the back of the Jeep. "He had a few things he needed to do at the bar first."

"I can't believe we're going to the hospital," Moira fretted. "I can't remember the last time Finn got hurt like this."

"Not since before he moved to the Clock," Chloe replied.

Lacey and I got into the back, and she gripped my hand. I had heard her crying in her room when I got back from the hospital. She looked exhausted. I gave her hand a squeeze. She leaned her head on my shoulder in reply.

Moira kept up a string of nervous chatter all the way to the hospital. Riel was waiting for us in the parking lot when we arrived. He gave Chloe a quick kiss and greeted us all. He appeared older, more weighed down today than I had ever seen before. Everyone was so affected by what happened; it hung heavy in the air.

I led everyone to Finn's room and tapped softly on the door.

"Unless you're bringing me something actually edible, begone," Finn called.

We all relaxed. He was in good spirits. I opened the door, and we filed in. Moira rushed over to a smiling Finn and gave him a tentative hug. Lacey was right behind her, grabbing his left hand, holding back tears.

"I'm okay, kid," Finn assured Lacey. "You know that."

Riel and Chloe were next, Chloe standing a little behind.

"I'm glad to see you, my old friend," Riel patted Finn's knee. "You gave us a scare."

"Nah, I got lucky. They keep telling me I had a guardian angel." Finn grinned at me. I was standing back by the door, strangely hesitant to approach.

"Well, we'll count the day Alexis moved to the Clock as a blessing indeed," Riel turned to me and smiled, too.

Chloe looked back and forth between Finn and me, a confused expression on her face. Her eyes did that weird thing again, like at the campfire. I stared, freshly aware of the strangeness and their shared secret. It lasted only a few seconds. Then her eyes went right back to normal, and she was joking with Finn about Superman being bulletproof.

"I got a sponge bath from a weirdly chatty nurse named Keith," Finn called over to me. "So, I swear I don't smell. It's safe to come closer."

My feet carried me to his injured side. I tried to act as normal as possible, but the sudden shyness I felt in his presence grew stronger the closer I came. I scanned him quickly and was happy that his coloring looked better today.

"Do I pass inspection?" His gaze was playful.

"Just checking for any new bullet holes," I joked.

"I'm proud to report that I've gone almost a full twenty-four hours without being shot," Finn quipped. "Take that, doubters."

Everyone laughed. I hoped I was the only one that felt the odd tension in the air. Moira plopped down the bag of baked goods on Finn's side table and started pulling things out. Lacey retreated to a chair in the corner and curled up like a cat, watching the room. Riel and Chloe chatted with Finn about his hospital stay. I settled on the chair next to Finn's bed and tried to shake off the weirdness of the moment. *You're visiting your friend in the hospital,* I coached myself. *Just like everyone else in the room.*

But my thoughts kept straying to yesterday: Laying in the bed next to him as he kissed my forehead, the fear in his voice when he asked me not to go when I went to get the nurse, and the way he looked at me when the nurse told me it was time to leave. There was something so intimate about the short time we shared alone here yesterday. I suddenly wanted everyone to leave so I could curl up next to Finn again. Something felt different between us since he showed up at my apartment and held me to chase away the demons. Had that only been two nights ago? God, the last couple of days had been a whirlwind.

A tap at the door drew my attention. It was the same nurse as the night before. Her face brightened as she took in the room.

"Quite the crew you've got here this morning, Detective," she chirped. "Looks like your gal brought some reinforcements."

Finn's eyes flitted to me, then back to the nurse. Heat flushed in my cheeks at being called his gal. I wondered if anyone else had noticed.

"They're only here for the dry turkey sandwiches, Linda," Finn replied.

"Oh, stop it, the food's not that bad," Linda the nurse waved him away. "You'd think the man had a five-star chef to cook for him every night the way he complains about hospital food. Miss Alexis, did you go to culinary school or something?"

"Haha, no, Moira's the baker here." I pointed to Moira, who grinned at the praise. "And we have a couple of friends who are bona fide geniuses in the kitchen. They own their own restaurant on 9-block, so Finn knows a good meal when he eats one."

"Well, you better call in an order for lunch, Detective, because the doctor said no to discharging you before then," Linda tapped Finn on the foot.

"What do you mean, discharge?" Moira asked. "It must be too early for that, right?"

"Oh, I agree," Linda nodded. "But your friend here seems to think he's just fine. Wants to head home as soon as possible. Can't say I blame him," she winked at me. My cheeks grew hotter.

"Finn!" Moira declared. "You're not seriously considering leaving?"

"I'd rather sit around in my bed than in a hospital bed," Finn confirmed. "I haven't even been here a full day and I'm bored out of my damn mind."

"We can bring you things to do, if you'd like," Moira coaxed.

"When did he say I could leave?" Finn asked Linda, ignoring Moira.

"If there's no sign of infection for the next five or six hours, he said he would consider it as long as you have someone to keep an eye on you at home." Linda looked up from what she was checking on the computer.

"I'm sure I could talk someone into it." Finn grinned at Linda, and she gave him a cheeky smile in return.

My face was nearly on fire with the implication. If our other friends knew Linda thought I was Finn's girlfriend, I might jump out the window behind me and take off running. Chloe already thought something was going on between us. Linda doing more girlfriend-talk would be sure to spark some suspicions. Finn and I were close friends. That was it. But even as I thought the words, a tiny part of me was calling me a liar.

"Well, if you're going to keep pushing the subject, I think I can get him to sign off on it for you," Linda sighed.

"You are the best," Finn beamed.

"And you're an ass-kiss," Linda chuckled. "All charm, this one."

"That he is," Riel agreed.

"You lot enjoy your visit. I'll go start gathering the information you'll need when you discharge, Detective. I'll also check in with the physical therapist we have on staff today and see if they can get in to talk to you about the recovery plan." Linda gave us a wave and was gone.

"Andre's still out in Tennessee." Riel sat on the edge of Finn's bed. "Who are you going to rope into being your nursemaid if you go home early?"

"I can take some time off work and come help," Moira offered. "Oh, but Cierra is off on maternity leave and Fred went to Kansas to see some family, so they might not grant it to me."

"I can pop by in the mornings before the bar opens," Riel added.

"You know I love you, Finn, but I think we'd end up murdering each other if I came to help." Chloe made a face at him.

Lacey waved and pointed to herself in the corner. Then she furrowed her brows, looked at me, shrugged and waved the idea away. She gazed out the window with a serene smile.

I groaned internally. Make it sound casual. Don't draw suspicion.

"I talked to the Chief this morning," I piped up. "He wants me to take a couple of weeks off, too, to process what happened. With Andre in Tennessee and you on leave, there wouldn't be much for me to do at the station, anyway."

Finn was already fighting back a smile.

"I can come stay with you for a couple of weeks." I fought to keep my voice casual. "There are only a few things I have to do for class next semester, but I think you'll survive me being gone a couple of hours at a time."

"Oh, that would work out perfectly," Moira clapped her hands together.

"What do you say, Finn?" Riel nudged him.

"I couldn't think of a better nurse," Finn joked.

"Just as long as I don't have to change your diapers," I quipped back.

"I went to the bathroom all by myself this morning. Thank you very much."

Everyone laughed.

"That settles it." Chloe suppressed a smile. "Alexis will stay with Finn while he's on the mend." The knowing tone in her voice was agonizing. "I'll take you back to the apartment before I go to work, Lex. You can pack what you need and come back here when he's ready to discharge."

"How are we going to get to my place?" Finn asked.

"I'll go get the Charger, then come here," I offered.

"You're going to drive my baby?"

"You won't be able to drive her, so yeah."

"Do you know how to handle her?"

"Keep it up and you'll be sleeping here until you can drive her yourself. Linda will love to have you around for another couple of weeks."

"Fine, you win." Finn held up his good arm in defeat.

"I always do," I smirked.

"We better get going," Moira waved us toward the door. "Finn, you call the second you need something!"

"I will. Thanks for coming, guys."

"Anytime, hun," Moira patted his arm.

"See you soon, my friend," Riel nodded his goodbye.

Lacey hopped up and waved.

"Briggs," Chloe saluted.

I pushed myself out of my chair as the others filed out.

"I guess I'll see you at home, babe," Finn cooed to me. His face was all mischief. I couldn't help but smile.

"I'm serious, no diapers," I shot back.

He let out a bark-like laugh as I shut the door behind me.

The sisters' conversation was considerably more relaxed now that they had seen Finn with their own eyes. Moira and Chloe chatted the entire way home, and Lacey stared out the window. I couldn't stop thinking about spending the next two weeks with Finn, just the two of us. Things were feeling complicated enough without basically living together for a fortnight.

But I did as I said and packed my things before Chloe dropped me off at the police station. I went inside for a bit to update the Chief on Finn's condition, letting him know he was likely being discharged today. The relief on the old man's face was clear.

In the parking lot, I patted the Charger on the hood before tossing my bag in the passenger seat. Once in the driver's seat, I had to readjust to reach the pedals. Finn was a good foot taller than me.

"Alright, Black Beauty," I whispered to the car. "Let's go get your man."

It was the smoothest car I had ever driven. Despite the circumstances, I had to admit it was fun to drive it. I parked it at the far end of the lot that so it was less likely to get dinged, as I knew Finn would have insisted, then made my way back to Finn's room. The door was already open, and Linda's distinctive voice floated through the opening. I knocked on the doorframe before entering. Finn was sitting up in bed while Linda took his blood pressure.

"There's our girl, back again," Linda chirped.

"I couldn't stay away," I joked.

Finn looked more lucid than he had since he woke up from his surgery. He smiled serenely at me. I fought off a blush.

"His vitals are looking great, sweetheart," Linda assured. "It's like he's a superhuman or something the way he's healing up already."

Finn's smile faltered, and my stomach dropped.

"Doctor says he can head home now if he likes." Linda removed the blood pressure cuff and slipped her stethoscope back around her neck. "And I'll be heading home, too. Damn double shifts will be the death of me. Let me go have one last chat with the discharge nurse and I'll be right back to help you get on your way."

She patted my arm as she swept from the room.

"Hey, roomie," Finn grinned.

"You're enjoying this a little too much." I chided, as I sat on the edge of his bed.

"How's my baby?"

"What?!" My stomach flipped.

"The Charger," Finn raised an eyebrow. "You didn't scratch her or…"

"Oh, stop it," I answered with relief. "She's perfectly fine and parked out in the middle of no-man's-land, just how you like her."

"You know me all too well, Henson," Finn leaned back against the bed.

"You are unhealthily attached to your car."

"It's the deepest and most meaningful romance of my life."

"That makes me sad for you," I teased. "Looking forward to heading home?"

"God, yes! Will you help me get changed out of this damn gown?"

"Are you sure you want me to…" I hesitated. "You don't have any clothes besides the ones you came in with."

"Riel dropped some stuff off for me." Finn pointed to the table.

A pair of gray sweatpants, a navy zip-up sweater, some white boxer-briefs, and sneakers were stacked neatly next to his hospital mug. Finn shifted his weight with a groan and put his legs over the edge of the bed.

"Hold up there, eager beaver!" I grabbed his left arm. "You're going to hurt yourself if you go too fast."

"Taking care of me already," Finn patted my hand. "Can you hand me my underwear before I take off the gown? You may be my temporary nurse, but I doubt you can handle the glory of my naked body."

I snorted. "All the bravado's back, I see."

I tossed him his underwear, and he leaned forward to put them on. His face spasmed, and he gasped, sitting back up immediately. I grabbed his arm to help ease him into a more comfortable position.

"Too much?" I asked. He nodded. "Let me help."

I took the boxer-briefs out of his hands and knelt in front of him. I guided his feet through the leg holes and eased them past his calves, then his knees, and onto his thighs. When I looked up at him, he was staring intensely at me. I swallowed hard.

"You're going to have to stand up so I can get these onto your ass," I urged.

Finn grasped my shoulder, and I helped him to his feet. I averted my gaze as I finished pulling his underwear into place. The motion felt strangely intimate. Without making eye contact, I grabbed his sweatpants and repeated the path of his underwear: feet, calves, knees, thighs, help him stand, then settled into place on his hips. I undid the snaps of the hospital gown at his right shoulder and eased it off under his sling. He hissed with pain.

"Did I hurt you?" I whispered.

"No, Allie," he answered through gritted teeth. "Not you. It's the bullet hole."

"Smart-ass."

I pulled the gown the rest of the way off and laid it on the foot of his bed. My eyes traced their way up from his chiseled abs, past his pecs, and to his injured shoulder, where a bright white bandage contrasted starkly against his tanned skin. When I met his gaze with soft sympathy, he was staring at me again. His gaze was electrifying. The air was thick with intensity.

Finn put a finger under my chin and examined my face. His eyes flicked down from my gaze to my lips and back again. He licked his lips and parted them slightly. Gentle pressure under my chin pulled me slowly towards him until we were only a few inches apart. I exhaled shakily. The tip of his nose brushed against mine and I parted my lips, ready for him.

A quick rap on the door had me leaping away. Linda bustled back into the room with a clipboard in her hand and a pen tucked behind her ear. I moved across the room faster than I thought myself capable. Linda glanced up from the clipboard and around the room between Finn and I.

"Sorry, did I interrupt?" Linda asked innocently. A small smile played around her lips.

The blush that erupted in my cheeks felt like fire. Finn ducked his head, but the corner of his mouth was turned up. I closed my eyes, wanting to be swallowed up by the earth. What the hell had almost happened? I could not let myself get too close like this. *Friend, friend, six-pack-ab-toting friend,* I chanted to myself.

"I need to go over some paperwork with you, then I'll give Alexis your care instruction packet and you can be on your way," Linda pressed on.

She talked him through the discharge paperwork. Finn signed clumsily with his left hand and Linda talked both of us through some basic care instructions. I did my best to keep my eyes off Finn's bare chest.

"Alexis, come on over here and I'll show you how to help the detective put on a shirt," Linda waved me over. "First, ease off the sling," she prompted as she demonstrated.

Finn inhaled sharply.

"Keep it together, Detective, you've got this," Linda soothed. "Then pull the sleeve on the left arm, wrap it around the back, and slowly ease the second sleeve up the affected arm. Stick with button ups and zip-ups for the time being. He won't be able to raise his arm over his head for t-shirts for a couple of weeks."

Finn was gritting his teeth as Linda pulled the sleeve of his injured arm up. Sweat beads were forming on his forehead. I frowned at the amount of pain this was clearly causing him and worried about having to put him through it myself for the next couple of weeks.

"Once we're zipped," Linda zipped up the sweater, "then you put the sling back on. Then your man is probably going to need some serious hugging and kissing to be talked into doing it all again the next time." She winked at me. My stomach flipped again.

"I'll grab a wheelchair if you want to pull the car up to the entrance, Alexis," Linda said.

"I don't need a wheelchair," Finn argued.

"It's hospital policy, I'm afraid," Linda replied. "If you fall on your way out, our insurance adjusters will be on my ass. Don't fight the system, Detective. We'll meet you out front, Alexis."

I nodded and almost ran out of the room. I took several deep breaths once I was back out in the cold late-December air. A few snow flurries had fallen. I shook myself mentally. If I was going to be alone with Finn like this, dressing him, helping him bathe, then I was going to need to have some serious boundaries to keep things casual.

You could do worse, you know. Chloe's voice rang through my head.

But, goddamn, would things get worse if something romantic happened between Finn and me and it didn't work out? I couldn't lose the Clock. My life was literally depending on this. A different, more ominous voice echoed in my head as I got into the Charger.

"My people will find you for me…"

I shuddered. I forced the image of him out of my mind and focused on the purring of the engine. Linda and Finn were waiting for me. Finn was still clearly put out by the wheelchair. Linda helped me get Finn into the passenger seat and I closed the door once he buckled his seat belt.

"He's lucky to have you, honey," Linda patted my back. "I can see how much you care about him. And that man is clearly smitten with you."

"What do you mean?"

"He kept saying your name in his sleep last night," Linda explained. "Called out for you a couple of times." She gazed adoringly at Finn, waiting in the car. "I know love when I see it and you two have it."

My heart pounded in my chest. Finn had called for me? Something inside of me moved, pulling my gaze to Finn. He raised a questioning eyebrow at me.

"You two hit the road," Linda directed. "I'm sure you can't wait to cuddle up together without me busting in on you every few seconds. You take care." She patted my arm once more and left with the wheelchair.

I slid into the driver's seat, trying desperately not to look at Finn, but knowing that I would have to at some point. We hadn't said a word to each other since the almost-kiss or whatever that had been. How the hell was I supposed to break this tension?

"Home, James," Finn cracked. He leaned his head back against the headrest and closed his eyes. "And don't forget the hugs and kisses you owe me for getting dressed." The corner of his mouth turned up.

"I'll have Andre see to that part as soon as he gets back."

We didn't talk at all as I drove Finn to his apartment on 11-block. When I first found out that he lived in the suburban part of town, I gave him a ton of shit about it. He told me he got lucky enough to find an empty place in the only apartment building in the neighborhood when he first moved out here. It was a nice one-bedroom that looked out over the water.

"Alright, you bourgeois bastard," I tapped him on the knee. "We've arrived at your fancy mansion."

Finn's eyes fluttered open, and he stared up at his building with a sigh.

"Never been so happy to see the place in all my life."

"I don't have a wheelchair for you, but do you think you can manage it up a few flights of stairs with me as a makeshift crutch?"

"I can walk just fine. I got shot in the shoulder, not in the kneecap, Allie," he argued as he opened the car door and undid his seatbelt.

"Please don't make my life more difficult with all the hyper-independent, masculine bullshit, Finn," I pleaded as I helped him out of the car.

I pulled his left arm over my shoulder. At first, he walked fine with his arm draped over me, but by the second flight of stairs, he was leaning on me more and more. We were both panting by the time I got him settled on his couch.

"I'm going to go get my stuff out of the trunk and I'll be right back," I declared. "Be thinking about what you want for lunch. I make a mean dried-out turkey sandwich."

"Ha ha." He settled back onto the soft cushion.

I took my time getting my things, steeling myself for a well-boundaried couple of weeks, taking care of my friend. *Friend, friend, friend.* By the time I got back upstairs, Finn was already asleep on the couch. I couldn't help but smile at the sight. I dropped my stuff by the side of the couch, pulled a blanket off the back, and tucked him in. I forgot all about the boundary conversation I had with myself as I tenderly brushed some of Finn's hair off his face.

Finn slept for three hours, muttering in his sleep. I busied myself with my laptop, checking to see what textbooks I would need for my upcoming semester and making sure I set everything up with my registration. I read Finn's care instruction packet from cover to cover. Then I made myself a not-dry sandwich for lunch and listened to a podcast while I did some light cleaning in the kitchen. Finn's house was already incredibly tidy, so there wasn't much else for me to do.

After all that, I rounded the couch and pressed my hand against Finn's forehead to make sure he wasn't running a fever. As I pulled away, his hand caught my wrist, and he pulled me down onto the couch beside him. His arm slid around my waist, and he pulled me close to him.

"What are you doing, Detective Briggs?" My voice came out more flustered than scolding.

"Forcing you to take a break," Finn muttered sleepily.

"How do you know I haven't been taking a break already? You've been sleeping this whole time."

"Because I know you," he countered. "If I sleep long enough while you're here, I'm going to wake up to every room painted a new color, new cabinets, and at least three stray cats all named Whiskers."

"You're terrible at naming pretend pets," I grumbled.

"Tell me I'm wrong," he challenged. He opened his eyes, and the intensity was still there when he looked at me.

"I only did a little cleaning," I admitted.

"Mm-hmm," he gloated.

"Shut up. What do you want to eat? It's dinnertime already."

"Let's order in," he suggested. "We can give Vijay and Vikram some business and give you a break."

"I don't need a break. I've only just started taking care of you! And you slept the entire time," I laughed.

"The only thing I need right now is my phone to call in our order and my best friend curled up next to me on the couch."

"Your what?" I raised my eyebrows at him.

"You heard me: my best friend." He rubbed his nose against mine.

"I'm your best friend now, am I?"

"Of course you are, Allie. Just don't tell Andre. It'll break the poor kid's heart."

"You know I'm going to start braiding friendship bracelets now that you've made it official."

He chuckled, and it rumbled in his chest. He pulled me closer until I finally gave in and put my head on his shoulder. I felt him press his face against the top of my head and he inhaled slowly. His warm breath as he exhaled made goosebumps erupt across my neck.

"I owe you, little siren. Big time," he whispered.

"I'll cash in on that later," I promised.

"I'm sure you will."

He pressed his lips against the top of my head. Once, twice, then over and over until I felt the tingles all the way down to my toes. God, it was going to be difficult to keep things platonic if he kept touching me like this. But did I want to keep things platonic anymore?

Two voices warred inside of me, and I had no idea which one to listen to anymore.

Chapter Nineteen

Finn

Vijay and Vikram delivered our dinner personally. Their company as we ate our food helped break some of the tension between Alexis and I. Ever since I'd woken up from surgery, I'd craved her presence. Having her close to me eased some of the pain in my shoulder. I don't know how that was possible, but it did. Maybe it was all an illusion from the narcotics they had me on, but I was too exhausted to question it.

After the brothers left, Alexis busied herself in the kitchen, cleaning up after dinner. It felt distinctly like she was avoiding getting too close to me again. I frowned. Was I making her uncomfortable? Brie's snide face popped into my head. I felt the urge to retch. *You're tugging her around like a toy duck on a string…* Even in my head, that bitch wouldn't shut up.

"Ready for bed?" Alexis snapped me out of my reverie.

"Huh?"

"Do you want to go to bed?" She repeated.

"Um, yeah. Strangely enough, after several naps, I'm still tired."

"Your body is telling you what it needs." Alexis held her hand out to me. "You've gotta listen to it if you want to feel better."

"Yes, ma'am." I let her pull me up from the dining table and slip under my left side again. "Lead the way."

She steadied me as we walked to my bedroom, then she lowered me onto my bed. She looked me over once, opened her mouth to say something, then hesitated.

"What?" I asked.

"Are you going to be comfortable sleeping in that?"

"I usually sleep naked." I wasn't even trying to be cheeky this time; it was true.

"I don't know if I can get you all the way there without needing to fill out those forms with HR, but I can at least get you started." She was joking with me, but she wore little spots of pink in her cheeks. "May I?" She pointed to my sweater.

"Be my guest," I offered.

She unzipped my sweater and slid my left arm out of the sleeve. I only caught myself subconsciously trying to flex when it made my shoulder burn, so I stopped. Alexis took off my sling and slowly, gently, slipped the sleeve off my right arm. I winced.

"Sorry," she whispered.

"It's alright."

"That was the hard part," she encouraged, replacing my sling. "Lay down, I'll get your pants off next."

"That's the sexiest thing you've ever said to me, Siren."

"Don't press your luck," she chuckled.

I laid back and her hands skimmed the band of my sweatpants. Despite myself, I felt a stirring in my groin. God, not now!

Her fingers hooked over the band, gliding first over the skin above my hipbones. She pulled my sweatpants off while I tried to fight off the oncoming erection. The white boxer-briefs she'd helped put on me earlier today would do little to hide my arousal. The last thing I wanted was for her to come face-to-face with my cock when I could tell she already felt uncomfortable helping me undress. I tried to shift my weight to reach for a pillow, but my damn shoulder cried out in protest. I gasped.

"Are you okay?" Alexis studied me with concern.

Her eyes traveled from my face to my shoulder. Then, to my horror, they skimmed over my crotch. Her eyes widened briefly, and then she looked away. I groaned internally. If a person could die of embarrassment, I would have done so right then and there.

"Do you need me to help you sit up?" she offered.

"I think so," I admitted.

She held out her hand to me and helped pull me up, gaze steadily set over my head. To make matters worse, my face came up right next to her breasts as she helped me shift sideways, preparing to lay me down. Her sweet scent was so intense it made my mouth water. The wild gnashed its teeth within. The urge to pull her down on top of me despite my gunshot wound reared up in me. It wanted to consume her.

Before I could make another move, she had pulled my comforter up to my waist and stepped back. My cock ached as I stared at her. She was blushing again. It endeared her to me even more. There was an innocence about her reaction that pleased the relentless cynic in me.

"Get some rest, bestie," she directed. "Good night."

She turned off the lights and shut the door behind her. My free hand strayed down to my cock. I rubbed myself to ease the ache, but then I remembered I would need her help to get my underwear off tomorrow morning and it would be hard to explain the…stain… if I finished. There was no way I could reach any tissues, and getting out of bed without help was not an option. Fuck. I pulled my hand back out of my underwear and rested it helplessly next to me. I was going to have to wait this one out the old-fashioned way.

But when I slept, I dreamt of her. Her mouth on my skin, her soft hand wrapped around my cock, my arms locked tightly around her, pulling her closer until we were indistinguishable from each other. I could almost smell her scent in the dream as I buried my face against her breasts, kissing them, sucking them as tiny moans of pleasure skimmed her lips. I kissed my way down her stomach, then trailed my tongue along the inside of her thighs. I was feral with lust, and I bit the tender flesh there. She yelped and tried to pull away, but the beast wouldn't let her. I held her greedily as I bit and kissed the insides of her thighs. Yips somewhere between pleasure and pain sputtered out of her uncontrollably.

Unable to hold out any longer, I thrust my thick cock inside her and released a guttural sigh of relief. Her moan was deep and satisfying. I held onto the back of her neck as I thrust into her, locking eyes. She stared me down, wrapping her arms around my neck, pulling me closer. I felt myself building as I fucked her, the delicious pressure gathering at the base of my cock. The second I came inside her, I jolted awake, my cock releasing in real life, spraying my cum against my underwear.

"Fuck," I cursed quietly. "Fuck." I tried to stop it, but it was beyond my control. I gave in and stroked myself, allowing the pleasure to course through me until I finished.

"Fuck," I repeated, relaxing against my pillows.

Alexis was moving around in the kitchen outside my bedroom. I checked the time. It wouldn't be long before she came in to check on me. I had to get rid of the evidence or risk mortifying her even more. Using my good arm, I pulled my underwear painfully off my body, cum spreading down my legs as I did so. I wiped myself down with my sheet and prayed to God that Alexis wouldn't notice it. I bunched up my underwear one-handed and tossed it at my laundry basket. It bounced off the edge, but made it in. I breathed an enormous sigh of relief as a knock came at the door.

"Hey, Finn, you up?" Alexis called.

I checked myself quickly, pulled my comforter back up to my chest, and took a deep breath. I smelled like sex and shame, but she wouldn't be able to smell it like I could. Thank God.

"Yeah, come on in," I replied as casually as I could muster.

The door opened and Alexis peeked in with a smile.

"You slept for a long time," she enthused. "How are you feeling?"

"I'm okay." I shrugged, but the motion sent pain spiking down my right side. "Son of a bitch," I moaned.

"No shrugs for you." Alexis hurried over and sat on the edge of my bed. She rubbed gently at the area around my bandage, trying to ease the ache. I focused on my breathing until the pain subsided.

"I think it's taking your brain a few days to remember that you've been shot." Alexis continued to massage around my injury. "Maybe I need to tie you down to the bed to immobilize you."

I groaned internally. Something like that was the last thing I needed to hear from her right now, with my bunched-up underwear only a few feet away. She smelled so impossibly sweet. She tied up her hair into the same bun she wore while we were camping. The serendipity of the moment wasn't lost to me. I wanted her then, and I wanted her now. What had gotten into me?

"Nurse Linda told me you needed to take your meds with food, so what can I get you for brunch?" Alexis asked.

You. I want you. Only you, the beast growled.

I shook my head, trying to clear the thoughts away. My mind felt more lucid today than the day before and part of me was loudly judging myself about this sudden return to the lustful beast from the woods. I needed to get this under control. But, God, she smelled so sweet.

"Earth to Finn." Alexis raised her eyebrows at me.

"Huh? Oh, sorry, still a little sleepy," I lied. "Um, eggs and sausage would be nice."

"Coming right up." She hopped up from my bed and left the room.

I groaned audibly this time. Two weeks of this. Two full weeks of having Alexis close to me, undressing me, dressing me, touching my bare skin... This was going to kill me if I didn't snap the fuck out of it.

I closed my eyes and envisioned the least sexy things I could imagine. I was running through visions of searching through the dump for evidence last year when Alexis returned with my food.

"I found a tray in a closet." She propped it over my lap and set down my food. "That way, you don't have to get up and down for meals until you feel better. Here are your meds: You need to take two of these and one of these," she portioned them out on my tray. "After you eat, I can help you up into the bathroom to pee, help you into a bath, then get you dressed. Just give me a holler once you've finished eating. I'm going to clean up the dishes."

"Thanks," I answered as she left the room.

I ate slowly, still a little nauseated, then took my meds with the glass of water Alexis had brought in. The food was exceptionally good, which made me feel even more grateful that she had been the one to volunteer to help me. After I finished, I kicked my sheets to the bottom of the bed beneath the comforter to hide them while they dried.

"Would this be easier for you if we got a bell?" I shouted.

"Let's not turn this into a trope," Alexis laughed as she came back in. She held out a hand to help me sit up.

"I have to warn you I'm naked," I mentioned casually.

"How did you manage that?"

"I got hot last night and took them off," I lied.

"Well, that's one less thing we have to worry about then. I'll keep my eyes on the ceiling while I walk you to the bathroom."

I took her arm to steady myself as I rose, ass out, and she kept her gaze high. She helped me to the bathroom. I was a lot better on my feet this morning, so she let me get myself into the bathtub to wash up while she waited outside the door. I wasn't allowed to get my wound wet, so showers were out of the question for now. The warm bath was welcome, though. While I cleaned up, she brought a new set of clothes in, eyes shut tight, and set them on the bathroom counter.

"Do you still want me to help you get dressed?" She asked through the door.

"I'll give it a shot on my own first," I replied, toweling myself off. It was the only safe approach after the events of last night and this morning.

I could get my underwear on while sitting on the edge of the tub, but ended up out of breath. The pair of black sweatpants took longer to get on, but my pride kept me at it until I had accomplished the task. I stared at the gray zip up she'd brought and sighed. I opened the door sheepishly.

"Hey, good work!" Alexis took in the sight of me in. "Two out of three ain't bad! And only on your second day at home."

Before I could even ask, she picked up the sweater and helped me get it on. She zipped it up, then replaced my sling. Then she patted my cheek and gave me a hopeful look.

"Do you want to relax in bed or on the couch while I get cleaned up myself?" Alexis asked.

"I wouldn't mind the couch, so I can watch a show."

"To the living room, then."

She let me walk on my own, but she hovered close by just in case. I still needed her help to lower myself onto the sofa. She covered my lap with a blanket, handed me the remote, and set my water-filled hospital jug on the end table.

"Think you'll survive without me for twenty minutes?"

"I think I can manage it." I rolled my eyes.

"Good. I'll be back soon."

I picked a familiar sitcom and settled into the couch while Alexis showered and got ready. I caught myself dozing a few times and startled back awake. My phone rang from my bedroom, and I cursed myself for forgetting it.

"Andre called." Alexis carried my phone in to me.

She was wearing a pair of yoga pants and a Led Zeppelin t-shirt, her still-damp hair resting around her shoulders. The honeysuckle scent was stronger than usual; it must be her body wash or shampoo. She sat next to me on my good side and pulled the blanket over her lap, too.

My phone showed one missed call from Andre, so I called him back. He checked in on my condition and updated me on the case. The Sheriff had let him interrogate the aunt, but she was tight-lipped. Andre was going back to try again in a few hours. She hadn't lawyered up yet, but the clock was ticking. I put him on speakerphone and the three of us talked about interrogation strategy. We ended the call with high hopes.

Alexis and I found a newer sitcom on one of the million streaming services and settled in to watch the afternoon away. It turned out to be a good one, and we both laughed and joked episode after episode. Some of the sexual tension was abating as we moved into our familiar, friendly rhythm.

Lunch came next, with a second round of meds. I could feel my body working to heal itself with a little help from my superhuman abilities. The pain was already significantly less than it was last night. But the meds kept making me sleepy. I fell asleep on the couch during our show. When I woke up, my head was in Alexis's lap, and she was running her fingers through my hair absentmindedly as she watched TV.

The next few days were almost exactly the same. We talked about everything except for the big secrets we each knew the other was holding. It didn't hang over us like I thought it would. We enjoyed each other's company. All our friends cycled through visits to check in and we spent most nights eating with someone and hanging out just like we normally would at the Pony. I needed Alexis's physical help to get around less and less, but she stayed to help around the house and keep me from getting cabin fever.

"So, we were thinking…" Chloe began one night during a visit. She had a mischievous grin on her face, and I braced myself. "Since you can't really come to the Pony for our annual New Year's party tomorrow night, we thought we might bring the party to you instead."

"Not the entire party," Moira clarified. "Just our closest friends. And you wouldn't have to do a thing! We'd bring the food and drinks, I'll do the decorations, you won't have to lift a finger."

"Or a shoulder," Chloe added.

"I read online that it's important to keep a person's spirits up while they're recovering. We thought this would be a good way to accomplish that."

"What do you think?" Alexis tapped me with her foot.

I considered it. My follow up with my doctor yesterday had gone well. It baffled him by how quickly I was healing. But I was less than thrilled when he told me he didn't want me in any crowded spaces yet. He was worried about my shoulder getting bumped and causing damage to the wound. I had weaned off the pain meds so I could safely drink at the party, but the doctor crushed my hopes with that one recommendation.

"Let's do it," I replied. "What else do we have left to do? We already finished all five seasons of our show."

"True story," she agreed. "I think it'll be good for you."

Alexis had worked hard to cheer me up on the way home from the doctor. She knew how much I needed something like this. I was ready to get back to my normal life. My leave officially ended on the second, and I couldn't wait to get back to work. Despite our best efforts, the walls of my apartment had started closing in on both of us.

"Yay!" Moira cheered. "I'll call everyone right now."

Call she did. The next evening, a little over a dozen of our closest friends were all crammed into my apartment. The only people missing were Andre, who was still working leads in Tennessee, and Riel, who had to oversee the chaos at the bar. Vijay and Vikram came early and helped Alexis prep the kitchen area for the food and drinks. The sisters came next with decorations, including a fully functional disco ball and a plethora of New Year's decorations.

My sling was more a formality, a reminder to still take it easy, but I was feeling almost normal again. I chugged a few beers and sang karaoke with Donna and Ricky. Then I danced with Lacey and played beer pong on my dining table with Taylor and a few others. Without realizing it, I visually tracked Alexis throughout the party, grinning anytime I saw her enjoying herself. She had done so much for me over the past two weeks. My chest burned the few times we locked eyes from across the room.

"The ball's about to drop," Moira announced, turning up the TV tuned to the celebration at Times Square.

"Start the countdown and find your lovers," Donna whooped.

"The year I finally get with Riel, he's not even here for me to kiss," Chloe lamented to Alexis.

"Sorry, girl," Alexis gave her a side-hug. "You'll have to kiss him twice as hard next year, then."

"You think we'll still be together?"

"Hell, yes! You guys are the power couple," Alexis assured.

"Thirty seconds," someone shouted.

"Be my New Year's kiss or lose me forever," Ricky wrapped his arm around Moira's waist with a dramatic flair.

Moira blushed and giggled. Lacey was already asleep on the loveseat across the room. Everyone else was sidling up to someone, arms wrapped around shoulders and waists, waiting for the big moment. The mood was light and triumphant.

"Finn, get your ass over here," Chloe demanded.

"You're a beautiful woman, Chloe, but I'm not risking that," I joked, moving over anyway.

"Not me, idiot. Gross!" Chloe made a face. "You're going to kiss Alexis. You owe her for wiping your ass."

"There was no ass-wiping involved," Alexis waved her arms. She was blushing.

"If I'm not getting any action tonight, I'm sure as hell going to make sure you do." Chloe pushed Alexis off the barstool and in my direction. I caught her by the elbow as she stumbled.

"Wow, you're not making this awkward at all." Alexis rolled her eyes at Chloe.

"What, Henson?" I smirked down at her, wrapping my good arm around her waist. "Afraid of a little kiss?"

"Ten!" Vijay shouted.

"Nine!" The room joined in.

"Eight!"

"Kiss him," Chloe yelled over the din.

"Seven!"

"Six!"

Alexis looked up at me, half shy, half challenging. My stomach did a backflip.

"Five!"

"Four!"

"THREE!"

"May I?" I asked.

"TWO!"

"What the hell?" Alexis wrapped her arms around my neck.

"ONE!"

"HAPPY NEW YEAR!" The room exploded with shouts and cheers.

With one last victorious smirk, I brought my mouth down on Alexis's. Her soft lips were slightly parted as our lips met. I tightened my grip around her waist as I kissed her soft and slow. I slipped the tip of my tongue into her mouth and tasted strawberries. She let out a soft sigh into my mouth and I smiled against her lips. My neck tingled as she sucked my bottom lip into her mouth, but even that light suction drove me wild with desire. She pulled me tighter to her and pressed herself against me. Our lips moved together expertly until she pulled away, slightly breathless.

"God damn," Chloe called over the sound of the celebration. "I think I almost came just *watching* that."

Alexis blushed once more, but laughed all the same. I still locked my arm around her waist. I had no desire to let her go. She didn't pull away, so I spun her in a circle and started slow dancing with her as Auld Lang Syne played through the TV speakers. She rested her forehead against my chest as we danced.

"Happy New Year, little siren," I whispered.

"Happy New Year, grumpy dragon." She gazed up at me, her eyes intense.

I leaned down once more and placed a soft kiss on her lips. She buried her face in my chest again, hugging me tight, and we continued to dance. It was a fitting end to the wild year this had turned out to be.

Chapter Twenty

Alexis

After our smoldering New Year's kiss, Finn and I had fallen asleep together on the couch while a bunch of our friends crashed on every other surface they could find. Only a few people stayed sober enough to drive home, so the rest stayed the night. Tangled bodies lay everywhere.

I woke up that morning with Finn's fingers laced in mine, cradled in his lap, with a blanket wrapped around us. When I stirred, his eyes opened lazily, and he smiled when he caught sight of my face. He kissed my forehead, sending tingles down my spine. I licked my lips and tilted my head back longingly. Mischief sparked in his eyes and his face started lowering toward mine.

Donna let out a deafening snore on the floor below us, and Finn and I both burst out laughing. With that, the moment was gone. The others woke up, nursing their hangovers, and we had breakfast all together.

Finn could take off his sling that morning and turned out to be surprisingly able-bodied again. After everyone helped clean up and left, I packed up my things and got ready to go home. Leaving was bittersweet, but heading home was a necessity. I was catching some serious feelings and needed some time away from our easy bond to work things out. Finn drove me home, disgustingly thrilled to drive the Charger once more.

"I can't thank you enough for putting up with me," Finn told me after parking in front of my building. "I don't know how I would have managed without you."

"What are best friends for?" I patted his arm.

"Do you need help with your bags?"

"Hell no! You're still technically in recovery. I can handle myself."

"I know you can," he smiled. "I'll see you at work tomorrow."

"See you tomorrow." I slid out of the car and grabbed my bags from the trunk.

Finn gave me a wave and drove off once he saw that I'd gotten into the building okay. I heaved my bags up the stairs and dropped them unceremoniously in the living room. I breathed a sigh of relief to be back at home. New Year's tradition or not, we'd kissed. Really kissed. That barrier was broken, and I was worried about the consequences of that choice. A million scenarios raced through my mind, some good, some bad.

I spent the rest of my New Year's Day, and my last day off, trying to distract myself from the intensity of the time I'd spent with Finn. I unpacked, did my laundry, cleaned my bedroom and bathroom, and tag-teamed cleaning the kitchen with Moira. No one mentioned what happened at the party, and for that I was grateful. Chloe spent most of the day with Riel at the bar since they hadn't been together the night before.

When I entered the think tank for my first day back at work since the shooting, things were buzzing. Finn was near the big board, writing notes and directing other cops and detectives. I squinted at the board from across the room and saw the name of the motel on 9-block scrawled at the top. The words "Vice" and "VC" were written on one side, creating two columns. I knew what that meant: what had started as a vice crime had morphed into a violent crimes case with Finn's shooting. A picture of Leticia was up on the board, as well as pictures of several men I didn't recognize. Were they Johns? Dealers? Right in the center of the board, in large, bold, red letters, circled several times, was one word: Bianchi.

There must have been a break in the case while we were out. Somehow, they must have traced either the shooting or the drugs, or both, back to the Bianchi crime syndicate. Was there anything in this town that they didn't have their hands in?

I saw the Chief walk into the breakroom, and I followed. With Finn occupied, I wasn't sure what my priorities were for the cases I was working. Andre still hadn't returned from Tennessee where he was working leads he had gotten out of Ramond's aunt.

"Good morning, Chief," I greeted.

"Ah, good to have you back, Alexis." Chief shook my hand. "How are you holding up?"

"I'm actually doing pretty well."

"Are you really?" Chief gave me a piercing look. His eyes were icy blue and adept. "I hear you spent most of your break taking care of Briggs. Did you get enough time to take care of yourself?"

"I think it was better for me to have something to focus on instead of dwelling on the shooting."

"I'm setting Briggs up with a therapist who contracts with the department. I can do the same for you if you need someone to talk to."

"I already got a couple of calls into my therapist. We met once last week online, and I have another appointment next week. But thanks for the offer."

"I'm glad to hear." Chief poured himself a cup of coffee.

"Seems like there's a lot going on out there," I pointed back to the think tank.

"You know Detective Briggs; the second he came in this morning, his foot was hard down on the gas pedal. He and Lot are comparing notes and we're seeing some parallels we didn't notice before."

"Is there anything I can do?" I grabbed a cup of coffee for myself.

"You already took care of the victim in this case. Not much left to do for it."

We walked out of the break room together.

"Any word on Leticia? The woman we were checking on at the motel?"

"No, Lot said she took off not long after they put Briggs in the ambulance. No one's seen her since. We've had black and whites out looking for her but..."

Chief's eyes went wide. I followed his gaze and my jaw dropped. Leticia herself was walking into the think tank. She looked like a terrified rabbit. She was clutching something in her hands. I hurried over to her and embraced her.

"Oh my God, Leticia, I'm so glad you're okay!" I released her from the hug.

"I'm okay..." Leticia's voice was quaking.

"Do you need to sit down? Can I get you anything?"

"No, I... uh... I wanted to bring you this." She held out her hands. She was clutching my coat. "I took it to the laundromat and made sure it was clean."

"Oh, Leticia, you didn't need to do that."

"Yes, I did." Tears rolled down both Leticia's cheeks. "You and Detective Briggs came out to help me and you got shot at for your trouble. You're good people. The least I could do was to bring this back to you."

"Thank you." I took my coat from her outstretched hands. "Where have you been? We've been trying to find you for weeks to make sure you were okay."

"I had to lie low for a little while. Word on the street was that the bullet that took down the detective was actually meant for me." She swallowed hard. "The higher ups didn't want me talking to the cops."

"What higher ups? Who would want to hurt you?"

"Leticia!" Finn's voice called from behind me.

"Detective." Leticia nodded to Finn as he approached.

"Are you okay?" Finn asked.

"I could ask you the same question." Leticia dropped her eyes to the floor.

"Good as new." Finn tapped his injured shoulder lightly. "Been worried about you, though."

"I..." Leticia stuttered. She looked back over her shoulder, then back at us. Her lip quivered, and she shifted from foot to foot.

"Is there something you want to tell us, Leticia?" I asked gently.

"Yes," her eyes welled with tears.

"Come on back here." Finn held his arm out and motioned towards the interrogation rooms. "Let's get you somewhere more comfortable and private."

We went into interrogation one and settled in the chairs. Leticia grabbed several tissues and dabbed at her eyes. I scooted my chair a little closer to her and waited.

"What's going on, Leticia?" Finn asked.

"I haven't been real honest with you," she sniffled. "The first time I met you, I told you it was a John that beat me up, but that was a lie. This…" She pointed to the fading yellow bruises on her face. "…wasn't a John either." She took a deep, steadying breath. "It's my runner that's been hitting me."

"Your runner?" I asked.

"Yeah, the guy who controls who me and the other girls go to for jobs," she explained.

"What other girls?" Finn pressed.

"All the other girls." Leticia glanced up at the door, then back to the table.

"All the other sex workers?" Finn continued.

"Yeah. There ain't a girl who pushes in this city who does it on her own. We all work for the same bosses."

"Who are your bosses, Leticia?" Finn's voice was suddenly urgent.

"I want to tell you, but you need to know that the second I walk out of this station, I'm a dead woman," Leticia gulped.

"We won't let that happen," Finn assured.

"They've got reach, Detective. Longer than you know. It'll happen," Leticia argued.

"If I have to put you in witness protection myself, I'll do it." Finn gritted his teeth.

My heart jumped, and my eyes dropped to the floor. I worked to control my expression to keep it neutral. I took a deep breath and hoped neither of them noticed my reaction.

"You can try, but I've come to terms with my fate," Leticia assured. "I can tell you the truth, but it's gonna be hard for you to do anything with it once you have it."

"You let us worry about that part. Who are your bosses?"

"The runner is just a link in the chain, so is his boss. But this," she motioned to the silver anklet with the red cherry charm she wore. "This is the mark of the girls who get run by the Bianchis."

My eyes bulged, but I held in the gasp that threatened to escape my lips. The Bianchis were trafficking these women. Drugs were supposed to be the name of the game for them, murder when things didn't go their way, but as far as I knew, no one had connected the syndicate with human trafficking. I could tell by the look on Finn's face that this was a revelation to him, too. This was huge. If it was true, Leticia was in horrible danger.

"Alright," Finn cleared his throat, but the timbre of his voice was off ever-so-slightly. He was shaken. "I'm going to have you stay here with Alexis until we can get a safe place sorted for you. Once I do, I'll have an officer with you at all times to keep you safe, okay?"

"I appreciate it. When I end up dead, I don't want either of you to feel bad about it. All my time in the Clock, you two and Andre were the only ones that ever gave a damn about me, aside from the other girls. If it's between getting my ass kicked and being used up by the assholes I work for or dying, dying's not that bad of an option to me anymore."

"We're going to take care of you, Leticia." I patted the back of her hand.

"Sit tight, okay?" Finn gave her an appreciative nod and left.

"You are so incredibly brave," I told her.

"Nah, I'm just sick of the life. I'm ready to be done with it. And if I can help you nice people stop these sick pricks on my way out, I'll be singing hallelujah for you on the other side. Here..." She unclasped the anklet and put it in my hand. "I don't want this shit anymore, but I think you can find some good use for it. Show it to my sisters and they'll know they can trust you."

I nodded, not sure what she meant. I tucked the anklet in my pocket for safekeeping. If nothing else, it would be a reminder to me of Leticia and her courage.

I sat with Leticia for the rest of the day. It took Finn ages to come back, but when he did, he had good news. They were going to take Leticia to a safe house far out of town. Nowhere in the Clock would be safe for her now. They wanted her as far out of the reach of the Bianchis as possible. She gave me a tight hug before they loaded her up in an unmarked car to take her to the safe house. I fought back the lump in my throat as they drove away.

Finn gave me a quick, wordless pat on the back, then hurried back into the station. He'd barely spoken to me all day. I wasn't sure if it was more out of busy necessity or regretful avoidance. The organized chaos at the office today had spared us any real one-on-one interactions, so it was hard to gauge.

Did I regret things? I wasn't sure yet. All I knew was that I wasn't as eager to chant *'just friends'* to myself as I was after the camp out.

The next two weeks at the station were concentrated almost entirely on the Bianchis; their drug running operation, pulling out files that were suspected to be hits or murders perpetrated by the syndicate, and now anything and everything they could gather that supported Leticia's claim that they were at the core of the human trafficking efforts in town. Chief gave me the task of reaching out to known sex workers in the area that I had already developed relationships with through my advocacy work. Eventually, he wanted to send me out onto the streets with either Finn or Andre to talk to the other women in their database who I hadn't met yet.

Things got really tense between violent crimes and vice for a while as they vied for control of the broader investigation. Each department thought they trumped the other. Chief was initially sitting it out until they finished their pissing contests. But one day it got to be too much for him, and he snapped at the entire station to get their shit together and focus more on doing their job than "measuring their peckers." I wholeheartedly agreed with the Chief on that one.

Out on the streets, things were also getting tense. Chief increased patrols during every shift, sex workers and known dealers were being watched, and vice conducted a few raids down at the warehouses and the docks where they suspected the Bianchis based their operations. Fights broke out, egos got big and bruised on both sides, and the innocent citizens of the Clock were a lot more hesitant to go out in certain parts of town, especially on 6-, 7-, and 9-block. I had even noticed a change in the atmosphere around 10-block.

Finn and I still hadn't talked much beyond office pleasantries. He sat in on some interviews I did with the women whose cases I had been assigned. But he was mostly caught up in running things on the violent crime side. He video-conferenced with Andre at least once a day to keep him up to date while Andre continued to track Ramond in Tennessee. Andre was pissed that he was missing out on the biggest break in the Bianchi case they'd ever had, but he was bound and determined not to return until he had Ramond in tow.

A few days after I watched Leticia and her plain clothes protector drive away from the station, I went back to school to start my second semester. My classes were just as fascinating as the semester before, and it was nice to step out of my job when I was with my classmates. I could breathe on campus in a way that I couldn't breathe at work.

Today, I was feeling like I was finding a new rhythm with the recent changes. I even had lunch with some friends on campus before heading to the bus to go home. When I was within sight of the bus stop, I noticed a familiar face sitting on the bench waiting for a ride, too.

"Selsha!" I called.

Her face lit up when she saw me. She waved me over and gave me a hug when I sat down next to her. I hadn't seen her since the disastrous Christmas party.

"I'm so glad to see you!" I squeezed her hand.

"Me too," she smiled.

"How have you been?"

"It's been… you know…" Her smile dropped.

"Is there something going on?"

"A couple of girls have gone missing lately," she confided. "I'm worried about them."

"Do you think something bad has happened to them?"

"That's what I'm worried about. Three girls in the past month stopped checking in and the bosses act like it's not a big deal. I tried to ask my runner about them, and he blew me off."

My heart dropped to my stomach.

"Your runner?"

"Yeah, it's...uh... it's complicated." She shifted in her seat and rubbed her hands against her bare arms to warm them up.

"Do you have the same runner as Leticia Johnson?"

"You know Leticia?!" Selsha's eyes went wide.

"Yeah, I'm her victim's advocate at the police station."

"Shit, you should know that she's one of the girls who went missing then. I hope she's okay." She wrung her hands together.

"I hope so too." I put my hand on the back of Selsha's. I wished I could tell her that Leticia was in safe custody, but I couldn't risk Leticia's safety for anything.

"Selsha, can I ask you a question?"

"Yeah..."

"Do you work for the Bianchis?"

She looked like I had slapped her. Selsha mouthed something, but no sound came out. Her foot starting jiggling and I noticed the anklet with the cherry charm. I reached into my pocket and pulled out the one Leticia had given me. I held it out to Selsha, and she froze.

"Who... where did you get that?" she whispered.

"A friend," I answered. "Listen, I don't want you to feel like I'm working an angle with you because of my job, but I'm genuinely worried about you if the Bianchis are the ones trafficking you. They are seriously dangerous people."

"You shouldn't be getting involved in this," Selsha warned, shaking her head.

"If people I care about are involved in this, then I am, too." I took her hand between both of mine. "You're my friend, and I don't want anything to happen to you."

"You're my friend, too, Alexis. But it's you who should be worried if you're sticking your nose into the Bianchis's business. If they see you talking to me and they find out you're a cop's pet, they'll hurt you...bad. Stay out of this."

"I can't. I want to help you," I pleaded.

"I wish you could," she whispered, a single tear sliding down her cheek.

A horn honked right next to us, startling both of us. My heart raced as a black town car with blacked-out windows rolled up. Selsha yelped and leapt up like it had electrocuted her. I hurriedly tucked Leticia's anklet back in my pocket.

"I have to go." Selsha opened the back passenger door.

A man in a dark suit was waiting in the backseat. He was wearing sunglasses, but I could tell he was staring at me. His expression was anything but friendly. Selsha slammed the door and the town car peeled out. What an awfully nice car and finely dressed escort for Selsha to be working for a simple, low-level pimp. My gut churned. The Bianchis were definitely involved.

I worried about Selsha the whole bus ride home, all the while rubbing the charm in my pocket. How many women were being trafficked, beaten, and exploited by the Bianchis? It made me physically ill just to think about it. The sick feeling intensified. I went straight to bed and took a nap once I got home. I never slept during the day, but this was too heavy.

When I dragged myself out to the kitchen for dinner, the sisters were already eating.

"Are you okay, hon?" Moira asked.

"Tough day," I shrugged.

"We made you some fettuccine if you're hungry." Chloe pointed to a pot on the stove.

"Thank you. I was dreading having to cook for myself, so it was going to be a cereal night." I grabbed a plate and started dishing up.

"We're going to the Pony after dinner. You should come with us." Chloe rubbed my back when I sat down. "It'll cheer you up."

Lacey's head suddenly whipped up so she could face me from across the table. Her eyes were big as she stared at me. I cocked my head to the side as I looked back. This wasn't her usual playful expression; it was something else, something intense.

"Yeah, come with us!" Moira urged. "You deserve a night out!"

"Okay, I'm in," I replied, still not able to look away from Lacey's strange gaze.

As soon as the words were out of my mouth, Lacey's eyes glazed over. She went from looking at me to staring right through me. Her eyebrows shot up, her whole face spasmed, and her mouth popped open into a little "o."

"Oh my God, Lacey?" I asked, alarmed. "Are you okay?"

Moira and Chloe shared a knowing glance, then scrambled up from the table.

"She's having one of her migraine episodes," Moira explained.

Chloe and Moira each took one of Lacey's arms, hauled her up from the table, and hurried her away to her room. I wanted to follow, but I had the distinct impression I shouldn't. I waited for them to come back, but only Chloe returned.

"Is she okay?" I asked, as Chloe sat back down to her food.

"It was a bad one," Chloe frowned. "We got her some medication, and she's past the worst part of it now. Moira's going to stay with her tonight, but you're still coming out with me."

"Are you sure?" I glanced back toward Lacey's room.

"Yes, totally. Lacey will sleep like the dead in the next ten minutes with the migraine medication in her system now. She'll be fine by morning."

"God, that was scary," I sighed, clutching my heart.

"Tell me about it," Chloe nodded. "It never gets any easier seeing her like that, no matter how many times it happens."

We ate in silence for the rest of the meal. I almost backed out on going to the Pony, but Chloe was insistent. She had promised Riel that she'd come tonight, and she wanted to make sure I had fun with our friends. I gave in. Chloe helped me get ready, even picking out my outfit. She grinned mischievously as she picked a top and skirt that showed off my breasts and legs.

"What am I? Your barbie doll?" I rolled my eyes.

"You absolutely are." She clapped her hands together. "And you look divine. You're going to knock the socks off of every guy at the bar."

"Just what I wanted: pairs and pairs of drunk men's smelly socks."

She looped her arm in mine, and we headed out. The streets were quieter than normal, but Chloe chattered the whole way, oblivious to the new tension on 10-block. The winter darkness was full and thick outside the rings of the streetlights and tiny snowflakes fluttered down around our heads. I pulled my coat tighter to keep out the cold and the strange chill hanging in the air.

The warmth of the bar was a welcome escape. Riel greeted us as soon as we entered. Donna ran over and gave me a tight hug, spinning me in a circle, before dropping me and running off to join in a game of beer pong. Finn was up at the bar, drinking a beer and chatting with Riel. My stomach did a little flip as Finn's eyes examined me from head to toe. The corner of his mouth turned up before he took another swig of his beer.

"Two of my favorite ladies!" Riel smiled as we sat down.

Chloe leaned over and gave him a kiss. He slid us each our favorite drinks. I sat in the middle, Finn on my right and Chloe on my left.

"Where are Moira and Lacey?" Riel asked.

"Home. Lacey got a bad migraine," Chloe explained.

Riel frowned, and I caught him exchanging a worried look with Finn. But before I could call them out on it, they were looking away from each other. Riel's signature smile was back on his face. I was thoroughly sick of this big secret, especially when it felt like it was being rubbed in my face. If Riel and Finn were so concerned about Lacey's migraines, they weren't just headaches.

"I made Alexis come tonight. She's had a rough day, and it's officially our job to cheer her up," Chloe announced.

"What kind of bad day?" Finn asked. It was the first personal question he'd asked me in weeks.

"I saw my friend Selsha around campus today. Remember her? I invited her to the Christmas party."

Everyone winced at the mention of the party.

"She's the working girl?" Finn asked, recognition in his eyes.

"Yeah. I did a little digging about her working for the Bianchis," I continued.

"You did what?" Finn's eyebrows shot up.

"The Chief wants me to spread my reach into the community, try to get some more information to help your case," I explained.

"That was risky talking to someone outside the station," Finn scolded.

"It would be riskier for Selsha if I hauled her into the station to ask her," I argued.

Finn frowned at me. I thought he would be excited to hear the near-confirmation Selsha had given me, but he was looking at me like a misbehaving child. My hackles were up.

"It's not just about the case, Finn. Selsha and all those other women are in serious danger if the Bianchis are pulling their strings. I couldn't sit next to her and say nothing!"

"It's not them I worry about being in danger after a stunt like that." Finn crossed his arms, eyes burning into me.

"I can take care of myself, thanks," I huffed.

"This is the opposite of cheering her up, Finn," Chloe admonished.

"I'd rather be sure she's safe than happy," Finn snapped back.

"It's not your job to worry about either," I argued.

Anger flared inside me, bigger than the situation called for. But I felt it anyway.

"I don't really feel like hanging out anymore," I pushed off the stool.

"I'll come with you," Chloe offered.

"No, you stay. You've been looking forward to spending time with Riel."

"I'll walk you home," Finn rose.

"No, thank you." I held up a hand. "In case you missed it, I'm not really craving your company right now."

I stalked over to the door, threw on my coat, and went back out into the cold. My cheeks were flushed with the intensity of my anger. My logical side knew it was about more than being scolded by Finn. If I was being honest with myself, the anger was mixed with a fair share of rejection. The first personal conversation with Finn after we kissed, and he treats me like a dumbass looking for trouble.

Nursing my hurt pride distracted me just enough that I nearly missed the movement out of the corner of my eye. But that half-second delay meant I didn't have enough time to defend myself when the shadowy figure snapped its hand over my mouth and its arm around my chest, pinning both of my arms to my side. A painfully familiar fear sent shockwaves through my body.

The figure was solid and strong as I fought against its grip. It dragged me backward into the darkness of the alley between the empty storefront north of the bodega and an apartment building two blocks from my apartment. Panic coursed through my veins, sparking every cell in my body to life.

Not again! Please, God, not again.

Another figure came into view, while the first pulled me deeper into the dead-end alleyway. I kicked and flailed, but whoever had me pinned had a vice-like grip. We passed underneath a flickering light, and my stomach dropped to my feet. I saw the familiar face of the Knuckle that picked a fight with Finn at the Christmas party.

"Hey there, little pet," the Knuckle taunted. "Been a long time since we seen your pretty face."

The man behind me chuckled cruelly, the sounded rumbling in his chest and into my back. I tried to break away again, but he only held me tighter. It was getting hard to breathe.

"Where's your master, baby?"

My captor clamped his hand tightly over my mouth. There was no way for me to answer, but they had no interest in what I had to say. This was all a part of their game; I could read it in his eyes. It made the hair on the back of my neck stand up.

"Ah, he's probably back at that bitch-bar struttin' around like he's a gift from the Gods." The Knuckle spat on the ground. "No matter. It's you we're looking for tonight. Humans like you are only good for one thing…"

He licked his lips. I blinked hard, staring at his mouth, wondering if I was hallucinating. But, no, it was happening. His teeth were getting sharper, and his mouth was growing wider. Thick brown hair sprouted all over his body. His nose elongated, and his eyes turned a beady black. His whole body was growing. Snaps and cracks sounded like every bone in his body was breaking. All I could do was stare in horror as the man in front of me morphed into a massive bear.

"Food…" the man-bear snarled, drool dripping from its jaws.

Whoever was holding me had loosened his grip enough for me to move. Before I came to the Clock, I'd taken a series of self-defense classes after my attack. The muscle memory I had developed from the repetition during those classes kicked in. I dropped my full body weight to the ground, slipping out of my captor's grasp. The Knuckle-turned-Bear lunged at me, but I rolled to the side. He collided with the man I had escaped from, and two warring roars sounded. I shuffled away from them, but it only led me closer to the dead-end wall.

More cracking sounds. A second bear-man was now standing next to the first. Holy fucking shit! What the hell was happening?

Both creatures launched themselves at me, and I scrambled to my right again. The claws of one caught on the arm of my coat, tearing it in three strips. My head smacked against the concrete as I ducked another blow. My vision went blurry. I tried to grab for my keys in my pocket, searching for my kubaton, but my fingers found only Leticia's anklet.

I reached for the closest thing to me, the metal lid of a garbage can, and held it between myself and my attackers. A pair of claws tore right through it, and I yelped. I ripped it to the left as hard as I could manage and dove toward the alleyway entrance.

My feet were too slow. Something caught my left leg and a searing pain exploded in my calf. I shrieked out in agony. Turning to look at the damage, I saw blood, my blood, dripping from one of the man-bear's jowls. If I had to guess the creature's expression, I would say it was grinning at me.

Two voices exploded within me: one that screamed for me to run and another that beckoned me to fight. But how the hell was I supposed to fight something I still couldn't believe was even real? Two men had turned into fucking bears right in front of my eyes! The only reason I knew I wasn't dreaming was because of the pain in my calf. No, this was a fight that I absolutely could not win. I had to run!

Without turning my back on the advancing beasts, I pooled my strength and prepared to escape. But my timing betrayed me once again. Before I could even get to my feet, one of the man-bears lunged straight toward me, its mouth on a direct collision course with my throat.

Chapter Twenty-One

Finn

I sat in a booth at the Pony, nursing both my beer and my bruised ego. Alexis hadn't lashed out at me like that since that first interrogation catastrophe. When she'd entered the bar, I'd had to scoop my jaw off the floor. She had on the sexiest outfit I had ever seen her wear. When she sat next to me at the bar, my mouth was already watering.

But then came the argument. I don't know why she was being so damn stubborn about it. I was only trying to look out for her. But that woman was too fucking independent for her own good. If she wasn't careful, I knew it was going to land her in trouble.

I took a deep breath to calm myself, and the hairs on my neck prickled. There was something in the air. Something bad… I inhaled a second time, focusing my senses. There it was again, stronger this time: adrenaline, fear, and a sour stench I recognized as the smell still lingering by the dartboard. A third deep breath sent horror through my entire being: honeysuckle.

In the distance, a scream.

I was on my feet in an instant, sprinting for the door. I knew in my gut what was happening, but I didn't want to admit it to myself. I knew that scream better than my own. The tone, the pitch, and the rhythm of that voice were like intimate friends of mine. Fear washed over me like a nauseous, cold sweat. I had let her walk home alone and now she was in mortal danger.

The beast inside of me roared from within as I sprinted down the sidewalk. Alexis's scent led me to the mouth of an alley. The scene in front of me made my guts twist. Two bear creatures were looming over Alexis, ready to pounce. I could smell the metallic tang of her blood.

Fury overtook me. I removed my clothes with lightning speed, readying for the fight. Heat rose from my chest and radiated through my entire being. I released the beast within me.

I shifted.

My body more than doubled in size, fur covering every inch of my skin. My teeth elongated, my snout taking the place of my nose, and a tail erupted from my tailbone. A feral snarl ripped from my throat as I leapt the length of the alleyway, straight for the creature about to kill Alexis.

We collided in midair before he could reach her. I started tearing at every inch of fur covered flesh I could find. A pair of powerful arms threw me backwards. I skidded across the cement on the pads of my paws, digging my claws down to get traction. Both bear creatures had abandoned Alexis and were coming straight for me instead. Good. I would enjoy ripping their throats out more than I had any other kill in my long life.

Both attacked me at the same time, each one approaching from a different side. They were powerful, but slow. I was quick, agile, and deadly. I knew everything about their kind, and it was about to be their undoing.

The blows and swipes they aimed at me while I leapt from side to side, clawing here, biting there, were chaotic. One lucky blow caught me against my still-healing shoulder, and I yelped. But that yelp quickly morphed into a guttural growl. I went from defensive dodges to offensive attack with one quick explosion of my well-trained muscles.

While I went for the one on my right, I noticed the one on my left changing its trajectory. It slid slightly before lumbering after Alexis, who had dragged herself about halfway back down the alley during the commotion. The terror in her eyes distracted me long enough to take a claw swipe to the side.

Ignoring the pain, I pushed off the bear I'd been fighting and latched on to the ankle of the one advancing on Alexis. It roared in agony as I felt my sharp teeth sever its tendons. I shook my head, jaw clamped tight, exacerbating the damage as much as possible. The creature fell on its side, no longer able to stand with the pain and the damage I was causing to one of its legs.

My body was lifted, then I was slammed to the ground from behind, the weight of the second bear's giant paws pinning me down. It roared in my face, saliva dripping from its mouth. It reared back its head, about to bite, but it stopped midway and howled in pain. A blue metal stick of some sort was protruding from its right eye. It used its paws to swipe it away, but to no avail. Alexis was standing behind me, hand bloody. That's when I realized the stick was the kubaton Alexis carried on her keychain. She had come to my aid.

The bear stumbled around the alley, trying in vain to extract the kubaton from its eye. Its features shrank until it changed back into one of the Knuckle crew from the fight at the party. Once again gifted with human hands, he ripped the kubaton out of his eye, and blood spurted everywhere. His cries of pain echoed down the alley as he slumped back against the wall.

I turned my attention back to the creature still next to me, far too close to Alexis. It lifted its head in her direction, and I jumped to my feet, putting my massive wolf's body between it and Alexis. The bear made one last, desperate attempt to get around me and to Alexis, but I saw it coming. I sank my razor-sharp teeth into its neck as it passed by, the momentum of its enormous body doing all the work for me. The sound of tearing flesh, the pull of tension and release against my jawbone, and I knew the job was done.

The bear flopped onto the concrete with a moan, pouring blood from its neck with every rapid pulse of its heart. Cups of blood poured out of its jugular and pooled at my feet. Alexis backed away with a gasp, hands flying to her mouth. She stumbled against a pile of trash and fell backwards onto it. I wanted to go to her, but I hadn't neutralized the threat yet.

I turned my attention to the Knuckle by the wall. But he was gone. The only evidence left behind that he'd even been there at all was Alexis's bloodied kubaton. I sniffed the air, using my heightened senses to check for any sign he was still lurking, but he was gone. He'd gotten away.

Once I knew it was safe, I padded over to Alexis to check on her. Her eyes were still filled with terror as I approached. She held up her hands between us and whimpered. It cut me to my core to see her afraid of me. I would never hurt her, not in any form. My wolf only wanted to protect her.

The sound of running feet drew my attention away. My muscles tensed, ready for another fight. But it was only Chloe and Riel who skidded to a halt in the alley's entrance. Chloe gasped and Riel swore. Alexis made an odd sound, likely a garbled call for help from the friends she could recognize. Riel held up his hands defensively as he entered the alley, head on a swivel. Chloe raced to Alexis's side and wrapped her in a tight embrace.

"I don't think it will hurt you, Riel," Alexis cried out as Riel approached me.

She had clearly mistaken Riel's stance as he checked for danger as a defensive approach towards me.

"Of course, he won't hurt you," Chloe soothed. "You're safe now."

"He?" Alexis looked back and forth between Chloe and I, me, still in my wolf form.

After checking to make sure the bear was dead, and assuring himself that no other danger lurked, Riel returned to the opening of the alley. He glanced both ways before gathering my discarded clothing and came back to me. The worry lines in his forehead made him look so much more the eternally old man he was than the young man he appeared to be.

"Alexis is hurt," Chloe declared.

I whimpered and took a step forward, my muzzle down, wanting to check the wound myself. But Alexis recoiled at my approach. I stopped in my tracks, not wanting to scare her more. Chloe pulled off her own coat and wrapped it around Alexis's calf.

"We need to get her to a doctor," Chloe insisted.

"I'm going to have to stay behind and make sure this all gets cleaned up before the wrong people see it." Riel rubbed the bridge of his nose.

"What the fuck just happened?" Alexis demanded.

"A bear attacked you," Chloe tried to soothe her, but Alexis pushed her out of the way and tried to stand. She faltered and resigned herself to the pile of trash she sat in. But she didn't relent.

"The dumbasses from the bar attacked me," Alexis growled. "Two mouth-breathers from the Knuckle Crew. Then they fucking turned into bears! Bears that could speak."

"Alexis, honey, I think you're in shock." Chloe tried to keep a straight face, but my heart sank. We had no way of talking our way out of this if those assholes had transformed right in front of Alexis's eyes.

"Stop bullshitting me, Chloe! I know what I saw. They turned into bears. *Bears*, Chloe! You all know exactly what happened and you're still treating me like I'm stupid."

I dropped into a sitting position and turned to Riel. He sighed heavily. Chloe opened her mouth to say something back, but Riel cleared his throat and she stopped.

"It's time," Riel relented.

"What are you talking about?" Chloe glared at him.

"It's time she knows. We thought keeping her in the dark would protect her, but look what's happened." He waved his arm around the bloodied alley. "She's lucky to be alive, and it's our fault."

I felt like a deflating balloon. He was right. This was our fault. Alexis had almost died because of her association with us.

"Finn?" Riel called softly.

Alexis searched the alley. When she couldn't see me in human form standing in the shadows somewhere, she turned to Chloe. Chloe was looking at me, and Alexis followed her gaze. I saw in the depths of her eyes the exact moment that the implication clicked. They widened and stared. I felt more exposed in that moment than I ever had at any other point in my life.

I rose and trotted behind a collection of garbage cans. Shifting back to my human form and standing naked in plain sight wouldn't do much to help keep Alexis calm. I shuddered internally as I prompted the shift. My limbs pulled back in on themselves, fur receded, snout shortened, and the change happened. The entire time, I kept my gaze locked on Alexis's. She watched me shift with a mixture of terror and fascination. Once my shift was over, I ran my hands through my tousled hair and Riel handed me my clothes. I dressed quickly, heat burning in my cheeks. It wasn't the nudity that bothered me; the shame came from Alexis watching me shift. It felt more intimate than being naked.

"Holy fucking shit," Alexis breathed.

"Yeah... about that secret," I sighed, slowly approaching her.

"You're one of them!" She pointed to the dead bear.

I bristled. "No, I'm not! Not exactly. God, there's so much to explain."

I dropped to my knees in front of her. Alexis stared at me, shocked. I wish I had told her everything before this moment, not waited until she stared at me like I was a monster.

"I... I'm a..." I struggled with the words.

"A werewolf," Alexis finished.

I couldn't help but laugh. "No, I'm not. I'm a shapeshifter. My shift just happens to be a wolf. Other shapeshifters take other forms."

"What the fuck are you talking about?"

"You seem to have found yourself befriended by the Fae community," Riel stepped in. I was relieved. He was always better with words.

"Fae?"

"Some would call us fairytale creatures, but that's the romanticized version of our history," Riel continued. "We prefer the term 'Fae.' We belong to an ancient race of beings that pre-date humans. There are many races of Fae, and you've witnessed several of those here tonight in their true form. Those 'bears' are really Berserkers, a race of Fae that are part bear but also have human form. They're…hitmen, assassins of sorts."

"Berserkers…" Alexis shook her head. The color continued to drain from her face.

"As Finn mentioned, he is another race of Fae, a Shapeshifter, a kind of Fae who have the power to take another form, usually animal, and embody the qualities of that creature in their human form: speed, strength, heightened senses, and so forth."

"Are the rest of you… shapeshifters, too?" Alexis asked. The wheels were turning in her brain, trying to process what was impossible to her only hours ago.

"No," Riel answered kindly. "As I said, there are many races of Fae. I am an elf." Riel ran his hands over the tops of his ears, and they elongated into tips. "It's a simple glamour to help me look more human."

Alexis looked at Chloe, but Chloe looked away.

"Yes, Chloe and her sisters are Fae as well. It is not my place to say what kind, for that is their story to tell when they are ready."

"The others? Our friends?" Alexis's eyes were tired and vulnerable. I wanted to hold her.

"Yes, they are Fae, too. Again, the type of Fae is their story to tell if they so choose."

"My God!" Alexis put her hands over her face.

"It's a lot to take in," Riel soothed. "It's one reason we keep to ourselves. Our existence has become the stuff of legends and childhood stories used to frighten humans. When humans find out about our existence, nothing good ever comes of it. That's why we haven't been honest with you. We were trying to protect you."

"Fat lot of good it did," I spat. Alexis's gaze shifted to me. I continued Riel's narrative, "Humans hate us, Allie. They fear us, they hunt us, and they try to destroy us. Riel came to the Clock with a few others and started a safe haven community here. More of us have joined over the years. It's the most peace a lot of us have known in centuries."

"Centuries?" Alexis's eyes widened again. "How old…"

"One thousand three hundred and eighty-two," Riel raised a hand with a sly smile.

"Five hundred thirteen," I grimaced.

"Older than time herself," Chloe squeaked.

"I… I don't… I have no idea what to say about this. Any of it…" Alexis slumped over.

"We'll have time to talk about it later," I answered. "Right now, we need to get you to a doctor. You're still bleeding."

She didn't reply.

"Is it okay if I pick you up?" I asked gently.

She only nodded.

I tenderly placed my arms beneath her, one behind her back and the other under her knees. I scooped her up and held her close against my chest. She was shivering; from shock or fear, I couldn't tell. Maybe it was better I didn't know the answer. God, I didn't want her to be afraid of me.

"Chloe, will you go back to the bar and get the others?" Riel asked. "I'm going to need some help to clean all this up."

"Of course," Chloe replied. Her head was low, and she avoided looking at Alexis. She hurried out of the alley, her heels clacking against the pavement as she jogged away.

"Go, I've got this," Riel prompted.

I carried Alexis out of the alley and back to my car. I set her in the passenger seat as carefully as I could. My heart ached as she let out tiny gasps of pain. This must be what she felt like after I got shot. It was agonizing.

My foot was heavy on the accelerator all the way to the hospital. A nurse's aide saw me carrying her across the lot and hurried out with a wheelchair. I refused it, not wanting to let Alexis go. The beast inside was snarling and protective. They shooed me out of the room in the ER after I laid her down on the bed. I sat in the waiting area, antsy and jittery.

Our secret was out. Only to one person, but the fear of a hundred other betrayals raked its way up and down my body. Fae attacked Alexis, and it was my fault. If I wouldn't have let the Knuckle Crew egg me into a fight at the Christmas party, then this never would have happened.

Alexis knew about us.

She was injured.

She was afraid of me.

She had seen me shift.

My brain was in overdrive. It was all too much. I pressed both hands against my head to slow the thoughts down or drown them out.

"Detective Briggs?" Nurse Linda approached me. "I thought I sent you two away weeks ago, but here we are again," she chided. But there was a solemn pull at the corner of her mouth.

"Is she okay?" I stood.

I knew there was no need to clarify who "she" was. Linda knew.

"It was a pretty nasty bite, but we've got her all cleaned up. The doctor started her on a round of antibiotics just to be safe and we've given her a rabies shot. We're going to keep her overnight to make sure she doesn't develop an infection. Would you like to come see her?"

"Does she want me there?" The question came heavy off my tongue and hung heavy in the air. My chest ached.

"Of course she does, Detective!" Linda patted me on the back. "She's hurting, hasn't said much, but her eyes keep darting to the door like she's waiting for someone to walk in. I have a feeling that someone is you."

But was she glancing at the door because she was terrified of who, or in my case what, would walk through it? Jesus Christ, what a fucking nightmare! I felt like I was being torn in two; half of me being pulled toward the front door to run fast and far, the other half of me needing to push open every door in the hospital until I found Alexis.

"Come on, darlin'. Your lady is waiting for you." Linda propelled me forward, deciding for me.

I let Linda lead me down several hallways and sets of doors, my mind still racing. My heart was pounding in my chest as she opened the door to room 118. A million different feelings exploded inside me when I saw Alexis's pale face looking back at me. Her expression was gut-wrenchingly difficult to read. I held my breath as I approached.

"I'll give you two some privacy." Linda slipped out and closed the door.

The silence was heavy between us in that room alone.

"You've got blood on your shirt," Alexis squeaked out.

The vulnerability wrapped around her every syllable was my undoing. I crossed the gap between us and knelt down on the floor next to her bed, then buried my face in her side. My arms looped her waist, and I held her. I couldn't tell if I was shaking, or she was, but it rocked us both. I couldn't bear to look into her face, terrified of what I might see in her expression.

But before my fear could engulf me, I felt her fingers slide into my hair and her arm rest across my shoulders. If it was difficult to keep my composure before, it was nearly impossible now as she held me and soundlessly comforted me. I swallowed hard, fighting back the emotional lump that rose in my throat. I took a deep, shuddering breath.

"Are you okay?" Her voice was soft and timid.

"Fuck no," I mumbled into her side.

I could feel her stomach contract as she chuckled once.

"Stupid question?" she sighed.

"The stupidest."

A long pause filled the air, and I felt her stomach contract again, this time to hold something in. "You killed a bear person, and you have a fucking tail," she accused. Then she broke down sobbing.

It was what I needed to pull me up out of my shame to face her. Her hands flew to her face, and she cried hard. I sat next to her on the hospital bed and wrapped her in my arms. Instead of turning away like I'd feared, she turned into me, burying her face in my chest. I held her tightly as she cried. Nothing I could say would make any of this okay, so nothing is what I said.

It was a long time before her tears ran out. When they finally did, she looked up at me through wet lashes and my heart skipped a beat. Before I could stop myself, I was kissing her. Gone was the impish victory, the hungry passion from our New Year's kiss. This was pure need. I needed to have her lips pressed against mine to reassure myself that she was here, safe. I needed to taste her to calm the anxiety that consumed me from the second I had heard her scream.

She clung to me as I kissed her, her lips as desperate and searching as my own. I pulled her into me, gently but firmly pressing her against my body, unable to get her close enough to quiet the terror and rage I'd felt as I watched the Berserker lunge for her throat. Every deep, consuming kiss was possessive. Soon she was gasping breathlessly into my mouth between kisses, and it only drove me deeper into need. I clutched her harder, kissed her deeper, and she melted into me.

I wanted to be inside her, craved the closeness with her that could only come from that glorious homecoming. Lust had nothing to do with what I was feeling. Something deep and abiding was rising within me that had been stirring for months. Holding her against me, breathing her breath into my lungs, clutching at her full lips with my own created a riotous need for her unlike anything I had ever felt before. And it scared me shitless.

A quiet knock on the door interrupted our solace. Alexis pulled her lips away from my hungry mouth. Her cheeks were pink, and her eyes were wide. She panted quietly, breathlessly, and my wolf simultaneously crowed its victory and demanded a return to my need-seeking. I couldn't let her go, despite knowing we now had an audience. She didn't pull away, though, so I pulled her back into my chest and held her as Linda came back into the room.

"Sorry to interrupt...again," she said gently, "But duty calls."

I didn't even look Linda's way. I closed my eyes and focused on the heat of Alexis's body against mine, the smell of her hair, and the intoxicating scent of the pheromones from her arousal. It made me want to run my tongue along every inch of her skin, lapping up her delicious taste. The adrenaline from the night was still coursing through me, and I could feel myself hardening as I inhaled her. If it weren't for Linda's presence and the small piece of logic screaming at me that Alexis was injured, I don't think I would have been able to stop myself from taking her if she was willing. I bit my tongue as the urge to ask Alexis if she wanted me as much as I wanted her rose like a tidal wave. I had no choice but to ride the wave, holding this beloved human creature against me as if she were about to be snatched away from me at any moment.

She was mine. And I was hers; desperately, ferociously, hopelessly hers.

Chapter Twenty-Two

Alexis

Finn refused to leave me once the visiting hours were over, and Linda didn't push it. He held me through the night, barely speaking another word. Linda seemed to sense the need we both had to be together, so she conducted her tests and checks around our tangled limbs. She smoothed back my hair and patted Finn on the arm often. When we were alone in the room together, we were kissing.

It was like I had been thirsting in the desert for days and found water at a spring. But the more I drank, the thirstier I became. Finn's lips roamed my face and neck. I laced my fingers in his hair and held him close to me. His tongue slid effortlessly between my parted lips time and again, meeting mine with eager ease. He slid his hand through the opening in the back of my hospital gown and traced trails of fire along my skin. I pulled at the front of his shirt, desperate to claim him for my own.

He hitched my injured leg up over his hip to avoid hurting me with our fervor. I could feel how hard he was as he pressed up against me. His hand on my bare back skirted down lower, stopping just above the curve of my ass. I whimpered. He growled and pulled me closer, sucking a spot between my neck and shoulder. He pulled back for a split second, staring at my face, eyes desperate. Fear and desire warred within their depths.

"Don't stop," I pleaded.

He groaned and pulled my mouth back to his. We were both panting between kisses. I had never felt something so all-consuming as this.

Nothing else mattered for those precious hours in the dark of that room but giving my mouth to him and taking his greedily in return. Fire burned and ached deep between my thighs. If it weren't for the constant unknown of when the next night check would be, I would have asked him, nearly begged him to sleep with me. My desire for him was that intense.

When I dozed around three in the morning, Finn was whispering unintelligibly into my hair in a language I'd never heard. The only word I could make out was my name, repeated over and over with something close to reverence. Not once did he relinquish his hold on me. I could feel him cradling me even in my sleep.

The sun streaming through the blinds pulled me back to the waking world. My muscles felt tight from sleeping half-reclined in the raised hospital bed. My urge to stretch and loosen them triggered the sudden realization of both the pain in my calf and Finn's noticeable absence. A quick check around the room confirmed that he was gone. My stomach dropped and a flood of rejection swept through me. I felt stupid for the knee-jerk response to the empty bed beside me.

I heard my door creak open, and my immediate thought was of Finn, but an unfamiliar nurse hurried in with a smile. My returning smile felt forced, but it was hard to mask my disappointment. I pulled the thin bedsheet higher up my waist.

"Good morning, Ms. Henson," the nurse chirped. "I'm Christine. I'll be taking care of you this morning before we send you on home. Linda gave me strict instructions to make sure you and your beau get special attention. I think she's grown pretty fond of the two of you." Christine winked at me. She checked my vitals, keeping up a constant stream of chatter.

As much as I tried to engage with Christine, my mind was pulling itself back into gear. The events of last night were replaying in my mind with frightening vividness. The sickeningly familiar fear as they dragged me into the alley awoke from the dark corners of my psyche. Then, echoing in my ears, came the cracking of the men's bones as they shifted from the moronic knuckle-draggers I'd grown accustomed to in the corner of the Pony into the monstrous bears who had tried to kill me. Images flashed before my eyes: the flimsy trash can lid I'd used as a shield, the bloodied saliva dripping from the bear's jowls, the bear lunging for me, the enormous white and gray wolf colliding with it in midair, plunging the kubaton into one of the bears' eyes, and then the wolf ripping the throat out of the other bear.

Christine was typing something into the computer. I tried to focus my attention on the clacking sound of the keyboard, but the next phase of memories was already breaking through the barriers I'd tried to place around them. Riel... Chloe... Finn. Finn the wolf, then Finn the man. Watching his features morph between animal and human had almost made me wretch. The familiar, comforting face of my best friend had been so alien and disconcerting.

He had saved my life. He had sacrificed his most closely, fiercely guarded secret to protect me. But I still felt afraid.

The logical, skeptical voice I carried as a protector was fighting against everything I'd witnessed and been told last night. Fae... fairytale creatures in the flesh and fur. Centuries, they had said, all three of them older than the length of any lifetime I could fathom. In the day's light, it felt almost laughable. But before the comforting bliss of denial could sweep in to save me, I remembered the strangeness my friends exhibited. As impossible as it seemed, I couldn't deny the serendipity of the explanation with the evidence I had gathered.

Despite all of it, I still wanted to reject it as truth. I needed to hear more, see more, before it could feel truly real. My cell phone blinked at me from the side table. I grabbed it as soon as Christine left to get the final clearance from the doctor to discharge me. No infection meant I could go home.

I argued with myself about whom to call, but the answer came to me. I dialed his number and listened to the trill of the ring, impatient. Would he answer? Had they told him?

"Lex!" Andre boomed joyfully.

"Hey Andre," I sighed.

"You don't sound too good. Is everything okay? Did that son of a bitch get shot again?"

"No, he's fine. As far as I know. It's me that landed in the hospital this time."

"What the hell? Are you okay? Did *you* get shot?" The words spilled out of Andre. "Fuck, I'm getting on a plane and coming home right now. Ya'll are going to get yourselves killed without me there to babysit you."

"Not shot, bitten." I swallowed hard.

"Bitten? By what?" His tone was shocked.

What had Riel called them? I wracked my brain for the word. It started with a "b…"

"Bitten by what, Lex? It's January, what could be out…"

"Berserkers," I blurted the unfamiliar, unnerving word. "A berserker bit me."

Silence greeted me on the other end of the line.

"What did you just say?" Andre's voice was deadly serious.

"Those Knuckle assholes from the bar attacked me in the street and turned into… berserkers, bear-people. They tried to kill me."

More silence.

"Finn saved me." My voice was suddenly thick with emotion.

"Finn…"

"Shifted."

Silence.

"Holy fucking shit," Andre released a huge breath. "My God, Lex, I am so goddam sorry. It never should have gotten this far. We should have warned you they were more dangerous than they seemed. Fuck."

"It's true?" I asked tearfully.

"You saw it with your own eyes, didn't you? How much did Finn tell you?"

"Riel and Chloe found us right after. Riel told me about the Fae. Not everything, but some. I still don't understand it… How could it be true?" I pleaded. "Can't you just tell me it was all a bad dream? Convince me somehow, Andre?"

Andre cleared his throat. "I can't, Lex. This isn't a dream. This is real. *We* are real."

"Riel said you were all Fae, but he wouldn't tell me what kind of Fae. I don't want you to feel like I'm being disrespectful or..."

"No," Andre cut in. "It's not a disrespectful thing to want to know about us. It sounds like Riel and Finn cracked the door on the secret, so I can't blame you for wanting to look into the room." He sighed again. "Speaking of dreams... I'm a sandman, a dream-weaver."

"You're the sandman?" I thought it couldn't get any stranger. I was wrong.

"Not *the* sandman, *a* sandman. There are generations of us, not just one. I can influence people's dreams, put people to sleep if I need to, and even enter a person's dream and communicate with them."

"Dreams... I... I don't know what to say to that..."

"How about, 'Wow, Andre, you're so impressive and magical! I wish I could be like you!'" he joked. "Are you mad I didn't tell you sooner?"

"Now that I know what the secret is, there's no way in hell I could blame you all for keeping it to yourselves. Fuck... Just... promise that you won't also turn into a massive bear and try to eat me, and I won't hold any of this against you."

"Damn, I wish I could have been there for you. I would have magically knocked their brains right out of their damn skulls for touching you. Are they in custody?"

"No, uh... Finn killed one of them." It was my turn to clear my throat. "I don't know what happened to the other one."

"The second I get back from this soul-suck of a case, I'll hunt that piece of shit down myself, I promise you that. How bad is it?"

"The bite hurts like a bitch, but they're sending me home in a bit, so I guess not too bad," I shrugged.

"As soon as you get home, call Riel or Vijay and Vikram. Have them make you a special poultice for it. Human medicine will only get you so far with a Fae injury. There could be some nasty shit in that berserker slobber, and we can't be too careful with you. I'm so, so sorry, Lex."

"I think I'll be okay; I need time to digest it all."

"Take all the time you need. We understand. I promise."

Christine returned with a clipboard in hand.

"I have to go, but thank you, Andre."

"Anytime, Lex. Keep me updated, okay?"

"I will. Bye." I hung up the phone.

"I ran into your boyfriend in the hallway." Christine smiled and raised her eyebrows at me a few times. "I sent that handsome devil to get his car so he can take you home."

No, not a devil. Not a dragon. A shapeshifter. Finn was Fae.

"The doctor cleared you to head home. She wants you to change your bandages daily and check for any signs of infection: redness, swelling, oozing, extra tenderness, and so on. If you see anything like that, call us right away.

Otherwise, stay off your feet for a day or two, then slowly start trying to put some weight on it. You can get a crutch or a cane if you need some extra support for a bit. No swimming or hot tubs until it heals and do your best to keep it clean."

I nodded as Christine ran down the list. My calf was throbbing.

"I think that covers it." Christine handed me the clipboard to sign the paperwork. "I just can't believe there are bears in the woods! You'd think that they'd all be hibernating this time of year, but you never know. Hopefully, your fella will have his cop buddies out looking for the thing that did this, so it doesn't hurt anyone else."

"I'm sure they're on it right now." I faked a smile.

No cops were out looking for the Knuckle that got away, but I had a strong feeling the crew from the Pony was. Maybe that's where Finn had taken off to this morning. How serious an issue would this be between the different kinds of Fae, I wondered.

A phone on Christine's waist rang, and she answered it.

"Okay, I'll bring her right down," she replied and hung up. "Your chariot awaits!"

Christine wheeled in a wheelchair and helped me out of bed and into it. She wheeled me through the halls, into the elevator, and out to the front area. It had only been a few weeks since I was the one waiting with the Charger to pick up Finn. Now it was him leaned up against his beloved car with his arms crossed, worry creases around his eyes, but a soft smile playing on his lips.

"Alright, you strapping, young gentleman…" Christine locked the wheels of the wheelchair. Both Finn and I winced at the word 'young.' "I relinquish your lady back to your care."

Finn held out a hand and helped me stand, one-legged, and shift into the passenger seat of the Charger. I used my hands to lift my left leg, then swung my right leg in after it. Finn shut the door and spent a minute talking to Christine in a low voice. Christine patted him on the shoulder and went back into the hospital with the wheelchair. Finn took his place in the driver's seat, and I felt suddenly self-conscious.

"You okay?" Finn asked.

"A little sore," I shrugged.

"I already got the pain meds they prescribed for you at the hospital pharmacy. We'll get you something as soon as we get back to your place." He revved the engine and took off. "I called Moira to let her know we're on the way and she's already got some breakfast made for you if you're hungry."

"Food's been the last thing on my mind."

"What has been on your mind?" Finn stole a glance at me as he drove.

"What hasn't been on my mind?"

"Food, we already covered that," he joked.

I rolled my eyes. "Tricycles."

"You've been thinking about tricycles?" Finn asked, sounding perplexed.

"No, I'm answering my question: What *hasn't* been on my mind? The answer is tricycles."

"Pelicans," Finn added.

"Oscar the Grouch."

"A venus fly trap."

"Bat guano."

"Gross," Finn chuckled.

"Well, now all of that is on my mind," I fake sulked.

"But seriously, Allie, what have you been thinking about?"

"Last night."

"I was worried about that."

"What part?"

"The everything part," Finn sighed and shook his head. "It's all a fucking dumpster fire. You shouldn't have been caught in the middle of it; any of it. I let those assholes get under my skin and they went after you because of it." I couldn't deny the fire in Finn's eyes as he spoke.

"Sometimes, a person goes after you because you're there, Finn. I might have just been an easy target," I tried to reassure. He had no way of understanding how acutely I knew that statement to be true.

"That's not it and you know it," he shook his head. "They went after you because of me, because of us. Human pet, remember."

"I remember very clearly," I shivered. *Humans like you are only good for one thing…*

"Berserkers look down on humans," Finn explained. "Lots of Fae do. Even I grew up seeing humans as inferior. It's an old bias, but it runs deep in our community. We didn't think about the consequences of getting too close to you so publicly."

"What do you mean?" The muscle was twitching in his jaw.

"It means we were selfish and stupid. Not everyone at the Pony is as forward-thinking as we wish they were. There are plenty of Fae in our community who see your association with us as a threat, maybe even an abomination."

"Ouch, okay…" I hugged myself.

"I'm not trying to insult you, Allie. I'm just being honest. We didn't think any of this through. You took us by surprise. I don't think anyone expected loving you as much as we all do."

"Loving?"

Finn's cheeks went pink, and he cleared his throat. "If you can't see how much we all adore you, you're not paying attention."

My stomach sank a little at the way he emphasized 'all.' I was getting too attached. Last night felt like it changed something between Finn and I, but I could feel the distance he was trying to create as he spoke.

We pulled up in front of my apartment. Finn sighed and ran his hands through his hair. He looked at me seriously, eyebrows furrowed and frowning.

"I don't think it's a good idea for you to come around the Pony for a while," he said.

"I wasn't planning on it," I replied. "The nurse told me to stay off my feet."

"No, I mean, I think we need to reconsider the amount of time we spend together," he continued. His expression was pained. "Not just me, everyone. It's sending a message."

My heart crashed down to my feet.

"What kind of message? That humans are more than a food group?" I was instantly defensive.

"No, Allie! Fuck, of course not!" He rolled his head back against his seat. "Not only is it putting you in danger of being used by asshole Fae to get at us, but it's also telling the less-than-friendly Fae in the area that we're…slipping."

"What the hell does that mean?"

"There is a delicate balance of power between the Fae that live here. Riel started the community, and he still leads it, but not every Fae thinks he's the right man for the job. Cavorting with a human could send the message that Riel is going soft. It opens things up for some ugly competition to step forward to challenge him. And those competitors obviously don't give a shit about using humans as leverage to hurt us."

"Where is all this coming from? Does everyone feel this way?" I was flabbergasted.

"Riel heard some things last night while they were out trying to get information on your attack. Things that put all of us in danger, Allie, not just you. We need to counter it before it gets worse. Riel and I agreed it's for the best. We…"

"So, you're breaking up with me?" I fumbled over the words. My cheeks flooded with heat at the implication, so I added, "All of you are? I'm being voted off the island?"

"Don't say it like that," Finn implored. "You mean more to us than you know, more than you should…" He sighed and looked away. The muscles in his jaw twitched. "What happened last night should never have happened."

His words were loaded. I knew he meant more than my attack. I stared at him until he met my eyes again.

"It shouldn't have?" I glared. My eyes were full of accusations.

"No, it shouldn't have," Finn answered, face blank.

"Noted." I flung open the door and used my right leg to stand.

"Let me help." Finn hurried out of the car.

"Stay the hell away from me," I warned, holding an arm out between us. He stopped in his tracks. "You wouldn't want to send the wrong message," I spat.

I hopped to the stairs and used the handrail to help myself up. I swore when I realized my keys had been in my coat and I had no idea where my coat had gone. I pressed the button to our apartment and Moira answered.

"Hello?"

"Can you buzz me in, Moira?" I snapped. I took a breath, not wanting to take my anger out on her. "It's Alexis, I don't have my keys."

"Oh, honey, of course," Moira answered. The buzz sounded, and I heard the lock disengage in the door. I grabbed the handle and swung it open with more force than I intended.

"Alexis," Finn called quietly.

"Go home, Finn," I growled, shutting the door behind me.

It was exhausting hopping myself up the stairs, but I made it. Moira was waiting with both the door and her arms open to greet me. She gave me a tight hug, then helped me over to the couch. The second I sat down, the tears exploded out of me. Moira cradled me while I cried.

Chloe and Lacey quietly came into the living and sat on the couch next to us. It was a tight squeeze. Lacey laid her head on my shoulder, and Chloe held one of my hands. I took a shuddering breath and calmed myself.

"Sometimes a good cry rinses out the pipes." Moira patted my back.

I cleared my throat, the conversation with Finn hovering over me. "As soon as I heal up, I'll pack my bags."

"What?" Moira gasped.

"No," Chloe protested.

"I know what happened to you was frightening beyond reason, Alexis, but we won't let something like that happen again. We'll protect you. All of us will," Moira added.

"Finn made it clear that I'm not welcome around you guys anymore. I think it's best if I moved out. I don't want to put you guys in a bad position."

"What did Finn say?" Chloe hissed. Her eyes darkened.

"He said my friendship with all of you was sending the wrong message to the Fae community. 'Cavorting' with a human was throwing off the balance of power and putting all of us in danger. He and Riel agreed…"

"Riel?!" Chloe gasped. "Fuck that!" She stormed out of the room and slammed her bedroom door.

We sat in awkward silence, not really knowing what to say. Chloe's voice was barely audible from her room; she must be on the phone. Had she called Finn? Riel? It didn't take long to find out.

"YOU DON'T GET TO MAKE THAT DECISION FOR ALL OF US, RIEL!" Chloe shouted. I cringed. I hadn't meant for her to get in a fight with Riel. Maybe I *was* screwing things up for my friends. It was quiet for a few moments.

"YOU AND FINN CAN BOTH GO FUCK YOURSELVES," Chloe shouted again. Something thudded against the wall and Chloe started to cry.

"I better go check on her." Moira hurried out of the room.

Lacey wrapped her arms around my waist and held tight. I rested my cheek on the top of her head. Even without words, I could feel how much she didn't want me to go. It made me wonder if her wordlessness was related to the type of Fae she was. I didn't have the heart to ask her.

Moira came back into the living room. "I made you some breakfast, Alexis. Let's get you settled at the table before your food gets too cold."

"Is Chloe okay?" I asked.

"No, but she will be," Moira sighed.

Lacey and Moira sat with me while I ate, Moira trying to keep up a conversation that avoided the two elephants in the room: my attack and the issue with the Fae. All I could think about was the betrayal that weighed heavy in my chest. The food I ate only added to the weight.

After breakfast, Moira made me a makeshift bed on the couch, with a pillow to elevate my injured leg, and we watched a movie. I was still considering finding a new place to live, but I kept it to myself. I would have to call Marshal Davis and get approval first. How could I explain the real reason I needed to move? He would think I'd gone insane. Maybe I could tell him I wanted to move closer to the University for the sake of convenience. That might work.

Around mid-afternoon, Chloe joined us in the living room again. Her eyes were puffy and rimmed with red. I held my hand out to her, and she took it wordlessly. We spent the rest of the day watching movies together and ordered takeout for dinner. None of us mentioned the phone call with Riel.

But I had made my decision. It was time for me to go.

Chapter Twenty-Three

Finn

No matter what I did, I couldn't find the Berserker's scent. Even in my wolf form, it was impossible to track after so much time had passed. Riel and the others had followed the drops of blood to the road, but he must have gotten into a car after that. His scent faded drastically, and the blood was non-existent past the sidewalk. I had left my car parked in front of Alexis's apartment while I channeled my anger at finding the piece of shit who attacked her.

Her face haunted me. The look she had given me as I told her she shouldn't be around us anymore was brutal. The difference between the way she had looked at me last night as I held her and during that impossibly hard conversation in the Charger was worlds apart. But it was for her own good. It was for everyone's good. I had realized that fucking horrendous truth this morning as I held her in my arms. After a night of immersing myself in her warmth, her goodness, her passionate perfection, all I could do was feel sick to my stomach. It wasn't towards her, no. Never. It was toward me.

I had been unendingly selfish the last few months. I let a human get too close to me and look at what it had cost. Brie had been right. I had pulled Alexis around like a toy on a string because being with her made me feel so good, better than I had in years. Not for a second did I consider the damage it could do to my friends—my family—and to Alexis. The image of the Berserker's bloody jaws was engraved on the backs of my eyelids. If I had arrived two seconds later, Alexis would have been dead. I almost puked when I looked down at her sleeping face and imagined it lifeless.

She could never be safe with me, with us. Pushing her away had been gut-wrenching, but necessary. My wolf growled dissent inside me. Fucking selfish...

My search proving fruitless, I made my way over to the Pony. I'd already spoken to Riel on the phone this morning, but there was a lot more left to discuss. Riel was sitting at the bar, his head in his hands. Before I could say anything, his phone rang.

I sat next to him as he answered it.

"Hey, beautiful," he greeted.

I couldn't hear what she said on the other end of the line, but I could tell Chloe was pissed. I sighed. She must have talked to Alexis.

"Yes, that's what we decided. It's what's best for everyone, Chloe," Riel frowned.

"YOU DON'T GET TO MAKE THAT DECISION FOR ALL OF US, RIEL," Chloe shouted through the phone. Riel pulled it away from his ear.

"You have to see the wisdom in this, my love. Alexis could have died last night. Keeping our distance protects her and it helps us protect our secret. I wish there was another way, but Finn and I discussed it all this morning. Nothing else makes sense. We need to keep our distance from Alexis."

"YOU AND FINN CAN BOTH GO FUCK YOURSELVES," Chloe shouted again. Then silence.

"She hung up on me," Riel sighed, setting his phone down.

"Can you blame her?" I asked.

"Never in all my days would I predict you siding with Chloe on something."

"You should have seen Alexis's face. No wonder Chloe is furious." It was my turn to put my face in my hands.

"I'm sorry you had to do that, my friend. I know how much you care for her."

"She'll never forgive me for it all. Hell, I can't blame her either. I'm an asshole."

"No, you're a good man, Finn. A good man in a hard position…"

"It sure as hell doesn't feel like it."

"Sometimes doing the right thing feels like the wrong thing," Riel rose.

"Where do we go from here?"

"We try to get back to normal. Stick close to our people. Ricky and some others are still out gathering information about the attack. What they've discovered confirms what Donna reported back; this attack wasn't only about a bar-room grudge. Someone was behind it. The berserkers were just the weapon, not the hand that held it."

"Who?"

"That's where people are getting tight-lipped. It worries me." Riel threw a rag over his shoulder.

"I'll see what I can do with my contacts through the station." I massaged the bridge of my nose.

My head was pounding. I barely slept last night. A part of me was worried the surviving berserker would come back and try to finish the job. The other, bigger part of me wanted to stay in that place with Alexis forever, wrapped up in each other. It had been less than thirty minutes since I watched her slam the door on me, but I missed her already. A deep ache was building in my chest.

A vibration in my pocket pulled me back from my misery. Andre's name appeared on my screen. I answered the call, dreading the conversation I would have to have with him about what had happened. He was going to put up a fight about Alexis, too. I knew it.

"Hello," I answered wearily.

"We got the sonofabitch, Finn!" Andre crowed.

"What?" My eyes widened.

"Ramond," Andre clarified. "We got him! Cowardly asshole was hiding at his cousin's dope den, but we got him. You should have seen the look on his face when I told him I was from Beckburg! Damn near shit his pants!" Andre was positively gleeful.

"Way to go, man," I encouraged, but my voice sounded hollow.

"Not the reaction I was expecting," Andre's voice fell. "What's up, Finn?"

"A shit ton," I answered. "A lot has happened since we last talked."

"Yeah, I heard," Andre sighed.

"Heard from who?"

"Alexis called me this morning. She told me about the berserkers. I can't believe it. All because of a bar fight?!"

"What else did Alexis say?"

"She told me you guys spilled the beans. She knows about the Fae, saw you go all wolfy, and I told her about my own special brand of amazing. Sounded like she was still trying to soak it in, but she wasn't freaking out, as far as I could tell."

"Is that all you heard?" I didn't know if Chloe or Moira had gotten a hold of him yet.

"Shit, there's more?"

"Riel and I had to make a tough decision," I hedged. I wasn't eager to tell him about Alexis, especially now he'd made such a monumental bust.

"What kind of tough decision? Is it about the berserkers?"

"Kind of," I sighed.

"Out with it," Andre demanded.

"We need to keep our distance from Alexis, Andre."

"What the hell are you talking about, Finn?"

"We let her get too close and it almost killed her. And we've heard whispers around town that Riel is getting soft, letting humans interfere with our business. The berserkers weren't acting on their own; someone sent them. Word on the street is that the attack was a message."

"So, we're just going to abandon her?" Andre sounded incredulous.

"We're going to back off to keep her safe," I corrected. But my stomach roiled. His assessment felt more accurate than mine.

Andre went quiet.

"I need you to back me up on this, partner," I pressed. "You've always had my back in the past. I need you to have it now."

"I've always backed you because it's always felt like the right call before. This doesn't feel like the right call, Finn."

"Andre…"

"I'll talk to you when I get back in town. I have to coordinate with the chief to transport Ramond. Later." The line went dead.

"He hung up on me," I told Riel.

"There's a lot of that going around today," Riel shook his head.

"I've gotta get to work." I stuck my phone in my pocket. "With Andre bringing Ramond back and the uproar with the Bianchis, they'll need all hands on deck."

"I'll keep you updated on our end," Riel waved me off and slumped into the back room.

Once I got back to the Charger, I glanced up at Alexis's apartment building. My wolf whined and urged me forward. I steeled myself against its influence. God, I wanted to bust up those stairs and take back everything I had said. But instead, I got in my car and drove to the station.

"Briggs," Chief called as I strode into the think tank. "Andre just gave me the good news! That's some solid work you two have done."

"That was all Andre, Chief. Save the praise for him."

"I bet Alexis is thrilled. Have you folks told the victim yet?"

My stomach clenched. "No, not yet. I want to see the piss-ant with my own eyes before I give Maria the good news. I'll get in touch with the DA today, see what we can get started."

"Sounds good. When Alexis gets in, follow up with her interviews with the sex workers around town. I've got a feeling they're going to be the key to the Bianchi mess."

"Alexis won't be in today." I swallowed hard. "She injured her leg and needs to stay off her feet for a few days. You should hear from her at some point soon."

"That's too bad," Chief frowned. "I'll call her now. Does she need anything?"

"Not that I know of. Her roommates will take good care of her."

"Alright, as you were." Chief headed back to his office.

I sank into my desk chair and leaned back. No matter where I went, reminders of Alexis would find me and stare me dead in the face. I flipped through my notebook and found her doodles, my gut doing a backflip as I traced the mermaid-siren with the tip of my finger. Even back at my apartment, I could still faintly smell her scent on the couch where she slept for the two weeks while she took care of me. My heart clenched.

After all she's done for me…

Was I abandoning her like Andre said? The hurt on Alexis's face haunted me. It broke me. I closed my eyes and brought up the image of the berserker going for her throat. That… that right there was why I was doing this. Why we had to do this; to protect her and ourselves.

"No rest for the wicked, Briggs," Chief called from his doorway. "We've got another headless body down at the dock."

"Fuck," I groaned, rising once more.

"Get on it," Chief ordered.

Uniforms were working the scene when I arrived. We were four slips over from where we found Ferret, but the scene was eerily similar. The smell hit me in the face the second I got out of my car. The closer I got to the body, the stronger the scent became. Just like the last crime scene, just like Dublin.

"Any ID on the vic?" I asked a uniform.

"No, sir. But he's got some dark red stains under his fingernails. Forensics thinks he might have gotten a piece of his attacker."

I bent down to examine the body. The hair on the back of my neck stood at attention. Another scent mingled with the stink of the penanggalan assassin: honeysuckle. My heart skipped several beats. I whipped my head back and forth, but the uniforms were the only other people around.

Leaning as close to the body as I could get without touching it, I inhaled again. It was unmistakable. Alexis's scent was all over the body. Another deep inhale brought another familiar scent to the surface: my own. I furrowed my brows. What the hell was going on?

My eyes raked over the headless corpse. Definitely male. His arms were thick with hair, and he was sturdily built. He stank of something familiar… a lingering stench by the dartboard. The realization struck me, and I swore.

It was the second berserker.

I almost missed his telltale smell masked by the horrible stench of his killer. That blood under his fingernails wasn't the penanggalan's, it was mine or Alexis's…or both. How the hell would I explain that one after forensics got a hold of it?

I strode away from the body and pulled out my phone. Riel answered on the second ring.

"Finn?"

"You can call off the search for the second berserker. Department found him first, sans head, down at the docks."

"The penanggalan?"

"Looks and smells like it."

"Then someone put a hit on him."

"But why?"

"Why do you kill an assassin, Finn?"

"Because he didn't get the job done… Fuck." White hot rage was rising inside me. "Someone powerful was pulling his strings, and Alexis is in the crosshairs."

"The million-dollar question is, 'Why her?'" Riel's voice was tight with worry.

I racked my brain. What could Alexis have done to draw the attention of the big bads? Her work since she came to the Clock was getting serious results. It was possible she was making some enemies. But most of the perps on her cases were low-level dirtbags. None of them were anywhere near powerful enough to merit a hit. But maybe the path she was walking was sending her in the direction of something bigger.

I turned and watched the medical examiner zip up the berserker's body. Alexis's attack wasn't a simple hit; it was a hit by a Fae assassin. Then that failed assassin was killed by another Fae. If Riel was correct about penanggalans, they were one of the most formidable, frightening Fae killers anywhere in the world. Whoever sent one after Ferret and the berserker had to have Fae connections. No one could control two different races of Fae without knowing what they were doing.

"Finn? You still there?"

"I need you to send someone into the medical examiner's office for a cleanup. The berserker has evidence under his fingernails that will link Alexis and I to the body. We can't exactly explain the real reason it's there. We don't need the heat from both sides."

"I'll send a team to take care of it," Riel assured. "All of this is connected somehow. The winds are shifting, Finn. I can feel something big approaching."

"How big?" My heart pounded. Riel's foresight was unmatched, save one Fae.

"Big," he breathed. "Bad. From multiple directions. Stay sharp."

"I will. Thank you."

I hung up and walked back to the Charger. On the way back to the station, I tried calling Andre, but he didn't pick up. He was probably on his way back to the Clock with Ramond. I left him a brief message about the second headless body, but I kept it vague just in case. As I drove away from the docks, I could sense eyes on me from the shadows. My wolf growled and my neck prickled.

It took a day and a half for Andre to come back with his prisoner. When he did, he received a hero's welcome. We saw to it that Ramond was thrown straight into our smallest and least comfortable cell to simmer in his own juices before we cracked down on him. Andre had already called Maria to give her the good news. He said she was terrified and overjoyed at the same time. Despite the victory, it only made me feel Alexis's absence more acutely. She was the reason we'd gotten anywhere on this case at all. Now she was missing the payoff.

"She's thrilled, in case you were wondering." Andre was tapping his pencil against his desk.

"Huh?" I turned to look at him.

"Alexis," Andre replied. The name alone shot a jolt of shame-wrapped pain through me. "I told her about Ramond. She's thrilled. Asked me about Maria right away." He was frowning at me.

"Don't start on me, man." I shook my head and turned away again.

"We've got to talk about it sometime."

"I already told you why Riel and I made the decision," I snapped. "Pushing it will not make it any easier. Everyone will be better off if she's not around anymore."

"You really believe that?"

The doubts crept up for the millionth time. Riel had talked to the rest of the crew. They had all agreed to pull away, but every single one of them was furious about it. Donna threw a chair. The sisters weren't speaking to either of us. They were ardently in Alexis's corner. The worst part was that was exactly where I wanted to be, too. Andre was the final holdout.

"What else is going to keep her safe?"

"We could," Andre argued.

I laughed humorlessly. "Alexis and I were closer than anyone and I couldn't keep her safe. All I did—all *we* did—was put her in more danger because of who we are."

"That's bullshit, Finn, and you know it."

"No, it isn't. A Fae attacked her, not some human junkie looking to rob her for his next fix. They went after her because of us... Fuck! If Alexis and I wouldn't have gotten into that damn fight..." I slammed my fist on my desk. Heads popped up to look at me, but I ignored them.

"What fight?" Andre asked.

"When Alexis got to the bar that night, she told me she was questioning one of the working girls she made friends with. But instead of bringing her into the station, Alexis had a friendly chat about her association with the Bianchi crime syndicate on campus, out in the open where anyone could have heard her."

"Finn." Andre's voice dropped an octave.

"What?"

"That's it." Andre moved to the big board where we were tracking connections. "What's the common denominator with the working girls? What's getting them to talk after years of silence?"

"Alexis," I answered.

"Exactly. We got Ramond and his dumbass cousin for going after Maria, and they're mid-level pushers for the Bianchi's drug ring. We only got that info because Maria trusts Alexis enough to talk. Leticia spills the beans about the human trafficking ring being linked to the Bianchis because she feels loyalty... to Alexis. More and more women are opening up, building our case against the Bianchis, because of..."

"Alexis." I swallowed hard. "Holy shit." I ran my hands through my hair. "Someone must have seen her talking to her friend and sent the berserkers after her. She's a walking liability to their syndicate and they know it."

"And Alexis doesn't." Andre slapped a sticky note with Alexis's name on the board.

"We have to warn her." I stood and made a move for the door.

"I'll warn her." Andre grabbed my shoulder to stop me. "Your name is shit at their place right now. Chloe might make you explode with a look if you show up."

I wanted to argue, but I knew he was right. It was taking every ounce of strength I had not to shift right here and race over. I was shaking with the effort.

"Still think we should back off from her?"

"More than ever!" I sat back in my chair.

"What?!"

"We need to get her the hell out of town. Far away from the Bianchis, far away from the Fae. We're going to get her killed." I ran my hands over my face. I felt bile rising in my throat.

"You can't be serious."

"I am. I can't believe you don't see it. Do you think buddying around with two Fae cops and all their human-hugging, disgraced Fae friends is going to make her seem like less of a threat? The Bianchis have an in with the Fae. There's no denying it now. We're dangerous to her on both fronts." Fuck, fuck, fuck. I gritted my teeth. What the hell had we done?

Andre didn't say anything. He was trying to work a way around my logic. But it was airtight. Being best friends with two Fae cops who were trying to take down the most powerful crime family in town was a death sentence.

Andre sat down, defeated. "I'll call." He picked up his phone and dialed Alexis's number.

"Put it on speaker," I demanded. He did as I asked.

"Hey Andre," Alexis answered. My chest tightened. Her voice... My yearning intensified.

"Hey Alexis, you got a minute?"

"Sure." She didn't sound at all like herself.

"We're working our cases, and we need to tell you something."

"Okay..." Her voice was guarded.

"You in danger, girl," Andre tried his best Whoopi Goldberg impression, but it fell flat. He sighed, "Shit. I don't know how to say this delicately, so I'll just put it out there. The Bianchis are after you. Someone sent those berserkers to kill you and when they failed, the Bianchis terminated the survivor."

"You're kidding me, right?"

"I wish I was. You're making trouble for them. Their girls trust you too much, like you too much, and that makes you a threat. We've got to get you out of town."

"No," she answered flatly. My rage flashed.

"What do you mean no?" I barked.

Pure silence on the other end. I scolded myself internally for the outburst. My jaw clenched with the effort of returning to my silence.

"Alexis?" Andre breathed.

No reply.

"It's not safe for you here anymore," Andre pleaded.

"I said 'no,' Andre. I'm not abandoning these women. They deserve someone to be a voice for them when they're too scared to speak for themselves. I'm not leaving."

"You don't get a choice in this, Alexis," I growled, unable to hold back. "If I have to drag you out of here myself, I'll…"

"I'm not leaving," Alexis asserted. The line went dead.

"FUCK," I yelled.

"Shit!" Andre immediately tried calling her back. It went straight to voicemail.

"What the hell is going on out here?" Chief walked over to us.

"The Bianchis are after Alexis," I explained. "We need to get her out of the Clock."

"Are you sure?" Chief asked, his expression shocked.

"We don't have it straight from anyone's mouth, but we're pretty confident," Andre replied.

"Have you told her?" Chief continued.

"Just did," I gritted my teeth. "She won't listen. Refuses to go."

Chief crossed his arms and frowned.

"We're going to make her, right?" I pressed.

"I'm afraid I can't do that." Chief shook his head.

"Why the hell not? You're her boss. Fire her! Suspend her! Hell, put her in witness protection and send her the hell out of here, for fuck's sakes!" I yelled. Everything inside of me was screaming for someone to see reason. I couldn't lose her. Not like this, not now, not ever.

"Watch your tone, Detective Briggs," Chief warned. "If Alexis doesn't want to go, then I can't make her go. I'm sure as hell not going to fire her. What safer place for her to be than the department?"

I bit my tongue.

"If you're sure she's in danger, we'll send patrols by her place to keep an eye on her. Other than that, without solid evidence, there's nothing else I can do." Chief walked back into his office and slammed the door.

"The Chief's right, you know. If Alexis doesn't want to go, we can't make her leave."

"Oh, I'll make her leave," I huffed. "If it's the last thing I do, I'll make sure she leaves the Clock and never looks back."

Chapter Twenty-Four

Alexis

"Valentine's Day is coming up," Moira swirled her wine glass.

"Don't remind me," Chloe sulked.

"I'm not trying to upset you, Chloe. I'm just saying, since we're all single and in desperate need of some cheering up, I thought maybe we could go to the concert down at the amphitheater on V-Day."

"Is anyone we know going to be there?" Chloe's eyebrows drew in tight.

"I haven't said anything to anyone else, if that's what you're asking. This would be a girls' night out. Lord knows we need one after being stuck in the house for so long!"

Our nightly visits to the Pony had come to a screeching halt after my attack. Finn and all the others were avoiding me like the plague and Chloe had broken up with Riel for trying to force her to unfriend me. The four of us were turning into a miserable, lonely lot and I knew it was all my fault.

To top it off, the Chief was having me work from home and sending hourly patrols by our place. Andre and Finn had convinced him my life was in danger because of the Bianchis. I wasn't as sure. If it was true, I was having a hard time giving a shit about it. A dark cloud had settled over my world, and it was proving almost impossible to shake.

"So, what do you think?" Moira prompted.

Lacey gave her an enthusiastic thumbs up. Her spirits had been down, too. I knew she missed her friends. The guilt stabbed at me again.

"Okay, I'm in." I tried to sound eager.

"Seriously?" Chloe eyed me skeptically.

"Why not? It's something to break up the monotony. And you love The Wild; I hear they're headlining."

Chloe grumbled and glanced at the door.

"Fine, I'll go," she conceded. "But only if we try to find dates. I couldn't stand being surrounded by couples sucking each other's faces off all night."

"What happened to a girls' night?" Moira protested.

"I love you all, but every night has been a girls' night lately. I need some testosterone in my life."

"Where are we going to find dates?" I asked with a raised eyebrow.

Chloe got a mischievous sparkle in her eye.

"No." I waved my hands emphatically. "No, no, no. We're not going to the Pony."

"The hell we're not." Chloe pulled me up from my dinner. "We're desirable, beautiful women in need of a little male company. And in the meantime, we can rub a few faces in our dalliances." She spat the last sentence with more than a little venom.

"I'm banished, remember?" I argued.

"What are they going to do? Throw us out?"

"Possibly," Moira answered.

"Not when they see us stroll in like sex on two legs. Just wait..." Chloe ran off.

She went from bedroom to bedroom, pulling out the sexiest outfits she could find for each of us. Lacey's sexiest outfit was a yellow sundress with sunflowers on it. Mine was a red sequined mini dress with a low V-neck. Chloe's was a little black dress with a slit up one side to her hip. Moira took her "sexy" outfit back to her room and brought out something more comfortable. Chloe shot her a frown.

"My leg..." I argued.

"...Is perfectly healed since Vikram brought you his magic mix," Chloe waved at my leg. "Plus, Vijay sewed up the rip in your favorite coat and brought it back, so you can't even argue that you'll be cold."

She was right. I couldn't argue with either point. The Fae remedy had taken away the pain and left only tiny, fading pink marks behind where the puncture wounds once festered. In a few days, it would look like nothing ever happened.

"We're doing this," Chloe persuaded. "Get your asses ready."

The three of us finally caved. We hadn't seen Chloe so focused on something since the breakup. If this is what she needed to move on, who were we to stop her? Maybe the regulars wouldn't be there, I lied to myself.

Red mini dress on, makeup at level ten, and a pair of red suede heels to match, and I was ready to go. We walked to the Pony arm-in-arm, Chloe grinning triumphantly the whole way.

Taron, the bouncer, let us in with wide eyes. Chloe tapped the tip of his nose with her finger as we entered. I chuckled. I had missed this side of her.

The bar was packed with patrons, lots I recognized, but also ones I didn't. I caught myself scanning the room for the familiar faces of my former friends. They were there, of course, like they always were. I locked eyes with Finn at the bar. His eyes went wide, and I looked away quickly.

Chloe led us to a table in the corner, far away from our usual spot, and ordered us a round of drinks from the server. Several men were already queuing up to talk with us by the time the drinks arrived. I could feel Finn's eyes on me from across the room, but I kept my gaze on the tall brunette I was flirting with. His name was Ben and a quick whisper with Chloe confirmed he was thankfully human. Ben kept finding excuses to touch my hair or my shoulder as we talked, and I gave him my most radiant smile. Heat burned in my cheeks as I felt the ever-watching eyes. The wicked part of me was hoping he was enjoying the show.

After about an hour, the men who had sat with us went to the bar to get a fresh round of drinks. My eyes wandered, but when they found the dance floor, my stomach dropped. Finn was dancing with Milani, her ass pressed up against his groin. Shame and fury erupted simultaneously in my chest. Everything about the picture was wrong. Finn couldn't stand Milani, and he hated dancing. Nevertheless, there he was, one arm wrapped tightly around her waist and the other roaming up and down her side.

I turned away quickly and caught Chloe staring at the dance floor, too, with a look of pure rage.

"That disgusting piece of shit," she hissed.

"Chloe, leave it," Moira warned.

Lacey was staring at the sight with a confused look. She studied me, and I gave her a strained smile. She looked back at the dance floor and frowned.

"Ladies, your drinks," Ben charmed, sitting down next to me.

Chloe instantly regained her composure, putting her hand on the thick arm of the Fae healer she'd been cozying up to all night. I forced myself to focus back on the group around our table, but the hairs on the back of my neck continued to prickle. I wanted to turn around and scream at Finn to focus on his new fuck-buddy instead of staring at me all night. But that would make me look like a lunatic. I was better than that.

By the end of the night, Moira, Chloe, and I had dates to the Valentine's concert at the amphitheater. Lacey was perfectly pleased with the handful of maraschino cherries she was taking home. Ben was a charming and interesting man. I was genuinely looking forward to going out with him.

The days passed faster now that we'd worked our way out of our slump. Ben and I texted every day, getting to know each other. Chloe spent several nights making out with the Fae healer named Jase on the couch. She giggled and flirted when he was around, but there was always a tiny look of longing in her eyes as soon as he left. He was not Riel, but Chloe refused to acknowledge or discuss it.

The morning of Valentine's Day came with a pleasantly surprising temperature increase. I opened my window to let in the cool, fresh air. As I was grabbing my backpack, my phone rang. Without checking to see who it was, I answered.

"Ms. Henson?" The voice was serious and low.

"Marshal Davis?" I gasped.

"I have some bad news."

My stomach fell to my feet.

"Okay." I sat on my bed and clutched the phone.

"They granted Cam Gunner an appeal."

My mouth dropped open, and I started to shake. Nausea swept over me. My vision blurred, and I almost dropped the phone.

"Turns out the prosecutor's office failed to turn over some evidence to the defense in his trial. Worse yet, Gunner's defense team talked a judge into the possibility of letting him out on parole until his new trial."

"That's impossible," I squeaked. "What about the other women? He… It wasn't just me…"

"They prosecuted him based on your case. None of the other victims survived to testify. Without the conviction in your case—this nail in the coffin— the sonofabitch might walk free."

"They can't do this, can they?"

"They can and they might actually get away with it," Marshal Davis confirmed. "But I want to reassure you that if it happens, you'll be safe. Witness protection will keep you out of harm's way. His 'people' he swore would come after you haven't caught even the slightest sniff of where we've stashed you, and Gunner won't either."

I swallowed hard. "Are you sure?"

"I'm positive. I'm the only one who knows exactly where you are. You're safe in my care."

The shaking didn't subside.

"I'll keep you apprised of the situation as it develops. Good day, Ms. Henson."

"Goodbye."

I could feel myself settling into shock. I thought the tears would start right away, but I sat frozen on my bed, staring at the wall. The sounds of the sisters bustling around in the kitchen, starting their day, floated down the hall, but everything sounded muffled. It felt like I'd been filled with rocks and wrapped in Styrofoam. I felt heavy. The sounds were so muted.

The front door opened and closed several times, signaling their departure. I was supposed to go to class, but my limbs weren't obeying my order to move. Instead, I watched the shadows on my wall shift and change as the hours ticked by. The shaking was the only constant.

I had no idea how many hours had passed while I sat on my bed. My phone pinged several times, but I couldn't bear to touch it. Whoever was trying to reach me would have to wait.

He could get out. If he did, he wouldn't stop until he found me. The second wave of nausea broke the spell. I launched off my bed and raced to the bathroom, completely emptying the meager contents of my stomach. Once I couldn't heave anymore, I collapsed onto the cold tile floor and surrendered to the feelings of hopelessness.

Everything was falling apart. I had lost my friends, Finn had abandoned me, and now the man who had tried to kill me was inches away from getting out of prison on a technicality. Whatever magical protection my friends could have offered me might have made this nightmare less terrifying, but they were all gone except for the sisters. From the little I knew about the kind of Fae they were, it was nothing that could shield me from a serial killer.

More hours passed.

The front door opened. Someone was home from work. The concert was tonight. I was going to have to tell the sisters I wasn't going. I dreaded the conversation. They would want to know why.

I peeled myself off the bathroom floor, rinsed my mouth out with water, and spat. I dragged my unwilling limbs into the living room. Moira was waiting for me. She had tears in her eyes.

"Moira? Are you okay?"

My own worries pushed aside the moment I saw the distress on her face. She didn't say a word, just wrapped her arms around me and hugged me tight. She smoothed my hair back and rocked me gently from side to side.

"We're not going to let anything happen to you," she crooned.

I pulled away from her grasp.

"Moira, what are you talking about?"

"I *know*," she whispered.

"You know what?"

She looked at me sheepishly, her cheeks turning pink. She seemed to struggle with what to say. I got the weird feeling I'd grown too accustomed to around my Fae friends.

"What do you know, Moira?" I pressed.

"I know what happened to you," she clamped her eyes shut. "I know why you came here."

My stomach clenched. "How could you possibly know that?"

"I… I can see… I can see the past," Moira's voice wavered. "It's my gift. The closer I am to a person, the clearer the picture. I know what that man did to you. I've seen it…" The last three words fell out of her mouth like a bombshell.

"You… you…" Tears flooded my eyes.

"I know about the phone call from the Marshal," she continued. "He might get out. But we won't let him find you. Chloe and Lacey know, too, about what happened. I'm sorry. It wasn't my place to ever say anything, but it was the only way to talk them into letting a human come live with us."

"You've known from the beginning?" I was in awe.

"Since I talked to you on the phone about the room for rent. That's when the first vision came. That's when I saw what you were running from…"

"I… I don't know what to say," I mumbled. The secrets never ended.

"Please don't be mad at me! I can't help what I see. I don't go looking for it. It just comes to me. I know it feels like an invasion, but I swear to you I haven't told another soul aside from my sisters. They've kept quiet, hand to the Gods." She raised her right hand to the square.

"I'm not mad," I assured. "If you can't help it, it's not like you snuck into my room and read my journal."

"I would never," she vowed, scandalized.

I sank down on the couch, my knees weak. Moira sat beside me and held my hand.

"What if he gets out?" I whispered.

"You're safe here."

The front door opened. Chloe and Lacey entered and spotted us on the couch. Chloe frowned, then that strange look came across her face. She was frozen for several moments, then her expression turned to one of horror. Lacey hid her face behind her hands.

"You can see it, too?" I asked.

"See what?" Chloe tried to play it off.

"I told her about my gift, Chloe," Moira explained. "No, Alexis, Chloe doesn't see the past like I do. She sees…something else."

"What?"

"I'm not ready to talk about it yet," Chloe shook her head.

"But you know what's happening. I can see it on your face," I accused. She nodded.

"Lacey?"

Lacey shook her head, but peeked through her fingers at me. She knew, too. The look in her eyes told me she had to know.

"He could get out?" Chloe lowered herself onto the couch on my other side.

"Yes," I acknowledged.

Chloe hugged me.

We sat on the couch for a long time. No one spoke. Lacey kept fiddling with a string coming off the corner of one cushion. She looked miles away.

Chloe's phone buzzed.

"It's Jase," Chloe explained. "He said they're going to meet us at the amphitheater in an hour."

"We don't have to go," Moira assured me.

"I don't think I have it in me," I wiped at my face.

"Of course," Moira patted my arm.

"But I don't want you to miss out. You three go. Lacey can be my stand-in with Ben."

Lacey's eyebrows shot into her hairline. She pointed to herself and the front door, then shook her head emphatically. It made me chuckle. A little light flickered back to life in my chest.

"No, no, we won't leave you alone," Chloe insisted.

"What about your testosterone shortage?"

"Men are a dime a dozen," she waved it off.

"Please, I don't want you three missing out on the concert, on Valentine's Day, because of me. I've already caused enough damage to your lives. Go," I urged.

"Will you feel safe staying here alone?" Moira asked.

I searched myself. "No."

"Then we'll stay." Chloe pulled my hand to her mouth and kissed the back of it.

I sighed, the immense guilt of what I was costing my friends overwhelming me. "Or I could suck it up and come with you."

"Did you just say, 'suck it up?' This isn't a scraped knee, Alexis. You found out that your attacker might get out of prison. Give yourself some credit!" Chloe was scandalized.

I brushed my hair out of my face and rose from the couch. The sisters followed me into my bedroom and watched with shocked faces while I washed my face and started applying fresh makeup.

"What are you doing?" Chloe asked.

"Getting ready for the concert."

"Are you sure about this?" Moira looked pale.

I sighed. "Either I can stay here and wallow in fear and misery, or I can pull myself together and go on a date with a handsome, perfectly human man on Valentine's Day. I think it will be good for me. Really," I insisted in response to their incredulous faces.

"If you're sure," Moira didn't look at all convinced.

"I'm sure. Unfortunately, I already wasted the entire day letting that monster invade my headspace." I cleared my throat. "I don't want to give him any more power over me."

"That's my girl," Chloe beamed.

Instead of going to their own rooms, the sisters brought their things into my room. We squeezed into my bathroom and got ready together. I chose a flowy blue blouse that matched my eyes and my favorite jeans and ballet flats. Chloe curled my hair and arranged it so that it cascaded over my shoulders. By the time we finished getting ready, I already felt calmer.

"Okay, let's go," Chloe prompted.

The amphitheater was all the way at the very end of 10-block. The air was still crisp and cold with the tail end of winter. I was glad the concert was at the interior portion of the amphitheater, not the open-air venue. Chloe and Lacey linked arms with me, and Chloe pulled Moira close to her other side as we walked. At that moment, I felt safe as we made our way down the sidewalk.

Ben, Jase, and Moira's date, Mishka, were waiting for us in front of the doors to the venue. Ben kissed the back of my hand, and I mustered a genuine smile. We hurried inside to get out of the cold. Scores of people were already lined up in the waiting area. The interior doors hadn't opened to permit entry yet.

We were chatting amiably when I caught a sharp motion out of the corner of my eye. Already jumpy, I whipped my head around. A wave of discomfort rolled over me as I caught sight of Finn and Andre, just a few people ahead of us. Milani and another woman were with them. Milani had snatched Andre's fedora off his head and was waving it around, cackling. That was the motion that caught my attention.

For a moment, my heart leapt with joy at seeing Andre again after so long. But the feeling was fleeting. I closed my eyes with a sigh. Why did Finn have to be everywhere I went? I wanted to have a pleasant night out. When I opened my eyes again, I saw Milani toss Andre's hat back to him before she draped herself on Finn's arm. His back tensed.

Lacey weaved her way through the people in front of us and tapped Andre on the shoulder. He turned and greeted her with a huge smile, followed by an enormous hug. I took a few steps back, hoping to fade into Ben's shadow. Lacey's face was beaming. Finn's keen eyes flicked from Lacey to the surrounding spaces. He knew Lacey never went anywhere on her own. I turned away to look for a bathroom to excuse myself to, but it was too late.

"Well, if it isn't the schoolmarm, Rode Hard, and little miss Fridge Vag," Milani's scathing voice sounded over my shoulder.

My whole body shuddered at the implication. My trauma lurched up from where I'd been barely suppressing it beneath the surface of my composure. I didn't want to turn back around. I wanted to run. But I forced myself to face her.

Milani was staring at me with a wicked grin. She wrapped her arm around Finn's and leaned into him as if she couldn't stand on her own. My stomach flopped. Andre, Lacey, and the other woman I didn't recognize stood behind them.

"And if it isn't the town bicycle," Chloe spat back. "Good to see you, Milani." Her voice was dripping with sarcasm.

Chloe glared at Finn with pure vitriol. "I see you've traded down, Briggs. Way down." Chloe ran her eyes up and down Milani's outfit.

"I think my sweet Finny got tired of waiting on your frigid friend there," Milani sneered, throwing a glance my way. "Why settle on a 2 when he can have a 10?"

"This is awkward," Ben breathed, moving closer to me protectively.

"I'm so sorry about this," I whispered to Ben.

Finn was staring impassively at us. He tightened his grip around Milani's waist when Ben put a reassuring hand on my shoulder. Finn's eyes were a dark, dancing flame.

"The only 10 about you is your IQ," Chloe bristled.

Moira put a hand on Chloe's arm to hold her back. Jase shifted uncomfortably beside her. Andre was looking at me with a pained expression.

"Do you always let your mommy fight your battles for you, princess?" Milani baited, looking right at me.

"I don't have a battle with you Milani," I sighed. "Enjoy your evening." I turned to walk away.

"I never understood what all the fuss was about with you, Alex," Milani drawled. I rolled my eyes. She knew my name; it was a stupid jab. "Everyone was *creaming* themselves over you and it turns out you're more trouble than you're worth, just like I thought. Just like everyone like you."

I knew what she was implying, just like all humans. My gaze flicked to Finn, my eyebrows raised. He stared back at me, jaw clenched. A cold wash flooded through me. That's where we stood, then.

"You're probably right," I replied.

Milani made a frustrated face. I could tell she was trying to get a rise out of me, but I'd spent too much time in police stations to be bothered by the likes of her. Being hard to rile was a part of the job description.

"I know I am, sweetheart." She sighed loudly. "Isn't it a shame that someone wasn't unleashed on you sooner and once they were, that they couldn't finish the job? It would have done us all a favor if they had."

I froze. A part of me knew she was talking about the berserker attack, but my trauma wounds were torn open fresh from this morning. It wasn't the berserkers I was afraid of being unleashed on me now. It was Cam Gunner.

Heat flooded my body, and panic rose in my chest. Everything and everyone were too close to me. I could feel the muscles in my back, pulling together, trying to make me smaller. The shaking started again. I had to get out.

Without another word, I pulled away from Ben and hurried out the front door. I buttoned up my coat and wrapped my arms around myself to keep out the cold. My body was shaking all over now. Every shadow that passed me on the street me made me startle. My head was pounding, and my vision was blurry around the edges. I sped down the sidewalk and crossed to the other side of the street.

I should have stayed home.

"Alexis," someone called.

I walked faster, fleeing from the familiar voice. He was the very last person I wanted to talk to right now. Despite the head start and my hurrying feet, he was behind me in a flash. He grabbed me by the arm to stop me. I threw his arm off me and spun to face him.

"Don't fucking touch me," I snarled.

"What the hell?" Finn glared at me.

"You've done a great job of staying away from me the past few weeks, Finn. Don't stop now." I tried to walk away, but he kept pace with me.

"You shouldn't be walking alone," he argued. His voice was icy.

"According to your date, I'd be doing everyone a favor if something happened to me on my way home. I guess it's too bad that the berserkers couldn't get the job done."

"She was out of line," Finn growled.

"I don't give a flying fuck what Milani thinks about me," I scoffed. "She's a vapid, self-centered Fae-bitch who's looking for an easy lay. If that's the kind of woman you're looking for, I hope you enjoy your jock itch."

"Is that what this is about?" Finn snapped. "You're pissed that I'm out with Milani. I don't owe you anything, Alexis. There was nothing…"

I spun on my heels and stuck my finger in his face, rage warping my vision.

"You self-centered asshole!" I yelled. "This," I motioned to myself, "has nothing to do with you and that bitch. Believe it or not, the world does not revolve around the magnanimous Finn Briggs. I have much bigger issues to deal with than who you're sleeping with today."

"Bullshit," he challenged. "You're mad you're not the center of attention anymore. No more Finn at your beck and call when your demons come to play."

I stared at him in shock. I was already teetering on the edge, but that comment sent me over. The shaking intensified. The disgust I felt brought back the nausea. Something flashed in his eyes, but it was gone in a moment.

"If you ever had any actual demons to begin with," he added, crossing his arms with a sneer. "I wouldn't know. It's a secret, right? Even though I told you mine, you still refuse to tell me yours."

"You really want to know what my demons are?" I hissed.

He lifted an eyebrow at me.

"Fine. Settle in, Shifter… I got a call this morning that the man who raped me then tried to kill me last year might get out of prison on a technicality. And if he gets out, I'm fucked. He's furious with me because I survived the attack, went to the police, and got him caught. The *fifteen* other women he did this to, *that we know about,* weren't so lucky. After he got sentenced to life without the possibility of parole, he threatened to send his friends after me to get even. So, I got put in witness protection, had to leave my whole life behind, and then got sent here to put up with your insufferable narcissism. So, there you go: My demons." I took a sarcastic bow.

Finn stared at me, slack jawed. The growing pity in his expression only pissed me off more. I put a hand up between us to cut off anything he was thinking to say.

"Do us both a favor; keep your distance like you promised. Stop pretending to give a shit about me or my demons, and go back to playing with your fuck buddy," I spat.

I turned on my heel once more and stormed away. My head was pounding harder than ever. The pressure in my chest had reached a crescendo, and it made me want to explode out of my skin. I needed to get home and take my rescue meds.

Then I was going to leave the Clock. Nowhere felt safe anymore. Least of all here.

Chapter Twenty-Five

Finn

I stared at Alexis's retreating back in horror. A thousand things rushed through my head at once. Her demons were worse than I ever imagined. She had been raped. She was the lone survivor of a serial killer.

Frozen to the spot, I watched her as she disappeared into the distance. No wonder she left the way she did when Milani lamented her survival from the berserker attack. That wasn't the first time Alexis had nearly lost her life at the hands of a psychopath.

Then I flew in like a damn wrecking ball and mocked her demons. I had confused her suffering with petty jealousy. Every time I came into contact with her after taking her to the hospital, I hurt her. I felt sick to my stomach about every word I had said.

After Alexis had left the amphitheater, Chloe launched herself at Milani. While Andre and Moira tried to pry them apart, I went after Alexis. I was trying to keep my distance, but the memory of Alexis's screams the last time I'd let her walk home alone haunted me. My cozying up to Milani was meant to push Alexis as far away as I could, but not at the expense of her immediate safety.

I needed to get her out of the Clock. We had to get her away from here to keep her safe, even if it meant turning myself into a soulless asshole in her eyes. I hated myself for all of it. But to convince her to leave, I could only hope to make her hate me enough to save her life.

But this was an extra complication. She had been in danger before I ever met her. I needed to find out everything I could about the man who had attacked her, the man who would have stolen her light from this world before I would have seen it for myself. My wolf was snarling at me to do something. I felt torn between going after her, demanding to know everything about her would-be killer so I could find him and annihilate him, and keeping to my charade. The boiling rage and helplessness rolled through me. I swore loudly and punched a streetlight. It creaked and swayed with the force of my blow.

"You are the worst, most vile piece of shit in the known universe, Finn!" Chloe's voice screeched through the cold air.

"Chloe, that's enough," Moira begged.

"No, it's not enough.," Chloe protested. "You know exactly what he's trying to do, Moira. He doesn't care if it tears Alexis apart in the meantime."

Chloe got right in my face. "You don't own her, Briggs. If she doesn't want to leave the Clock, you can't make her. If you don't fucking watch yourself, I'm going to tell her everything. And I mean *everything*. Every look, every thought, every desire, all of it."

"You wouldn't," I challenged.

"Watch me," she hissed. A drop of dried blood lingered at the corner of her mouth from her scuffle with Milani. "Alexis is our family now and I'll be damned if you keep hurting her with your white knight complex. Back the fuck off or I'll make you regret it for the rest of your days." Her eyes turned black as she glared at me.

"Chloe, don't," Moira warned.

"Chloe!" Andre jogged up behind her and spun her around just as my head started to pound with pressure. "This isn't going to fix anything."

"Get off, Andre, you goddamn coward." Chloe shoved Andre away.

"What the hell did I do?" Andre threw his hands in the air.

"It's what you didn't do," Chloe accused. "You couldn't bear to stand up to Finn, even though you disagree with what he's doing. Then you just stood there while that bitch went after Alexis. You egged Finn on with Alexis nonstop with your dream pushing, then cowed like a dog the moment he snapped his fingers and told you to heel."

"Woah, who flipped your bitch switch?" Andre snapped back.

"She told you." Chloe turned on me once more, accusations all over her face.

I couldn't speak. My mind was still spinning. I wanted to lash out at Chloe, but the sense of overwhelm I felt held me back. A loud part of me felt like I deserved the dressing down she was giving me. I wanted to fight, but who was the real enemy here?

"She told you what happened to her," Chloe repeated. "You know what she's been through now. You still think isolating her from everyone who cares about her, everyone who could actually protect her, is the right call?"

Maybe it was pride and ego, maybe it was something else, but I didn't respond. I didn't know the answer anymore. I needed time to think. I turned wordlessly from the chaos of the scene and strode away, fists clenched.

"Yeah, walk away, Finn. It's what you're good at," Chloe yelled after me.

I shook my head and sped up. I needed to get out of here. I needed to go to the woods to think. My wolf whined to be set loose, and I didn't feel like denying it any longer. I broke into a full sprint, using every ounce of my speed to get out of here. I left the Charger behind; I was faster on foot.

The second I entered the first line of trees in the woods, I threw off my clothes and shifted. My wolf came to life with a vicious snarl. I ran. As hard and as fast as my four legs could carry me, I launched myself through the woods, desperate for some kind of release. My legs pumped, my heart pounded, and my breath clouded the air. But no relief came. The turmoil inside me only increased. It split me in two and it wasn't just me and my wolf that vied for control anymore. It was life with Alexis and life without her.

One part of me was pure selfishness. I craved her, desired her, and wanted her in every single way. She was unlike anyone, human or Fae, that I had met in all my centuries on Earth. I thought my life was complete before her, but now there was a throbbing, aching hole inside me in her absence. I wasn't whole before her, and I worried I would never be whole if I succeeded in my plot to push her away.

The other side of me wanted to protect her from the vicious world she'd stumbled upon. She was all goodness. The forces she was facing with her stubborn resolve wouldn't stop until she was destroyed piece by piece. If I drew her to me, kept her close, I could end up losing her, anyway. There was no way I could survive that pain. I would rather know she was alive and safe, hating me, somewhere else than to watch my selfishness put her in the devil's path. So, I guess both sides of me were purely selfish. I now knew I had no interest in living in a world in which Alexis didn't safely exist.

Despite failing to find relief in my wolf form, I ran myself to exhaustion. Part working out my aggression, part self-punishment, the running at least left me too tired to stay conscious. I curled up under a tree and slept, welcoming the escape from my current reality. But my dreams were not so kind. They intensified everything that plagued me in waking. It was a fitting punishment for all my fuck ups.

A few days after the Valentine's fiasco, Alexis returned to work at the station. The patrols they sent out to watch for further Bianchi hitmen found nothing and our contacts on the street said things were strangely silent. The Chief felt strongly that she was safer at the station than at home, so he pulled her back in. I had decided against being outwardly oppositional to drive Alexis away, but I kept a cordial distance. Andre took over coordinating with her on cases while I focused on running the leads with the Bianchis. When we had to be in the same room together for any reason, she refused to even meet my eyes. I sarcastically congratulated myself on such a hollow victory.

This morning, Andre and I were about to get a chance to sit down and take a crack at Ramond. When we first got Maria's case, she told us that an unknown assailant had assaulted her on Ramond's order when she stopped taking his phone calls. After she grew to trust us, thanks again to Alexis, she told us it had been Ramond himself who beat her up because she didn't want to be sold anymore. When the cops got involved, he took off to "visit his cousin" and didn't come back. But it didn't stop him from sending Maria the message to keep her mouth shut via a beating from Cousin Ronaldo.

"Good cop, bad cop?" Andre asked, rubbing his hands together before we entered Ramond's cell.

"Isn't that our natural way?"

"More and more lately."

"What does that mean?" I shot him a look.

"You've been 'bad cop' for weeks. You're miserable, my friend. Any idiot on the street could see it. It's written all over your face."

"And?"

"And that's not what I want for you, man." Andre gripped my shoulder. "You think it's enjoyable watching the light totally fade out in you?"

"No one said it was for your enjoyment," I snapped.

"I see your dreams every night," Andre confided. "It's a damn hellscape in there."

My cheeks flushed.

"Knock that shit off, then. I didn't ask you to be my bedtime babysitter."

"This is exactly what I'm talking about, Finn. You're being a complete dick to just about everyone. I get that you're trying to push Alexis away because you think it's going to keep her safe, but you're pushing everyone away. I've spent a hell of a long time backing you up over the years, but I'm reaching my limits, too."

I looked away from him and clenched my jaw. I'd been in a foul mood for who knows how long, but he didn't deserve the shit I'd been shoveling on him. What could I say? How could I defend myself when I knew he was right?

"Look, I get it, man." Andre circled me to make me face him again. "I know how you feel about her. You may not be ready to admit it to yourself yet, but I see it. You're scared shitless that something's gonna happen to her. But, you think ghosting her is going to change that? The truth is, if you keep this shit up, you're going to lose her either way."

"I never deserved her in the first place," I mumbled.

"Nah, you didn't," Andre replied.

I glared up at him, surprised. He was grinning at me. I rolled my eyes and shook my head.

"You deserve something good, man. And Alexis, she's good."

"Briggs! Alvarez! Your boy's ready," a guard called from the booth.

We headed through rows of automated locked doors, my mind spinning. Andre picked a hell of a time for a heart to heart. I needed to get my head in the game. I needed to watch Ramond sing like a damn bird.

"Ramond! Good to see you again," Andre greeted, arms wide. "Did you miss me?"

"Fuck you, pig," Ramond spat on the floor.

"You did miss me," Andre cooed, sitting on the chair across from his cell.

"Who's your guard dog?" Ramond lifted his chin at me.

"Detective Briggs," I answered with a low growl.

"He your boyfriend?"

"You're testy today," Andre tutted.

"What the hell do you expect? You assholes arrested me at my niece's quince, hauled my ass back to the fuckin' Clock, then threw me in here for no reason."

"No reason, huh?" I glared. "You had nothing to do with what happened to your ex-girlfriend, Maria Benicio?"

"Nothing happened to that whiny bitch. She couldn't handle being with this much man, so she split. No loss."

"We might believe you if she was only your girlfriend, Ray, but that's not what we heard." Andre shook his head.

"What'd you hear?" Ramond perked up. Interest. Noted.

"A few things here, a few things there," Andre kept it vague. "What we want to know is what *you* say. But keep in mind, we've heard a lot from a lot of people."

"What'd that bitch say I did?"

"We know it wasn't 'all this man,'" I motioned mockingly to him, "that she couldn't handle. Sounds like you were pimping her out to fuel your 'drug habit.'"

Ramond's face grew hard.

"The look on your face says it all," I gloated.

"I don't know what you're talking about." Ramond crossed his arms.

"See, we don't believe that Ray," Andre leaned forward. "We have it on good authority that you were trafficking Maria. Not just from her testimony either, we have a few Johns who are happy to sell you out to get some leniency for their charges."

"You tell me the names of those rat bastards and we'll see how happy they are to sing."

"You gonna send tough, scary cousin Ronaldo after 'em?" I taunted.

"Aww, yeah, about that." Andre gave him an apologetic look. "Ronaldo's already down at County for beating up Maria. He's ready to sing, too. You'd think family ties would be stronger than a plea deal, but I guess not." Andre addressed the last sentence to me, and I smirked and shrugged.

"Son of a bitch!" Ramond shoved his chair over and began pacing his cell.

"What we're saying is we've got your balls in a vice," I smirked.

"You're looking at hard time, my friend. Assaults, witness tampering, human trafficking… But we also know that you're a little fish in a big pond, Ray. We know this is bigger than you and Maria. If you're willing to make a deal yourself, tell us about your bosses, then we might make something happen."

"I don't have no damn bosses."

"Oh, but you do," Andre sighed.

"Not a single woman gets sold in the Clock without the Bianchis's say so. A limp dick like you wouldn't dare go toe-to-toe with them just for a little extra drug money."

Ramond's eyes went wide. Andre suppressed a smile. There it was: Confirmation.

"I don't know what you're talking about," Ramond claimed.

"Faking ignorance isn't going to get you anywhere, my friend," Andre chuckled. "Your only chance at ever seeing daylight again is if you talk."

"Anyone who even thinks about narc-ing on the Bianchis doesn't see anything ever again. Period. Just ask the ferret." Ramond scoffed. "Good luck."

Ferret? I fought the muscles in my cheek to avoid a grin. Ramond was giving away more than he should. Sounds like Ferret was about to flip on the Bianchis and lost his head for it. He must have known something important to get the headless treatment from the penanggalan.

"We don't need luck, Ray. We've got witnesses," Andre smiled.

"Bullshit."

"The Bianchis are going down," I promised. "If you want to go down with them, that's fine by me." I started to walk away. "Let's go, Andre. This cowardly piece of shit isn't important enough to know anything we need. Let's release him back onto the streets and let the Bianchis think he squealed."

Andre rose, but Ramond called out to stop me.

"Yo, wait, wait, wait," he begged.

"You got something to say?" Andre asked.

Ramond hesitated.

"You gotta cut me a break."

"That depends entirely on what you're offering." Andre sat back down. I strode back over and leaned against the wall.

"If, and I mean if, I knew something about the Bianchis, how do I know I wouldn't end up headless like a former snitching associate of mine?"

My ears perked up. He had to mean Ferret. Ramond knew a lot more than we originally thought he did.

"We've got ways of keeping you safe. But you've got to cooperate or we're happy to let you reap what you've already sewn," Andre said.

Ramond paced his cell for a few more minutes. Andre and I let him stew. Silence was one of my favorite weapons against a perp. Make 'em sweat.

"You swear you won't send me back out there?" Ramond finally asked.

"You give us the right information and you'll be too valuable to us to risk your neck like that," I confirmed.

He screwed up his face and sat on his bed. He stared at Andre and I. Andre looked at him with something bordering on amusement. I stared back with indifference.

"Fine," he cracked. "But I want a sweet-ass deal."

"What do you know?" Andre leaned back in his chair.

"I was a runner for the Bianchis. Not drugs, women. Maria was just one bitch in my brood. It only took a few sappy promises, and she did whatever I wanted," he bragged.

My rage flared. It took everything I had not to reach through the bars and strangle him. I took several deep breaths to calm myself.

"How many women?" Andre continued while I bit my tongue.

"Eight for me. Other runners do more, others do less."

"How many runners?"

"I don't fuckin' know! Like six maybe? We don't have picnics together or nothin'."

Anywhere around fifty women, I calculated. Shit. More than we'd clocked.

"How do we know you're telling the truth?" I asked.

"Guess you're gonna have to trust me," he smirked.

"You have any evidence to back up your bullshit?" I raised an eyebrow at him.

"I got plenty of insurance tucked away, if that's what you're askin'."

"Proof?"

"Yeah, proof. Fuck, what do you think I'm stupid or something?"

I shrugged.

"So, what's this buy me?"

"We'll need more than that to get the DA to agree to a deal. Give us something specific we can take to them," Andre explained.

"Here's somethin'. The Bianchis have a way of knowing who's their girls, a way to keep track of 'em. It's the mark of the cherry. Every girl's got one."

My mind flashed back to Leticia. Alexis showed me the anklet Leticia had given her; it was adorned with a small cherry charm. It was solid evidence that corroborated Leticia's testimony. We had them.

I nodded to Andre, and he nodded back.

"We'll see what we can do for you," Andre rose.

"That it?" Ramond was incredulous.

"Like I said, we have to talk to the DA about your deal. We'll be back. Until then, make yourself comfortable."

"You get me somethin' good, and I'll give you something real nice in return. Hard proof, you hear me?" Ramond shouted.

We walked off as he yelled at our backs. Once we were out of the holding area, and far out of earshot, Andre whooped. Despite the cloud hanging over my head, I grinned.

"We got 'em. We got 'em!" Andre enthused.

"He was a lot easier to crack than I thought he'd be."

"I might have laid the foundation for that on our way back to town. A few slip-ups about people going missing and dead bodies around the dock while 'talking to my partner on the phone.' Putting the fear of God in him."

"Well done," I congratulated.

"What can I say?" He popped his collar.

"What other proof do you think he has?" I wondered.

"I guess we won't find out until we bring him a shiny new deal."

"Nothing too shiny. He's still the piece of shit who beat up Maria and put her and a bunch of other women through hell."

"I'll get on the phone with the DA as soon as we get back." Andre pumped his fist. "I can't wait to tell…" He stopped short and glanced at me.

"Tell whoever you want," I feigned nonchalance.

"Think about what I said, Finn," Andre urged. "If we can wrap things up with this case, nail every single of those Bianchi bastards, then the threat goes away. What then? You still going to push Alexis away? Try to repair the damage? Rethink your approach and what it's costing. And selfishly, I miss my friend."

"You make whatever decision you want to make about being friends with Alexis," I sighed, remembering Chloe's angry assertion that Andre asked, 'How high?' when I told him to jump.

"I already have," Andre replied. "But, for the record, I wasn't talking about Alexis. I miss the real Finn. That bastard has grown on me over the years, but I haven't seen him since before I left town. I'd like to see him come back again."

Andre gave me a nod before heading off to call the DA. I watched him go, battling myself once again. If we wrapped the Bianchi case, disassembled it piece by piece, and threw the lot of them in prison, would Alexis be safe? Or would she just be facing more threats from the demons she left behind?

It took a few days of cajoling, but the DA got back to us about a deal for Ramond, hinging on how usable his "proof" turned out to be. Andre and I planned to head back over to the jail in the evening to continue working him.

A string of assaults on 4-block kept us busy all morning. Just as we were about to leave, we got a call from the jail. Andre took the call while I waited for him to wrap up. He listened intently, the smile he had worn slowly slipping off his face.

"He's what?!" Andre asked, eyes wide.

His eyes got wider as he listened to the voice on the line.

"Fuck! We're on our way," Andre slammed the phone. "Ramond's dead. FUCK."

"What?!" I shot up from my desk.

"Guard went by after lunch, and he was unresponsive on the floor. When they opened the door, he was already dead."

"You've gotta be fucking kidding me." I slammed my fist on the table.

"Instead of catching a goddamn break, we just caught another case."

"I gotta see this for myself. Let's go."

When we got to Ramond's cell, his body was face up on the floor. The medical examiner was already there, waiting for us to complete our investigation of the scene. Andre went off to interview the guard who was on duty, and I went into the cell to examine the body. A part of his shirt had been undone, maybe to check for a pulse, but something else caught my eye.

"Trent," I called out to the crime scene photographer. "Come here."

"What's up, boss?" Trent asked.

"There's something here," I motioned to Ramond's chest.

Trent raised his camera while I continued to unbutton Ramond's jail-issued shirt. Beneath the fabric, written in red marker across Ramond's chest, were the words, "Tell the bitch to watch her back." Aside from the clicks of Trent's camera, we both went silent.

"Andre," I called out.

Andre appeared by my side, took one look at Ramond's chest, and swore.

"I'll get on the phone with the detectives in New Mexico right away. We'll make sure Maria gets plenty of extra coverage. Shit," he cursed as he left the cell.

"Whoever Maria is, I hope she has better luck than this poor bastard." Trent shook his head. I glared at him, and he retreated from the cell.

After gathering what evidence I could, I went back to the station, straight into the chief's office. When I told him about Ramond, his fury was evident. He called over to the jail and ripped the jail superintendent a new asshole. Chief wanted the same answer I wanted: How did a prisoner end up dead on our watch?

I went home totally demoralized. We'd gotten a small glimmer of hope that we could finally put the Bianchis away, and it was gone in an instant. Not only was Ramond dead, but now Maria was in danger because the syndicate knew she'd talked. I nursed my injured ego with an entire bottle of whiskey and passed out on the couch.

I woke up with a raging headache, still clutching the empty whiskey bottle. I tossed it aside in disgust and went straight to the bathroom for some painkillers and a hot shower to rinse away the stink of failure and shame. By the time I got out and dressed, I took one look at the clock and swore. I was two hours late for work.

I grabbed my phone and raced down to the Charger, throwing myself into the front seat. I had already missed four phone calls from Andre. After the last call, he'd left me a voicemail.

"We've got another body up by the University. Northwest side near the tree line."

I hurried through the Clock and made my way to 5-block. The crime scene tape was already up and there were almost a dozen cop cars surrounding the area. I flashed my badge and went under the tape, heading for the tree line. The scene was buzzing. Every cop I passed took one look at me and blanched. It annoyed the hell out of me being gawked at for my late-arrival hangover.

I caught sight of Andre talking to the Chief. His face was drawn, almost sickly. When he looked up at me, his eyes were red. My feet carried me faster without me consciously telling them to. The hairs on the back of my neck stood straight up as he watched me approach with a look of dread.

"What do we have?" I asked Andre and the Chief.

"Another body, no head." Chief's features were pinched.

"Shit. So soon after the last? It's escalating."

They both nodded wordlessly.

"Any guess on the identity of the victim?"

They exchanged looks before looking back at me.

"What?" I asked, looking over to where the forensics team was busying themselves around a shape on the ground.

"We're pretty sure we know the identity of the victim based on the clothes she's wearing," Andre's voice wavered.

"She? Female victim this time? Who do you think she is?"

They exchanged strained looks again. The wind picked up and blew across my face. I sniffed the air. My blood ran cold.

"No," I mouthed.

I took off in the direction of the body. No, it couldn't be. Before I could get too close, Andre grabbed me from behind to stop me. I shoved him off me and ran toward the lifeless form on the ground. When I was close enough to make out the details of the body, I skidded to a stop.

The coat.

Her coat.

The same damn coat I had seen a hundred times was wrapped around the headless body. The coat that hugged her hips. The coat Andre teased her about never switching out. The coat with a mended sleeve from the aftermath of the berserker attack. The coat that smelled like honeysuckle.

No. No, no, no. This wasn't real. It wasn't her. It couldn't be.

Panic consumed me. A full-body shiver swept from head to toe. My head and heart we throbbing as I considered the possibility. But my mind rejected it outright.

Andre caught up to me, tears welling in his eyes, just as I pulled out my cellphone. I dialed her phone number and held my breath. The connecting tone sounded at my end. To my horror and utter despair, Alexis's favorite song rang through the trees from the pocket of the lifeless, headless body. My blood went cold.

My knees hit the ground. My phone landed in a shrinking patch of snow, the tone ringing out from my end while Alexis's song haunted the trees from the other. Something inhuman bubbled up from my chest and came out of my mouth in a strangled yell. It tore from my throat.

Again and again and again, I yelled. My tortured shouts could barely give voice to the wrenching torment that wracked my body. Every cell was in pain. Every good thing that existed in the world shattered around me in that moment of endless despair. The heads of every cop were bowed, avoiding my agony.

Andre knelt beside me and wrapped both arms around me. He was crying, shoulders heaving. He was saying something through his tears, but my brain wouldn't process it. All my mind could hold on to was the fact that Alexis was gone. I wanted to claw my way out of my skin. It hurt to breathe. It hurt to think. I wanted to lie down next to her and die, too.

Someone pulled Andre away, then a pair of hands pulled me up and half carried me over to a squad car. They sat me in the passenger seat, my legs collapsed against the running board, head leaning against the door frame. I stared toward Alexis's body. I was repulsed by it and drawn to it at the same time. I wanted to see her face until I remembered she didn't have one anymore. My stomach lurched, and I leaned over and vomited all over the ground at my feet.

I had pushed her away. I left her alone. Now she was gone.

"Briggs... Finn," Chief's voice was husky. "I'm so sorry."

"Alexis." My voice was barely above a whisper.

"I know, son." Chief patted me on the back.

I barely felt it. My body was numb. I felt hollow. Ramond's glassy stare from yesterday popped into my mind.

"It wasn't Maria," I choked out.

"What?" Chief raised his head to look at me.

"The warning on Ramond..." My vision blurred.

"Tell the bitch to watch her back," Andre's voice was empty, horrified.

"It was Alexis," I sobbed. "It was Alexis."

Chapter Twenty-Six

Alexis

With everything that had happened this year, my studies were seriously suffering. I'd spoken with my professors about my injury, the stress of my job, and they were incredibly understanding. As I walked out of the education building, I felt a little better. One of my first midterms was this morning, and it had gone well. I was hopeful things were back on track.

As I walked to the bus stop, I noticed a crowd of students gathered at the North end of campus. My curiosity piqued, I followed the hurrying feet of my fellow students and wound up at the edge of the smattering of woods. Familiar yellow crime scene tape was wrapped in a wide perimeter around the entire area. I scanned the crowd of police officers for a familiar face. One of the rookies I recognized was standing near the perimeter, holding back the onslaught of curious college students.

"Hey Tran," I called, pushing my way through the crowd. "What's going on?"

"Alexis, hey," he greeted. "Hell if I know. We've been here all morning. There was a big hubbub a few hours ago, sounded real bad, but nobody's told me nothing. They told me to keep out the riffraff." He motioned to the gathering crowd.

"Does that include me?"

"You convinced Chief to switch out the old coffee pot for one of those fancy coffee pod things, so you can get away with damn near anything in my book." Tran lifted the tape for me to pass under.

"Thanks, Tran, you're the best."

I walked tentatively along the grass, scanning the scene, trying to figure out what could have brought what seemed like the entire Beckburg police force to one crime scene. It had to be massive. Something with the Bianchis, maybe?

Over to my left, near a group of squad cars, a fight was breaking out. I stopped to watch and realized it was Andre scuffling with Finn. Finn was ashen-faced and screaming something, trying to fight his way out of Andre's clutching arms. The Chief was grappling with them, trying to get them under control. What the hell could have gotten Finn so riled up? He looked feral.

Half annoyed, half worried, I stalked over to knock some sense into both of them. This was no way to behave at a crime scene. As I approached, Finn was yelling something about finding and killing the son of a bitch who did this. They were all so consumed by the scuffle that they didn't even see me stop a few yards away.

"What the hell is going on here?" I demanded.

All three of them fell completely silent. Their heads whipped around in my direction in perfect unison. They looked like someone had slapped them.

"What?" I asked.

"Alexis?" Finn squeaked out. His face was white as a sheet.

His gaze shifted over to his left at the trees, then back to me. I raised my eyebrows at him. He pushed off Andre and ran straight at me. I braced myself, thinking he was going to attack me too, but when his body slammed against mine, he pulled me into a rib-crackingly tight embrace.

"Holy shit, holy shit," he breathed. "It's you. Oh, my God. Holy shit."

"Finn, what the hell?" The hug muffled my voice against his chest.

He pulled me away from him, just far enough that he could look down into my face. His eyes searched my features hungrily. The shadows of the beast I knew lay within him crossed his expression. His eyes were wet and rimmed with red. Once he saw what he was looking for in my features, he pulled me tight against him again.

"My siren…" Finn crooned, his body shaking against mine. "You're alive. Thank God! I can't believe you're here. You're safe. I'm never letting you out of my sight again. You're alive." His voice was thick with emotion.

I pushed against him gently, worried that something in him had cracked. He refused to let me get far. Eyes devouring me, hands clutching. Andre was standing next to us, tears streaming down his cheeks. He was smiling and crying at the same time.

"What is happening?" I asked, bewildered.

"We thought you were dead," Andre's voice caught on the last word.

"Why would you think I was dead?"

"We found a body." Andre jerked his head to the left. "She was wearing your coat. She has your phone."

My coat?

My coat!

My heart crashed to the bottom of my feet.

"No," I breathed.

I struggled to free myself from Finn's embrace, but he held me back. I needed to see it for myself. If my coat was on the body…

"Let me go, Finn," I pleaded.

"You don't need to see that," Finn argued.

"I have to! I have to see her face."

"You can't," Andre helped Finn restrain me.

"I have to!" I repeated.

Finn took my face in his hands and made me look at him. The sorrow in his gaze was immense. "There isn't a face to see, Allie."

His statement didn't make sense to me. I had to see her face to be sure it wasn't her. Or that it was her. I wasn't sure which. But if she didn't have a face… I looked around me, the gravity of the scene sinking in. Nearly the entire department… Only one thing would merit this kind of response: the Bianchis. And the last two dead bodies they had found connected with the Bianchis didn't have…

"Oh God," I moaned. My legs gave way. Finn lowered me to the ground before I could fall.

"Do you know who it is, Lex?" Andre knelt beside me.

"It's Selsha," I sobbed.

"The sex worker you talked to before your attack?" Chief finally spoke up. He looked like he'd aged ten years since I last saw him.

I nodded.

"I'll go run her info." Chief walked toward the collection of squad cars.

"Why was she wearing your coat? And your phone?" Finn demanded. "We thought it was you!"

"I gave her my coat this morning," I explained. "She was leaving the Clock, getting away from the work they were making her do, and she came to say goodbye to me. She was shivering, and she told me that the Bianchis stole her coat and wouldn't give it back. But she couldn't take waiting anymore. So, I gave her mine. I was in a hurry to get to an exam, so I must have forgotten my phone in the pocket. I should have stayed with her. God, no… Selsha…"

Finn's eyes went wide. "The Bianchis stole her coat? Are you sure?"

"Yes, she was so upset about it. It must have meant so much to her. When she first told me she was a sex worker, she said her bosses took something from her and wouldn't give it back unless she worked for them."

"Fuck," Finn swore.

"What is it, Finn?" Andre asked.

Finn dropped his voice low. "Selsha was a selkie."

"What?!" Andre looked over his shoulder toward the woods. "How do you know?"

"I knew a colony of selkies when I lived in Scotland a couple hundred years ago. I know their scent. When Alexis pointed her out to me at the Christmas party, I could smell it on her."

"What's a selkie?" I asked.

"It's a type of Fae; they're seals, but they can remove their coats and take human form when they want to go on land," Finn explained.

"And if the Bianchis took her coat, she'd do anything they asked to get it back." Andre added.

"I don't understand." I stared between the two of them.

"A selkie can't turn back into their true form without their coat. They trapped her in her human form without it. Whoever had her coat could control everything about her," Finn went on. "Withholding a coat from a selkie is barbaric. They belong in the sea with their families. If they're on land too long, it can become excruciating for them, physically painful, to be away. It's torture," Finn replied.

"And that cements our Fae connection with the Bianchis. They sent the berserkers out, they're controlling the penanggalan, and they were withholding a coat from a selkie. They have to be Fae, Finn." Andre frowned.

"How are we supposed to manage that?" Finn shook his head.

"We'll figure that out later." Andre helped Finn lift me to my feet. "You need to get Alexis out of here. Whether that hit was meant for Selsha or not, you were probably right about the threat on Ramond."

"But Selsha," I argued.

"We'll take care of her. I'll see to it myself. I promise." Andre hugged me. It was harder than usual with Finn refusing to let me go, but he didn't seem to mind having to hug us both to manage the feat. "Go on."

"You don't have to tell me twice." Finn pulled me away from the scene.

I didn't fight as he walked me out of the trees, across the grass, and under the crime scene tape. The numbness was already creeping in. He tucked me into the passenger seat of the Charger with one last desperate look at my face. I closed my eyes against the reality that my friend was dead. Not just dead, slaughtered. The thought that she had spent the last year or more of her life in constant agony without her coat was heart-wrenching. Who could be so cruel?

The moment Finn took the driver's seat, he grabbed hold of my hand. His breath was labored, and his grip was tight. I could feel him shaking. For weeks, he had ignored me. Now he was acting like I would disappear into thin air if he stopped touching me. I kept my eyes closed for the entire ride, not ready to face him.

Selsha was gone. I should have stayed with her. I was in such a rush to get to my test; afraid a delay would spin me out further in my schoolwork. She was clearly afraid when I stepped off the bus and found her waiting for me at the bus stop. I could feel her shaking when I embraced her. She was leaving, she said, and she wanted to say goodbye. She was going to be near her family. Now I knew why she had only said 'near' instead of 'with.' She had no way to be with her family without her coat, and the Bianchis would never have relinquished it to her. It was too painful to think about. I shoved it to the back of my mind, tucked it away where I could pretend that my friend had made it safely home to her family.

"Alexis," Finn whispered.

I opened my eyes and looked at him. His expression was tortured. The grief still lingered in his face. My heart gave a squeeze. Regardless of how angry and betrayed I felt still, I hated to see him in pain.

"I know you hate me." Finn's voice was low and intense. "I don't even care that you do. Even if you hate me for the rest of your life, I'm so fucking grateful that you're still here." He swallowed hard. "You have no idea…"

Finn looked away. He swallowed several times, struggling to continue. When he turned back to me, a tear was making its way down his cheek. I reached up to wipe it away. He turned into my hand, burying his cheek in my palm, and closing his eyes.

"I thought you were dead," he croaked. "For two miserable, godforsaken hours, I thought you were dead." His shoulders heaved.

"I'm still here," I whispered.

Finn doubled over and wept. I imagined how I would feel if our positions were reversed; if I had been convinced that they murdered him and saw what I thought was his mutilated body right in front of my eyes. My whole body rejected the image. Bile rose in my throat. Despite his behavior over the past weeks, I knew exactly how it would affect me. It would rip my heart out of my chest.

I leaned over the center console and held him. He was shaking as he cried. His whole body was wracked with his sobs. My tears slid down my cheeks and peppered the back of his white-collared shirt. I don't know how long we sat like that.

When his wave of grief subsided, he sat up and pulled me over the center console into his lap. He cradled me like a child, just like he had when he came to comfort me the night my demons came to devour me. His fingers laced their way through my hair, and he inhaled. It felt like he was drinking me in. God, how I had missed his warmth.

"I won't leave you again," he vowed. "Ever."

He nudged my face upward with his nose, and chin until our faces were inches apart. His eyes were burning. I felt a warm flood roll through my chest.

"I'm in love with you," Finn admitted.

The warmth from my chest radiated out into the rest of my body.

"I have been so damn in love with you for so long that it feels like you're a part of me," he continued. "I've been a fucking idiot. But I swear to you, I thought I was doing the right thing. Everything I've done since that damn camping trip has been to keep you safe. I'm fucking miserable without you. I love you, little siren."

I licked my lips, a rush of emotions going through me. These were the exact words I had longed to hear since I held his hand in the hospital after he was shot. But the pain of the last few weeks was still raw under the surface.

"Please say something," Finn begged.

"Damn you, Finn Briggs," I muttered, shaking my head. "I've been rehearsing the ass-chewing I was going to give you for weeks and you say something like that."

A smile perked up at the corner of his mouth.

"You are a complete asshole. I knew it from the moment I met you."

His growing smile faltered.

"But… you're *my* asshole." I touched his face. "You are not a perfect man, Briggs. But you stick fiercely to what you think is right. I can't fault you for that, and I never will. I don't want to be without you. Even when you're being an impossible, stubborn dick, I want you. You are my best friend. And I love you, too."

Finn laughed once, another tear rolling down his cheek. His voice was thick with relief. He pulled my face to his and kissed me. It was deep and soulful. Our lips fell into a familiar rhythm. I felt those hard feelings I'd been nursing lighten a bit.

"Let's go inside." Finn pushed open the door and helped me to my feet.

He had taken me to his apartment. He laced his fingers through mine as he brought me up to his place. He checked and double checked the locks before pulling me onto his lap on the couch.

"Whatever else you need to say to me, I want you to say it now." He brushed my hair out of my face. "Let's get everything out, because after this, I want to surrender to you completely."

I took a deep breath. "You left me," I stated simply.

"I did." His eyes were sad.

"Then you convinced my friends to stay away, too." The regret was all over his face, but he didn't interrupt me. "It was the loneliest I have ever felt. Regardless of the reasons you may have had, you took so much away from me."

"I can't imagine what that felt like. You need to know that everyone hated me for it. They love you and I convinced them the same way I convinced myself that it was for your protection."

"You can't decide what's best for me without consulting me. It's completely unfair."

"You're right," Finn nodded. "I should have respected your perspective. I acted out of fear, and it clouded my judgment. It's no excuse, but I have never been so afraid of losing someone. I've watched thousands of people in my acquaintance die in a thousand ways, but thinking about what almost happened to you with the berserkers sent me over the edge."

"I understand." I dragged my thumb across his cheekbone, wiping another tear. "But now that you know about my past, I hope you can understand why I can't live life in a place of fear. I did that for almost a year after my attack, and it gutted me. When I first came to the Clock, fear was all I had. Then, I found you… all of you. You helped me feel safe again. Being part of this family that you've created here made me remember my strength and helped me come back to myself. The fear is still there sometimes, but I don't want to let it rule me. Not again."

"I should have talked to you. I know I have control issues, but it was unacceptable what I did. After that night with you in the hospital, I finally had to be honest with myself about how I felt about you. You weren't just my best friend anymore. Hell, it would have been torture enough to come that close to losing you if you were only my best friend. But thinking about losing my best friend and the woman I love rolled into one was…" He shuddered.

I could feel the depth of his conviction as he explained. I still didn't condone his choice, but I understood it. There was one more thing I needed to know.

"If we do this," I motioned between us, "Then I need to know that something like that will never happen again. If it does, no matter how much I love you, I have to walk away. I owe it to myself."

"I swear to every God." Finn grasped my face in both hands. "So long as I live, I will never push you away like that again. I don't think I would survive it if I tried. It was almost literally tearing me in two."

My heart surged. I could never doubt him with the look on his face. I nestled deeper into his arms.

"What do you mean, it almost tore you in two?"

"My wolf was very unhappy with me for pulling away." He shook his head.

"Your wolf?"

"Being a shifter means being of two minds; human and beast. It's like when you say, 'A part of me wants this, but another part of me wants that.' My wolf has a drive of its own. It's both me and not me at the same time. It's hard to describe."

"So, you and your wolf sometimes want different things," I clarified.

"Very different things," he chuckled. "Like when we went camping, my wolf was infatuated with you. The woods are a source of magic. That's why Riel came to the Clock. Going there reconnects us to that magic, rejuvenates us, it's why we go camping so much."

"Like kids in a candy store," I laughed, remembering their unrestrained joy.

"Exactly. My wolf is more powerful in the woods, surrounded by that ancient magic. I couldn't stop thinking about you the entire time we were camping." Finn ran his fingers slowly up my arm. It gave me goosebumps. "My human logic kept trying to keep things platonic, but my wolf is all instinct: protection, consumption… desire." His eyes burned through me. "The real reason I kept my distance was because I was trying to keep my wolf under control." He smiled, his eyes far away while he reminisced. Then he burst out laughing.

"What's so funny?" I pulled his arm tighter around my waist.

"You're going to hate me," he chuckled.

"Been there, done that." I rolled my eyes. "Tell me anyway."

"The second morning we were there, I mean first thing in the morning, when we were all waking up… I heard you…" Mischief flashed across his face.

"You heard me…?" I scanned my memory, trying to remember the day he was referring to, but nothing came to mind.

"In your tent…" he hinted.

"In the morning…" I racked my brain.

"In that very noisy sleeping bag," he pressed.

It hit me.

"Oh God," I groaned.

"Oh God indeed," Finn barked a laugh.

"You heard me…"

"Taking matters into your own hands," Finn finished for me. "Yes, siren, I did. And with these heightened senses of mine, I could smell it, too."

"You're kidding me." I covered my face in shame. "Was it bad?"

"No, siren, it was the opposite." He tried pulling my hands away from my face. "You smell like honeysuckle. When you're aroused, the scent intensifies. I can smell your pheromones and when you were touching yourself, it was so intense I could taste it. It drove me wild." His voice was low and gravelly.

I peeked through my fingers at him. He was looking at me with a mix of humor and desire. He licked his lips.

"What were you thinking about while you were doing it?" he asked, his hand sneaking below the hem of my shirt and finding the skin of my waist.

"You weren't the only one who was having less-than-platonic thoughts during the camping trip," I admitted. "It was your fault!" I playfully pushed his chest. His touch on my skin was sparking goosebumps all over my body.

"How was it my fault?"

"Your little striptease at the pond got it started, then I kept having… dreams about you."

"Well, I can take credit for the stripping, but you can thank Andre for the dreams. At least the first night, until I got on his ass about it."

"Oh, God, I forgot he could do that." I shook my head.

"He did it to me, too," Finn admitted. "I was just quieter about the aftermath than you were," Finn smirked. "Although… I heard you masturbating after the second night. Did you still dream about me after Andre laid off?" His fingers slid across my side to my stomach, skimming along the top of my jeans. I sighed.

"Yes." My cheeks felt hot. "I guess I didn't need Andre's twisted form of 'help' after all."

"I guess you didn't." Finn took my chin between his fingers and pulled my face to his. "Do you want to tell me what you dreamed about?"

"You, me, fur blankets, and the best sex of my dream life."

"Hmmm," he licked his lips again. "What if I told you it took everything that I had to stop myself from coming into your tent and making that dream a reality?"

I felt heat rush through my whole body. A tingling ache awoke between my legs. I slid one arm around his neck and my other hand slipped up the back of his head into his hair.

"I'd say I would have welcomed the intrusion."

"What a waste," he lamented with a sly smile. "All this time, I could have been worshipping you, wasted."

"We don't have to waste any more time now," I nudged.

"God, my little siren, how I've wanted to hear you say something just like that."

Finn stood abruptly from the couch, making me squeal with surprise as he scooped me in his arms. He carried me into his bedroom and threw me playfully on the bed. I scrambled back to sit up against the headboard.

"Redo," he smirked, unbuttoning his shirt quickly, tossing it to the side.

He grabbed the back of his undershirt and dragged it, discarding it as well. I watched him hungrily. His belt came next, falling to the floor with a clatter. Then his pants. When he was down to nothing but the same pair of maroon boxer briefs from the pond, he paused.

"Kismet," I chuckled, pointing at his underwear.

"It's like the Fates themselves destined it." Finn winked.

He came to the foot of the bed and crawled up from the bottom over my body, like the predator I knew he was inside. He nuzzled his face against my neck and sniffed. He looked me in the eye and licked his lips.

"Honeysuckle," he growled.

His lips crashed down on mine. I put one arm around his neck and the other grasped his bare back. I pressed my fingers hard against his skin, pulling him closer to me. His tongue slid past my lips, meeting my own. I swirled my tongue around his, then playfully pushed it back out of my mouth. He grinned against my lips. It was my turn to slip the tip of my tongue into his mouth, running it slowly against the underside of his top lip. He pressed me back against the headboard.

He knelt over me, one knee on either side of my hips. Both hands slipped under my shirt to claim the skin of my sides. I shoved him over to a sitting position and straddled him instead. He studied me with a mix of surprise and intrigue.

"Redo," I whispered.

I pulled my shirt slowly over my head, my hair falling gently against my back and around my shoulders as I did. I threw it to the floor and bit my lip as I stared straight into Finn's hungry eyes. He drank in the sight of me in my black lace bra. His hands settled on my hips, clutching me closer to his groin. I settled my weight on his lap and could feel his erection straining against his boxer-briefs. I could feel the wetness growing in my panties.

"It's not red, but it's not bad," Finn teased, staring at my bra.

"Unlike you, I have more than one pair of underwear."

He pushed me backwards off his lap onto my back, cushioning the back of my head with his hand.

"That's not true and you know it," he growled playfully. "You know more about my underwear than anyone on Earth, since you had to dress me."

He hovered over me, running his fingers from my neck, down between my breasts, all the way to my stomach. The touch was fire and ice. His hand made its way to my jeans, unbuttoning and unzipping them in a flash. His gaze only left my face to glance at my underwear. He groaned as he stared at the matching black panties I wore.

He pulled back, resting on his knees again, and slowly slid my jeans off my hips and legs. Tossed aside like the rest of our clothes, he ran a hand up each leg, stopping before he got to my hipbones, his thumbs tracing the insides of my thighs. It made my whole body quiver.

"God, I want you," he whispered.

"Do you?"

"More than I've wanted anything else in five centuries," he growled, lowering his face to my stomach.

He pressed his tongue against the skin above my navel and dragged it up to the bottom of my bra. When he stopped, he kissed and sucked at the spot. He exhaled against my skin.

"God, baby, you taste so good," he sighed.

"I do?" I was suddenly self-conscious, remembering his heightened senses.

"Incredible," he assured. "I want more."

He peeked up at me through his lashes before pressing his mouth against my stomach once more. He licked and kissed his way around my stomach and sides. I laced my fingers in his hair, clutching him while I sighed my pleasure. He roamed his way down to the top of my panties, then looked up at me with a frown.

"What?" I asked.

"This is getting in my way," he pouted, biting his lip, slipping one solitary finger over the top of my panties. His eyes were wild, pleading.

Words betrayed me, so I nodded my consent shyly. He grinned wolfishly at me. Instead of pulling them down with his hands, he skimmed his teeth against my left hipbone and grabbed the fabric with his teeth. My panties slid off at his command, his nose skimming behind in their wake, all the way down my legs. Only once they were off me did he take them in his hand, twirling them victoriously around on the tip of his finger before he sling-shotted them across the room. He stared, drinking me in.

His hands traveled up my legs once more, spreading them further apart, his eyes locked on me laid bare before him. He licked his lips, centering himself between my legs, then sliding each arm under my legs and grasping my hips. I was panting with anticipation when he looked up at me. The wild expression he wore made the heat in my core spike. He pressed his lips against the inside of my thighs, making me tense against the tickling of his scruff.

"I like it when you do that," he hummed against my skin.

He kissed and licked his way from one thigh to the other, grazing his lips over my tender center, but not quite making the connection yet. It was driving me wild. I clutch at the back of his head, pulling him toward me, desire driving every move.

"Do you want me, little siren?"

"Yes," I panted.

"Beg me for it," he raised an eyebrow at me.

"Please, Finn." I ran my fingers through his hair. "I want you."

The plea did its job. Finn pulled my hips toward him with a possessive tug, his mouth sinking into me. His warm tongue found my clit in an instant, and I moaned. I arched my back, bringing his face against me. He licked and sucked me, sending bolts of pleasure through my body. His entire focus went to consuming me. My body pulsated with the rhythm of his movements. I draped both legs over his shoulders as he continued to pull at my hips.

"God, yes," I moaned. "Oh, Finn…"

His tongue moved slowly back and forth against my clit. The pressure was building inside me. He was relentless in his pursuit.

"Don't stop," I begged.

He clutched my hips harder, his pace never wavering as I built. My breath came in quick gasps. He sucked and stroked with expert precision.

"Oh God, I'm going to come," I moaned.

He grunted, and his fingers dug into my sides. I arched my back harder, tipping my head back. The moment of unstoppable release came, and my orgasm rocked me. I gasped and moaned as I rode the wave of the pleasure that he'd coaxed out of me. Not once did he stop his perfect performance as I came. It wasn't until my panting slowed and my grip on his hair faltered that he came up for air. He was grinning triumphantly.

"You have quite the high opinion of yourself, Finn Briggs," I scolded playfully.

"Am I wrong to?" He crawled up from between my legs, kissing and licking up my body as he did.

"I refuse to answer that question on account of it feeding your ego."

He grinned at me.

"God, I could feast on you all day, Allie," he nuzzled against my neck. "You taste sweeter than I ever imagined. And I imagined a lot," he chuckled.

"I bet you did." I ran my fingers down his muscled arm.

"Did I satisfy you, little siren?" He whispered in my ear.

"Not completely."

He pulled back to look at me with surprise. I laughed at the scandal on his face. The side of his mouth pulled up in a grin, determination filling his features.

"Challenge accepted," he growled, wrapping his arms around my waist and pulling me on top of him.

I straddled his hips, my chest pressed against his, and our mouths connected once more. His lips were hungrier than ever. One of my arms snaked around his neck while the other drifted down between us. My hand explored his muscular chest, down his hard stomach, and slipped beneath the band of his underwear. I found what I was looking for. His hard, full cock was waiting for me. The second my fingers slid down its length, Finn pulled away from my mouth and gasped. It was my turn to grin victoriously.

"Your touch is amazing, baby," he crooned. "Oh God, touch me more."

My lips came back down on his and we kissed passionately as I stroked his cock. He was long and thick, making me dripping wet with anticipation. When I slid my hand lower, cupping his balls, he moaned loudly into my mouth.

"Do you like that, love?" I whispered huskily, gripping him.

"Yes, siren," he moaned, his hands gripping my bare ass. "Uh, you're making me so hard."

"I want to see you," I pulled away from him.

He tried to pull me back down, but I swatted his hands away. I used my free hand to pull down the top of his underwear and pulled his cock out with the other. I bit my lip as I took in his size. He stared up at me with desire and pride.

"Is the ego still warranted?" His eyes danced.

"All of your cockiness suddenly makes sense. Pun intended."

He laughed.

I pulled his underwear the rest of the way off. I lay back down against his chest, my hand still working his length. He pulled my mouth to his once more and kissed and bit my lower lip. His hands skimmed up my back and started working my bra strap. It didn't take long before I felt it release. He slid the straps off my shoulders. I sat back once more, letting my bra slide down my arms.

"Fuck," Finn breathed. "You are the most beautiful thing I have ever seen."

His eyes raked my body, hands sliding up to cup my breasts. His hands kneaded my breasts gently, fingers trapping my nipples. He rolled my nipples as I hovered over him, pulling at his cock. The sensation sent sparks through my core.

He sat up, one arm circling my waist in a tight hold. He held his other hand briefly around my throat, tipping my head back toward the ceiling. Then that hand trailed down to my right breast. He massaged it while he kissed my neck. Then his lips and tongue trailed down to my left breast. He took my nipple into his mouth and sucked. I sighed. His tongue flicked against it, heightening the glorious sensation. He alternated between flicking and sucking at my nipple while his other hand grasped at my other breast. I continued to work his cock with both hands. We were both gasping and panting as we touched each other.

"The way you touch me," Finn huffed. "It sends fire through me. I don't want you to ever stop. God, siren."

His hand left my waist and passed by where I was massaging his cock. He pressed his palm against me, slipping two fingers inside me. I gasped, but started moving my hips, rubbing against his palm.

"That's my girl," he coaxed. "Come for me again."

His fingers dug deeper inside me, moving in a come-hither motion until he found my G-spot. I let out a high-pitched yip, and he chuckled. Heat flooded my cheeks.

"Don't be embarrassed, baby," he crooned. "I love every sound."

He brought my mouth to his and kissed me passionately. His tongue went back to work against my lips and in my mouth. He pulled his hand away from my breast and put it on the small of my back, helping to move me against his other hand. He released my mouth and pulled back with a smile. I tried to kiss him, but he pulled back out of my reach.

"I want to watch you this time," he teased. "I want to see the look on your face as I make you come."

I redoubled my efforts against his hand. I was still gripping his hard cock, using it more for leverage than pleasure now. His fingers were so deep inside me, moving so deliciously that I couldn't help the sounds that came out of my mouth.

"You're so wet for me, siren," he praised. "Fuck, you are so sexy. Every inch of you is perfect. God, I fucking want you. Come for me like a good girl," he coaxed.

The praise was all it took. I threw my head back and came hard. What came out of me was more of a yell than a satisfied groan. I closed my eyes.

"No, baby, don't close your eyes." Finn put a hand against my cheek. "Look at me while you come."

I did as I was told, locking eyes with him. The intensity that sparked between us as I rode his hand was palpable. I could taste his desire and satisfaction in the air around us. His eyes were dark fire as he reveled in his glory.

I collapsed back on the pillows the second my orgasm abated, trying to catch my breath. Finn hovered over me once more, grinning. I smiled back up at him and pulled his mouth down on mine. He kissed me slowly, leisurely. I spread my legs, pulling him down closer to me. He responded wordlessly, moving his legs to fill the space between mine.

"I need you inside me, Finn," I whispered against his lips.

He moaned. "I want to bury myself so deep inside you that I never come back out," he growled. "But I can't promise it will be gentle." His mouth curled into a smirk.

"Who said anything about gentle?" I seduced, lifting my knees to his sides, my hands resting on his ass.

"Are you sure you're ready for me?" He was panting.

It was taking massive effort for him to restrain himself. He was all eagerness. One arm was propping him up, the other was clutching my left hip. I brushed my finger against the faint scar from the bullet wound on his shoulder.

"Take me, Finn. I'm yours."

He groaned at the invitation, sliding his cock inside me in one fluid, passionate motion. I moaned as he filled me up. He pushed himself deep inside me and paused, panting. His eyes drank in my face. He smiled and kissed my forehead.

"I love you," he vowed.

"I love you, too," I breathed. "Now show me."

Chapter Twenty-Seven

Finn

Alexis was tight and warm around my cock. Being inside her was like coming home. I moved my hand to grasp the back of her neck. The way she was looking at me made me feel like the luckiest bastard in the world.

I rocked my hips back and forth, moving inside her. I started slowly, but a desperation was building inside me. It made me move faster, harder, consuming her, consuming me. She wrapped her legs around me and lifted her hips to meet my thrusts. We moved together in perfect unison, both gasping, both moaning, bodies slick with sweat. The more I moved inside her, the greater my need for her grew.

Alexis pulled at my arm, leveraging me onto my back, rolling over on top of me. She settled her weight on top of me, grinding against me. I settled back into the pillows, watching her move. Her body was poetry. I couldn't stop touching her.

She pressed her hands into my chest, pinning me down. She smiled at me and my already pounding heart did a flip. I sat up, wrapping my arms around her, needing to be closer to her. We kissed, and she ran her nails gently down my back. It gave me shivers.

I moved my mouth to her neck, licking and sucking the spot over her jugular. I could taste her so acutely at that spot. My wolf was alive inside me, triumphant, giving greater need to every touch. Alexis rode my cock, our limbs tangled together. The walls of her pussy clenched around me as she lifted and lowered her body in my lap. I slipped a hand into her hair, pulling gently to expose her throat to me. I trailed my tongue from the hollow of her neck up to her chin, pressing a kiss there once I arrived. She sighed contentedly.

"I love you, Alexis," I whispered in her ear.

"I love you, Finn," she whispered in mine. She sucked my earlobe into her mouth, and I growled throatily.

"Are you growling at me, or is that your wolf?"

"We both like that," I replied.

"What else do you like?" Her voice was smoky, breathless from exertion.

"Being with you."

"You're already with me."

"That's all I ever wanted."

"Now you have me, I'll let you ask for a little more," she sucked my earlobe again.

"Stay with me." My voice became husky with emotion. "Always."

She pulled away to look at me. Her eyes were soft and glistening. She sank into my lap, my cock settling achingly deep inside her. Then she stopped moving.

"I may not live to be five hundred years old, but whatever years I have left, I want to spend them with you."

I held her face tenderly, pulling her mouth to mine. I kissed her softly, my lips just grazing hers. My lips traced along her face, down her neck. Between every kiss, I whispered, "I love you."

Her body resumed its motion against mine. I maneuvered our bodies back down to the bed, Alexis on her back, me on top once again. My lips claimed hers possessively, the need growing inside me once more. I lifted one of her legs, adjusting her position so I could plunge deeper and deeper inside her. My hips rolled against her, my breaths coming in huffs. I felt myself building deep in the base of my cock.

We locked eyes. I drank in the sight of her, ecstasy written all over her face. Her hands gripped my biceps as I worked. My muscles tensed and I had to force myself to slow down, calm the frenzy inside me, and enjoy the moment. But I couldn't slow the building pressure. My face contorted, and I came. I grunted and moaned as my orgasm rocked through me. The all-consuming pleasure traveled all the way down to my feet. I continued to thrust inside Alexis and then heard her cry out, too. Worried that I had hurt her, maybe forgotten my strength and let go too much, I touched her face. But she was smiling at me.

"Did you…?" I panted.

"Yes," she chuckled, brushing my hair back from my face.

"Again?"

"Again," she confirmed.

I collapsed next to her, throwing my arm around her waist. My mind was blissfully clear. I breathed hard into the pillows, trying to catch my breath. Alexis rolled to her side, and I turned to look at her. She was glowing.

"My God, you're beautiful," I panted.

"You're not bad looking yourself."

I pulled her into my arms and kissed her forehead. My heart was pounding. All the fear, all the worry, and all the stress that had plagued me for months was gone in that moment. Alexis shivered against me. I pulled a blanket from the bottom of the bed and covered us with it.

"Thank you," she whispered.

"You're welcome, little siren." I pressed my lips against her forehead again.

"I guess I can't call you grumpy dragon anymore." She nuzzled my chest.

"Why not?"

"You're still a grumpy bastard sometimes, but I guessed the wrong mythical creature," she explained. "I never would have guessed you were a shapeshifter."

"I like my nickname," I argued. "I want to keep it."

"You don't want to be my grumpy wolf instead?"

"Whatever you want to call me, as long as you call me yours." I kissed the top of her head.

"You are mine." She lifted her face to mine. "And I am hopelessly, ridiculously, yours."

She kissed me slowly, then burrowed back into my arms, her back against my chest. I held her close, reveling in the warmth of her body. My heart rate slowed, but I felt a glorious burning in my chest. She loved me. She was safe. She was mine.

. . . . .

My muscles twitched, pulling me out of my dreamless sleep. Alexis was lying next to me, my body curled around hers. My heart gave a tug as I felt the rhythm of her soft breathing against my chest. I laid a soft kiss on the peak of her shoulder. My nose trailed down the arch of her neck, inhaling as I went. Her sweet scent was mixed with my own musky one. I smiled; it intensely pleased my wolf that we had marked her as our own.

"If I weren't such an understanding woman, the sniffing would get a little creepy," Alexis warned sleepily.

"I can't help myself," I answered, burying my face in her hair. "You're intoxicating."

"I'll take that as a compliment." She rolled over to face me.

"You should." I kissed her.

"What time is it?"

"Who the hell cares?" I pulled her closer.

"Don't you think we should check in?"

"I would prefer to pretend the rest of the world doesn't exist," I frowned. "There's too much shit out there to worry about. All I want to do is lay here with you."

"You are ridiculously charming." She kissed me again.

"It's a crime to pack so much charm into one man." I puffed out my chest. "You are one lucky woman."

I rolled to hover over her. Her soft, brown hair was spread out on the white pillow below her head. She smiled up at me, blinking the sleep away.

"You really are an angel," I beamed.

"You're just saying that because I finally let you see me naked."

"That," I looked her naked body up and down appreciatively, "Was definitely a perk, but I've known you were heaven sent since I saw you only mostly naked."

She pushed me off her, and I laughed loudly at the playful gesture. She swatted me several times before moving to get off the bed.

"Hey, hey, hey," I grabbed her arm. "Where do you think you're going?"

"I'm not allowed to go to the bathroom," she raised an eyebrow.

"I promised not to let you out of my sight." I kissed her fingers.

"I'm not ready to breach that relationship barrier yet. There's nothing sexy about watching a woman pee." She rolled her eyes.

She walked around the side of the bed toward the bathroom.

"But I can certainly enjoy the show as you go." I stared.

She gave me a cheeky wink over her shoulder before disappearing behind the door. I relaxed back against the bed, both hands behind my head. My mind was awash with happiness. It was a stark difference between the way I felt now and the misery I wallowed in only twenty-four hours earlier. The reality of the last few days tried to push its way to the front of my mind, but I fought it off.

The sound of the shower starting in the bathroom was a welcome distraction. I grinned to myself, sliding out of bed and heading for the door. One soft pull proved that Alexis had left it unlocked. I slid it open a crack and glanced in. Alexis was in the shower, running her hands through her wet hair. I immediately got hard watching the water drip down her luscious skin.

I wolf whistled and Alexis looked up at me with a tolerant grin.

"Mind if I join you?"

Her grin widened ever so slightly as she took in my stiff cock.

"It would be my pleasure," she beckoned.

I slid open the shower door and stepped in.

"You bet your fine ass it will," I promised.

I joined her under the hot spray, ducking my head under. She stepped out of the way enough for the both of us to stand beneath the water. I pulled her to me, sliding my hands over her slick ass. She looped her arms around my neck and pressed our bodies together.

"How did you sleep?" I asked.

"Better than I have in a long time. You?"

"Same," I kissed her forehead.

"You talk in your sleep."

"Do I? What did I say?"

"You called for me," she beamed up at me. "Apparently, you did the same thing when you were in the hospital. Linda told me."

"I'm not surprised," I chuckled. "Did I say anything else?"

"That you will do whatever I want, no matter how ridiculous the request, including but not limited to…"

"Liar," I laughed, pushing her against the wall of the shower with a gentle hand.

"It was worth a shot," she shrugged.

I looked her body up and down, biting my lower lip and running my hands through my wet hair. She looked back at me with a challenging, almost defiant expression. She reached out a hand and traced the curves of my chest muscles, exploring my body. With just the tips of two fingers still in contact with my skin, she dragged her touch down the center of my chest, over my abs, and stopped at my navel. I watched her with hungry anticipation. My cock was already throbbing and ready. She spared me one last mischievous glance before following the light trail of hair below my navel and leading into my pubic hair.

My cock strained up to meet her hand. Her feather-light touch ran from the base of my cock all the way to the tip. I bit my lower lip to suppress a moan. Her hand spread wide and wrapped itself around my length, drifting up and down my shaft. I steadied myself against the wall behind Alexis, just over her shoulder. My other hand caressed her face.

"Do you like that?"

"Yes," my voice was gruff.

"I think you'll like this even more."

She kissed my lips lightly. I chased her with my mouth as she pulled back with a smirk. She released my cock, and I gave her a little pout. She laughed once, then grabbed both my hips, lowering to her knees in front of me. My head dropped back, and I sighed, the realization hitting me. My cock gave another throb. I looked down at her and her face was waiting.

"I want you to watch," she purred.

Alexis leaned forward, her hands still on my hips, and her tongue eased its way past her lips. I quivered with anticipation. In an agonizingly slow fashion, her tongue reached the head of my cock, and she swirled it around.

"Oh God," I breathed.

She licked up and down my shaft, holding me in place. I watched with a mix of fascination and desperation. Her licking seemed to last an eternity, the rest of her mouth approaching, then retreating against my head. My entire body tingled, waiting for the moment she would take me into her mouth. The warm spray of the shower on my back heightened the sensation.

Finally, she licked the underside of my head one last time, then slid it into her mouth. Her mouth was warm and wet. She wrapped her lips tightly around my cock, swirling her tongue around the tip. I grabbed the back of her head and let out a deep-throated moan. I wanted to push her head forward, moving myself deeper into her mouth, but I held back. I loved when she took control, and I was eager to see where she would take me.

Grasping my hips, she pulled me forward, taking me deeper. My shaft slid into her mouth and her swirling tongue continued to explore me. She began moving her head back and forth, sucking me hard. Beads of ecstasy exploded over every inch of my body. I ached deep in my core, feeling the preliminary build to my release. I fought the sensation, not wanting this delicious feeling to end in my frenzy. Not yet. I'd waited so long to be with Alexis, I wanted to prolong every moment.

One of her hands left my hip and made its way to my balls. Another jolt of ecstasy. She fondled my balls and sucked up and down my cock. I stared down at her in awe, watching my length disappear and reappear past those beautiful pink lips of hers. She looked up at me through her eyelashes and my knees buckled. I couldn't believe she was mine.

I lost all track of time while she pleasured me, grateful that living in an apartment meant almost unlimited access to hot water. Otherwise, I was sure the spray would have long turned cold against my back. I gently pressed against the back of her head, falling into rhythm with her agonizingly slow movements up and down my cock. Then, with one last tight, hard suck, she pulled back and my cock slipped out of her mouth.

"Oh, fuck," I swore, throwing my head back.

Alexis stood, dragging her hands up the lengths of my legs as she did. I was panting. She was grinning. She kissed me enthusiastically, that expert tongue of hers working its way into my mouth. I devoured her in return, making our kisses deeper.

"How was that?" she crooned, running her hand up the back of my neck into my hair.

"You… are a goddess," I smiled against her lips. "And I'm going to worship you for the rest of my days."

My insatiable hunger took over. I grabbed her below her ass and lifted her up, her legs instinctively wrapping around me. Pressing her back against the wall for leverage, I lifted her up and dropped my own hips, aligning our bodies for the plunge. My tip found her opening, and I thrusted, burying my pulsating cock deep inside her. Our synchronized moans echoed around the bathroom. She was dripping wet and oh, so warm.

She held on around my neck, pulling my face into her collarbone, her head tipped back against the wall. I wrapped one arm around her hips and propped myself against the wall with the other. I wanted to go slow with her, but my body had other plans. The torturously slow way she had sucked me off had turned me ravenous. I pumped in and out of her hard and fast.

"God, Finn," she cried out. "Oh my God, that feels incredible."

My wolf sparked to life. I let out a guttural snarl and slammed into her even harder. I buried my cock all the way to my balls. I could feel every wall of her pussy.

"I made love to you earlier," I whispered in her ear. "And now I'm going to fuck you until you come for me and scream for more."

She clutched me closer to her, another moan rasping from her throat. My mouth found its way to her neck. I kissed, sucked, and bit my way all around her neck and shoulders. My thrusting cock was relentless. I could feel the muscles of her pussy contracting around it, driving me wild with passion. Her wet skin slid against mine so perfectly, reducing the friction and allowing me deeper access inside her.

Then every muscle in her body tensed, and she let out a yell. Every breath was an echoing release as she came rhythmically around my swollen cock. She pulled my hair hard, and I grunted as my head snapped back, mirroring hers.

"Oh my God," she yelled. "God, Finn, fuck! Yes!"

I didn't relent. Not able to see her beautiful face, I focused on the feel of her. I pounded into her pussy, the slapping of our bodies coming together a welcome symphony.

"Fuck me, Finn," she begged. "Fuck me hard."

"Yes, oh fuck yes," I obeyed, fucking her harder and harder. "You take me so well, baby. You take all of me. Take my cock, baby."

My release came quick. I wouldn't have been able to stop myself if I tried. My yell was all animal as I came exploding into her. She tightened her legs around me, pulling me deeper. I pressed her against the wall, burying my cock all the way as it pulsed out my cum. I needed to bury my seed deep inside her. It was pure instinct. Pure wolf. I had to mark her, declare her mine.

We were both panting as I opened my eyes to look at her. Her face was flushed, her chest heaving. My grin was wicked and triumphant. She pulled my mouth to hers and kissed me again. Again, I devoured her. My cock buried deep; my tongue mimicked its depth inside her mouth. Her arms were vice-like around my neck and shoulders, her legs crossed tightly around my waist. I poured myself into her, giving into the need to become one with the woman I loved.

When the wave of intensity subsided for both of us, Alexis slid off my body, reached around me, and turned off the water. I handed her a towel, and we both dried off. I couldn't stop looking at her and, even though we didn't speak, the way she returned my gaze spoke volumes.

"I realized I didn't actually have time to wash anything," Alexis noted.

"That was by far the dirtiest shower of my life," I chuckled, wrapping my arms around her from behind.

"Wanna try again?"

"I don't think anything would get washed if we tried another round," I rumbled in her ear.

"Damn," she fake-sighed. "I guess I won't be getting clean again until I go back to my place."

"Oh, didn't I tell you?" I cocked my head to the side. "You're never going back to your place. You live here now. Forever. With me."

She laughed, and I could feel it against my chest.

"About the color of the walls..." she teased.

"Don't even think about it."

I lifted her off her feet and she squealed. I carried her back into the bedroom and collapsed on the bed with her still in my arms. She pulled me tight around her and kissed my arm. I nuzzled against her neck and breathed her in.

"I know." I stopped her before she could say it. "Creepy. But you'll have to get used to it. Your scent calms me. Grounds me."

"No, not creepy," she corrected. "It feels nice to be loved like this."

"Good. Are you happy, little siren?"

"Yes, very."

"I'm never going to let you go, Alexis," I breathed. "You're my happiness."

"I missed you so much, grumpy dragon. The world was grey without you in it."

"We'll never have to be without each other again. I promise."

Chapter Twenty-Eight

Alexis

We cuddled in bed for hours, talking almost nonstop, totally lost in one another. Time didn't exist for us. It wasn't until Finn's stomach growled loudly that we made any attempt to extricate ourselves from the bedsheets. I risked a glance at the clock when we entered the kitchen; it was five a.m. I slipped on Finn's white dress shirt and buttoned it with a cheeky grin.

"It looks better on you than it does on me," Finn said. "And that's saying something."

"I think it looks better off you than on you." I ran a hand down his bare chest.

"All this is all yours." He pulled me into a quick kiss before putting his underwear on.

I made us omelets for an early breakfast. Finn never strayed far while I puttered around the kitchen. Most of the time I spent at the stove, his arms wrapped around my waist, his head alternating between resting on the top of my head and nuzzled against my neck. After the weeks of distance, we were both craving nothing but closeness. When I tried to sit in the chair next to him at the table, he shook his head and pulled me onto his lap. Eating was a challenge that way, but we were both more content.

After we ate our fill, we gravitated back to the bed. After sleeping most of the day away yesterday, I wasn't particularly tired, but I found so much comfort tangled up with Finn that I didn't feel like being anywhere else. Anytime the pain of what was happening outside the walls of Finn's apartment popped up, I would bury my face in Finn's chest. Each time it happened, Finn would sense it and wordlessly comfort me. I could feel the weight of all my fears hovering around the edges of the safe, happy bubble we had momentarily created together. I wanted to prolong as long as possible the crushing blow it would be to face reality. One worry snuck its way through.

"Finn?"

"Hmmm?" he murmured, kissing the tip of my nose.

I had wrapped us up under a soft faux fur blanket. Finn had been relaxing with his eyes closed and I had been reading a book I'd started while I was caring for him after his gunshot wound. In the book, there was a character who reminded me forcefully of a certain bitch we knew.

"Why were you cozying up next to Milani?"

His eyes opened, and he frowned.

"I was trying to get you to think you meant nothing to me," he admitted. "I thought if I broke your heart, you'd leave the Clock. Honestly, I just wanted you away from the Fae and the Bianchis."

"Why did you think you'd break my heart? You didn't know how I felt about you yet."

"I had a pretty good idea." He brushed his fingers against my cheek. "The way you kissed me at the hospital… It felt different."

"I could say the same thing about you."

"I'm sure you could. Shifting breaks down my walls. And shifting in front of you, not knowing if you'd run or scream and think I was a monster, it was… terrifying. Vulnerable. Intimate. I'd fought so hard to keep the truth from you. But when you let me come to you in your hospital room, held me, comforted me, when I was the reason that you got hurt, all that was gone."

"I'm sorry. I understand how scary that was for you. I wish you didn't have to expose your secret like that. I know it was important for you to honor it."

Finn pulled me closer. "I would do it again a thousand times over to keep you safe. I wish I had been honest with you sooner. The others wanted to tell you, but I kept hanging on to the oath we made to each other. …But I've been thinking about that, too. If I'm completely honest with myself, the reason I didn't tell you was less about the oath and more about the fear of how you would react. Humans rarely take the news well."

"It sounds like you've had some pretty terrible experiences with humans finding out about you."

"Yeah," he dropped his gaze. "We lost a few friends. Like I told you that night, humans fear us. We were hunted and some people I really cared about lost their lives because our secret got out. No matter the century, it's always the same result: death."

"Finn, I'm so sorry." I cupped his face in my hands.

"Me too." His eyes were full of old sorrow.

"I hope you didn't feel like I was a danger to you or the others."

"No, not you. Other people that might have found out through you, though maybe. And if you didn't take it well or if you were afraid of us, afraid of me, I thought you'd bail. It didn't take me long to get so attached to you that my fear of losing you, even just as a friend, outweighed everything else."

"If you were so afraid of losing me, why did you try to get me to leave the Clock?"

"Loss comes in different forms, love." He ran his fingers up my back. "Before your attack, loss was not being around you anymore. After your attack, my reality became not having you on this earth anymore. If I had to choose which loss to suffer between the two, I chose the first."

I nodded. If I had to make that choice, I probably would have done the same. I still had a slight ache in my chest thinking about the past few weeks, but it bothered me less.

"Just promise me no more Milani."

"On my honor," he nodded, brushing our noses together. "Not my finest hour, to be sure. But I swear, nothing happened with her. Only what you saw at the bar and the almost-date to the concert. I wanted you to hate me, but I still have my limits."

"So, you knew I saw you in the bar?"

"I made sure of it; that was the whole point, after all. ...God, you looked hot as hell itself that night. You almost broke me. And watching that bozo sidle up next to you, touching you, made me sick to my fucking stomach. I wanted to tear his throat out."

"Jesus, Finn, that's dark."

"That's my wolf," he shrugged. "As far as he was concerned, you were his—ours—and he wanted to protect that claim."

"No throat-tearing," I warned. "Unless it's life or death. Deal?"

"I think I can manage that," Finn chuckled. "Despite my recent track record, I don't make a habit of getting into fights. It draws too much attention. My job is to blend in."

"I know exactly what you mean."

"How so?"

"Witness protection, remember." I raised my hand.

"Vividly," Finn's eyes darkened.

The outside had inevitably broken in. I could feel the sudden tension in Finn's body. A shiver rippled through me. Finn pulled me tighter against his chest.

"Will you tell me about it?" Finn asked. "Your assault?"

I hesitated. I knew the question was coming, but I still felt unprepared for it.

"Maybe later, but not now." I swallowed hard.

"Okay." His eyes were dark, but his expression was soft.

"I want to tell you everything, really I do, but I want to pretend we're a normal couple for a little longer." I gave him a soft kiss.

"What's not normal about a five hundred- and thirteen-year-old Fae Shifter detective and a beautiful, brilliant human social worker in witness protection? We're the poster children for normalcy."

Finn pulled me on top of him, and I snuggled into his chest.

"Normal is overrated, my precious siren. You were born to be extraordinary. You deserve an extraordinary love; and I'll do my damnedest to give it to you."

"Tell me about your abilities." I traced my finger around his pecs.

"I'm super charming, super virile, and incredible in bed."

"I meant your Fae abilities."

"In my human form, my senses are heightened. Compared to a normal man, I'm faster, stronger, have more endurance, and have faster reflexes. In my wolf form, my senses are unmatched; the speed, strength, endurance, and reflexes are unrivaled; my instincts are sharper; and I'm a killing machine if I have to be."

"How often do you have to be?" I shivered again.

"More often than I cared to admit in my youth, but seldom now."

"So, your teenage years? Early twenties?"

"My first century or two," he flushed. "Time moves differently when you're immortal."

"You can't die?"

"Oh, no, I can die. Almost all Fae can die. But our death has to be caused by something. We don't die of old age."

"You forgot to mention that in your list of superpowers."

"I forget about it sometimes. It's just the way my people are."

"It blows my mind, even now." I shook my head. "If I hadn't seen it with my own eyes, I still wouldn't believe it."

"Were you afraid of me when I showed up in my wolf form? I mean, before you knew it was me?" Finn's voice quivered slightly.

"Strangely, no. You—the wolf-you—stopped the berserker from killing me. Then you were fighting them off, trying to keep them away from me. I could tell that you were there to protect me, not to hurt me. It's hard to explain. It's like a part of me recognized you deep down."

"Is that why you stabbed one of them in the eye?"

"He was going to hurt you," I explained. "You were in trouble, even though I didn't know it was you yet. And your wolf was stunning; so beautiful and ethereal. Fierce, of course, but I felt such an intense need to make sure nothing bad happened to you...it... whatever." I made a face at his bemused expression. "What?"

"I'm surprised, that's all. The look on your face when I tried to get close to you made me think you were terrified of me. And my wolf is incredibly pleased with himself at your compliments, by the way."

"He should be. He's incredible. Even though I was in shock, I kept feeling the urge to reach out and touch his fur."

"You can touch me in any form, any time, Allie," Finn grinned. "I crave you—your touch, your body—in every form." He kissed.

The way Finn talked to me was unlike any other man I'd ever been with. It was akin to being worshipped. It was intoxicating. I could feel my arousal stirring once more. Finn smirked at me.

"How am I ever supposed to keep something secret from you with those damn superpowers?" I fake-pouted.

"You can't...at least not *that* secret," Finn boasted. "You're lucky I can't read minds."

"Can any of our friends?"

"Not in the traditional sense, like tune in and hear your thoughts, no. But some can read a person based on other things."

"Like Moira can see your past," I nodded.

"She told you?" Finn cocked an eyebrow.

"Yeah, the morning I got the call from the Marshal. She knew my entire story before she even met me. Do Fae siblings usually have the same powers? Chloe and Lacey haven't told me what they can do, but it makes me wonder."

"It depends on the type of Fae. For example, if your parents are elves, you're an elf. You and your siblings will have the same abilities, mostly. Some might have more influence over water while another has more influence over the wind, but they can both influence the elements. A shifter, like me, is going to have the same ability to shift as their siblings, but they might shift into different animals. It depends on what the environment demanded of your magic during your first shift. I'd say powers are in the same ballpark for all Fae siblings, but it's not always identical. If you mix lines like different types of Fae interbreeding, all bets are off. You never know what powers will manifest at what level or if new powers develop when a multi-Fae child is born."

"Are there many of those types of children?" It fascinated me. It was the first time we'd talked openly about the Fae.

"No, not many. Most Fae are old-fashioned and stick to their own kind when it's time to settle down. But it's not unheard of. Dating around between types of Fae is really common, though."

My stomach clenched at a sudden thought, heat rising in my cheeks. I wanted to push the thought far away, but my curiosity demanded to know the answer to a suddenly very important question.

"What about… Fae and humans?" I blushed harder. "What happens if they… intermingle…"

"Ah, love." Finn tucked my hair behind my ear. "Do you mean, what happens if I knock you up?"

"Very delicate, Finn." I rolled off him and lay on my back, staring at the ceiling while worry and embarrassment painted my cheeks.

Finn chuckled softly. I refused to look back at him. We'd had unprotected sex twice now. What if my birth control failed? What would it mean for me as a human being in a relationship with a Fae? I felt the bed move as Finn rolled over to his side to face me.

"Siren…" He put his finger under my chin and guided it over to face him. "Don't worry. Humans and Fae have been 'intermingling' for thousands of years. It's safe, I promise. No matter how much I want you, I would never put you in a position to get hurt if I wasn't one hundred percent sure it was safe for you." He kissed my forehead. "And… if at some point we want to have children, yes, our kids would be Fae. They would have the same powers as me, probably muted to some extent."

"Woah there, pal," I raised an eyebrow at him. "We just started dating less than 24 hours ago. Let's not go rushing into anything."

"No rush," he smiled. "But I know what I want. I want a life with you. We have years to make the big decisions; I want to let you know that I'm open to the idea. God, we'd make the most beautiful babies."

He leaned in and kissed me. It gave me tingles. He wanted a future with me! Fae babies aside for now, I couldn't help but be thrilled at the idea of being with my best friend for the rest of my days.

"What are you smiling about?" Finn asked.

"You want to make babies with me."

"I want to make everything with you," he crooned. "I wouldn't say no to practicing the baby-making again."

"Are we covered, though? I mean, I'm on birth control, but does birth control even work with the Fae?"

"Human birth control is useless…"

"Fuck…" I recoiled.

"But… I take a Fae remedy every month that serves as birth control for us. It's airtight, trust me. Several centuries of… 'activities,' and still not a kid in sight."

"Oh, thank God!" I exhaled. "With everything else we're facing, I have no idea how I'd cope with a magical pregnancy."

Finn slid his hand down to rest over my stomach. He stroked the area reverently. His eyes sparkled as he gazed at me.

"I don't know, my love. I don't think there's a damn thing on earth that you can't cope with. It turns me on to imagine you with a swollen belly, growing my child, our child. Wolves mate for life, you know." He chuckled, "Never in a thousand lifetimes would I have guessed my mate would end up being a human."

"Are you disappointed?" I put my hand on top of his hand as it continued to rub my stomach.

"What's the extreme opposite of disappointed?" He kissed me lightly. "Whatever it is, I'm that. You are more than I ever dreamed. Everything I always wanted and everything I didn't know I needed. I am so goddamn in love with you, Alexis."

"Still waters run deep," I sighed.

"Huh?"

"When I first met you, I had no idea you were capable of this much passion. Thank you for opening yourself up to me despite the losses from your past. If you hadn't, I would have missed out on so much."

"You have a way with people, Siren," he brushed his thumb against my cheek. "I don't think I could have stayed closed off to you if I'd tried. Chief brought you in to get victims to open up, but they weren't the only ones who found you irresistible. That's *your* superpower."

"Well, if it can't be invisibility or flight, I guess that's an acceptable one," I smiled.

Finn's phone rang. I reached over to grab it from his nightstand, but he wrapped his arms around my waist and rolled me away from it. He pinned me playfully to the bed.

"Let it ring," he smirked, kissing my neck.

"What if it's something important?"

"There's nothing more important to me than this," he motioned between us.

"This isn't going anywhere." I pushed him back and kissed the tip of his nose. "You don't have to answer it. Just see who it is."

Finn sighed heavily, rolled off me, and grabbed his phone. He had missed the caller, but his brows pinched together when he checked his call log. He looked at me and sighed again.

"It was Andre." He showed me the screen.

"Call him back. I'm not going anywhere."

"Anyone else and I'd…" Finn started.

"I know. Call him."

I tried to fight off the frown that drew the corners of my mouth down. As much as I hated the idea, recoiled from it, I knew we had to face the outside world again at some point. The back of my neck prickled as the reality of our circumstances stalked up behind me. Finn hit redial and held the phone to his ear.

"Hey man," Finn greeted.

I waited and watched Finn's face intently as Andre spoke. I could make out the timbre of his voice, but not any of the words he was saying. Finn's eyebrows pulled together, and his worry lines appeared.

"The fingerprints match? You sure?" Finn asked.

His frown deepened.

"Yeah, we can do that."

Finn paused and glanced at me. My stomach sank. Reality.

"We'll be there soon." Finn hung up the phone.

"They got a positive ID on Selsha, love." Finn pulled me back into his arms.

The tears sprang to my eyes immediately.

"They need us back at the station. With Ramond dead and another Bianchi murder victim, we've got to gather everything we have to nail these assholes. Are you up for it?"

A firm resolve was already forming in my chest. "Put away the assholes that killed Selsha? You bet your ass I'm up for it."

I pulled out of his arms and gathered my clothes from the ground.

"Quick stop at your place?" Finn raised his eyebrows at my day-old clothing.

"Real quick. I want to get to the station ASAP. Those women need us to put the Bianchis behind bars before any more of them end up missing or dead."

Finn dressed rapidly, his eagerness matching my own. The delicious solitude we had created was a needed and welcome break, but the fire had awoken once more in both of us. Maria and Leticia were safe, but dozens more women were not. I may not have been able to save Selsha... or the women Cam Gunner had killed, maybe not even helped them get justice after death, but I was sure as hell going to try to save the women the Bianchis were controlling.

After a change of clothes, we arrived at the station. Andre was deep in conversation with Lot and Olivier. He didn't notice us come in until Finn was right next to him. I stood back and watched him join in the conversation. Ever since Olivier shared his flippant and disgusting attitude about Leticia and other sex workers, I had zero interest in interacting with the man. Despite the obvious intensity of the conversation, Andre kept shooting glances at me over his shoulder, smiling each time he met my eye. It took me a few glances to remember that I had been dead to him, too, not too long ago. My heart gave a grateful squeeze.

"Alexis," Finn beckoned me over. "You knew Selsha the best. How do you think they found her?"

"Look who's back from the dead," Olivier raised an eyebrow at me.

"Selsha was around campus a lot," I answered, ignoring Olivier. "They would always send a town car to pick her up near the bus stop. That was her area."

"But she wasn't working that morning. She was leaving, right?" Andre asked.

"Yeah, she was." Selsha's scared yet deliberate face popped into my mind.

"If her runner hadn't dropped her off, then how did they know where she'd be?" Andre mused.

"Remember what Ramond said," Finn tapped Andre's arm.

"What did that weasel say?" Olivier snapped.

"He said the Bianchis had a way of keeping track of their girls." Andre answered. "Cell phone tracking, maybe?"

"Why don't you ask him?" I pressed.

"Unless you have a Ouija board, sweetheart, he won't be saying nothing." Olivier flicked his toothpick from one side of his mouth to the other.

"He got capped in holding," Lot explained. "We don't know how or who yet, but we'll find 'em."

My heart sank. All of that work tracking him down to get justice for Maria...gone. How could the Bianchis have gotten to him in holding?

"Could you reach out to some of your contacts, Alexis?" Finn asked. "Maybe they'll know something."

"I can try," I replied. I could call Maria first, then Leticia. They ran the least amount of risk by talking. They were safe for now.

"I doubt any of your whores are going to know anything, even if you could get them to talk," Olivier spat. "If they did, they'd end up like the headless bitch in the woods."

Before I could stop myself, my fist collided with Olivier's nose. It was like I'd lost all control of my senses. Finn and Andre's arms shot out to restrain me. Olivier stared at me in shock. Lot grabbed Olivier's arm, but there was a glint in Lot's eye and the corner of his mouth was fighting to turn up.

"WHAT THE FUCK, YOU STUPID BITCH?" Olivier screamed.

"You talk to her like that again and I'll finish the job she started, you filthy piece of shit," Finn growled, pointing his finger in Olivier's face.

Blood was gushing from Olivier's nose. He was using his hand to stem the flow, but it was getting into his mouth. Otherwise, I doubt he would have stopped his tirade. Lot yanked on his arm and pulled him back.

"C'mon, let's get you cleaned up," Lot urged, handing him a handkerchief.

Olivier spat into the handkerchief. "This isn't over."

Lot led Olivier out of the think tank toward the locker room.

"Holy shit, Lex," Andre's eyes were wide. "Remind me never to piss you off!"

"You just assaulted a cop," Finn sighed.

"Yup," I acknowledged.

"Do you know how much trouble that could get you into?" Finn sat me at his desk.

"Yup," I nodded, still a little shocked myself.

"Do you regret it?" Andre asked with a sparkle in his eye.

"Nope." I gritted my teeth.

"I'm not saying he didn't deserve it…" Finn started.

"That prick has been asking for a knuckle sandwich as long as he's been on the force," Andre shrugged.

"But what happens when the Chief finds out about it?" Finn held my hand up to examine it for signs of injury.

As the adrenaline declined, a throbbing ache developed. I winced as Finn brushed his fingers along my knuckles. His sensitive ears picked up the sharp intake of breath, and his eyes flashed to my face. He glanced around the think tank, then brushed his lips softly against my knuckles. I smiled at him.

"It's about damn time," Andre smirked. "Anything you want to tell me?"

Finn's cheeks flushed a little. He sat on the edge of his desk and straightened his collar. Andre looked back and forth between us with a knowing smile.

"Alright, yes, we're together," Finn relented.

"Yes!" Andre pumped his fist in the air. "Goddamn, you two. We thought you'd never pull the trigger."

"We?" I asked.

"All of us. Literally all of us. Like everyone at the Pony. We even had a pool going at one point, but we got bored with waiting and we scrapped it." Andre chuckled.

"Good to know you all were taking such a keen interest in our dating lives." Finn rolled his eyes, but he was smiling.

"On to more important business," I sighed, flexing my hand. "With Ramond dead, how are you guys going to get the information you need to nail the syndicate?"

"Let's put a call into Maria, see if she knows something," Finn suggested. "She was one of his girls, after all. She might have a better idea than the rest since she lived with him. That's how he continued the charade of being her boyfriend to keep her on the line for so long."

"Do we tell her about Ramond?" Andre asked.

"We can't keep it from her. We owe her the truth," I sighed. "She may not have gotten justice through the system, but maybe it will give her some peace of mind to know that he'll never hurt her again."

"Ms. Henson?" Chief Whitmer's holler startled me. He was beckoning to me from his doorway.

Finn and Andre followed, but Chief held up a hand to stop them.

"Just Ms. Henson," he warned.

They returned to their desks, and I entered Chief's office with a lump in my throat. He motioned for me to sit before settling in his chair. He crossed his arms over his ample stomach and sighed.

"How's your hand?" he asked with a deep sigh.

"Chief, I…"

He held up a hand.

"I didn't peg you for the type, Alexis." He pinched the bridge of his nose.

"I'm sorry, sir. I shouldn't have. Detective Olivier was saying disgusting, reprehensible things about Selsha and her death. I lost my temper…"

"Detective Olivier is an asshole," Chief stated. My eyes popped wide at the declaration. "Everyone here knows it. You're not the only one who has wanted to break his nose, which you probably did according to the EMT Lot snagged in passing. I'd be lying if I said I never had the passing urge. But violence is never acceptable in my precinct."

"I understand, sir." I hung my head. After all this, I was about to lose my job.

"However, given what I know about your history, I understand your response," Chief added. I chanced a look at him. His eyes were kind. "Not that I condone it," he warned. "But I understand it. You've been through more hell in the past couple of years than most people go through in a lifetime. You're a damn good advocate and letting you go wouldn't serve anyone or anything aside from Olivier's ego. Normally, I'd put you on administrative leave, but the bigger picture here needs you if we're going to take down the Bianchis. So, promise me you'll keep your fists to yourself, and I'll let you walk out of here with mandated therapy to manage that temper."

"But I'm already in therapy," I reminded.

"Well, isn't that lucky for the both of us?" his eyes sparkled. "Now get the hell out of my office and go do your job. No more bullshit, Ms. Henson. Those women need you."

"Yes, sir," I rose, and he gave me a nod.

"Out," he waved me off.

I left his office, letting the tension melt away. I'd gotten off ridiculously easy, and I knew it. The immense respect I already had for the Chief multiplied tenfold. I couldn't help but feel incredibly grateful that Marshal Davis had sent me his way, and he'd been open enough to let me join his precinct.

"Are you fired?" Andre asked once I got back to their desks.

"No, it all worked out. Mandated therapy, but that's it."

"Aren't you already in therapy?" Andre cocked an eyebrow.

"Yup," I smiled.

"God bless the chief," Andre shook his head.

"You got lucky, Allie," Finn reminded.

"I know. Let's go make some phone calls and hope that luck holds out."

I led the way to interrogation one. When we called the contact number we had for Maria, her abuela answered. Maria was at work, but Abuela said she'd pass along the message and have her call us back as soon as she got home. Leticia was next. She answered straight away, but she had no more to give us. Ramond hadn't been her runner. She suggested a few names of friends she knew who were run by Ramond and wished us luck in 'finally taking those bastards down.' We made plans to find some women Leticia suggested we talk to while we waited for Maria to call us back.

When 9:00 p.m. rolled around and Maria still hadn't called us back, my anxiety skyrocketed. I imagined a hundred terrible scenarios. Finn took my hand under the table to soothe me. Andre kept reassuring me she probably worked late. Another hour went by and still nothing. Andre called the number again and her mother answered this time. Maria had picked up a double, so she wouldn't be home until around 2:00 a.m. But her mother assured us she would have Maria call first thing in the morning.

With nothing left to do for the evening, we called it a night. Andre suggested heading over to the Pony. Finn seemed eager to get back to his place. I suppressed a knowing smile but urged him to stop by the Pony for a bit. I wanted to see my friends again. He relented, knowing that he'd dug his own hole on that one. He was the reason I hadn't seen everyone in so long, and he seemed to accept this detour as a part of his atonement.

Walking through the front doors of the Pony was like coming home again. The second my friends saw me walk in holding Finn's hand, they cheered and whooped. They swarmed us at the entrance with a many-armed hug. It felt like no time had passed between my temporary exile and my joyously welcomed return. We laughed, drank, talked, and danced until the wee hours of the morning.

Riel waved the last of the stragglers out of the bar around 3 a.m. With the door locked behind him, he rounded on us with a smile. The others were smiling, too.

"Is it time for the human sacrifice already?" I asked. Everyone laughed.

"We owe you an explanation," Riel began.

"Finn already told me everything," I waved it away. "I know why you all took a step back."

"That's not the explanation we owe you." Vijay guided me to a barstool and sat me down. "It's this one." He and Vikram moved to stand in front of me and bowed low. "Our names are Vijay and Vikram Burman. We are hobs, formerly known as domestic hobgoblins. Our gifts are apparent in our love of cooking and caring for a household unseen. It's a pleasure to officially make your acquaintance."

Vijay and Vikram moved to the right, and Donna took their place. She was grinning from ear to ear. "My name is Aradonna, daughter of Arethusa. I'm a nymph, a Naiad-born nymph, but a Thyiad-made by the grace of Dionysus. I am daughter of the River-gods and have powers over water. Glad to meet you as myself." She pointed a finger at a near empty glass and a large drop of water floated up, danced around my head, then made its way into Andre's open mouth. They both laughed.

Next came Hiro, "Konnichiwa, I am Hiro Hakuseki. I am zenko kitsune. We are fox people with great powers of intellect and image weaving…illusions." She gave me a shy smile, spun on the spot, and transformed into a stunning copper-colored fox with one, two, three… nine tails! Hiro capered around the room before spinning once more and resuming her human form. My mouth was agape.

Ricky, Grace, and Taylor came up together next. "Evening, m'lady," Ricky bowed. "Ricky O'Leary, leprechaun extraordinaire, at your service. Everything you've ever heard about us is true." He winked, flipping a gold coin in my direction. It disappeared before it reached my waiting palm.

"Grace of the Winter Woods, friend," Grace curtseyed. "A proud pixie." She waved her hand and shrunk to the size of a cell phone, sprouting beautiful gossamer-like wings. She flitted close to my face and stuck her tongue out at me playfully, then disappeared with the tinkle of a bell. Then, she reappeared in her full size on a tabletop all the way across the bar.

"Taylor Aspenbud, wood sprite. Lover of nature, friend of the trees, and keeper of all things that grow." Taylor ran her finger against a wilting flower in a vase and it bloomed powerfully back to life. She handed it to me with a smile.

"We've already been introduced," Riel came to the center now, "But under circumstances much less ideal. I am Riel Yannalor Lonaurin of the Elven clan Erendriel. I have dominion over the elements. Your servant, miss," he bowed to me.

I looked around the room at my friends, my heart full to bursting. They were showing me their truest selves, their most sacred secrets. Moira was beaming at me from the corner where she sat with her sisters. Lacey waved enthusiastically to me, but Chloe wouldn't meet my gaze.

They were the only ones who didn't come to stand in front of me to declare themselves or their powers. I deflated a bit, but tried to keep in mind the seriousness of what my friends were doing. The sisters had been unendingly loyal to me. It was all I could ever ask of them and more. Even if they never shared what race of Fae they were, I would always feel honored to be so loved and cherished by them.

"Now, if you don't mind," Finn cleared his throat and pulled me into his arms, "I'm going to take my girlfriend home with me."

The crew whooped and whistled. The heat rose in my cheeks, and I swatted Finn on the arm. He pulled me close to him and we left the bar together. My last view of the bar was the grinning faces of my friends. Never, in all my days, had I felt so thoroughly loved.

Chapter Twenty-Nine

Finn

Alexis was taking forever in the bathroom. It was nearing four in the morning, but I was anything but tired. The craving I had for Alexis was unending. My body was alive with anticipation as I listened to her moving around just a few yards away.

Tonight had been a good night. Although I wasn't thrilled to share her with the others, I'm glad I'd agreed to go to the Pony. My friends—my family—had given Alexis the greatest honor of our people: A Greeting Ceremony. I didn't know it was happening until Vijay and Vikram took their places in front of her. My face was sore from smiling. They accepted her fully. She was one of us now. It gave me a deep sense of peace I hadn't known I was missing.

The sound of the bathroom door opening drew my eager attention. Alexis stood in the doorway, freshly washed, in panties and a form-fitting tank top. I was instantly hard.

"My God," I shook my head, "You are everything."

I held my arms out to her, and she slipped right into them, joining me on the bed. I held her tight against me, my heart thrumming to have her close once more. I placed a long, reverent kiss on her forehead. She truly was everything to me.

"They trust me," she whispered into my chest gleefully.

"Of course they do, baby," I purred. "I told you how much we all adore you. Your dumbass boyfriend was the one thing standing in the way of that greeting happening a long time ago."

"My boyfriend is kind of a dumbass, isn't he?" She kissed my collarbone.

"Say it again," I growled happily.

"What? That my boyfriend is a dumbass?"

"Your boyfriend," I hummed.

Alexis looked up at me. Her smile made my heart squeeze. She scooted up higher on the bed, so we were face-to-face, our noses barely touching.

"Finn Briggs is my boyfriend," she boasted.

"Hell yes, he is!" I kissed her. "And my girlfriend punched an asshole today."

"Hell yes, she did," Alexis chuckled.

"I want you." I lifted her chin and kissed her again. "God, I want you."

"If I had known punching Olivier was what it took to get an invitation into your bed, I would have done it a helluva lot sooner."

"Baby, you have a permanent invitation in my bed." I ran my hand over her ass and squeezed.

"And you, my dragon, have a permanent invitation inside me," her eyes sparked.

She pushed me gently onto my back and climbed on top of me. She slipped her hand beneath my underwear and pleasure jolted through me as she grasped my cock. Before I could register much more, she had pulled it out of my boxer-briefs and was hovering over me. With her free hand, she slid her panties to one side and centered herself over my waiting cock. I licked my lips and waited hungrily.

My tip penetrated her wet pussy as she lowered herself slowly onto me. My relief at being reunited with her in this way came out in a long sigh. She settled herself on top of me, burying me deep inside her. She rocked her hips back and forth, running her hands up my stomach and chest.

"God, you're so warm," I blinked lazily. "I could do this forever, you know."

"You want to be with me forever?" Her voice was smoky.

I sat up and weaved my hands into her hair. "Like this? Every single moment of forever, Allie. A few feet out of my reach is too far after the weeks I punished us by staying away. Of all my regrets, that's the worst one. I should have declared my love for you in that hospital room and never left your side."

"You had the berserkers to worry about." She shook her head, slowing the movement of her rolling hips.

"No, not that hospital room," I corrected. "Mine. When I woke up after surgery and you were there, I fell head over heels. Hell, I'd been falling a long time before that, but that was the moment I really knew how far gone I was."

"Is that why you kissed me on New Year's?"

"Yes." I grasped her hips and moved her on top of me, desperate for the delicious sensation she created in me to continue. "God, you tasted incredible. And the way you kissed me back…" I moaned.

She ran her fingers through my hair, and my scalp tingled.

"It made me hope you felt the same way. …Fuck, you feel good, Siren."

"You belong inside me, Finn," she breathed, her breath warm against my skin.

"Yes, I do." I peeled off her tank top.

Her nipples were tight, pink, and tempting. I licked my lips, saliva exploding in my mouth as I stared at her breasts. I shifted her weight and rolled her onto her back. My mouth enveloped the flesh of her breast as I took over the synchronization of moving bodies.

Her hands slid under my boxer-briefs and cupped my ass. I flexed my glutes, and she chuckled. She pushed me deeper as I fucked her lazily and feasted on her tits. My dick dragged back and forth against the edge of her panties, heightening the sensation throbbing through me. Her head tipped back, exposing her beautiful throat. I wrapped my hand around her neck and gripped it gently. I could feel her pulse under my thumb. It was the most beautiful, satisfying reassurance. She was alive; she was here, and she was mine.

Alexis pulled at my underwear, sliding them down my legs, and I kicked them off impatiently. Her eyes traced up my body. I reveled in her appreciative gaze.

"What made you fall in love with me?" She traced the peak of my nipples, making them pebble under her touch.

"Your fire," I huffed, resuming my slow rhythm inside her. "Your brilliance, your kindness…" I punctuated each truth with a stroke of my pulsing cock. "Your tenacity, your resilience, your beauty, your loyalty. God, everything about you. I fucking love you, Allie."

"I love you, Finn." Her eyes glistened with welling tears.

I lowered myself closer and wiped the moisture away from her eyes, kissing her cheeks softly. "Don't cry, my love."

Her hands rested on the back of my neck, staring right into my soul.

"What do you see when you look at me like that?" I asked.

"I see you," she smiled. "The real you, wolf and all."

"Do I scare you?" The worry still nagged at the back of my mind.

"Of all the things in my life, you scare me the least." She kissed me lightly on the lips.

"I'm not just another demon?"

"Far from it, my grumpy dragon." She pushed me away gently, sliding out from underneath me.

I watched as she peeled her soaked panties off and stood next to the side of the bed. I stroked my cock as I gloried in her every tiny movement. It was wet with her juices. I ran a finger over the tip, shuddering at the sensation, then brought the finger to my mouth. The combination of her taste mixed with my own was intoxicating.

"Here I stand, completely and utterly bare, defenseless, and vulnerable in every single way, and all I feel is safe. Seen. Loved. No fear."

I moved to the edge of the bed and pulled her back to me. She knelt over my lap, pulling my cock back inside her as she resumed riding me. My mouth found hers wordlessly. We consumed each other, communicating with our lips and tongues, sighs and moans, what no words could ever adequately convey. She was a part of me. That deep, abiding feeling I felt when I was with her exploded into an enduring assurance that I had found my true equal, my soulmate.

My arms tightened around her waist, and I stood, carrying her across the room to the top of my dresser. I leaned her against the wall and drove myself deep inside her. She gasped.

"Did I hurt you, baby?"

"A little," she confessed.

"I'm sorry, Siren." I pulled away.

"No," she pleaded. "Stay." Desperation saturated every syllable.

"I'll be more gentle."

I slipped my tongue under her nipple and sucked it into my mouth. She exploded across my tastebuds. Her moans sounded more like purring. My wolf awakened, ravenous to make those sounds turn to keens of pleasure. I slipped my cock out of her, and her eyes popped open, her lips forming a pout. I chuckled.

"Don't be disappointed, beautiful." I stroked her cheek and spread her legs wider. "I'm nowhere near done with you."

I bent over with a grin and saw the desire flame in her eyes. My tongue found her clit as if it had visited a thousand times. Her body was familiar in all the right ways. I ran my tongue back and forth along that delicious rosebud, sucking and flicking. She gripped my head with both hands, holding me tightly against her. I ran one hand up to her breast and kneaded her tender flesh. My other hand slipped next to my mouth, two fingers sliding into her sweet pussy.

With other women, oral had been an unpleasant chore, but with Alexis, it was akin to worship. I whispered oaths against her warm, wet slit, vowing to make her my altar. Her breaths became ragged and her clutching fingers spasmed. She was close to coming. I grinned against her pussy lips. She deserved every pleasure. I swirled my tongue with longer, slower strokes, moving my fingers inside her in a synchronized rhythm.

"Come for me, baby," I demanded in a throaty whisper. "Come undone for me."

My words pushed her over the brink to her salvation. Her voice rose in a song of ecstasy and release as I continued to eat her out. My tongue replaced my fingers inside her as I lapped up her juices. My wolf growled, shaking to be released. I held it back, fighting the urge to explode into the animal I was deep inside. When the urge finally subsided, I straightened up before her with a satisfied smirk.

"What was that?" she heaved.

"That was an orgasm, baby," I chuckled. "And there's plenty more where that came from."

She laughed and pulled me close, kissing my lips. "I meant the growl."

"You heard that?"

"Mm-hmm." She dragged her tongue along my upper lip.

"We want you," I growled again.

"Your wolf..."

"Is eager." I ran a finger along her clit, and she gasped.

"Show me." She grabbed my cock possessively.

I raised an eyebrow at her.

"Not literally," she laughed. "I don't think I'll ever be ready for...that..." She raised her eyebrows back at me. "Show me the eagerness."

She slid off the dresser to stand in front of me. My wolf leapt. I closed my eyes and granted it access to my limbs without giving it space enough to prompt a shift. A snarl ripped from my lips, and I spun Alexis around, pressing her against the dresser. Without thinking, I plunged my cock back inside her from behind, one hand wrapped around the front of her throat and the other sliding from her stomach straight to her clit once more.

The wild took over our tangled limbs. I fucked her so hard that it slammed the dresser against the wall. She yelped yeses and pleas to the Gods as my cock invaded her. I could feel my tip pressing against the deepest parts of her pussy. My wolf worked through me, stroking her clit and reveling in the sound of my body slamming against her ass. My mouth licked and sucked her neck, hovering over her jugular, hungry to bite into her neck and suckle her lifeblood. I bit into the firm skin of her shoulder, marking her as mine.

Holding her tight, I spun us back over to the bed, bending her over the soft mattress. She spread her legs wide to receive me and my wolf howled its approval. I rutted deep inside her, grabbing her hips for leverage. The sounds Alexis made became just as animalistic as my own. Her hands tangled in the sheets as she gripped the mattress. I let myself give in completely to my baser instincts as I fucked her. She called out my name, and without warning, my cum erupted. I threw my head back and grunted, pumping every last ounce of my seed into my mate.

Her knees buckled, and she collapsed onto the bed as her pussy milked my waning cock. Her ass muscles tightened as I pulled myself out, shooting one last glorious jolt of ecstasy through me as it squeezed my hypersensitive tip. I fell to my knees beside her, my head still swimming with the intensity of my orgasm. We were both gasping for air, trying to pull ourselves back from the edge of oblivion.

"By the Gods," I swore. "That was…"

"The best damn sex of your life?" she finished.

"Holy shit, yes." I climbed, weak-legged, back on the bed, pulling her up with me. We lay side by side on our backs.

"It's a good thing you take Fae birth control," her chest heaved. "Otherwise, I'd probably get pregnant just *thinking* about what you just did to me."

A laugh burst out of my chest. I took her hand and brought it to my mouth, kissing her fingers one by one. Sweat glistened across her forehead. I gave her a triumphant smirk.

"If you keep making me feel this way," I panted, "You'll make me want to stop taking it altogether. My mating urge is intense with you."

"No Fae babies yet," she scolded.

"Yet?" I grinned wolfishly.

"Yet," she chuckled. "When the time is right, I'll let you fill me up. Make us a few of those beautiful babies you were thinking about."

"Yeah?" I pulled her against my chest.

"Yes, Finn. I've been thinking about it since you mentioned it earlier. I can't think of anything more incredible than carrying a part of you inside me, making life with you."

"I want you now," I growled, arousal spiking once more.

"I don't think I'll be ready for another round for a while." She put a calming hand on my chest. "You?"

She palmed my flaccid dick, and I groaned. She was right. That last few minutes was going to keep me soft for a while. I nuzzled her neck and inhaled her. She was beginning to smell like me a little, wrapped in my sheets and arms, marked by my cum. It didn't dull the honeysuckle, but weaved its way through it and around it.

We held each other silently for a long time. My heart beat its way back into a normal rhythm. I strained to listen and heard her precious heart settle into its normal pace, too. I pressed soft kisses against her neck as I breathed her in.

"Can I ask you a question?" Alexis broke the silence.

"Anything," I answered, pulling back so I could see her face.

"Why won't Chloe tell me what kind of Fae she is?"

I sighed. I figured this question was coming.

"I mean, I thought we were close…" Alexis's eyebrows drew together.

"You are close, love," I soothed. "Chloe hasn't ever let a human get this close to her. It scares her."

"Why?"

"A long time ago, Chloe told her human lover that she was Fae. She thought he loved her. Maybe he did once, but after he found out about her, things changed…" I remembered listening to Chloe tell this story the night we came together to swear the oath. It made my stomach turn.

"Did he hurt her?"

"Worse," I swallowed hard. "He hurt Lacey."

Alexis's eyes shot wide. "What?!"

"The sisters are connected not just by blood, but by their Fae powers. Chloe's lover used her identity to figure out Moira's and Lacey's, too. Lacey is…" I paused. I thought about how to be honest with Allie without exposing information that wasn't mine to tell. "Lacey is a uniquely powerful Fae. There are many, many people, both human and Fae, who would try to use her gifts for their own selfish purposes, despite the costs."

"The costs," Alexis frowned. She was quiet a moment before her eyes widened. "Her migraines?"

I nodded.

"Her gift causes her pain?"

"It got worse after he abused her powers. Sometimes it's agonizing for her."

"Oh my God," her eyes watered. "Lacey? But she's so pure and innocent."

"She is. It's a big reason we've worked so hard to keep our secret. It's a necessary protection for the rest of us, sure, but it's vital to keep Lacey safe."

"And Chloe's lover?"

"He used Chloe to get to Lacey and used her. They got her away from him with the help of some other Fae, but she hasn't spoken a word since."

"That's why she's mute? Dear God…"

"The way he used Lacey traumatized her. And Chloe has never forgiven herself for it."

"How awful." She moved in closer to me.

"Now do you understand?" I kissed her forehead.

"How could I not? The next time I see her, I'm going to tell her she never has to tell me a thing. I love her no matter what. God… poor Lacey… I love them so much, Finn."

"I know, baby," I soothed. "We all do. And they love you back. You know that, right?"

She nodded. I wiped the tears that slid down her cheeks. Shifting our weight, I pulled us under the sheets and held her close. I whispered reassurances to her in both English and Gaelic until she fell into a deep sleep. I watched her, my heart full, until sleep claimed me next.

Whatever sleep we got, it wasn't enough. My alarm blared too early. I pounded it back into silence with a grunt. Rolling back into Alexis's warmth, kissing the spot between her shoulder blades.

"Alarms are the devil," she murmured.

"Don't worry, I sent it back to hell."

"Does that mean we have to get up and face the world again?" She had a slight tremor in her voice.

"Yes, love. But we'll face it together." I smoothed her hair back behind her ear.

She nuzzled in closer, and I wrapped my arm around her waist, letting my hand drift softly back and forth across her stomach. I'd dreamt of our children. I smiled to myself.

Alexis groaned as she extricated herself from my arms and the sheets tangled between our limbs. I followed suit, tossing one last disgusted look at my alarm clock. We showered together, washing one another between kisses and lingering touches. I watched with keen interest as she put on her makeup and did her hair, searing every tiny detail into my memory. I gripped her hand as we drove to the station, savoring her skin against mine, not looking forward to the professional distance we would have to maintain once we got to work.

I parked in the station lot and took Alexis's chin gently between my fingers, planting one last lingering kiss on her juicy lips. She smiled and brushed her hand against my cheek. Walking into the station was a rude awakening from the bliss of my apartment. Lot and Olivier were talking to a small group of uniforms in the corner. Olivier cast us a death glare, his anger flaring as he stared at Alexis. I bristled, moving my body subtly in front of her to interrupt his line of sight. The purple bruising around both of his eyes mollified me.

We settled at my desk, trying to ignore whatever was in the air around us. Luckily, Andre strolled out of the break room with a half-eaten bagel clamped between his teeth. His eyes lit up when he saw us. He made his way to join us, pulling his chair between our desks.

"Things are tense around here today," Andre whistled. "Chief fired the guards who were on duty when Ramond was killed. Autopsy came back; poison."

"Chief thinks the guards did it?" I asked.

"I doubt it." Andre took another bite of his bagel. "My best bet is he's making an example out of them for letting something like that get by 'em. Unacceptable," he shook his head. "Olivier came in off his meds or something, screaming at a couple of rookies for not refilling the water on the coffeemaker. I don't know what crawled up his ass and died, but you both better steer clear of him."

"Done," Alexis shrugged. I glanced at her knuckles. Faint traces of bruising painted her fair skin. My heart flared with pride.

"Ms. Henson?" A timid-looking tech with horn-rimmed glasses approached my desk.

"Yes?" Alexis confirmed.

"We've finished processing some things from the University crime scene and Chief Whitmer cleared me to return them to you." The shy man held out a plastic bag with Alexis's cell phone and Leticia's anklet with the cherry charm. "I'm afraid the coat was too far gone, so we disposed it of."

Alexis's face blanched. She stared at the bag, still as a statue. My stomach roiled at the memory of that crime scene. The ring of her cell phone haunting the woods and damning me to a life without her. I swallowed back the bile that rose in my throat.

"I'll take that." Andre stood and took the bag. He signed his name on the clipboard, then the tech scurried away. "Do you want me to hold on to these for you for a while?" Andre asked softly.

"Will you?" Alexis whispered.

"Of course, Lex," Andre squeezed her hand. "I've got you."

"Thank you," she wiped at her eyes.

"It's okay, Siren," I soothed. "We're here with you."

She swallowed hard and nodded.

The phone on Andre's desk rang behind us, pulling us out of the living nightmare that bag of evidence reawakened. Andre grabbed the receiver, tucking the phone and anklet, still sealed in the evidence bag, into his coat pocket as he did.

"Alvarez," Andre answered. His eyes lit up, "Maria! I'm so glad to hear from you. Give me a minute to transfer you to another line so Detective Briggs and Alexis can get in on the call, too." He waited a minute while Maria said something, then pressed a few buttons on his phone.

"Let's head into One." Andre set the receiver down after checking that the call had indeed transferred to the other line.

We hurried into interrogation one, Andre pulling the phone to the center of the room and pressing the speakerphone button. My jaw clenched. Please, God, let her have something for us!

"Maria, are you still there?" Andre asked.

"Yes, I'm here," Maria's voice replied.

"Maria, we're so happy to hear from you," Alexis sighed. "How are you holding up?" She repeated the greeting in Spanish.

I sighed, mentally scolding myself for not bothering to learn Spanish when Andre offered back in Chicago. It would have made things a lot easier for all of us. But, as Maria answered in Spanish and both Alexis and Andre answered in kind, whoever wasn't speaking translated what was being said into English for me.

"My job treats me very well," Maria updated. "Mama and Abuela are so happy to have me home. They are both getting older and it's nice for them to have a younger back in the house, if only to carry the weight of their gossiping." She chuckled. It was the first time I'd heard her make a joke. I grinned as Alexis translated it for me with a smile.

"Good to hear, Maria," Andre replied. "We're so sorry to bother you, but we have some news." He swallowed hard. "You know we caught Ramond, but I'm sorry to tell you he was killed in police custody. Someone poisoned him."

Silence greeted us from the other end of the line. We looked back and forth at one another, waiting for her to reply.

"Aye Dios Mio," she finally uttered. I knew what that meant, at least. "He's really gone?"

"Yes, he is," Andre confirmed.

"Who?" she asked.

"We're working to find that out now. It will not end with him, I promise. We'll see this through to the end, no matter what."

"I know you will," she sighed. "Am I in danger?"

"No, Maria," I assured in English. "You're safe. We've got our eyes on you, I swear."

She was quiet again for a moment.

"What do you need from me?" Maria's voice quivered.

"We're so sorry to ask more after you've already given so much," Alexis apologized. "But with Ramond dead, we're at a loss. If there was any other way of finding you justice and ensuring your safety, we wouldn't have called."

"I understand. What do you want to know?"

"Are you sure?" Alexis's eyes were worried.

"I'm positive. Ask me anything."

Pride swelled in me as I listened to the strength in Maria's voice. She had gone from being a terrified victim to being a brave survivor in such a short time. I had to admire her courage.

"Did Ramond have any hiding spots at his place? Someone where he'd stash something he didn't want found? He mentioned having hard evidence against the Bianchis. We need that evidence." Andre leveled with her.

"Ramond never talked to me much," Maria started. My hopes fell. "But anytime he wanted to be alone, he would go to the basement. I didn't want to go down there; so many spiders…"

"The basement… okay, got it. Anything else?" Andre coaxed.

"Sometimes, when he was down there, I would hear this sound through the vents. It was like chalk on cement, but hollow. I'm sorry, that probably doesn't help."

"Don't apologize, Maria," Alexis urged. "Anything is helpful right now, right, Andre?"

"Absolutely," he confirmed.

"That's all I can think of, but if I think of more, I will call you back right away."

"Thank you, Maria. You are incredible," I said.

"Be safe, all of you," she answered in English. "Adios."

Andre hung up the phone.

"Is the warrant on Ramond's place still active?" I asked.

"Yep," Andre confirmed. "Last one to the Charger is a rotten egg." He had a fresh sparkle in his eye.

"I can make some more calls while you're gone," Alexis offered.

"No way. You're coming with us." I motioned for her to follow us. "I meant it when I said I'm not letting you out of my sight. I don't trust anyone else to look out for you like we can until every single member of the Bianchi syndicate is rotting behind bars."

Crime scene seals on the door secured Ramond's house on 9-block. We notified Chief that we were checking it out to keep the chain of evidence consistent. The whole place was filthy and reeked of fish that's been left out too long. It didn't take long to find the door down to the basement. The old wooden stairs creaked and groaned as we descended. Just like Maria promised, there were spider webs everywhere.

The basement walls were half stacked stone foundation and the top half crumbling red bricks. It was a small space, no bigger than a couple hundred square feet. We all donned gloves and spread out to look for clues. I tried smelling around for something, but all I could detect was damp earth.

"Anything?" I asked the room at large.

"Not yet," Andre sighed.

"Chalk on cement," Alexis muttered. "I don't see any chalk or drawings on the cement floor. She said she could hear something like chalk on cement through the vents."

I shifted my gaze upwards, looking for a vent. I found one in the northeast corner of the room, up near where the wall met the ceiling. For Maria to hear something, it would have to be close to the vent itself.

As I moved closer to the vent, Alexis stumbled into me, headed the same direction.

"Vent," she pointed.

"Good eye, junior detective," I smiled. "Shall we?"

We moved into the space and started looking around, Alexis focusing on the North wall and me on the East. I tapped a torn cardboard box with my foot and a mouse skittered away from it, seeking the safety of the darkness beneath the stairs. The space had already been searched, but we had to be missing something.

"Chalk on cement," Alexis continued to mutter. "Chalk on cement…"

I could feel my frustration rise with every minute we searched. Evidence like this never came easy, but I was eager to find it so we could nab these bastards and put this all behind us. But I couldn't find anything out of the ordinary.

"The walls!" Alexis burst out. I jumped.

"What?" Andre hurried over.

"Have either of you ever built a brick wall?"

"Can't say I have." Andre lifted an eyebrow.

"I helped a friend landscape her backyard before I moved here. We used bricks to make a garden wall. My friend kept forgetting to put mortar on the tops of the last layer before stacking the next. Every time she did, it would make a sound like something scraping across cement. That's what kept reminding her to go back and put on the mortar."

"The bricks." I saw exactly where she was going. "Check the bricks. Start up near the vent and work your way around. Andre, start right there. Allie, start on the left, and I'll take the right."

I ran my gloved finger around the joints of the brick wall, looking for a weak spot. The mortar was separated and deteriorating in most places, so it was tough to narrow down where to look. I started tugging on random bricks, checking for any movement.

"I've got something," Andre called.

I whipped around. He was pulling on a brick at waist height below the vent. The brick slid out cooperatively, scraping as it went. Andre grinned.

"Chalk on cement," I nodded. "Way to go, Maria."

Andre continued pulling brick after brick from the wall, Alexis and I waiting eagerly behind him. When the hole was big enough, he grabbed a small flashlight off his belt and shined it through the middle. The anticipation hung thick in the air.

"There's something in here," Andre announced.

He passed me the flashlight, and I held it while he reached in with both hands. Andre pulled out a worn, two-toned orange and brown Nike shoebox. With a puff of air, Andre blew off the fine layer of dust that had settled on the lid. I cleared a spot for the box on the battered brown desk to our left and we gathered around as Andre opened it gingerly.

Inside was a stack of photographs, a leather journal, an SD card, and one of the now-familiar anklets with a broken cherry charm dangling from it. I slipped the SD card into an evidence bag and sealed it; the secrets it held would only be accessible once we got it back to the station. Andre and I started flipping through the photographs.

"These look like photos of the girls Ramond was running." Andre frowned.

"I've got a few of what looks like a meeting down at the docks," I added. "Some known associates of the family, but there's... wait! Here's one of the whole damn family! Big Dominic, Lorenzo, Leo, and even little sis Francesca."

"Shit, this one has Ferret in it. Look!" Andre passed a photo to me. It was Leo, the enforcer of the family, grabbing Ferret by the neck.

"That's a direct link," I crowed. "Fuck yeah!"

"Guys," Alexis was running her gloved finger over the anklet. "I know how the Bianchis track their girls."

She turned the broken cherry charm around to reveal a tiny microchip in the center. Andre's eyes grew round. He reached into his pocket and pulled out the evidence bag with Alexis's phone and Leticia's anklet in it. He pulled the anklet out and turned the cherry charm around between his fingertips.

"That's how they found Selsha," Andre whispered. "The anklet."

"No," Alexis shook her head. "She told me she threw hers down the garbage disposal."

"Not hers, Leticia's," Andre corrected, holding it aloft. "It was in the pocket of your coat."

"How did they know Selsha had it?" Alexis cocked her head to the side.

"They didn't," I gritted my teeth. My stomach churned.

"Were they coming after Leticia and just happened across Selsha instead?" Andre puzzled.

"No," Alexis's voice got hollow. "They were coming after me. They saw me with the anklet at the bus stop when I was talking to Selsha. Her runner did, I mean. I was showing it to Selsha to let her know she could trust me."

"Holy shit," Andre swore.

"That's how they knew where you were the night of the berserker attack, too." I threw down my gloves and ran my hands through my hair. "We got into a fight about you talking to Selsha that night. They saw you with the charm and they tracked you down when they figured out you were taking their girls off the job. The attack at the University was their second shot. They sent the penanggalan to finish the job when the berserkers couldn't do it, but they wound up catching Selsha on the run instead."

Heat was rising in my throat. My wolf was snarling. Just thinking of how many times Alexis had faced almost certain death and escaped by the skin of our teeth was making me sick with rage.

"It really is my fault that Selsha died," Alexis gasped.

"No." Andre shook his head fervently. "It's their fault." He shoved a finger at the picture of the Bianchis. "Those filthy fucking bastards did this, not you. It's them. It's always them. And this treasure box might be enough to get those sick fucks off the street for good."

"Let's get back to the station." I pulled Alexis to my side. "I have a feeling that little SD card has a hell of a lot more to tell us."

Chapter Thirty

Alexis

Despite Andre's and Finn's reassurances, the guilt weighed heavy on my heart. Selsha had almost gotten away. That damn anklet... In my coat. It should have been me. I shivered at the thought. Despite a constant stream of conversation between Andre and Finn in the front of the Charger, Finn kept glancing back at me. There was so much I wanted to say to him: the grief I felt, the fear that slithered up my spine when I thought about Selsha's last moments, and the ever-lurking possibility of Cam Gunner getting out of prison on a technicality.

"Chief," Andre hollered as we crossed the think tank. "We have something you're gonna wanna see."

"Whatcha got?" Chief tugged the waist of his slacks higher.

"We'll tell you all about it in Porter's office." Finn didn't break stride as he headed to the rear of the station.

"Tech? Color me intrigued."

Chief followed us back to Porter Miller's office. The wiry, just-out-of-college kid with horn-rimmed glasses was shocked as we piled into his office and Chief closed the door with a snap. He sputtered a few times before offering a polite greeting.

"We need you to see what's on this, Porter." Andre handed him the SD card.

"What's that?" Chief asked as Porter busied himself at his computer.

"Maria clued us in to Ramond's favorite skulking spot and we found this hidden in the brick wall of his basement." Finn put the box and its contents on the desk to our right. "Pictures of the women Ramond was running, meetings down at the dock, Ferret getting squeezed by Leo, and the whole damn Bianchi family right in the center of it all."

"I flipped through this journal of his on the way back to the station and Ramond was quite the bookkeeper," Andre continued. "Every John, every drop-off, every penny earned, every time he made a 'deposit' to the Bianchis, and each complaint that ever crossed Ramond's brain about how he was getting screwed out of what he thought he was due."

Chief pulled on a pair of gloves from Porter's desk, his big hands nearly bursting out of the small purple rubber, and flipped through the pictures and the journal himself. With every picture and every page he turned, his grin grew wider.

"I'm in," Porter declared. "Not even password protected..."

We all turned our attention to Porter's screen.

"It's got backups of the pictures you've found, plus a few more. There are some audio files, too." Porter explained.

"Play 'em," Andre and Finn commanded in unison.

Porter clicked on the first audio file. Static grated my eardrums. Then what sounded like clothes rustling and heavy breathing came next. A minute and a half passed with no additional sound. Finn tapped his finger impatiently on the desk.

"Why the fuck did you change the drop-off spot?" Ramond's voice broke the muffled silence.

"Had to," came a second voice.

The sound of hard sole shoes walking on concrete... Echoes of dripping... Horns off in the distance...

"I got better shit to do than play hide and seek with your crooked ass all night," Ramond complained.

"You act like pushin' whores is a noble occupation," the second voice sounded much closer this time. The tone was familiar, but it was still too garbled to distinguish. Ramond must have hidden the recording device under several layers of clothes.

"The bosses send their regards for your continued service protecting the family," Ramond sneered.

"I'm sure they do," the mystery voice responded on the recording. Someone spit something.

"I know that voice," Andre declared, staring at the screen.

"Hey, fuck you, man! These are new kicks," Ramond complained. "Spit your damn toothpick at your own fuckin' feet, not mine."

I gasped. Finn swore.

"Pause it," Chief commanded, fury in his voice. Porter did as he was told.

"That fucking rat!" Andre turned to look at the Chief.

"Olivier." Finn's face looked dangerous.

The Chief nodded. Even in the dim light of Porter's office, the red fury coloring Chief Whitmer's face was obvious. The precinct had a defector, and that defector's name was Detective Olivier. God, the number of times I'd cringed away from that voice since I punched the pompous asshole in the face...it was him on the recording, without a doubt. The second voice on that tape was Olivier's, and he was collecting a payoff from Ramond on behalf of the Bianchis.

"Where was Olivier the day Ramond was killed?" Finn growled.

"I'm not sure," Chief answered. "But I'm sure as shit about to find out."

"You think he took him out?" Andre asked.

"The whole precinct knew Ramond was about to sing. Olivier probably ran to his pocket-stuffers, shitting his pants the whole way," Finn acknowledged.

"Who better to eliminate someone in police custody than a cop? Access to any space, no one questioning why he was there. It would make for the perfect cover."

"Should we nail him, Chief?" Andre asked.

Chief was silent for a few moments, the muscle in his jaw clenched tight.

"No, we don't. No one breathes a word about any of this. Do you all understand?"

We nodded our heads in agreement. Poor Porter's green face meant he was probably about to throw up.

"Porter, you lock this damn door and finish processing what's on that SD card. Do not let another soul in here unless it's me. You three didn't go to Ramond's place and you sure as hell didn't find any evidence." The Chief collected the box, pictures, and journal and slid it under his jacket. "We play this one close to the chest. Olivier might not be the only rat on the ship. I've got some thinking to do before anything else goes down, you hear?"

"You've got it, Boss," Andre saluted.

"Briggs?"

"Yes, sir." Finn crossed his arms tightly over his chest.

"Ms. Henson, keep your fists to yourself," Chief nodded to me.

"I'll keep them tight to my sides until you say otherwise." My voice was bitter, hard.

A million thoughts were rushing through my head. Olivier was owned by the Bianchi family. He knew what they were doing to those women, and he padded his pockets instead of protecting their lives. He mocked Leticia's plight at the motel and then spewed his filth about Selsha after she was so brutally murdered. That mewling piece of shit probably murdered Ramond to protect his own ass. He deserved everything that was coming to him.

On the drive to the Pony after work, we were all in a dark mood.

"What if the Chief can't make charges stick to Olivier?" I worried aloud.

"He will. Chief Whitmer is the kind of chief that never stops being a cop even after he rises up the ranks. He's got something up his sleeve, I guarantee it." Andre assured.

"And if he weasels his way out of it somehow? Cops a plea deal?"

"Then we'll take care of him our way." Finn's voice was dark.

Normally, the thought of what Finn was capable of made my stomach turn, but not this time. If anyone deserved to have his throat ripped out, it was the man who vowed to protect the helpless and turned his back on their exploitation, rapes, and murders instead. I could feel the heat of my anger radiating through my chest.

We carried our storm cloud into the Pony. As we passed our friends throughout the bar, they gave us curious looks. Riel greeted us with a furrowed brow and tilted head.

"Later," Finn promised. Riel nodded knowingly.

We tried to loosen up as the night progressed, but with little luck. The sisters joined us a few hours after we arrived, and I could tell by the looks on their faces that they could read and see what was going on. I wondered how much they knew about the Bianchi crime family and the reach they had in the Clock with both humans and Fae alike.

Chloe kept casting glances at Riel when she thought no one was looking. Things were still icy between them despite Finn and me resolving our issues and getting together. My heart gave a guilty squeeze. When things settled down, I would have a one-on-one with Chloe and make this right. I couldn't fix their issues for them, but I could damn sure speak up about the loyalty Chloe showed me in one of my darkest hours. I hated to see them unhappy apart.

After last call, the few stragglers still left filtered out. We stayed behind. I could sense the bouncing urgency Finn carried to speak to Riel about our case. Finn held me close throughout the evening, none of the sexually charged eagerness in his touch this time. His energy was possessive tonight, protective despite being surrounded by friends. But with the news of Olivier's betrayal, I shifted my gaze from face to face around the bar all night, scrutinizing every move, every glance our way. Was Olivier the only wolf in sheep's clothing?

"What did you learn?" Riel sat down at our booth with a sigh.

"We've got the goods on the Bianchi family," Finn suppressed a grin.

"But there's been a fox in the henhouse," Andre added.

"Who?" Riel looked back over his shoulder.

"Olivier," Finn grimaced. "He's been in bed with the Bianchis for God knows how long. The Chief is on it, but we still have a few questions we need to find answers to before we confront the Bianchis."

"The Fae connections, you mean," Riel nodded. "We can't have the entire police force walking into a potentially dangerous situation and risk exposing the existence of the Fae."

"Exactly," Finn confirmed.

"Let's start from the beginning," I suggested. "What do we know?"

"The Bianchis have Fae hitmen," Andre said. "They sent the berserkers after you because you were causing a ruckus with their girls. And they send out the penanggalan to clean up the big messes."

"Why send the berserkers when you have the penanggalan, though? It's like throwing a pocketknife when you have a bazooka." Andre scratched his chin.

"For show?" Chloe piped up.

"To send a message?" Moira ventured.

"What's the difference between the two?" Riel pushed.

"Results, for one." Finn frowned and pulled me closer. "The berserkers failed, and the penanggalan is three for three."

"I don't think the Bianchis sent the berserkers, intending them to fail," Andre argued. "Why send an ineffective hitman? No. The Bianchis weren't planning on someone interrupting the hit." He nodded to Finn. "Maybe they didn't know how protected Alexis would be, how much she's integrated into our Fae community."

My heart dropped and gave a squeeze at the same time. It was strange discussing my murder attempt so casually. But we had to look at this objectively if we wanted to figure out the connection between the Bianchis and the Fae.

"Aside from the success rate, there's a significant difference in delivery," I sighed. "The berserkers were messy, emotional, it was personal... fun for them." I suppressed a shudder and Finn kissed the top of my head. "Is it that way for the penanggalan?"

"Not even close." Andre shook his head. "The crime scenes with the headless victims are frustratingly clean. There's an emotionless precision in the kill. Quick, efficient, effective. That's the MO."

"Sending the berserkers was a message, then. The kill from the berserkers would be carnage." I could feel Finn's growl roll in his chest as he spoke. "But the kill from the penanggalan would be a clean disposal. Sending the berserkers after Alexis would send the message to everyone in the community, human and Fae alike, that fucking with the family means a messy end."

"Or send us the message... you the message... to back off their business," Riel said seriously to Finn. "They have to know you're a Fae cop. The berserkers would have told them as much. You know too much about their business on both fronts."

Finn's body went rigid around mine. I rubbed the top of his forearm and leaned further back against his chest. Had it really been that personal?

"What about the other victims?" Chloe asked. Her eyes darted nervously between me and Riel. "Why did they meet their end the way they did?"

"Inside job, outside job." Andre's eyes got big. "They were taking care of their own business, their own people, with the penanggalan. According to Ramond, Ferret may have been about to rat out the Bianchis. The berserker failed his assignment, and then Selsha was on the run. Even if Alexis had been the target with the last attack, they would have had no other choice but to send the penanggalan after the berserkers failed. How many hitmen does one crime family have hanging around?"

"Makes sense," Finn said through gritted teeth.

"The penanggalan isn't about sending messages, it's about cleaning up the trash," Andre shifted in his seat. "That's gotta be it. Ferret ran afoul of the family, got offed. Berserker, same thing. I guarantee if we traced back other similar deaths, we'd find the same thing. It's business... cost of doing business," Andre shook his head.

"What else do you know about their connection with the Fae?" Riel prompted.

"They knew enough to keep a coat from a selkie to get her to do their dirty work," Finn said. "Someone in the organization knows Fae lore at a minimum. They sure as hell didn't get that information from the berserkers."

"Do you think the penanggalan is their inside source?" Moira offered.

"Could be." Andre tossed his fedora on the table and wiped his brow with the back of his hand. "Riel did some digging on them after Finn got back from Chicago. Penanggalans are witches that learned to take the form of the floating head and trailing entrails by hanging out in a tub of vinegar. It's a complicated spell, so it means the witch who does it is powerful. Normal looking human by day, creepy ass motherfucker by night."

"So, team Bianchi included a witch, berserker squad, and an imprisoned selkie at minimum," I counted off on my fingers.

"Three very different races of Fae working for one family is strange..." Riel sipped at his beer. "What would bring them together like that?"

"What brought you guys together?" I looked around at my Fae friends. They stared back at me blankly. "Riel did, right?" Everyone turned to Riel. "You guys all found your way to a powerful leader. Someone you knew you could trust..."

"...Because he's one of us." Finn's eyebrows shot up and he caught Andre's eye.

"A powerful Fae leader," Andre nodded back to Finn with an identical, knowing expression. I knew that look. They'd figured it out.

"Holy fucking shit." Finn ran his hand through his hair.

"The Bianchis are Fae," Andre finished for him.

Moira gasped. "No! How could they be? We would know, wouldn't we?"

"A powerful force," Riel said, more to himself than to us. "Whispers in the Fae community of another rising power. Someone who could challenge the peaceful hold we have on the Clock."

"You came here because of the magic in the woods," I continued. "Is it so unbelievable that other Fae came here for the same reason?"

"Not unbelievable at all, Alexis," Riel nodded. "I've been so blind."

"But we would have seen something like that," Chloe looked at Moira.

"Not if something was blocking your sight," Riel shook his head.

"What the hell could possibly block Moira and..." Andre started.

"Nothing," Chloe snapped. I could feel the fear and panic in her voice.

"That's not true, Chloe," Moira grabbed her hand and held it tight. "I'm not infallible. I can't see everything without a lot of concentrated effort, you know that. I haven't been looking for something like this."

"Lacey?" Andre whispered, looking at Lacey snoozing on a tabletop across the bar.

"We wouldn't know, would we?" Chloe's eyes got watery.

"Finn, what was it you told me about Fae siblings?" I asked.

He looked back and forth between Moira and Chloe with a worried glance before answering me. "That their powers are usually within the same realm. Why?"

"Could the penanggalan have siblings?"

The bar went silent. A shiver went down my spine. Everyone stared at me, then at each other.

"I mean, you said that the penanggalan must be a really powerful witch to do what she does. I'm not a Fae expert by any means, but if she can do that kind of magic, could a sibling of hers do a different magic to block you guys from seeing what you normally see?"

No one answered me. We sat in silence for what seemed like forever. I shifted uncomfortably in my seat, Finn's breath tickling my ear. I was feeling stupid. Had I made some kind of Fae faux pas?

"Alexis, you are a freaking genius," Andre burst out. "It's the fucking Bianchis. The Bianchis are witches and warlocks! They'd have the pull with other Fae, be enough of a force to rally Fae around them and be a big enough threat that it's pinging Riel's magical radar."

"How did you make that kind of leap?" Chloe asked.

"From what Riel says, penanggalans rarely go around doing other people's bidding for them." Andre explained. "They're not errand runners and guns for hire like the berserkers. Since they're powerful enough in their own right, they don't need to run looking for bigger bads to protect and shelter them. They do their own dirty work, pick their own victims. We were wrong; the penanggalan isn't some kind of hired hand doing their bidding. She's none other than Francesca Bianchi herself. Leo may be the hammer, but she's the fucking scalpel."

"It fits," Finn confirmed. "Lorenzo and Leo are ravenously protective of Francesca. We chalked it up to big brother behavior, but maybe it's more than that. She's their most effective weapon against deserters in the ranks. Run afoul of them and lose your head at the hands of this seemingly demure, pretty little package."

"Riel, what do you think?" Chloe borderline whispered.

Riel's frown was so deep it carved lines across his otherwise perfectly smooth face. Worry was dancing in his eyes. My gut was telling me that Andre's theory was pretty close to the mark. It made perfect sense to me, but I knew so little about Fae culture and powers. Riel had thousands of years of knowledge and experience.

"There's no way we can be sure, but it is a strong possibility," Riel admitted.

"We have to know for sure before we send a few dozen human cops right into the middle of this shitstorm," Finn argued. "I crossed paths with my share of witches and warlocks in the 17th century, and I've steered clear since. They're not all bad, like any other type of Fae, but the bad ones can be fucking terrifying."

"We need to get close enough to them to find out for sure." Andre rubbed the bridge of his nose.

"No," Moira protested. "It's not safe. Even if they turn out to be perfectly human, they're crime lords, Andre. You'd be risking your lives!"

"I agree, it's too dangerous," Chloe bit her lip. "But... maybe there's another way." She stared meaningfully at Moira. Realization dawned on Moira's face.

"Moira?" Finn's voice was worried.

"I..." Moira cleared her throat. "I can try. It's been centuries since I've done it, but I can sure try."

"Try what?" I asked.

"We have access to some ancient magic, my sisters and I," Moira explained. "There's a ceremony of sorts we can perform to tap into it, open ourselves up to clearer sight. Then I can see the past more clearly, search into the timelines around the Bianchis, and get some answers."

"Is it safe?" The tension in the air made me wary.

"It's... intense," Chloe admitted. "But it's familiar magic. We used it all the time for thousands of years. We can do it. Especially if it means keeping the rest of you out of the lion's den."

"The warrants for the Bianchis will come down the pipeline soon with what we found tonight," Finn warned. "We don't have a lot of time."

"We'll do it tonight," Moira swallowed hard.

"Are you guys sure about this?" I reached out for their hands. They both squeezed my hands reassuringly.

"It's the right thing to do," Moira stood up, brushed the creases from her skirt, and held out a hand to Chloe. "Sister?"

"Let's go," Chloe rose with her.

"Be safe," Riel pleaded. Chloe gave him a sad smile.

We watched as they gently woke Lacey. Lacey's big eyes were full of deep understanding as she examined their faces. She nodded to us, a determined lilt to her chin, before they disappeared into the darkness outside.

"Are they going to be okay?" My throat felt tight.

"The sisters are the most capable, powerful Fae force I know." Andre patted my shoulder. "They'll be fine."

"You all should go home and get some rest. I have some reflection of my own to do this evening." Riel drained the last few drops of his beer.

"Come on, Siren, let's go home." Finn pulled me to my feet, and we left.

Our drive was silent. Finn's thumb traced a path back and forth along the back of my hand as he drove. We dropped Andre at his apartment, and he gave us a halfhearted 'Goodnight, lovebirds' as he got out of the car.

When we got back to Finn's place, we peeled off our clothes and melted into each other in bed. Finn held me tight. We didn't need to speak to convey our thoughts and feelings. We could both feel the intensity of what was happening around us. Just being together was enough to keep us both grounded.

I woke to my favorite song playing from the pocket of Finn's suit jacket. It was a familiar sound, but I couldn't quite figure out why it made my stomach drop. I blinked my eyes open slowly.

"NO!" Finn cried, jackknifing to a sitting position next to me. "NO!" His face was sleepy panic and agony.

"Finn," I cradled his face in my hands. "What's wrong?"

"Alexis!" He called out, his eyes unfocused.

"I'm right here, Finn. Look at me."

Once his eyes finally settled on mine, his tense body went limp in my arms. He sounded like he'd run a marathon. His arms snaked around my waist, his grip painfully tight.

"Finn, honey, what happened?"

"I called you," his voice was muffled. "I called you and it rang from her pocket."

The realization dawned on me.

Selsha.

Her poor, mangled body wrapped in my coat. Finn called my phone, and it rang from my dead friend's pocket. He thought it was me. I was dead to him only days ago.

"Oh, dragon," I held him closer and kissed his hair. "I'm so sorry. I'm here. I'm here with you."

"I know." He took a shuddering breath. "I know."

He pulled me with him as he lay back on the bed. His mouth took mine in a deep, possessive kiss. Desire sparked within me instantly. His hands were all over my body, his tongue slipping in and out of my mouth. I slid my leg over his hip and ran my hand down the planes of his stomach to touch him.

My phone rang again.

"Fuck," Finn growled.

"I'm sorry, I'll turn it off."

"I should have let Andre keep it. I thought you might need it."

I hurried over to the source of the sound.

"Can you do me a favor and change the ringtone, love?" Finn's voice was tight.

"Of course, I'll do it right..." My breath hitched, and I froze.

The name on the caller ID was one I desperately didn't want to see. I stared at my tainted phone. I wanted to throw it across the room as the doom spread through my limbs. But I answered it anyway because I knew I had to.

"Marshal Davis?" I asked.

"Ms. Henson," Marshal Davis replied. "I have bad news. Seriously bad news."

My heart dropped out through the bottoms of my feet.

"They released Cam Gunner from prison on parole yesterday. I've been trying to contact you since I got word, but you haven't been answering your phone. The son of a bitch didn't check in with his parole officer this morning. It looks like he skipped town."

My ears were ringing. I could hear every word the Marshal was saying with painful acuity, but they still sounded far away. Panic was ballooning from the center of my chest, expanding, filling me up. My body was shaking.

He was out.

"Ms. Henson?"

"I'm... I'm here." The words were a painful echo of the assurance I'd just given Finn.

"We already have a team out looking for him. We're still confident that he doesn't know your location, but you need to be on guard, just in case. You know what that animal is capable of better than anyone, so I'll save any more warnings."

The bile was rising in my throat. My knees buckled, and I grabbed the armchair for support. My eyes went unfocused.

"He's coming after me, isn't he?" I squeaked out.

"You're a smart woman, Ms. Henson. I'm going to level with you. He made some threats as he was leaving the prison. Your name came up more than once. I've already contacted Chief Whitmer and apprised him of the situation. He assured me you'll be under the constant, watchful eyes of some of his best officers. Stay vigilant. I'll be in touch."

The line went dead.

"Allie?" Finn touched my shoulder, and I jumped. "Baby? "

The phone slipped from my grasp and hit the floor with a dull thud.

"He's out," my voice trembled.

The shaking rocked my whole body. Finn pulled me close, his skin warm against mine. It was my turn to collapse into his arms.

"He's out. They can't find him. He's coming for me."

Finn's body went stiff. I shook like an earthquake against his perfect stillness. A rumbling growl was gathering in his chest. After several long moments, he carried me back over to the bed, pulled the blankets over us, and continued to hold me. I don't know how long we stayed locked together as I fought the urge to vomit.

Once my body had exhausted itself and gone still, my eyes desperately sought Finn's gaze. He stared back at me, fire and ice. He emanated a frighteningly powerful aura as he drank in my face.

"I'm ready to tell you now," I whispered.

He frowned but nodded his assent. I took a deep breath and readied myself to show him my demons.

"I was going to graduate school in Iowa, working on my master's degree in social work and...uh..." I cleared my throat. I hadn't told anyone this story since I sat on the witness stand over a year ago. It felt like the story itself was getting caught in my throat.

"I was walking home from the library late one night after studying for an exam. My apartment was off campus, and I was nearly home when someone grabbed me from behind and pulled me into the alcove of the building next to mine. He called me by name. I didn't recognize his voice. He told me he'd been watching me, and he'd picked me for a special project of his. He said he didn't go off-script very often, but he was…hungry."

My tears painted my cheeks. Finn's breathing was labored. He ran his hand through my hair and kissed my forehead.

"He told me not to scream and held a knife to my neck. He forced me to take him to my apartment. Once we were there, he tied my arms to the posts of my bed with my shoelaces and he raped me…"

The images of that night flooded my consciousness. The smell of cigarettes… The feel of his calloused palms on my skin… The way he'd reveled in my terror…

"He bragged about himself the entire time. I tried to shut him out, but my mind latched onto the names of the other women he said he'd 'played' with before. So many of them… It was his job, he said. Sniff them out. Hunt them down. Teach them who they belonged to." I shuddered.

"I knew he was going to kill me. I was already working as a victim's advocate, and I knew he wouldn't be telling me all of this unless he planned for me to never speak it to anyone else. A part of me wanted to die just to make it end. But those names… those other women… I knew I had to do something or there would be more names. More women. They needed me."

"Hours had gone by, and he was… cleaning himself up, getting dressed. I had been working on getting my hands out." I rubbed my wrists. "I got my left hand out first, then untied my right hand when he turned his back. He had left the knife on my nightstand. He saw me as I reached for it and he jumped at me, so fast, so far… But I had just enough time to angle the knife and it caught him in the chest. I pushed him off me, grabbed my phone, and ran."

"I ran right into my downstairs neighbor, Mrs. Hogan, while she was bringing her dog in from going to the bathroom. She took me into her apartment, got me some clothes, and sat with me while she called the police. Banging on her door while we waited for the cops to show up... but her dog was a pretty ferocious mastiff. I think Brutus's barking kept him at bay and then the sirens scared him off."

"They took me to the hospital, took my statement, did a rape kit, and I did my best to recite the names of every woman he'd mentioned. The next couple of weeks were a blur. The cops found him trying to make a run for it on a bus, knife wound and all. Afterwards, I… I fell apart after it. I found out his name, and it haunted me: Cam Gunner. I started therapy and moved in with a friend since I couldn't stomach being at my apartment anymore. We went to trial. I testified more for those other women than myself. They found him guilty. After his sentencing, he threatened to have his family find me and kill me, so they put me in witness protection and sent me here."

I sighed heavily. Once the words started, I couldn't stop them. They flooded out of me as I was cradled in the arms of the man I loved. He didn't speak a word the whole time. His expression was a mix of pity and fury. As my body shook with the visceral remembrance of my assault, his trembled with what I could only assume was barely bridled rage. The shadows of his wolf played in the depths of his eyes.

"And now he's out. He skipped parole. They don't know for certain where he is, but I know he's coming. Something deep down in me feels it."

"I won't let him touch you," Finn growled. "I'll rip the fucker limb from limb if he gets within a hundred miles of you."

His vow felt so real, so earnestly delivered, but it didn't chase away the fear like I hoped it would. I knew Finn would do anything to protect me, but could he protect me from this? He was magically powerful, capable. I wanted so badly to believe he could, but the fear...

He took my face between his hands.

"I will protect you," he promised. "I will always protect you. Even if it means my life. I won't hesitate. Ever."

No words would come. So, I kissed him instead. Gently, fervently, and let my lips communicate what my voice couldn't. I believed him. I trusted him. I loved him.

But I was still afraid.

It was Finn's phone that interrupted our kiss this time. He moved away from me only as far as he had to in order to reach it. His eyes flickered from the phone then to me, then back again, his face conflicted.

"Briggs," he snapped into the phone. "Chief?" His tone changed instantly.

Finn listened intently for a long time. I couldn't hear the words the chief was saying, but I could hear the urgency in his tone. Something was happening. Olivier? The Bianchis? Another body?

"Understood. I'm on my way." Finn hung up.

"The warrants are in. They need me at the station. We're going in tonight to make the arrests."

"Okay, let's go." I struggled to get my limbs to obey.

"The Chief doesn't want you to come to the station," Finn gritted his teeth. "Olivier's still there. Chief has a plan for him, and he's worried about your safety since you decked the asshole. If things go bad when Chief puts his plan in place, he thinks Olivier might try to hurt you."

"I have to be there," I protested. "It's not like you're going to take me to the scene for the arrest, but I at least want to be at the station when it all goes down."

"Olivier will be at the station while the rest of us are out on the bust. Chief won't let him anywhere near the Bianchis now that we know where his loyalties lie."

"He's going to leave him at the station alone?"

"He'll have babysitters that are in the know."

"What am I supposed to do, then? Just stay here?"

"Yes, that's exactly what you're going to do. I'm going to call Riel to come stay with you while I take care of this once and for all. He'll keep you safe while I'm gone."

"Finn, that's not fair! You can't leave me here while…" I rose to follow him as he dressed.

"Do you think I want to leave you?! Like this? Now?! After what you just told me? How terrified I know you are? If I could rip myself in two so part of me could go nail these fuckers and the other half could stay with you, I would do it. No question. But the Chief gave me explicit orders and no time to plead your case."

"You're not leaving me behind again," I spat.

His face fell. I had wounded him. A part of me didn't care, though. This was just as much my case now as it was Finn and Andre's case. I wanted…no, *needed* to be a part of this. Finn was staring at me wordlessly, war in his eyes. My inner voice became conflicted at the pain in his gaze. Would it really be so different sitting here waiting for the news versus sitting at the station? I knew I would feel equally helpless no matter where I waited.

I took a deep breath to steady myself.

"Okay, I'll stay here."

"Are you sure?" Finn's voice was tight. "I promised I would never make a big decision without your input again. You tell me what you think is right and I'll back you."

"Even if it means catching hell from the Chief? Or ending up at the station with Olivier?" I asked.

Finn swallowed hard. "I trust you. No matter what."

I thought it over. My knee-jerk reaction to being left behind was fading, and my logic was kicking in. If I went to the station, Olivier would be a threat. As long as my safety wasn't secure, Finn would worry, and a worried Finn would be a distracted Finn. That would put him in danger. Nothing was worth that kind of risk to me.

"Call Riel. I'll stay." I sat back on the bed.

"If that's what you really want."

"What I want is for my badass boyfriend to catch those Fae sons-of-bitches and put them somewhere they'll never see the light of day again. If I can't be there to watch it myself, you'll owe me a play-by-play the second you get back in one completely unharmed piece. You got it?"

"I swear on my life." He finished buttoning his shirt and kissed me.

He swept out of the room, cellphone in hand, and called Riel. I laid back and stared at the ceiling. I didn't want Finn to be away when fear was still coursing through me. But we didn't have a choice. This was bigger than both of us. All I could do was trust Marshal Davis when he said Cam Gunner didn't know my location. I didn't know the full extent of Riel's powers, but if he was the leader of the good Fae in the Clock, I knew he could protect me.

"Riel has to wrap a few things up at the bar, but he said he would be right over." Finn hurried back into the room, pulled on his holster, and checked his sidearm. "I called Moira and left her a message as backup, but God knows what kind of shape they're in after last night."

"My God, I completely forgot about that. Do you think I should call and check on them?"

"No, when they're done, rested, and ready, they'll have answers for us. They understand the urgency and the stakes. I hope that time is soon. I don't know if I can delay the Chief. If things go sideways in a magical way, I'm not sure how much Andre and I can do on our own to protect the entire force. I hate going in blind."

"Then maybe you need more than just you and Andre. Can you rally the troops? The magical ones?"

Finn frowned. The muscles in his jaw spasmed.

"Once I know the Chief's play, I can call in the Fae cavalry to wait in the wings. We'll need to be careful. We'd be risking a helluva lot to protect a few dozen human cops."

"You'd be risking the exposure of the Fae, I know." I pulled the blankets tighter around my shoulders. "You've had to make that choice before, and I don't envy your position any time you've had to make it."

His phone rang again.

"Andre?" Finn answered. His frown deepened. "Shit, that soon?" His eyes flickered to mine. "Riel's going to stay with her, but he's not here yet. I'll explain later." He ran his free hand through his hair. "Fuck… Okay, yeah… I'm coming." He hung up.

"I've got thirty minutes between now and when they light the fuse." Finn sat on the edge of the bed next to me.

"Go then, they need you more than I do right now," I forced a serious smile.

"That's not true and you know it," he caressed my cheek.

"I'll keep just fine until Riel gets here. I promise."

"Swear to me you won't leave this apartment, not for anything."

"I'll be right here waiting for you when you get back in one piece, dammit," I ordered. "Now go."

He grabbed my face with both hands and kissed me firmly. "I love you more than anything, Alexis."

"I love you, too, Finn."

With that, he was gone. A chill ran through me at the sound of him locking the apartment door behind him. The walls felt like they were closing in on me. There were enemies all around us and I wasn't sure how I was going to make it through the next few hours while I waited helplessly as they raided the Bianchis. All the while, the threat of Cam Gunner loomed in the darkest corners of my mind. *Hurry, Riel*, I prompted in a whisper.

Fearing the dragging of every second, I got up and dressed in a pair of black leggings and a comfortable vintage t-shirt Chloe and I had found at a swap meet. I cobbled together a light breakfast and barely tasted it as I stared at the door in anticipation.

Finally, there was a knock.

"Riel?" I called through the door.

"Riel got held up, so he sent me to give you a message," a female voice answered.

"Milani?!"

"This shit wasn't my idea, so just open the hell up so I can tell you and leave," Milani's scathing voice replied.

With the sisters indisposed and Finn calling the rest of our friends to help with the raid, Milani must have been the only one left for the favor. Simultaneously puzzled and disgruntled, I opened the door. The disdainful retort was ready to roll off my tongue the second I saw her smirking face.

"What's the message, Milani?" I forced away the litany of profanity, ready to burst out of my mouth at the sight of her. "Riel could have called me."

"Oh, he could have. But there was a little fire in the woman's bathroom. It'll take him just long enough to put it out that he's going to miss this."

"Miss what?"

"The message," Milani's smirk grew wider.

"For the love of God, Milani, what message?"

"To keep your filthy human nose out of Bianchi business, bitch." Milani took three slow steps back, and another figure emerged from the shadows.

I barely had enough time to register the grinning face that haunted my dreams before pain exploded on the side of my head and I fell into darkness.

Chapter Thirty-One

Finn

The station was in chaos; I'd never seen it this way before. Every uniform and detective crammed themselves into the think tank. People were shouting, elbows were pushing through the crowd, and it was a damn fight just to get to my desk where Andre sat waiting for me.

"Was she pissed?" Andre asked over the din.

"Alexis? She wasn't doing back flips, that's for damn sure," I sighed.

"I can't blame her. She's sunk just as much into this case as we have. It sucks to miss out on the payoff. Especially since it's all because of that piece of shit." Andre lifted his chin towards Olivier and Lot huddled in a corner together.

My neck prickled at the sight of the murdering asshole. Lot caught my eye. His features pinched. Did he know his partner was a rat? Was he in on it himself? I had to trust that the Chief had all that handled. I needed to focus on getting all these clueless humans through a Fae fight without letting them know that's what it was. I'd made a few calls to my Fae friends on the drive here. They were eager to help; a plan was already in motion.

"Why did you send Riel to babysit her? You that worried about Olivier?"

"No," my stomach rolled. "You know the attack I told you about from before she came to the Clock?"

"How could I forget? You're not the only one making a secret angry hit list of people who've hurt Lex." Andre ran his palm over the butt of his sidearm.

"She got a call this morning. He's out, and he skipped out on his P.O. She's terrified that he's headed this way." Her face flashed in my mind. My wolf whined.

"Son of a bitch! You've gotta be kidding me." Andre's face was incredulous. "How the hell did she talk you into coming here, then?"

"It was her call, not mine. But I figure all I can do is go after the more immediate threat. I can't bury my teeth into Cam Gunner's neck yet, but I sure as hell can do my best to rid us all of the Bianchis. It's one concrete thing I can do to keep her safe. We'll deal with the other if it comes to that."

"Fuck, man. I'm sorry. Ya'll can't catch a break."

"Tell me about it."

The Chief emerged from his office with a thick black bulletproof vest stretched tightly over his barrel chest. Not the type of man to send his people into a fight while he sat back at the office, he looked ready to pounce. He surveyed the scene with a frown. His mouth opened, but before he could speak, his expression changed to surprise. I followed his gaze and saw the sisters pushing their way through the crowd.

"Moira? What are you doing here?" I chastised.

"Alexis was right," Moira panted. Andre drew in closer to us. Moira's face was drawn and ashen. "Two brothers and a sister, thrice blessed, long lineage. The head, the arm, and the core…"

"You're speaking in riddles, Moira," Andre whispered. "What does all that mean?"

"They're witches," Chloe confirmed. "Powerful ones. But if I can get close to them, I can find a weakness. We're coming with you."

"Chief won't let that happen," I argued.

"We'll be discreet. Stay in the shadows. You're going to need us, trust me. After what Moira saw, you'll need all the help you can get… and you already know that." Chloe's eyes went unfocused as she stared at me. "You called the others. They're coming, too."

"It was Alexis's idea," I nodded.

Lacey gasped. Her eyes went wide and her whole body went rigid. Moira and Chloe each grabbed her by an arm. The second her sisters touched her, they went rigid, too. All three sets of gray eyes clouded over. Holy shit, not here!

"Past, present, and future," Moira's voice was a barely discernible monotone. It was her, but not her at the same time. I had only seen this happen once before in all the years I had known them. My back tensed.

"We three," Chloe intoned.

Lacey gasped again, her eyes coming back into focus. She locked eyes with me, her mouth opening and closing like a fish out of water. Everything inside me was screaming a warning. My wolf paced within me as intuitive dread flooded my system.

She forced a small squeak. The think tank was still in chaos, no one paid any mind to the strange scene unfolding at the back of the room by our desks. Another squeak and a soft cry.

"Lacey?" I placed my hands on both sides of her face. The power surging between the sisters jolted through me like an electric shock, but I didn't release my hold. My instincts were howling. "What do you see?"

Her face went from pink to red to purple with the effort she mustered. Her eyes were wild with urgency. She took a deep breath and tried again.

"He…" she forced out. Andre swore softly.

"He… has… her," Lacey breathed. Her face screwed up in pain, but she persisted. Every word was an agonizing labor. "The hunter has her."

Lacey's hands flew up to her head, and she fell to her knees in a silent scream. Moira and Chloe snapped out of it simultaneously and knelt on the floor next to Lacey, comforting her. Three sets of eternally wise eyes stared at me in horror.

A sick chill washed over me. The same terror I'd felt at the edge of the woods on campus clamped across my chest. A hunter… A relentless killing machine. Fae.

"Gunner?" Chief's voice snapped me back. But he wasn't speaking to me; he was talking to the sisters.

Chloe nodded to him. Horror, looks of horror from all sides.

"You knew?" I accused. "Alexis?"

"Go," he commanded. I'd never heard fear in the old man's voice, but that one word was drowning in it. "Both of you, GO NOW!" he thundered.

Andre grabbed my arm and pulled me through the crowd. My brain fought against the gut-twisting realization.

He had her.

He had her.

A hunter.

Fae.

It all came back to the Fae.

"Fucking DRIVE, Finn," Andre screamed at me.

I barely registered that I was behind the wheel of the Charger. Everything snapped into place at once. My wolf and I snarled in unison as I slammed my foot on the accelerator. Cam Gunner had Alexis. I had to get to her.

We tore up the stairs to my apartment. The door was ajar. I roared in frustration, knowing already that only emptiness waited for us within. Droplets of blood dotted the doorjamb. I could smell Alexis in the metallic tang of it.

My feet obeyed my nose, following the scent back out of the building. Her scent was strong, fresh. But it stopped at the curb.

"He put her in a car. FUCK," I yelled.

"Finn, Andre!" Riel was running down the sidewalk at us.

"Where the hell were you?" I charged at him, blinded by my rage.

"Milani set a fire at the Pony. She said she had to use the bathroom. The smoke detectors went off a few minutes after she left," Riel explained.

My wolf demanded to be set loose. I was barely holding myself together.

"A hunter took Alexis," Andre spat. "You were supposed to be here with her." He grabbed Riel roughly by the front of his black vest. "Who gives a shit about the Pony?"

"A hunter?" Riel's face fell. "The attacker is Fae?"

"I smell her," I growled. Alexis's wasn't the only female scent in the air. "Milani. She was here."

"She set the fucking fire as a distraction," Andre pushed Riel away. "There were no signs of forced entry. Alexis wouldn't have opened the door unless it was for someone she knew. It was Milani, that foul, lying succu-bitch."

"We can put the pieces together later. If Alexis is in the clutches of a hunter, our time is woefully short. We must find her," Riel paced, his shoes scuffling along the sidewalk.

"Her scent ends here," I raged. "How the hell are we supposed to find her?!"

Andre's eyes went unfocused, flicking back and forth rapidly. He was dream hopping.

"I found her," Andre crowed. "She's unconscious. It's not a dream, but I can reach into her mind."

"Do it," I demanded.

His face screwed up in concentration. Sweat beaded along his forehead. His eyes moved faster and faster as he worked.

"Darkness... it's muffled... fear... cold... she's bound... an owl... she knows this smell..."

"Andre!" I urged.

His eyes flickered faster.

"Taylor told her about these flowers... sweet rocket, that's what she called them. She recognizes the smell!"

"He took her to the woods." My feet were already moving. "Taylor told her about the flowers in the woods."

"Go find her," Riel ordered. "I'll deal with Milani." He looked dangerous. Good.

Andre and I launched ourselves into the car and headed for the woods. Andre's eyes bounced back and forth as he maintained his connection with Alexis's unconscious mind from the passenger seat. He gripped the handle of the door so tightly that it made his skin blanch.

"She hears a voice... male... deep... she's terrified of it. The smell of cigarettes..."

"Can you tell what he's saying?" I begged.

"It's muffled..." Andre's voice was pinched.

"Push," I prompted.

He took a deep breath and was silent for a while. The sirens on the Charger blared and the red and blue lights danced across my dashboard as we raced through town. My foot was heavy on the accelerator.

"Let me in all the way, Lex," Andre whispered.

I risked a glance at him. His whole body shuddered. He was in.

"...happy to see you kept so well in my absence. We have the Marshal to thank for that. It's nice to have so many useful, well-placed ticks tucked in our pockets. I'll make sure cousin Leo sends him a little bonus." Andre repeated the words Alexis's mind was absorbing.

The red I saw had nothing to do with the lights on my dash. Snakes at every turn. Betrayal after betrayal.

"It's nice to be home again. That cell wasn't at all to my taste. So long without a playmate. The family tells me you've been meddling. Isn't it funny? You went from a pleasant distraction, a mistake, a flaw in my perfect record, to an actual part of my job. Hunting down all of those runaway whores and snuffing them out for years has always been a delicious treat, but you've been my biggest thrill. Not one of those cherries put up a fight quite like you."

"Son of a bitch!" I slammed my hand against the steering wheel.

Andre gasped. He emerged from her mind, gulping air like a drowning man.

"He hit her, and she woke up. Fucking go, man!" Andre commanded.

The implication of what's we'd just heard hung heavy in the air. All of this was connected. Every enemy led back to one singular source.

The second my feet hit the ground in the parking lot on the south end of the woods, the faint scent of honeysuckle mocked me on the breeze. We hit the tree line running; me tearing off my clothes, Andre gathering them behind me as I outran him. Fear and rage ripped through me, and the shift came easily. My wolf and I merged into one with a snarl.

Alexis's scent exploded through my muzzle. Pure instinct took over and pulled me forward. Never in all my centuries had I moved so quickly. My wolf and I nearly flew through the woods where we'd first fallen in love with Alexis, desperate to get to her in time.

Her scent was getting stronger. I was nearly there. Please, Gods, don't let me be too late!

My ears perked up as I heard the frightened tones of Alexis's voice ahead. I pushed myself harder, my paws thudding against the hard ground. Launching myself off a fallen log, I burst into a clearing surrounded by tufts of flowers. The sight in front of me had me roaring.

A thickly built man with circular burn scars running up his forearm held Alexis by the hair. He tied her to a tree, her body straining away from the psychopath before her. Silver duct tape covered her mouth. A guttural growl burst out of me as I advanced.

"A guest!" Cam Gunner grinned at me.

Another snarl rolled across my lips.

"No regular guest, either. You're the shifter. I've heard so much about you from the family." He licked his lips.

Alexis's eyes were locked on me. My guts turned inside out at the sight of caked blood in the hair around her temple. White hot rage coursed through me. I advanced on my prey.

"Oh, I don't think you'll be coming any closer," Gunner mocked. He yanked Alexis's hair, and she cried out in pain. I stopped in my tracks.

"Good choice, shifter. My friend Alexis and I were just catching up. I've missed so much since she put me in a cage." He twirled a section of Alexis's hair around his finger.

"Imagine my delight when I learned that she'd stumbled across a few of my close, personal friends here in the Clock. You killed one of them, if I understand correctly; ripped his throat out in the same way you're fantasizing about doing to me now. But don't fret your wolfy little head about it. Bygones and all that."

He ran his hand across Alexis's cheek. I was nearly bursting out of my skin to get to her. But one wrong move and the hunter would snap her neck. His kind was pure instinct. Hunt. Kill. It was rare for them to play with their mark in this way.

"It's difficult to carry on a conversation with a dog," Gunner sneered. "Why don't you do us all a favor and take your human form again? It would fascinate me to hear your take on Alexis's current condition."

I shook my head, still laser-focused and ready to pounce.

"Uncle Dom said you were stubborn. Good," he grinned. "It wouldn't be any fun if you weren't."

He pulled out a large knife. I took a step forward, growling, until he held the knife to Alexis's throat. I stopped dead.

"Hunting bitches for the family has gotten so tedious. It's hardly challenging. But Alexis," he sighed. "She's been a challenge. We had her sent here to keep until my release, but we had no idea she'd ally herself with the fluffy Fae. This is going to be a genuine thrill. I simply can't decide whether to kill you first while she watches or consume your human whore in every way while you bleed out slowly on the dirt."

He threw his head back and laughed. It was a split-second moment, but I took advantage of it. I launched myself across the clearing, aiming for his throat. But he was ready for me. He swung the knife between us and caught me across the side. I yelped, my paws hitting the ground, and I skidded backwards. He backed away from me, tossing the knife back and forth between his hands. I barely registered the pain in my side, the adrenaline sharpening my focus.

I lunged again, and he dodged it with ease. His face was wild and gleeful. My frustration flared. He could dance around and play his game all he wanted. This piece of shit was living on borrowed time.

We circled each other, both waiting for the other to make a move. He tried to head fake me, but I was patient despite my desperation. Without warning, he flashed forward, knife slicing through the air. I pushed off the tree behind me and met him midair. Another sharp pain splintered through my left hip. Before Gunner could pull away, though, I twisted my body around and buried my teeth into the arm holding the knife.

A heavy blow struck me in the chest, throwing me backwards. I landed hard on my back and struggled to regain my footing. My senses warned of another approach, and I was able to pull myself out of the way seconds before Gunner plunged the knife into the ground where I had just been. I made a move to jump on his back, but my injuries were making me sluggish. He threw me off with ease, and it took all my strength to leap out of the way of another knife strike.

My last move landed me on the far side of the clearing, away from Alexis. Her eyes were wild with fear. She strained against her binding, crying out muffled sounds from behind the duct tape. Gunner looked back and forth between Alexis and I, a wicked grin spreading across his face like a disease.

"Don't tell me the noble shifter has fallen in love with the hapless human," he sneered. "They told me you were unhealthily attached to your little pet, but no one said anything about love. That settles it; I bleed the both of you slow and painful. You lucky star-crossed lovers will get to watch the light fade out of each other's eyes."

In a flash, he had Alexis by the hair once more, knife to her exposed throat. I threw myself at him. Once again, the swiftness of his kind bested my own. The cold steel slid across my chest, and I landed in a heap a few feet away.

"Time to die, bitch," Gunner snickered.

The knife contacted her skin. My limbs wouldn't obey me fast enough. I was going to be too late. I was going to watch Alexis die.

Before the knife could do more than prick her skin, Gunner howled in pain. He dropped the knife and clutched his head with both hands, falling to his knees. His screams echoed through the woods.

"No, it's time for *you* to die, bitch," Andre thundered.

He stood at the point in the clearing where I had entered, arm extended, hand clenched like a claw. His eyes were clouded black, his face full of fury.

"Who are you?" Gunner wailed. "What are you doing to me?"

"I am a living nightmare, horror personified," Andre's voice reverberated through my chest. It barely sounded like him at all, reaching bass tones not part of his normal register. He was in the depth of his power.

"I am every demon from every dream. The very darkness from which you crawled. Your mind belongs to me in sleeping and in waking."

Gunner's eyes popped open wide, staring at the space before him. His screaming intensified, and he started punching the empty air as if he were fighting something off. Andre advanced on him slowly, the power of the woods palpable in his gait. Here, at the source of our magic, he didn't need Gunner to be asleep to invade his mind.

As Andre held Gunner in a waking terror, I limped over to Alexis. My sharp teeth made quick work of her bindings. She fell to her knees and threw her arms around my middle, burying her face in my thick fur. I nuzzled her closer, my eyes not leaving Andre and Gunner.

"Death would be too great a gift for you," Andre continued, towering over the wretched heap that was Cam Gunner.

I growled my dissent and stalked over to his side, drawing on the power of the woods and the power within me to heal my wounds and renew my strength. I bared my teeth at Gunner while he continued to fight the nightmares only he could see. I reveled in the stench of the fear he emanated.

"You can see their faces, can't you? Every woman you hunted, every woman you violated. They've returned for their vengeance. I am their arbiter. I will grant them the retribution they so rightly deserve." Andre made a forceful movement with his hand.

Gunner stumbled back, once more clutching his skull. His screams weaved their way through the trees. The mighty hunter was nothing more than a quivering weasel at the hands of this skilled sandman.

"They made me," Gunner shrieked. "They made me do it! It was my job to hunt down the deserters. No one escapes the Bianchis. No one! Just like none of your little cop friends will escape the docks tonight."

"Those women you killed?" Alexis's voice was hoarse, but fierce. "Who were they?" She gripped my fur to steady herself.

"Cherries!" He squirmed. "Cherries, cherries, cherries! Traitorous cherries. Dead cherries! You and your friends will die, too. They'll see to it tonight."

Alexis stared. I could read the fury and devastation in every line of her face. I snarled my intent. She gave me one solitary nod. It was all I needed.

As Andre held Gunner in his invisible grasp, I stalked forward. I licked my chops, a grin spreading across my wolfish face as I opened my mouth. Not a single ounce of pity or remorse flickered within me as I ripped the pulsing jugular out of that monster's throat. He gurgled, spasmed, screamed once more, and then was still.

Andre lowered his arm and took a steadying breath, his eyes back to warm brown. It only took one look at Alexis's face before he looped his arm around her waist and pulled her into a hug. She cried as he held her, running his hand from the crown of her head down her back to soothe her.

The time for my wolf was spent, and he willingly ceded his control back to me. I shifted once more and pulled myself to my feet. While my wounds weren't gaping and fresh with the magnification of my healing abilities, they still ached with every move. Without a single thought for my state of undress or the blood—both my own and not my own—staining my skin, I went straight for Alexis.

Wordlessly, Andre shifted her into my arms. She burrowed into me, and I enveloped her completely. I inhaled every blessed inch of her, letting her familiar scent wash away the horror of what had just happened. I berated myself for leaving her side as her tremors rocked us both.

"We ha…have to go," she pulled back to look me in the face. "He said they were going to die. They know we're coming. It's a trap. We can't let them kill all those innocent men and women."

"Siren, I'm not taking you anywhere near those maniacs," I argued.

"We don't have a choice. We have to go now!"

She extricated herself from my arms and walked away. Andre handed me my clothes, his face serious. Alexis was already cutting through the trees. Not a moment of hesitation. My heart swelled with pride. She was the most ferocious creature I ever beheld. I threw on my clothes and ran to catch up with her. She held my hand silently as the three of us hurried back to the car.

"Call the Chief," I told Andre. "Warn him… if it isn't already too late."

Chapter Thirty-Two

Alexis

The Chief's phone rang and rang. No answer. Next, they tried the radio. Nothing. No one answered at the station, either. Something was wrong. We stopped at the station first. Finn insisted I stay in the car with him while Andre went inside to see what was up.

"Are you okay, Siren?" Finn reached out a tentative hand.

"No, I'm not. And I don't think I will be for a long time. But that's not important right now."

"Of course it is," Finn argued. "Baby, look at me."

I kept my eyes on the station. It was taking every ounce of energy I had not to fall apart. One look at Finn's face and my tenuous hold on my emotions would break.

"Siren," Finn's voice was low.

My throat ached with the effort of holding back my tears. Finn's hand found my cheek and softly turned my head toward him. I closed my eyes, the watering in them intensifying, threatening to betray me.

"Alexis, love, look at me." He stroked my cheek.

I finally peeled my eyes open. Finn's gentle, strong, beautiful face was there to greet me. Thank God he had wiped the blood away from his mouth.

The blood…

The tears fell. I collapsed into his waiting arms. He stroked my hair, kissed the top of my head, and whispered reassurances softly in my ear.

"Thank you for coming for me," I choked out.

"Always, Siren. I will always come for you," Finn replied.

He kissed me, hands cradling my face. Enveloped in his warmth, his familiar scent, my heart settled back into a familiar rhythm after hours of pounding against my chest. He leaned his forehead against mine with a sigh.

"I'm never letting you out of my sight again."

I choked out a laugh. "You make me sound like some pathetic damsel-in-distress. I had a pretty clean record of taking care of myself until the last couple of years. My need for a knight in shining armor used to be zero."

"It'll probably never be zero again now that you're an honorary Fae. Although, I can't take credit for this save. I turned out to be just the distraction until Andre arrived."

"Yeah, your badass bestie was pretty amazing." How we were talking about what had happened so casually was beyond me. But it was familiar, soothing, and so needed.

A movement out of the corner of my eye pulled my attention back to the station. Andre was jogging back to the Charger. He threw himself back into the car.

"Nothing. Station's empty. I tried the radio again, but comms are down. Hit the gas, man."

The engine roared back to life, and we were speeding through town once again.

"What's the plan?" The tension in Andre's voice was palpable.

"We can't know until we get there." The muscle in Finn's jaw clenched. "I just pray to God that the Pony crew is there. Without them, the entire force could already be…"

He didn't need to finish his sentence. We all knew. Firearms and academy training were sickeningly inadequate against the Fae. Finn squeezed my hand once.

"Then what's our plan?" Andre asked.

"Cut the head off the snake," Finn spat.

"That's some thick irony."

"Turnabout is fair play."

"Straight for the sons-of-witches themselves, then." Andre agreed.

"Just like we did in the Market Street assault."

"You're reading my mind."

My mind was buzzing. Without powers, what role could I possibly play in this that wouldn't end up with someone I loved having to throw themselves between me and an enemy? Finn and Andre knew exactly what they had to do. Where did I stand in all this?

"Where do you want me?" I asked.

"By my side every second, where you belong," Finn answered, squeezing my hand.

"We've got you, Lex," Andre added.

Their words were both reassuring and concerning at the same time. They already put themselves at risk to save me once today. I had to be sure they wouldn't need to do it again. But the more I tried to think up my own plan, the more oppressive my thoughts of Cam Gunner became. The godforsaken smell of his cigarettes, the scratchy tone of his voice in my ear, his hot breath on my skin.

I shuddered. It made me want to crawl out of my skin and shriek at the top of my lungs. Fuck that piece of shit. That murderer! He killed them. He killed all of those women who were just trying to get away from a life of exploitation and dehumanization. The cherries… Just like Maria and Leticia and Selsha…

The terror gave way to a pulsating rage. I wasn't a violent person by nature, but I felt a sense of karmic satisfaction as Finn ripped the taunting vocal cords out of Cam Gunner's throat. The part of me that held deep compassion for human suffering was noticeably absent at that moment. But Cam Gunner had no humanity. He deserved his fate. But he wasn't the only enemy here, just another damn puppet. Everything came back to the syndicate. It was time to take those motherfuckers down. Hard.

The Charger skidded to a halt, barely out of view of the edge of the docks. Vengeance fueled my every step, blurring out the fear, as I hurried close behind Finn and Andre. Movement from the shadows brought both Finn and Andre's pistols straight up, their posture tense.

"It's us." Riel stepped into the flickering halo of the aged light posts.

The rest of our friends emerged from the darkness behind him. My heart skipped a beat. I felt a combination of gratitude for their presence and concern for their wellbeing. For all we knew, we were about to walk into hell itself. But the determination and ferocity on each face filled me with courage. This must be what a real family felt like.

"Alexis!" The sisters rushed to me and wrapped me in a tight group embrace.

"We're so glad you're safe," Chloe breathed.

Lacey's face was tear-stained. I kissed her forehead and wiped the moisture from her cheeks. Moira sniffled and dabbed her own eyes. My chest tightened and the need to break down threatened to overcome me once more. I clenched my jaw and swallowed my grief. The time for that would come after we put these bastards down.

"We worked out a plan," Riel started, but Andre interrupted him.

"It's a trap. Gunner was another Bianchi hitman. The Bianchis know that the force is coming. We've gotta switch things up."

"Finn?" Riel frowned. "You make the call, then. Where do you need us?"

Shouts echoed around the corner toward the docks.

"We need a read on the situation first. There's no way we're going in blind. Chloe?"

"I've got this." Chloe pulled away from our huddled hug. Her eyes went dark as she spread her arms to her sides, fingers splayed. Static electricity crackled across my skin, and I shivered.

"What's she doing?" I whispered.

"She's reading the scene," Moira replied. "You remember what I see?"

"The past?"

"Yes. Chloe sees the present. That's what she's doing now. Gathering a picture of what's happening beyond our sight."

Lacey's wide eyes met mine. She tapped her forehead, pointed to her eyes, then pointed into the distance. Understanding washed over me.

"Moira sees the past, Chloe sees the present, and you see the future," I whispered.

Lacey smiled sadly and nodded. She leaned her forehead against mine and sighed, her fingers tracing the new wounds blossoming on my face from the abuse I suffered at the hands of Cam Gunner. It all made sense now; her headaches were visions.

"You knew he had me?"

I felt her nod.

"It was you, wasn't it? You sent Finn."

Lacey took a shuddering breath and nodded again.

"You saved my life." My voice cracked, heavy with emotion.

"Sister," she whispered so softly that I almost didn't catch it. She put her hand over my heart.

My heart swelled in my chest. My tears fell freely. I don't know if I was more overwhelmed because Lacey had just spoken to me for the first time or by the beauty and love in the word she had spoken. I smoothed her hair and kissed her on the top of the head.

"Sister," I agreed and hugged her tight.

"Thirty-eight thugs are standing between the cops and the warehouse by dock three. Twenty-six cops, guns drawn, the Chief calling out the Bianchis using a bullhorn." Chloe screwed up her face and frowned. "Something's blocking me from seeing inside the warehouse. That's where the witches must be. I need to get inside to see past the block."

"We need to split into two groups then," Finn commanded. "Hiro, you do your thing between the cops and the thugs. Make 'em see hell if you have to but get their eyes off each other before there's a shootout. Vijay, Vikram, Taylor, Grace, Donna, and Ricky, you'll stay outside with Hiro and give her cover. We don't know who is human and who's Fae on their side, so watch yourselves and each other. If things get out of control, do what you have to do to protect the human cops."

They all nodded at his instructions.

"The rest of us will work on getting Chloe close enough to break through whatever spells they've cast to see what we're up against inside that warehouse. Let me be clear: The Bianchis can't make it out in one piece. We do what we have to do. Keep the promise we made to each other when we came to the Clock; we keep ourselves safe from any and every threat, no matter what."

More nods. I could feel the power my friends emitted pulsating in the air around us. I swallowed hard. They would take no prisoners tonight.

The group divided; Hiro and the others slowly creeping through the shadows towards the shouting while the rest of us waited for them to work their literal magic. Every muscle in my body tensed. Every sound seemed to echo in my ears. I gripped Finn's bicep as he peered around the building where we took cover.

"Chloe, what do you see?" Riel touched her gently on the shoulder.

"They're almost there. Ricky teleported behind the line of the Bianchi's men. He's making noise, drawing their attention away from the others. It's working; everyone's looking away." A bead of sweat slid down Chloe's temple. "There she goes. She's singing. By the looks on their faces, it's working already. God, she's good. It's like watching bees getting smoked."

I breathed a sigh of relief.

"...Wait! There's a group near the back... they're moving, whispering to each other. Vikram sees them. He's gone invisible, but I can sense his intentions... He's made his way over to them. He's listening. They're Fae. They know we're here."

"What kind of Fae?" Andre squinted into the distance.

Chloe took a breath and furrowed her brow. Moira and Lacey each took one of her hands and their eyes went dark, too. The electric charge in the air intensified.

"Two trolls, a Grendel, a satyr, three harpies, and a goblin," Chloe's voice echoed.

"They must have some sort of protection spell. Hiro's illusions should work on humans and Fae alike," Riel mumbled.

"Vikram is back filling the others in. Cover your ears!"

Before I could react, an unearthly screech filled the night. I fell to my knees, hands over my ears, but the shriek bounced around inside my skull. My stomach roiled, and I fought the bile that rose in my throat.

"Fire!" Chloe shouted.

But it was too late. The dilapidated wood building we sheltered behind burst into flames, and we were all blown off our feet. The shrieking continued.

"They know we're back here," Andre shouted over the din, helping me to my feet.

"We have to move." Finn was pulling Lacey away from the flames, patting at a lock of her hair that had caught fire.

We scrambled away from the burning building and out into the open. Here we had a full view of what was happening. The entire Beckburg police department stood slack jawed, staring at nothing. Just across from them, an equally bewitched group of criminals shared the same fate. But that was the only calm in the picture. Three winged women with sharp faces were launching fireballs at our friends. Vijay was shielding Hiro and covering her ears, forsaking his own, as Hiro fought to maintain the illusion for the humans. The others were scattered, dodging the flying flames.

As we took shelter behind a stack of crates, I saw Donna sprint toward the dock, her arms moving in deliberate, fluid motions. She skidded to a halt and dropped to one knee, her hands splayed, arms outstretched. An enormous wave of water rose from behind her, launching toward the winged women. A direct hit knocked them off their feet, and the screeching halted. Donna continued waving her arms, commanding water toward every fire, extinguishing them with a cacophony of hisses.

Two gigantic men lumbered forward, roaring, shoving crates and bodies out of the way as if they were one and the same. Ricky and Vikram ran out to meet them head on. My heart seized in my chest. How could they survive brute force like that? The men collided, and I had to force myself not to shut my eyes. But Ricky and Vikram matched the goons blow for blow.

Taylor took the chance to join Donna near the docks and waved her own hands. I watched for something to happen with the water, but was shocked to see tendrils of seaweed rise from the depths instead. Ropes of the green tendrils shot through the air and wound themselves around the dripping wet winged women and a man with short horns spouting from his temples. The women shrieked again, and my hands flew back up to my ears. But the shrieks were short-lived. More seaweed wound around their mouths, silencing them.

A jagged piece of metal whizzed past me, grazing my face. The sting of the cut made me gasp and stagger back. Someone grabbed me by the arm and pulled me down further. I hadn't realized how exposed I had become as I anxiously watched the fight unfolding.

"Stay down, Siren. They'll be fine." But the look on Finn's face made me doubt the confidence he'd tried to infuse in his tone.

"More than half of them are subdued. Now's as good a time as any." Andre pulled his head back down as well.

"Follow me." Finn crouched low and started off on a diagonal course.

I hurried behind him, and the others followed. I tried not to look around as I cradled my cheek, but the urge to check on my friends was too strong. A short man with grizzled hair and pointed teeth had Grace tightly by the arm. Her face was panicked.

I stopped in my tracks. A guttural growl rolled from my chest through my bared teeth. I grabbed the first thing I could find, an old harpoon, and ran at him. He buried his sharp teeth in Grace's forearm, and she cried out in pain. Without hesitation, I buried the tip of the rusty harpoon into the man's side. He howled but released Grace. He turned on me with an evil sneer, clutching his bleeding side.

I sneered right back at him, holding the harpoon between us. He lunged at me. But stopped suddenly in midair and flew backwards, colliding with a lamppost with a crunch. He fell to the bottom in a limp pile and didn't move again. I turned to see who had helped me. Ricky gave me a cheeky salute before running back over to help Vijay and Vikram fight off the two huge men.

Moira grabbed my arm and pulled me back in line with the others as we navigated toward the warehouse. "You are so stupid and so wonderful," she choked out, wiping at her face.

"Thanks."

My hurried footsteps landed heavily on the sodden ground. My heart was pounding and the adrenaline from helping Grace pumped hard through my veins.

We rounded the corner of the warehouse when Chloe grabbed Finn's arm, yanking him to a halt.

"Grendel," Chloe shouted, pointing at a beast of a man covered in fur.

The Grendel stood between us and the entrance to the warehouse, his chest heaving, teeth bared. He looked like Bigfoot and a wild boar had gotten together and had a very tall, ugly baby. He spread his long, clawed fingers and roared at us.

Finn snarled, taking a step forward, but Riel grabbed his arm to stop him.

"You're strong, my friend, but a Grendel is stronger." Riel gave him a significant look. "Stand back."

Finn hesitated, but threw me a look over his shoulder. He nodded once, then stepped out of Riel's way. Riel closed his eyes, held his hands across his heart, and started whispering something I couldn't hear through the noise of the fight behind us.

"What's he doing?" I asked Moira.

"You're about to see why Riel is the leader of the good Fae." Chloe stared at Riel in awe.

"Brace yourself." Moira put a steadying hand on my shoulder.

The Grendel advanced on us with long, lumbering strides. He roared again, saliva dripping from his jowls. Before he could come within arm's reach, Riel swirled his hands gracefully above his head and the wind howled. The Grendel searched for the source of the noise but gave up and continued his approach. There was no fear or urgency in Riel's expression, just calm determination. The flame in his eyes made him almost unrecognizable.

A long-clawed swipe from the Grendel missed Riel's face by inches. I gasped, lurching forward, but Moira kept me still. Finn was growling from deep in his throat, body tensed to spring should his friend need help. The wind continued to howl. I could feel it gathering around us, swirling and circling the place where we stood huddled together.

It suddenly reminded me of Riel's campfire story about the man and his friend, the Wind. Recognition dawned on my face as I looked at Chloe. She grabbed my other shoulder and widened her stance, a proud smirk at the corner of her mouth.

The Grendel raised his arm for another strike. I sucked in a breath and held it hostage in my lungs. Riel forced his arms down to his sides and a massive burst of wind rocketed through the air toward the Grendel, pounding like a thunderclap. I felt the blowback of the force and would have fallen if not for Moira and Chloe's steadying hands. The Grendel flew back through the air, tossed like a rag doll. Riel looked like he had expended no effort at all. The Grendel may as well have been made of tissue paper.

Chloe let go of my arm and strode to Riel's side. Lacey's small hand slid into mine as she stared after her sister. Chloe's eyes went pitch black once again as she faced down the furious creature before them. It ran towards Riel and Chloe, fangs bared. Chloe's hands shot out in what I thought was a defensive stance, but the Grendel howled in agony and fell to the ground.

"What is she doing?"

"She's cutting his thread," Moira explained.

"She's what?"

"She's killing him." Her tone was melancholy.

"How the hell is she…"

But another agonized roar from the Grendel tore through the air, cutting off my question. Now it wasn't just saliva oozing from his mouth, it was blood, too. His eyes bulged and his body shook. I averted my eyes. Even though this man was a monster, had obvious intentions of hurting or killing us, I still didn't enjoy witnessing his suffering. Lacey buried her face in my shoulder, and I hugged her tightly. I wasn't the only one who felt that way.

The howls eventually ceased. Another loud thunderclap echoed around the docks, and I looked over in time to watch the Grendel's body splash into the sea. His blood seeped into the grain of the wooden boards where he'd fallen. I understood better why Riel's power made him a natural choice for a leader, but I couldn't help but wonder why Chloe wasn't the more obvious choice. I had never seen that kind of raw power in my life.

"Let's get to the doors," Andre urged us forward.

We dashed the rest of the way. Andre and Finn each grabbed a handle and pulled at the massive sliding doors, but they didn't budge. Finn snarled and tried again, the veins in his biceps popping, but still nothing.

"Is it a spell?" Finn asked Chloe.

"Not that I can feel."

"You mean it's just a fucking lock? Can we break it?" Andre examined the doors.

"I can help," a voice tinkled behind us.

Grace limped over to us; Donna's shirt tied around the bite on her arm and blood seeping from a tear in her pant leg. She took a breath and shrunk down to her pixie size. I watched her flit to the lock and squeeze herself right in. The seconds turned to minutes as we stood and waited. A series of mechanical clicks and scrapes signaled that whatever she was doing was working. A final loud click and Grace was back out and back to her human size with a pained grin.

"You go somewhere safe and get off that leg, Grace," Moira smoothed her hair back. "You've done enough tonight." Grace nodded and hobbled quickly away.

"Ready?" Finn asked Andre.

"Hell no. But here we go anyway." Andre grabbed the other handle once more.

They pulled, and the doors rolled open with a grating groan. It was dark inside the warehouse. Something about the space made the hair on the back of my neck stand straight up. Lacey was trembling beside me. I squeezed her hand, trying to reassure her.

"Finn?" Riel took in the darkness with narrowed eyes. "Anything?"

"Looks empty." Finn peered into the space, his right hand on the butt of his holstered gun.

"Can you ladies read anything yet?" Andre glanced between the open doors and the sisters.

"Not yet," Moira shook her head.

"I can feel the spell, right here," Chloe motioned to the space between the doors. "We won't be able to get a feel for anything until we're past the doors and in the warehouse."

"It's a risk," Andre sighed.

"One we have to take." Finn looked at me with serious eyes.

I nodded.

Finn clenched his jaw, drew his weapon, and stepped over the threshold. I held Lacey's hand firmly as we followed Finn, my eyes refusing to adjust to the darkness beyond vague shapes and shadows. I was grateful for Finn and Riel's sharp vision as they scanned the space for threats.

"Stay back," Andre directed in a whisper, his gun held aloft.

The sisters and I stopped where we were, my senses straining to gather information. Riel, Finn, and Andre's footsteps seemed to echo loudly through the enormous room despite the care I knew they were taking. My muscles were tensed for an attack. Every tiny sound sent my heart racing. Every breeze that blew the scent of moldy wood across my face made me shiver. I huddled closer to Moira and Chloe, bringing Lacey with me.

"Forty-one heartbeats," Chloe whispered. Her breathing was labored.

"Pain, fear, degradation…" Moira intoned to my left. "Triumph, victory, desire…"

"We're through the spell," Andre acknowledged. "Where are they, ladies?"

Blinding white lights buzzed to life above us. My arm flew to my face, shielding my eyes from our violent re-emergence from the darkness. Someone else was here. I could feel it in the air despite my temporary blindness.

"Four heartbeats close," Chloe's voice was all quiet desperation. I wondered why she was still whispering until I remembered everyone in our group was close enough to hear her or had sensitive enough hearing that they could, but the unseen threat might not.

"You have no idea how long I've waited for this moment," a booming male voice called.

I opened my eyes just a slit, looking toward the noise. The voice was distinctly accented in a way that reminded me of the reality show from New Jersey that an old roommate of mine used to watch religiously. Despite the intensity of the fluorescent light now flooding the warehouse, I could make out four figures directly across from us against the far wall.

"If it ain't the infamous Finn Briggs himself," the voice continued. It seemed to come from the heavyset man in the middle. I blinked and rubbed my eyes again. "The hotshot donut-sucking, human ass-kissing, dog-breathed, son of a bitch who can't keep his nose outta other people's business."

The forms were coming into clearer focus as my eyes adjusted. Three men and a woman dressed in sharp business attire contrasted starkly against the sodden squalor of the wooden warehouse. The men were dressed in dark, tailored suits and the woman was in a tight fitting red mini dress.

"And right by his side, his trusty brown bitch," he waved his hand toward Andre.

Anger flared in my chest. The urge to punch the asshole for his racist bullshit was strong enough to send my feet forward a couple of steps. Lacey pulled my arm, returning me to her side. She tapped me on the shoulder until I met her gaze. She gave me a significant look. The intent was clear in her gaze. She glanced over at the enemies, who kept their distance, then to each of her sisters.

I followed her gaze first to Chloe, then to Moira. Both of their eyes were pitch black. Chloe's breathing was heavy again. Moira's eyes flitted back and forth rapidly. They were working. Moira was consuming their past like pages in a novel. Chloe was absorbing their present.

"Can she cut their threads?" I whispered.

Lacey shook her head. She slouched her shoulders and mimicked a yawn. Then she pointed to the group across from us and flexed her biceps.

"It takes a lot of energy and they're too strong," I sighed.

She nodded, then bit her lip, looking at her sisters once more.

"And you brought quite the posse with you, huh? Isn't that somethin'?"

My vision was back to normal, and now I could make out the features of the speaker. He looked to be in his sixties, but God knew how old he truly was. His face was puffy, and he had the perpetually rosy cheeks I recognized as long-term alcohol addiction. White roots peeked from beneath his slicked-back black hair. That must be Big Dominic, head of the Bianchi family.

The man to his left was built like a professional wrestler. The veins in his thick neck might pop any second, and his hands reminded me of the paws of berserkers. He sneered at Finn and Riel, sizing them up. He had to be the enforcer, Leo.

That left the shorter, stockier man with diamond stud earrings on Big Dominic's left: Lorenzo. He tapped his foot and flicked a toothpick back and forth between his lips. Olivier's smug-ass face immediately came to mind. Looks like the traitorous little sycophant picked up his toothpick habit from a friend.

Francesca, in her tight red dress, stood stiff and silent, her eyes scanning the room. Her bleach blonde hair cascaded over one shoulder. She licked her lips hungrily as her eyes fell on Finn. I bristled, but kept still.

"Is that the elf, there?" Big Dominic pointed at Riel.

"You know who I am." Riel stepped forward, hands tensed at his sides.

"You're the big-bad goody two shoes, ain'tcha," Dominic chuckled, his belly bouncing.

"I'm the leader of the benevolent Fae," Riel replied smoothly.

"Benevolent," Leo snorted.

"Keep your mouth shut," Dominic snapped. "We don't want to offend our guests."

"Yeah, calling us names and sending your attack dogs after us isn't offensive at all," Andre sneered. He held his gun stiff and straight in front of him.

Finn was staring at the Bianchis. I expected him to be mirroring Andre's ready stance, but his gun was only half raised. His shrewd eyes were narrowed, and his nose twitched. I wished I was close enough to talk to him, but he was already half the length of the warehouse away from me.

"We wouldn't have needed to send our associates out if you hadn't come here to our stoop, and interfered with our business." Dominic ran his hand through his hair. "But that's a pattern with you, isn't it? You just can't stop interfering." The last three words he punctuated with loud claps as he walked in our direction. "Now, I can excuse the odd weasel going to jail, a little product ending up in the hands of the cops… It's the cost of doing business. But when you start plucking my cherries and killing my Fae, I gotta step in and do something about it."

His eyes landed on me. Lacey shook behind me, burying her face between my shoulder blades. I stood up taller, chin level with the ground. Nothing brought me more pride than knowing I'd played a significant role in "plucking his cherries." Selsha's face flashed in my mind and the rage and grief wove its way back in, thickening my resolve.

"What did you expect? That you'd get to run your little criminal empire without us coming after you?" Finn barked.

"Who's 'us?' You and your little cop friends? Or these pathetic little Fae who follow an elf?" Dominic continued moving toward Finn.

Andre inched forward, falling in next to Finn. Riel was a few paces behind them and to the side. He settled himself in the line of sight between Francesca, who had broken off a little from her father and brothers, and us. Francesca cocked her head far to the side, far enough to be unsettling as she raked her eyes over me and the sisters behind me.

"Either way, we weren't going to sit back while you took over the Clock," Finn continued. "The Clock is ours and you made a huge mistake bringing your 'business' here."

"Yours, is it?" Dominic chuckled. "Maybe it used to be, but it ain't no more."

"Says who?" Andre scoffed.

"Do you know how easy it was to slip in here and turn your people?" Lorenzo piped up. His voice was surprisingly shrill. "We coulda tossed that cop a nickel, and he woulda flopped on you. And that succubus of yours," he giggled,

"She practically begged us for the high life in exchange for your secrets. Your hold on this place ain't near as tight as you think it is."

"Oh, yes, Milani. Shame what you did to poor Milani, Elf. Our boys found her babbling like a loon in her penthouse. But don't worry, we put her out of her misery. We've no use for a neutered succubus." Big Dominic gave Riel a wicked grin.

After what she had done to me, I felt no love lost for Milani, but my stomach gave a lurch at the suppressed glee in the man's voice. She may have been a treacherous bitch, but she was a person. They talked about her like she was a used tissue; soiled and disposable. It was the same way they treated the women they trafficked.

"You killed her?" Riel stared, wide-eyed.

"You killed her first by taking her powers," Big Dominic accused.

"It didn't mean you had to kill her," Riel argued.

"Better dead than human," Leo glared at me.

Finn let out a guttural growl.

"Ooh, touchy, ain'tcha," Big Dominic chuckled. "We had it on good authority that you didn't mix with humans, wolf. It gave Brie quite the shock that her old bed-buddy was fuckin' a human."

"What the fuck," Andre swore.

"We did our homework," Leo gloated. "Eyes and ears, asshole, eyes and ears everywhere."

"It sounds like you keep shitty company," Andre spat, his face curled in a sneer.

"What about your company, you boot-licking coward?" Lorenzo squeaked back at Andre. "Is it a kink of yours to get bossed around?" He motioned to Finn.

But another movement drew my attention away; Francesca was creeping closer and closer. Her grotesquely tilted head peered past me, landing on Chloe and Moira, their eyes still dark with searching. I watch the comprehension dawn on her face. She opened her mouth, but I beat her words with some of my own, desperate to give the sisters the time they needed to find the answers they were seeking.

"Sounds like *you're* the cowards," I shouted. "Always sending other people to do your dirty work for you."

"Ah, the human pet!" Big Dominic turned up his nose at me. "If I wanted you to speak, bitch, I woulda put a treat on your nose."

Finn lunged at Big Dominic, but Andre grabbed his arm just in time. The Bianchis laughed. Despite the insult, I felt no fear. After facing down the monster that had haunted me for years, the fear was gone. Standing here with my family, all I felt was a ferocious urge to protect.

"In your case, I shoulda sent my daughter to take care of you," Big Dominic continued, curling his lip up at me. "Seeing as how the others couldn't get the fuckin' job done. Right, Franny?"

Francesca gave her father an ingratiating smile. Her eyes flickered to Lacey's form huddled behind me, then back to her father's gaze. She gave him a tiny nod, and they broke into identical evil grins.

"NOW!" Big Dominic bellowed.

Sparks shot from the fingertips of each of the Bianchis. Spells blasted from each side. They had corralled us, spreading out as they distracted us with threats and betrayals. Finn dropped his gun and shifted with a snarl, dodging to the right as he lunged toward Leo. Riel waved his arms, blowing the spells off the mark. Andre fired a few shots at Lorenzo, but they ricocheted off the spells, and Andre had to dive out of the way to avoid being hit by his own bullets.

Francesca launched herself at Chloe and Moira. I had the advantage of being closer to them, though. I grabbed their arms and threw myself and the sisters behind a stack of boxes. My elbow protested with a sharp sting as it collided with the corner of a box. Moira and Chloe's eyes returned to normal. I shuffled around, staying low, trying to pull Lacey further back.

"Did you guys get what you…"

Something hit me hard in the back, burning across my shoulder blade. I cried out, spinning around. Chloe patted the spot, putting out the flames that had blossomed there. I glimpsed Francesca advancing on us; the others fighting in the background. Finn yelped and my stomach lurched.

I picked up a splintered 2x4 board, ready to square up against Francesca. Chloe pulled me backward, spinning me to face her.

"The Bianchis have the rest of the women they traffic locked in a room there, three doors down to the left," Chloe whispered, pointing at a door in the far corner of the warehouse. "You need to get them out of here. If things don't go their way, the Bianchis have a plan to use them as leverage against us."

"I can't leave you guys. The Bianchis have something up their…" I argued.

"We know," Moira interrupted. "We've seen everything. Get those poor women to safety. What they've been through…" Moira's voice was thick with emotion.

Another blast bounced off the wall behind us. I threw my hands over my head to protect myself from the explosion of wood. I looked around the warehouse at the people I loved so much. The Bianchis were feral as they fought. I knew in that moment that all I could do here was become a distraction. I was no match for magic. But here was something I could do; something I was meant to do. My place wasn't here in the middle of my friends and our foes, but firmly between those innocent victims and their abusers; just where it always had been.

"I'll take Lacey with me. She'll be safer with me. But are you going to be okay?" I asked.

"We'll be fine," Moira affirmed.

Chloe kissed Lacey's forehead and gave her a reassuring look. Lacey's eyes were swimming with tears. I grabbed Lacey's hand once more and rose to a crouch, preparing to run.

"Francesca…" I motioned past the boxes.

Chloe rose to her full height, eyes darkening around the edges. "Don't worry," a grin spread across her face, "I can handle this bitch."

"Let's go," Moira took off, and I followed, towing Lacey behind me.

Moira waved us toward the door, but skidded to a halt behind a pillar where Andre hid. She started whispering urgently into his ear as Lacey and I continued to run. Another blast of sparks came within inches of my face, reminding me of the burn in my shoulder. We slammed against the door, and I yanked on the handle. It refused to budge. I tucked Lacey into the corner before backing up to break it down. Finn and Andre had taught me to kick near the handle. I braced myself against the doorjamb and kicked as hard as I could, ducking as spells bounced against every wall.

The door gave way with a crunch. I took Lacey by the hand once more and took in her frightened expression.

"Let's go change the future for those women," I declared.

She nodded, a smile lifting at the corner of her mouth. We ducked another spell, then hurried through the door to free the Bianchi's "cherries."

Chapter Thirty-Three

Finn

I dragged my claws along the wet cement floor as I skidded backwards. A flash of intimately familiar brown hair sped through my periphery. My heart gave a tug as Alexis and Lacey raced for a door in the corner. The two seconds I took to watch the love of my immortal life flit through my vision were two seconds too long. Electricity shot through me, making my limbs jerk, until I fell to the floor in a heap.

Leo cackled, picking up a discarded crowbar. I tried to shake off the blow, but my limbs wouldn't obey me. I bared my teeth at the bastard as he approached. Leo smashed the crowbar against a rotting pillar, splinters flying. The roof above us groaned.

Alexis's face was front and center in my mind. I had intended to keep her close, but knew now I was an idiot for thinking that I could protect her and fight witches at the same time. I had to do my part to protect my people. I felt defensive of my friends—my family—but the ferocity I felt radiating from every inch of my body was something different. It was visceral, animalistic in every sense.

Alexis had become my home, my heart, and my purpose. I had nearly lost her once tonight and I would do everything to keep her safe, even if that meant losing my life. She was a part of me now and if I lost her, I would lose myself. It would mean death either way.

The crack of the crowbar hitting another pillar pulled me back to the immediate threat. I snarled at Leo, now only a few feet away from me. He wasn't blasting spells at me anymore, the way his family was across the room. This vindictive fuck liked to make his point the old-fashioned way. My snarl curled up into a smirk; if that's how he wanted it, that's exactly how I would give it to him.

Channeling the magic I had so freshly reaped from the woods only hours ago, I felt my body shuck off the shock that left me reeling. Pressing the pads of my paws against the ground, I leapt through the air at Leo. But instead of going for the throat as he expected, his fists already up by his face, I went low. I collided with his shins full force, knocking his feet out from under him. He flipped over my head as I ducked beneath him and whipped around 180 degrees to face him again. He swore loudly as his head cracked against the cement.

"C'mon you fucking pussy; fight me like a man. Put those fucking teeth away and let's settle this hand to hand." Leo clambered back to his feet.

I prompted the shift, but Alexis's voice in my head stopped me. Don't rise to the bait. Be smart. If I shifted back into my human form, I would be at a disadvantage. It would be akin to pulling my punches, with no guarantee that Leo would pull his. In fact, that's probably exactly what he wanted. The Bianchis knew more about us and our abilities than we ever knew, thanks to Milani's backstabbing bullshit. I had to use what I knew about them from years of detective work to counter all that.

Think, don't react. What's the opposite of what he expects me to do?

He was already advancing on me again, his eyes sparking yellow. He fired a spell in my direction. I jumped to the side. Hmm... at a distance, he attacks with spells. Up close, it's the crowbar or the fist. Which one would give me the upper hand? Without help from the others, I was ineffective at a distance, and they had their hands full. Close encounter it is...

Another spring forward had me just out of Leo's reach. He took a mighty swing with the crowbar. It was close enough that I felt it graze the tips of my ears. He held the crowbar more towards his stomach, readying for an attack from high or low this time. Shit, this fucker learned quick. We circled. I waited.

His patience spent, Leo lashed out with the crowbar again. My senses prickled a few seconds before he brought the crowbar down toward my head. It gave me just enough time to leap to his side and grab hold of his left elbow with my jaws. I dug my sharp teeth into his flesh and heard the bone crunch as I clamped down with all my might. He roared, flung his arm around to shake me off, but only accomplished more crunching and tearing in his elbow. His dominant arm now torn and bloody, the crowbar fell to the ground with a clatter.

Leo's other fist collided with my side with rib-cracking force. I released my hold and hurried outside his reach once more. His face was purple with rage, his left arm hanging limply by his side.

"IS THAT ALL YOU GOT, ELF?" Big Dominic bellowed to my left.

When I saw Leo turn to look in his father's direction, I chanced a look around at my friends. Riel was locked in defensive mode with Big Dominic. I wanted to scream at him. Now was not the time to be a pacifist. But all that came out was a growl. I contemplated shifting but stopped myself short of initiating the change. Riel was perfectly capable of taking care of himself... if he stopped trying to be his usual fucking benevolent self.

A few yards away, Moira's hand was locked on Andre's shoulder as they circled Lorenzo. Without a direct connection with the magic from the woods, Andre couldn't pull the same power he did on Cam Gunner with a fully conscious Lorenzo, the fire building in his eyes as they flicked back and forth. Moira was powering him up like a battery, and Andre was reading every moment of

Lorenzo's past through Moira's sight, devouring it like a perp's rap sheet. I grinned, seeing Lorenzo's smirking ignorance at what was about to come his way.

Chloe and Francesca were further away from the others, powers forgotten. A flurry of fists and feet showed them as evenly matched. When one threw a punch, the other blocked or dodged. Unlike Riel, Chloe was furiously pouring her all into the fight. That woman couldn't pull a punch if her life depended on it. Francesca ducked under Chloe's right hook and ran a long, sharp fingernail across Chloe's side. Chloe cried out.

I watched what happened next in slow-motion: Riel wheeled around, full attention toward Chloe's cry of pain. His power surged, and he blew Francesca twenty feet backwards, away from Chloe. But with Riel's back turned, Big Dominic's grin grew grotesque in its wickedness. He launched a spell at Riel's back and Riel flew forward onto his face. He went still. The entire room watched with bated breath. But Riel didn't stir.

The walls of the warehouse shook violently as the air was pulled from the room. I could feel the charge building to my far left and I knew that feeling. I had felt it myself in a much smaller measure when Chloe was going for me after the Valentine's Day incident before Andre stopped her. But there would be no stopping her this time. I couldn't read Chloe the way she could read me, but I knew what she felt for Riel was as deep and powerful as what I felt for Alexis.

There was about to be hell to pay.

I launched myself behind a stack of boxes as Moira pulled Andre behind a pillar. Chloe's form was visible through a split in the stacks. Her eyes were pitch black and her form was rigid. I realized she wasn't just going to cut the man's thread; she was about to make him suffer.

Lorenzo hurried over to Francesca and Leo was still guffawing as he pointed to Riel's sickeningly still form on the concrete when it happened. Chloe's shriek sounded the alarm like a banshee heralding his death. Her hands came together, then she thrust them forward, the rush of air the only sign that something was coming Big Dominic's way. Big Dominic stumbled backward a few steps as the force hit him, then looked around at his children with a smug expression.

"Is that all you…" the smirk slid off his face just as his head and shoulders slid off his torso. His disfigured body twitched a few times and then he went still.

The Bianchi children all cried out in unison, Francesca and Lorenzo rushing to Big Dominic and Leo sprinting at Chloe with a roar. I was ready for him, though. Speed was my ally in getting to Chloe before Leo got his hands on her. I threw myself between them. Chloe collapsed against the back wall, breathing hard, as Leo locked his arms around my chest, crushing the breath out of my lungs. How he could apply such force with the injuries I had inflicted on his arm had to be pure adrenaline or powerful magic.

"Fuckin' finish 'em, Franny!" Lorenzo pointed a bloodied finger in our direction.

As I struggled for air, Francesca sat next to her father's body, closed her eyes, and mumbled something with haunting rapidity. Lorenzo pulled out a vial of clear liquid and poured it over her body. I sniffed. Fuck. I knew that smell. My eyes bulged, not because of Leo's grip, but from the shock of what she did next.

Francesca's head rose off her shoulders, spine and entrails still attached. Her now hollow body fell backwards onto her father's severed chest. The already angular features of her face sharpened, and the smell of vinegar and rot assaulted my nose. Her eyes snapped open, and her grin spread from ear to ear. My guts twisted as I watched Francesca in her penanggalan form advance on us.

Everything in my finely tuned senses screamed at me to fight or flee. I felt the animalistic terror the penanggalan inspired deep in my core. Leo threw me to the ground between him and his floating head of a sister. I heard him chuckle as the back of my neck prickled, instinct urging me to do something, anything. But, for the first time in my long life, I froze.

Moira shouted something at me from their hiding place, but I couldn't make out the words. The only sound I could focus on was the squelching drag of the penanggalan's intestines across the filthy floor. Leo circled to my right; his right arm cradling his injured left one. He leaned against a pillar, clearly satisfied to watch the show instead of finishing me on his own.

A shot rang out. The penanggalan floated back several feet in the air, a hole in the center of her forehead. She blinked lazily in the direction of the shot, locking eyes with Andre. His gun was still raised, waiting for her to make another move. She shrieked an ungodly shriek and flew at Andre.

I found my feet again as Andre fired off four more shots, some hitting their mark, others ricocheting around the room and lodging themselves in walls and crates. But nothing stopped her. A bullet to the brain wasn't even enough to slow her down. She was unstoppable. I knew we were fucked with her in this state, but it didn't stop me from running full speed at Andre, trying to reach my partner's side before the penanggalan could get there first.

But I wasn't the only one thinking of backup. Lorenzo was hot on my heels, blasting spells as we ran. Without a clear strategy, I used my momentum to throw my bulky body against the penanggalan's eerie floating head. I rolled into a pile of garbage, but whatever magic fueled the penanggalan kept her upright and floating a few feet away. She stared me down and that frozen feeling returned. It was only Lorenzo's voracious swearing that drew her attention away from me long enough for the fear melting down the back of my neck to cease.

Andre had Lorenzo in a chokehold, but he was losing his hold as Lorenzo flailed and grabbed at him. Moira scurried under Lorenzo's swinging arm and gripped Andre's shoulders. Her eyes went black, and Andre nearly sizzled with the electricity of her channeled power. Releasing the chokehold, Andre instead put both of his hands on the sides of Lorenzo's head and whispered in his ear. Lorenzo stopped flailing and his face went sickly pale. His eyes slid in and out of focus. Then the screaming started. Whatever nightmares Andre had in store for him were between Lorenzo and the devil himself.

Both the penanggalan and Leo made moves toward their screaming brother. Once again, I gained my composure and launched myself into the fray to run interference. Despite his head start, Leo was no match for my speed. I locked my jaws around his right calf. His momentum threw him face down on the floor. With another chomp and jerk of the head, I severed his Achilles tendon. Leo screamed, launching a spell that hit me in the face. It burned like acid. I backed up, pawing at my face, trying to wipe the pain away.

The penanggalan's shriek turned my chest to ice. With Andre preoccupied with Lorenzo, Moira pulled away to deal with the penanggalan. She picked up a shovel and held it defensively between herself and the disembodied terror. I knew she'd pumped so much of her own power into Andre that she must be exhausted herself. I tried to move her way, but the pain from my face was spreading through my paws. They wouldn't obey me.

The penanggalan whipped her entrails upwards, wrapping them around Moira's arm. Moira shrieked as a sizzling sound and the smell of burning flesh rose in the air. She dropped the shovel and fell to her knees. I redoubled my efforts to get to her, pushing myself with my hind legs as the front half of my body ached and burned. A sharp blow to my rib cage reminded me that Leo wasn't out of the fight. I yelped. The crowbar struck true this time; the cracking of several ribs was its witness.

Moira's sobs echoed, gutting me, calling for me. Riel was still lying lifeless on the floor, blood pooling beneath his face. Andre was locked on to Lorenzo, eyes dark as night, no external sights or sounds entering his consciousness. Chloe called out to Moira, dragging her own exhausted body across the grimy floor in a desperate attempt to save her beloved sister. For the first time in centuries, I felt helpless, hopeless.

Leo hit me again with the crowbar, more ribs cracking and breaking. The air whooshed out of me, and I fell to my side. Between the agony of the spell and the crowbar, I couldn't move. Moira's echoing screams taunted and haunted me. I snarled my frustration, anger, and impotence. Whimpers escaped my muzzle as I continued to push myself forward. Another blow and my vision blurred. This could be it, the end.

But then, there was honeysuckle.

Chapter Thirty-Four

Alexis

Lacey and I searched frantically for a second exit, but it was useless. We exchanged worried glances, both knowing that the only way to lead these women to safety was back the way we came. Back toward a bunch of fighting Fae...

We had found 37 women chained in a filthy room with no toilet or beds. They assured us they hadn't been there long, but the faraway looks in some of their eyes told a different story. It took a while for them to trust us, but then a few of the women who knew me from my work around town and at the station vouched for me. A woman with strawberry blonde hair and beautiful freckles asked me about Selsha. I swallowed back the bile that rose with the feelings of failure. Lacey pulled a pin from her hair and picked the locks on the chains.

Now we stood in the hallway with victims to protect as I stared at the door that would lead us back into the cavernous warehouse. Loud, echoing noises on the other side of the door meant the fight wasn't over. Lacey's eyes went out of focus for a few seconds, and her sweet face went pale.

"What do you see?" I whispered.

She grabbed my wrist. It felt like my head had been plunged into a bucket of icy water before I could take a breath. Visions of what was happening on the other side of that door darted and zapped through my mind. A deep ache wrapped my consciousness as I watched a headless woman floating before a screaming Moira. Riel lay lifeless and unmoving on the floor. Big Dominic's bisected corpse lay next to a woman's headless body. Andre had Lorenzo trapped, Chloe was dragging herself across the floor, and Leo was beating Finn, still in his wolf form, with a crowbar.

Moira's screams pulled me back to reality. Lacey collapsed to the floor with her head in her hands. The women behind me exchanged terrified looks.

"I have to get in there." I knelt next to Lacey.

She did her best to nod.

"Stay here with them." I stroked her hair.

I stood and turned to the women we had freed. "No matter what you hear, do not leave this hallway until me or one of my friends comes back."

"What if you don't come back?" A woman with a bruised face asked.

"One of us will. I promise."

I steeled myself before hurrying through the door.

The vision Lacey had shown me unfolded right before my eyes. The situation was dire. Who did I run to first?

Whimpering from Finn pulled me in his direction without conscious thought. Leo was raining blows on him with a crowbar one-handed, his left hand sickeningly limp at his side. I grabbed a broken beam that had fallen from the ceiling and sprinted, slipping on a puddle of blood from Big Dominic as I ran. I righted myself before using my momentum to swing the beam as hard as I could at the back of Leo's head. Leo gurgled and fell forward. I hit him three more times over the head with as much force as I could muster. The cracking, crunching sounds made my stomach turn.

When Leo stopped moving, I threw the beam to the side and knelt next to Finn. I ran my fingers through his soft fur and kissed the top of his head. My eyes scanned his large furry form to assess the damage.

"Finn, how bad is it?"

He whined in reply, his muzzle burrowing into my hand. Moira screamed again. Finn's eyes locked on mine. I could feel the tortured urging in his gaze. Without needing to hear the words, I knew he was telling me to leave him and go to her.

My heart split in two. The only thing that would keep Finn from going to Moira himself would be mortal wounding. He was in terrible shape. But if I didn't move now, I stood to lose my whole family to the terror of the penanggalan.

Another fierce, pleading look from Finn was all it took to get me to my feet. I jumped over him and raced toward Moira. I grabbed a discarded shovel and swung at the floating head. It made contact with an echoing clang, but she barely moved in response. Moira was on her knees screaming, the penanggalan's intestines wrapped around her arms, burning red welts into her skin. Tear tracks streaked Moira's dirty face. The penanggalan was grinning, gaze focused and furious.

A rage like I have never known rose inside at the sick pleasure Francesca was getting from torturing one of the sweetest people I had ever known. I swung the shovel again at her head. Another echo and again, no movement. She wouldn't let go.

Her intestines were wrapping around Moira's arm and slithered their way around her throat. My first thought was that she was going to strangle her. But the utter horror of Selsha's headless body haunted me even in waking. This was how the penanggalan beheaded her victims. She was going to kill Moira.

Chloe was screaming Moira's name as she continued to drag herself painfully across the floor. I had to stop the penanggalan. Andre was the only one still standing aside from me and he was still grappling with a struggling, screaming Lorenzo.

Attacking the head was useless, so I changed my tactics. With a guttural scream, I raised the shovel over my head and brought the sharp side down on the intestines dangling between the disembodied head and Moira's arms. Again and again, I hacked at them.

The penanggalan shrieked, and the intestines retracted. Blood spurted from sections I had mangled. She turned her horror on me, and Moira collapsed in a heap. I saw the intestines coming before they could reach my blood-soaked shoes. I dodged out of the way and swung as hard as I could at the head again. This time it knocked her off balance, wobbling several feet to the left. Dodging and swinging the shovel, I positioned myself between the penanggalan and Moira's body.

The penanggalan shrieked at me again, fury in every line of her face.

"Back the fuck off, you flying bitch," I yelled.

A gaping hole in the middle of her forehead made me retch. *Gunshot wound*, my mind registered. Someone had shot her in the head and nothing. How the hell was I going to kill this thing if the others couldn't?

I glanced over my shoulder, and Chloe was cradling Moira's body. She was sobbing and calling her name, running a gentle hand over the welts up and down her arms. When she looked up, we made eye contact. A few of my own tears escaped.

"Chloe, I don't know what to do," I called.

"Salt," Chloe cried. "SALT!"

"I don't know what that means!"

But I didn't have time to get more clarity. Finn's growl alerted me to turn back around. The penanggalan was on a speedy trajectory my way. Wielding the shovel, I tried to swat at her, but she blew right past me and straight at Chloe. Her entrails flipped through the air and wrapped around Chloe's throat. Chloe's hands shot up as she tried to free herself, her eyes bulging. I ran after the penanggalan, but Chloe shook her head at me.

"Salt," she gurgled.

I raised the shovel to attack the penanggalan once more, but before I could swing it, someone pulled the shovel from my hands. I whipped around, ready to fight, but was relieved to find Andre behind me. Lorenzo was across the room, lying flat on his back, glassy eyes wide with terror, unmoving.

"I've got this," Andre pushed me behind him.

"Chloe keeps saying 'salt.' What the hell does she mean?"

"I have no fucking idea, but you better figure it out quick. Not even a fucking bullet right between the eyes can stop this bitch." Andre started swinging at the penanggalan. "Hurry, Lex!"

I spun on the spot and started running through the massive space. Where the fuck was I going to find salt? Was there a kitchen? Should I go back through the door and look? Chloe's gagging sounds echoed around me. No, there wasn't time.

Frustrated and terrified, I shoved over a stack of crates, frantic in my search for something that could help us. But there was nothing but barrels of stinking fish. I kept running, kept searching as Andre's shouts became shriller. I cried as I ran, knowing that at any moment, Chloe would be dead, and it would be my fault.

I couldn't save her. I couldn't save any of them.

My toe snagged on something, and I crashed to the ground. My hands reached out to break my fall and collided painfully with scratchy cement. I swore, my palms pounding and aching immediately. My palms were bleeding, stinging, burning. The floor was gritty as I forced myself back to kneeling. Something was lodged in my bleeding palms. I picked at it.

Salt!

My eye caught on what I'd tripped on. It was a large bag of ice melt, the stuff I used to use for melting the snow in our driveway when I was a teenager. Sodium chloride; fucking salt!

The bag was already half empty. Despite the burning pain in both hands, I snatched it up and lifted it over my shoulder. Stumbling as I ran, I made it halfway back to Andre when I saw Lacey's little head bob through the door where I'd left her with the Bianchi's victims. Shit! Lacey wasn't a fighter. I waved her back, but she shook her head. When her eyes landed on her sisters, her face contorted. She moved like she was going to run to them, but stopped herself.

She came running to me instead.

"I told you to stay behind. You're not safe here," I chided.

Lacey pointed at the bag on my shoulder, then at the bodies of Francesca and Big Dominic. The echoing of the shovel strikes rang in my ears. She pointed to the bag and the bodies again.

"Do I pour salt on the bodies?" I asked.

She shook her head. She patted the top of her head and shook her head 'no' again. Then she grabbed at her neck and pointed down.

"Not on?"

Lacey made a circle with one hand, then mimed pouring something into it, like water into a cup. The realization hit me.

"Not on, IN!"

Lacey nodded so hard her shoulders shook.

"LEX, HURRY!" Andre shouted.

I ran at the bodies of Francesca and Big Dominic. It was a bloody, gruesome scene. I set the bag down and pulled Francesca's body into a seated position. Lacey scooted the bag of salt over to me, not able to lift it with her tiny frame. I retched at the smell of vinegar and gore seeping from Francesca's body.

As if the penanggalan could sense something was happening with her body, she shrieked an unholy shriek and released her hold on Chloe. She rocketed our direction. Andre swatted at her and gave chase.

"The salt, Lacey, hurry," I urged.

I held the body while Lacey cupped her hands and dipped into the bag of salt. The penanggalan was only feet away. My heart slammed in my chest. The penanggalan's bloodied entrails whipped out in front of her.

I released the body and pulled Lacey's head down as they snapped over us like a whip. They were so close that it blew my hair around my face as they sailed over our heads. I grabbed the body again, hauled it up, and held it tight, my whole body shaking with fear. The penanggalan's entrails were coiling back, preparing for another strike.

"Now, Lacey," I urged.

Lacey dumped the handful of salt into the penanggalan's empty neck cavity. The penanggalan shrieked but kept coming.

"More!"

Lacey scooped another handful and dumped it again. More shrieking. The penanggalan was slowing down. Lacey scooped and dumped over and over again, as quickly as her hands could move.

Just as the penanggalan was about to reach us, it fell to the floor with a thump. The disembodied head rolled to a stop at my side and continued to shriek in agony as a sizzling sound came from her neck. Smoke rose from the gaping hole. The shrieking stopped, and the penanggalan stared lifelessly at me from the ground.

It was over.

I pushed the body away in disgust, and Lacey helped me stand. My hands were burning like they'd been lit on fire, but it didn't stop me from pulling her into a tight hug. It was impossible for me to take my eyes off the penanggalan, though. That face would be seared into my memory, joining the ranks of Cam Gunner in my nightmares.

Andre skidded to a stop beside us and wrapped his arms around us both. His skin was slick with sweat. He kissed the top of Lacey's head, then mine.

"Thank the Gods," Andre huffed. "You fucking did it!"

I could feel the relief wash through me, but my mind immediately turned to Finn.

"The others!" I pulled out of Andre's hug and hurried over to Finn.

Andre raced over to Riel, and Lacey made her way to Chloe and Moira. I wished I could have eyes on every person I loved, but in this moment, I only had eyes for Finn. He was lying on the floor where I'd left him, but he'd shifted back into his human form. One arm was holding his ribs, and the other was stretched out in the direction I'd come from.

"Finn, honey, wake up," I knelt beside him, brushing his hair out of his face. But he didn't move. "Finn," I pleaded. "Come on, Grumpy Dragon, wake up!"

I lifted his wrist and felt for a pulse. My heart skipped a beat when I couldn't find it right away, but I moved my fingers a little more toward the center and found a faint rhythm. I put my fingers beneath his nose next and waited. Light, warm breath tickled the pads of my fingers. The tears of relief started to fall. He was alive! But he was injured. We had to get him to the hospital.

"Andre?" I called.

"Is that son of a bitch still alive?" Worry coated every syllable.

"Yes, but he's hurt. Riel?"

"It's bad. He's unconscious, but I can't see into his mind. He's slipping away. We've gotta get them outta here."

I swung around to find the sisters. Moira and Chloe were prone on the ground, Lacey kneeling between them. Her eyes were bright white and glowing. I watched in awe as she waved her hands from the tops of her sisters' heads to their feet and back again, over and over. Light filtered from her fingers and into their still bodies. After several passes, both Moira and Chloe took a heavy breath and sat up. Lacey threw her arms around their necks and cried silently. They cradled her in return. Moira and Chloe's bodies were covered in angry, red welts.

"Lex, you stay here with the others. I'm going to go see if it's clear outside. If the others are okay, they can help us with Finn and Riel." Andre gave my shoulder a squeeze and took a hitched breath as he looked down at Finn. "Don't go dying on me now, dumbass."

Andre hurried out of the warehouse. I held Finn's hand, running my fingers over his knuckles, kissing the back of his hand over and over. The full weight of what had happened settled heavy in my chest. I couldn't stop the wracking sobs that shook my shoulders.

"You can't leave me," I scolded Finn. "I just found you. We haven't had enough time yet. You promised me you were going to live forever. Don't lie to me about this one. Anything but this one."

The prospect of a future without Finn in it was excruciating. My whole life I'd ached for something like what we shared. Despite all the pain from his past, he let me in. He made me a part of his family, they all did. If his heart stopped beating tonight, I don't think mine would ever beat again.

"Stay with me." I laid my head on his bare shoulder.

His breathing was slowing. His chest barely moved at all. Purple bruises and red marks spotted his torso. Leo and the crowbar. God knows how much damage they did.

"You have to stay," I whispered. "You promised me. We were going to have beautiful Fae babies, remember?" My tears fell onto his face and slid down his cheeks.

Finn took one last small breath, then stilled.

My whole body was numb. I barely registered when Andre came running back into the warehouse with Vikram, Vijay, Ricky, and Donna all looking worse for the wear. Vikram and Vijay lifted Riel and hurried gingerly back out the door. It took Andre, Ricky, and Donna to lift Finn from the floor.

"You have to let him go, honey," Donna urged. "We've gotta go."

"I can't," I sputtered.

"You have to, sweetie." Donna pulled lightly on my arm, and I reluctantly released Finn's hand. It fell limply to his side.

My body shook with sobs as they carried him away. The sisters hurried over to me. Chloe and Lacey held me up as I tried to stagger after Finn. I could barely keep my feet.

"I'll go get those poor women," Moira said.

"Don't let them see all this," Chloe warned. "They might ask questions and Gods knows they've been traumatized enough."

Chloe and Lacey ushered me out of the warehouse. The dock was still wet from Donna's waves. When we rounded the corner, the cops were busy handcuffing the remaining human lackeys. They barely noticed us slipping through the shadows. We'd almost made it to the Charger when I heard the Chief call my name.

"Alexis." Chief hurried up behind us. "What the hell happened in there?" He pointed over his shoulder at the warehouse.

I opened my mouth to respond, but no words came. He examined my bruised face, bloodied hands, and shaking body. Chloe held my arm protectively.

"This is one of those things, isn't it?" Chief asked.

"What do you mean?" Chloe's eyes narrowed.

"One of those unexplainable things that happens around here more often than I care to admit," Chief replied boldly.

Chloe stiffened. But Chief's eyes were kind. The old man must know more than he ever let on. I swallowed hard and cleared my throat.

"Our friend Moira is bringing the women out." My voice was scratchy. "Thirty-seven victims in total. You'll take care of them?"

"Of course. I'll see to it personally that those women make it back to the station safely. Then we'll get them some accommodations until we can question them." Chief looked around the scene. "The Bianchis?"

"Dead. All four of them. In the warehouse. It's... it's going to be hard to explain the state of the bodies," I admitted.

Chief sighed. "Don't you worry about that. I'll take care of the cleanup. I'll call Briggs and Alvarez in the morning, and we'll take it from there. Get outta here, Alexis. We'll debrief later."

My heart lurched. I didn't have the words to tell him about Finn. I don't know if words like that even existed in any language.

Chloe and Lacey guided me to the Charger and helped me into the back seat. Chloe drove like a bat out of hell, all the while gripping Lacey's hand like her life depended on it. I leaned my head back and closed my eyes, breathing in Finn's familiar scent embedded in the leather upholstery. The tears returned with a vengeance. My whole body ached.

The reality of what happened was slamming against my consciousness. I gritted my teeth and tried to force the inevitable conclusion away. Instead of letting the emotional pain overcome me, I focused on the physical pain that wracked every inch of me: my back, my face, my hands, my knees…my everything.

When I opened my eyes, we were pulling into an all-too-familiar parking lot. But it wasn't the one I expected. Instead of the glaringly bright white lights of the hospital parking lot, Chloe was parking the Charger in the small lot outside the woods. My heart stopped. I'd been here once before tonight, and I almost hadn't made it back out.

Chloe and Lacey hurried out of the car. I recognized Vijay's hunter green Bronco and Ricky's obnoxiously yellow Mustang convertible already in the lot, empty of passengers. It was only when they realized I hadn't exited the backseat that Chloe turned around. She motioned frantically for me to follow. My limbs felt frozen.

"Come on, Alexis, we have to hurry if we're going to catch up to…" Chloe paused, hand resting on the now open back door. Her eyes unfocused for a split second, her face drawn and tired, then came back into focus. "Oh, Lex, I'm so sorry. I didn't even think…"

"Why are we here?" I rasped. "We need to get them to the hospital."

"This is where Riel and Finn need to be right now. The hospital will come later. But there is something they can get from here that no hospital on Earth can provide. Without this…" Chloe's breathing hitched. She cleared her throat, dabbed at her eyes, then went on, "If they can't connect them to the source here, our guys may never wake up again."

"What if it doesn't work…" The tears were flowing down my cheeks again.

"It has to," Chloe swallowed hard.

She reached out her hand to me. It was shaking. The stakes were high for us all, but in this moment, I wouldn't have gotten out of the car if it wasn't for Chloe. Although I knew that Cam Gunner was dead and gone, his specter felt heavy here, mere hours after he took me to end my life in the very woods we love so much. The smell of cigarettes haunted my nose still.

"Finn," Chloe reminded. "You can do this for Finn. Moira would tell you that you don't have to go in if you don't want to, but she's back there and I'm here. I'm telling you that you'll never forgive yourself if you don't get your ass in those woods now."

She was right. I knew she was. It didn't make it hurt less; it didn't make it easier, but it was true, and we both knew it. Finn came here for me. Now I was going to run into the dark for him. That's what love is: running into the unknown and praying you make it out together.

I tightened my hold on Chloe's hand, and without another word, we started running. My throat was tight, my lungs burned, but I ran. My body ached, my fear prickled, but I ran. *Finn*, I chanted to myself. *Finn. Finn. Finn.*

We burst through the last line of trees, and we were back in the clearing where we'd camped months ago. This is where I'd first started falling in love with

Finn. It was fitting. This is where I truly found him; I just prayed with everything in me that this wouldn't be the place where I lost him, too.

Andre and Vikram knelt next to Finn's body on the ground near the picnic table. They must have clothed him during the drive over. Chloe ran to where Ricky, Donna, and Vijay surrounded Riel a few feet away. The moment I saw Finn's ashen face, every other feeling inside me shrank to almost nothing. I was achingly familiar with fear, but the fear I felt seeing him still and broken was nothing I'd ever felt before. I came to the Clock with fear as my only companion. Finn had changed that for me. They all had.

"What can I do?" I fell to my knees by Finn's head.

"Talk to him, Lex," Andre replied. "Call him back."

He and Vikram were chanting something in another language. It was like a song, low and soft. Their deep voices ran goosebumps up my arms. They held each other's wrists, arms straight over Finn's body. The others were chanting, too.

I took Finn's hand and brought it to my lips, smoothing the skin of his knuckles with my kisses. He was so still. I held his hand tighter.

"Finn, don't you dare do this to us," I scolded. The pleading sorrow from before had become a fiery, angry refusal. "You have too much left to do here. You're not going anywhere, dammnit, so breathe."

The chanting continued. I felt the energy vibrating from the earth below me as my friends drew on the power from the woods. Chloe had her forehead pressed against Riel's. She was chanting loudest, hardest. Even Lacey's lips were moving in sync with the others, although I don't think any words were coming out.

"I'm not going to let you go. Do you hear me?" I continued. "We need you. All of us. You are going to leave whatever heaven you found on the other side and get your ass back here immediately."

Andre took my hand. My body gave a jolt as the power he and Vikram were channeling surged through me, too. It ran up and down my spine, circulating through every space, sparking every cell to attention.

"Keep talking," Vikram urged.

"Andre would hate having to partner with anyone else at work. You know how anti-social he is."

Andre snorted a laugh through his chanting.

"Vijay and Vikram need you, too. Who else is going to eat through an entire bowl of abandoned potato salad next New Year's?"

Vikram's lip twitched up at the corner. The chanting was growing louder all around me. Chloe was watching me with wet eyes.

"Chloe needs you. There're a million snarky fights she still needs to have, and no one else pisses her off as well as you do. Moira needs to fuss over you. Lacey needs you to finish teaching her how to play pool. Riel needs you to help him keep an eye on the Fae, so they're safe here like they deserve."

Chloe held my wrist as I continued to grasp Finn's hand, fingers interlaced. The tingling surge inside me intensified. Vikram held onto Andre, still with one arm, reaching across the small gap between Finn and Riel, and took Vijay's hand.

We were all connected. The chanting was at full volume now. The only words I could make out of the foreign sounds were Finn and Riel's names. I wasn't the only one calling to him.

"And *I* need you. I need you to roll your eyes at me when I convince you to let me eat in your car. I need you to slow-dance with me to my favorite songs at the Pony, even though you hate dancing. I need you to hold me when my nightmares keep me up at night. I need you to tell me stories about all the centuries you've been on this Earth before me and all the years that we'll be here together."

Tears slid down my aching cheeks. I could feel the pleas each of my friends were silently making through the power coursing through us. Images from our past as a mismatched family flashed vividly through my mind. I could feel the love saturating these moments through the eyes and hearts of each one of my friends. Distinctly different waves of power brushed across my skin, each of them feeling unique to the powers of these incredible people.

Wind whipped around us, howling through the trees. My body shook with the intensity of what they were drawing from the ground beneath us. My knuckles were white from my grip.

"Now PUSH!" Andre shouted.

The power that had been circulating through us built to a crescendo. My friends grunted and shouted, chanted and yelled as I felt that power pull in from the other side of our circle and collect in me and Chloe. My ears popped and my voice joined the yells of its own accord. Every ounce of what they'd pulled from the woods filtered through Chloe and I, down into Finn and Riel, where we each clutched the men we loved. Where Finn and I's hands were joined, I felt the burning surge pass through me and into him. Without knowing how, I knew that Chloe's hand on Riel's chest felt the same.

The flood of power seemed to last forever. I screamed Finn's name and heard Chloe yell for Riel. One last rush of power washed over me, and then it stopped.

Finn and Riel simultaneously jackknifed into a sitting position, gasping for breath. Finn's intense green eyes popped open and immediately searched his surroundings until they landed on mine. His arms shot out, pulling me into his lap. He cradled me against his chest, breathing in the scent of my hair, as his fingers clutched at my back and waist.

"Alexis," Finn panted. "Siren."

I let the sheer weight of this horrific day collapse on top of me. I cried the hardest I ever had in my life. Finn held me and rocked me. I reached out for Andre and pulled him into our embrace. He was crying, too.

When most of my tears were spent, I pulled away to examine Finn's face. It was still pale. He was wincing in pain, but he was alive! I drew him into a deep kiss, and he responded eagerly. Not a single thought for our onlooking friends. He feasted on my mouth like a starving man. When I pulled away, it was my turn to be breathless.

"I heard you," Finn whispered, brushing my hair back from my face. "I heard you calling to me." He chuckled. "Little Siren, not even Death can resist your call."

"Good," I hiccupped. "You tell that asshole to stay away. You're mine."

"And you're mine, Alexis. I love you."

"I love you, too."

Finn cradled my face in his hands. "I need you, too, love. I need you to tell me when I'm being an arrogant asshole. I need you to help me loosen up and enjoy myself. I need you to deface my work notebook with your doodles. And I need you to carry my children, our children, and love us for the rest of our days together."

"Fae babies?" A smile lifted at the corner of my mouth.

The beautiful, familiar, mischievous glint sparkled in his eyes. "You bet your fine ass we're making Fae babies." He chuckled, which was immediately followed by a groan.

"Maybe you all should wait on making me an uncle until after we get you to the hospital," Andre quipped.

"Valid point," I nodded, brushing my fingers across Finn's chest.

"It's time to let your girl go so we can take you to see your favorite nurse," Andre prompted, holding out a hand to help me up.

Finn's gaze burned into me. "Never," he replied. "I'm never letting this one go."

Chapter Thirty-Five

Finn

Nurse Linda almost had a conniption when she walked into my recovery room and found Alexis and I once again in her expert care. Thirteen broken ribs, a punctured lung, and a ruptured spleen were the only injuries left after my friends brought me back from death. The power they'd channeled from the woods and pushed into Riel and I had healed everything else before we'd even pulled into the ER bay.

When I woke up from surgery, Alexis was sleeping on the couch next to my hospital bed. God, she was the most beautiful thing on the planet. I watched her sleep, the love I felt for her swallowing the pain and the pull of what was left of the anesthesia. I ached to call out her name, coax her onto the bed with me so I could hold her. But I held my tongue. After what she had been through yesterday, she needed her sleep.

The last few moments of consciousness I'd had before succumbing to my injuries in that fucking warehouse were filled with Alexis. The penanggalan was heading straight for her and I couldn't stop it. I couldn't protect her. But she had saved herself. She had saved all of us.

After passing out, I still felt her presence before it all went blank for a while. She had been speaking to me. I couldn't make out what she said, but the pain in her voice tore holes through my insides. I tried to make my way back to her, but I couldn't.

It wasn't until they started calling for me in the woods that I was able to find myself again. I was somewhere else, somewhere indistinct, when I heard her voice. My eyes weren't working, but I heard her loud and clear. I followed her voice through the darkness until I felt a power beyond anything I've ever known lift me into the air and force me back into my body. Pain exploded from my battered shell, but there she was: Alexis. She was my peace, my calm, my love, and my life.

She lay on the uncomfortable hospital couch, just ten feet away from me now, but it felt like miles. I cleared my throat. She stirred. I couldn't help it. I was a selfish bastard.

"Finn?" Her voice was joy and relief. "I'm sorry, I must have dozed off. Are you okay? Are you in pain? Do you want me to call…"

"Shh, baby. It's okay. All I want right now is you." I held my arms out to her.

Once she was in my arms, I could breathe again. "I'll never get tired of the way you smell," I sighed.

"Well, I haven't been able to shower for a couple of days, so take it all in, baby," she teased.

I tipped her chin up and kissed her. "I'll never get tired of the way you taste, either."

"Good," she purred, kissing me again. "Because you have a hell of a lot of tasting left to do, and so do I."

She slipped her tongue in my mouth, and I groaned. My cock twitched. Glad to see *that* was still working. I tried pulling her closer, but my ribs protested, so I settled for running my hands under her shirt and around the bare skin of her sides and back. My wolf whined internally. We both wanted to devour her.

"God, I need you right now," I moaned into her mouth.

"We have plenty of time, love," she smiled.

Despite my repeated protests of never knowing which breath would be our last, Alexis convinced me that sex would have to wait until I was in better shape. My consolation prize was a hell of a lot of kissing and groping, though. Having almost lost everything that we shared, my fingers thirsted for her touch and drank like men trapped in the desert for decades when they found her again.

A sharp rap on the door pulled us apart. I was hard as a rock and pissed about the disruption. I fucking hated the hospital if for no other reason than the constant interruptions. Alexis slid out of my bed, tossing a pillow over my crotch with a cheeky grin, and settled back on the couch.

"You have no idea the things I'm going to do to you when I'm back on top, Siren," I growled.

"I look forward to finding out," she winked.

The sharp knock came again. I gritted my teeth, rubbed at my erection, and leaned back in bed. "Come in," I barked.

"Glad to see that you're still in one piece, kid," Chief Whitmer came around the privacy curtain. My irritation abated instantly. I needed to know what happened, every detail.

"Chief, what's the situation?"

"I don't want you to worry about that, right…"

"I'm not going to rest until I know."

Chief glanced at Alexis, and she nodded. She was probably just as eager to hear the news as I was. As we drove from the woods to the hospital, she'd talked to Moira on the phone. All the women who had been trafficked by the Bianchis were safe. That was the most important thing.

"Where do you want me to start?" Chief rubbed the bridge of his nose.

"From the minute I left the station to find Alexis." I reached out a hand to Alexis, and she took it.

"We finished setting up the raid. Olivier was picking up too much at the station, so I sent Olivier and Lot on a wild goose chase to keep that piece of shit in the dark. Lot had no idea Olivier was dirty; he took it pretty hard. We cut off our comms so Olivier wouldn't catch wind of what we were up to. I'm sure he would have fed us to the wolves. But they knew we were coming, anyway. Maybe he already passed word."

"It was a trap, Chief. They knew," Alexis confirmed.

"Did the Bianchis say so?"

"No," Alexis swallowed hard, and I squeezed her hand. "Cam Gunner did. He's related to the Bianchis. He bragged about being one of their hitmen and going after women that escaped the Clock."

"Holy Mother of God…" Chief shook his head. "Poison fruit doesn't fall far from the rotten tree, does it?"

"No," I spat. "And now that we're on the topic of poison fruit, we have a marshal that needs handling. He got pocketed by the Bianchis, too. That's why he sent Alexis here to the Clock."

"That rancid son-of-a-bitch!" Chief's jaw muscle twitched. "I swear I didn't know."

"I know." Alexis took a deep breath. "Otherwise, you wouldn't have sent Finn and Andre to save me."

"Don't you worry, we'll get that fucker," Chief vowed. "What about Gunner?"

"Dead," I confirmed. "He…uh… was attacked by an animal in the woods right after we got there."

"An animal, huh? Just like Alexis was mauled by a bear?" Chief's eyes sparkled with suppressed suspicion.

"What happened at the warehouse?" I dodged.

"Like I said, they were waiting for us." Chief allowed the redirect, but I could feel the questions building in the wily old man. "Both me and the negotiator tried talking the lackeys out of the way, but they were armed to the hilt. We had to hold for a long time, trying to convince them to let us patch in a call to the big boss. They weren't budging. Then something really strange happened…"

Hiro's illusion. How the hell was I supposed to explain that? I hadn't talked to her about it, so I had no idea what they'd been shown. After being hauled out of the warehouse, I had no idea what scene we had left them in the aftermath, either.

"What strange thing?" Alexis asked, a little too innocently.

"They all surrendered out of nowhere, but when I checked my watch, over an hour had gone by. I'm not one to sleep on the job, but it felt like just that, like I'd been asleep that whole time and woke up to a pack of dirtbags giving up and lining up for the squad cars."

Chief eyed me, waiting for my response. I held my tongue and nodded. With no answers coming, Chief went on.

"That's when I saw you coming out." He motioned to Alexis. "When you told me the state of the Bianchis's bodies was going to be hard to explain, you weren't kidding."

Shit. Without Riel or me to facilitate a clean-up, Chief and the squad had walked right into a Fae murder scene. We were going to have to get a handle on things immediately.

"By the look on your face, Briggs, something tells me I don't want to know the actual explanation. There are things going on here in the Clock that defy normal explanation, aren't there?"

I looked at Alexis. She pursed her lips and gave a small shrug. She wasn't going to say anything. I knew she would protect our secret no matter what. But the Chief knew something. Maybe he'd known something for a lot longer than he'd let on. I struggled with the weight of the moment. Do I let on? Can we trust him? As the seconds stretched out between us, I made a call; one that I hoped I wouldn't regret.

"Yes, sir. There are."

Alexis's eyes went wide. She squeezed my hand. I squeezed back hard, both to reassure her and to steady myself.

"I can't tell you much. It's not mine to tell. But there are forces beyond human understanding. The Clock is... unique, and so are some of its residents. Myself included."

"Alexis?"

I didn't expect the laugh that exploded out of her. She gave the Chief a genuine smile and shook her head. "I'm as normal as you, sir."

"Alvarez?"

I didn't respond.

"Alright." Chief adjusted his holster. "I've had a feeling for a long time. This complicates things a bit, but I bet I've got you and those special residents to thank for a lot of the good that happens in this city."

"Unfortunately, a lot of the bad, too," I sighed.

"The Bianchis?"

I nodded this time.

"Well, ya'll saw to that problem, too."

"Chief, it's vital that no one else..."

But Chief held up a hand to stop me. "I've lived too long and seen too much to look a gift horse in the mouth. You've already confirmed my suspicions, and I don't need much more than that. I trust you and Alvarez to keep doing what you've been doing and keeping things straight. I'll come up with answers that'll satisfy the big wigs. It won't be hard seeing as how they'll be claiming all the credit for wiping out the Bianchis before the next election; the how doesn't much matter to them. I talk, you keep those special folk in line. Fair?"

"More than fair, sir." Relief washed over me.

"And you, my dear," he rounded on Alexis. She flinched. "Unless you plan on heading back home to your family now that Gunner is out of the picture, I'd like to offer you a full-time job with us. We couldn't have done any of this without you."

My heart stopped. I hadn't even considered the possibility that Alexis would leave the Clock. But the Chief had a point. Whatever life she had before this one, it was ready and waiting for her to return now that she was safe to do just that. I stared at her face, eagerly awaiting her response.

"I'm already home. My family is here." Alexis gave me a radiant smile, and my stomach did a backflip. "I'll gladly accept your offer, Chief."

"Happy to hear it. Well, I've got a jail overloading with lackeys, a morgue full of hard-to-explain bodies, and an entire police force to debrief. You two take whatever the hell's left of your sick leave and stay out of my station for a few weeks. I've got work to do."

Chief patted me on the arm and gave Alexis a tired smile, then left.

"I can't believe you told him." Alexis sat next to me on the bed.

"I didn't feel like I had much of a choice. Without me or Riel to smooth things over before the cops saw the scene, we're in desperate need of someone on the inside to help. Chief is the only man I can trust for the job. Do you think I made a mistake?"

"No, I don't. If Chief's known about the Fae to some degree, he's had plenty of time to take advantage of that knowledge. He hasn't," she shrugged. "He didn't press you for more, so I think you can call it safe for now. Maybe he'll have more questions down the road."

"Maybe…"

"But that's a problem for future-Finn. Right now, we have to focus on getting you better…again." She furrowed her brows in mock annoyance.

"It's not my fault that I keep ending up here," I waved around the room.

"I'm certainly not complaining! I had a taste of the alternative and, I have to say, I wasn't a fan. You're not allowed to die, Finn Briggs, and that's that."

I chuckled, snaking one arm around her waist and pulling her back down beside me.

"It's hard to slay a dragon," I reassured. "Especially one with a siren to protect it."

"Damn right," she agreed.

"Are you really going to stay?" I whispered, a small nagging bit of doubt consuming me.

"You really think I would go through all this just to pack up and leave tomorrow? You've got another think coming, wolfy. I've earned my place in the Clock, and you'll have to do more than pretend to date a succubus this time to get me out of here."

"Don't remind me," I groaned.

"It's okay, I'm just teasing," she reassured. "I'm staying, Finn. I meant what I said to the Chief. You're my family. And we've got a lot of living to enjoy together."

"Starting now." I nuzzled into her neck and breathed her in. "Honeysuckle," I sighed.

"I love you, too, creep," she chuckled.

"I love you, Alexis."

My stay in the hospital was short. As usual, my own powers, magnified by the power imbued in me by my friends, sped up my healing process. Nurse Linda threatened to retire if she saw either of us back at the hospital within the next year. I joked that the only reason we'd want to come back would be to bring a new life into the world, not to save one. She got teary-eyed and shooed us away into the Charger.

The second we got back to my place, I carried Alexis to my bed, and we stayed there for days. We made love constantly, never seeming to get enough from each other. After a little persuading, Alexis called the sisters and told them they were going to have to find a new roommate because she was moving in with me. They'd already started the process. We should have known. Despite our mutual eagerness to start a family, we decided to hold off on trying for kids so we could enjoy each other for a while.

"As much as I would love to continue living in our love nest," Alexis gestured to my messy bed... our messy bed, "We promised that we'd meet everyone at the Pony."

I stretched my arms over my head, popping my back. There was no persuading her. I watched her dress in a pair of comfortable jeans and a simple blue tank top. Since my quick foray into the underworld, I found pure bliss in memorizing every tiny intricacy of my life, especially Alexis. Gratitude was my new best friend, and I had it in spades for her.

The Pony was nearly empty of regulars by the time we arrived. The last few stragglers were paying their tabs and stumbling to the door. Our friends were all waiting for us. Riel stood behind the bar looking more frail than usual, but better than he had when we last saw him at the hospital. Chloe was back with him; she had taken over running the logistics at the Pony until Riel was back to 100%. Everyone greeted us with enormous smiles, and it made me happy to see how much joy that simple gesture brought Alexis.

"You're here!" Moira clapped her hands together. She gave us each a quick hug. "We have something for the both of you! Come sit down, Alexis."

Alexis sat on the stool Moira waved her into. Everyone created a circle around her, with the sisters right in front of her. I realized what was coming and how much it would mean to Alexis.

"Why do I feel like we've done this before?" Alexis raised an eyebrow.

"Because we have," Chloe replied. "But we didn't get a chance to participate last time. Now we want to make it right."

Moira, Chloe, and Lacey took several steps forward, hands entwined.

"I am Moira, seer of the past."

"I am Chloe, seer of the present."

"She is Lacey, seer of the future," Moira and Chloe intoned.

"We three are one," Moira added.

"We are the apportioners, the spinners, the alloters, the unturnable," Chloe continued.

"We have guarded the destinies of humankind since time immemorial. We are the Fates," Moira smiled. "And we are beyond blessed to know you and count you as one of our own, Alexis."

"I'm sorry we didn't make ourselves known to you sooner." Chloe took Alexis's hand. "That was my fault. You have proven yourself true at every turn. Forgive me for not having more faith in you."

"There's nothing to forgive." Alexis pulled Chloe in for a hug. Moira and Lacey joined in. "Thank you for trusting me with your whole selves."

Taylor sniffled, and I saw Donna wipe a tear.

"Now, it's my turn." Alexis hopped off the stool and stood before the group. "My name is Alexis Henson. They sent me to the Clock as a part of the Witness Protection Program. The man who tried to take my life failed in more ways than one. Not only did I survive him twice, but he also inadvertently gave me a life better than I ever could have imagined by getting me sent here. Thank you for opening your hearts to me and accepting me as your own. It means more to me than I think any of you know."

"Group hug!" Donna yelled.

I shook my head but joined in, anyway. Maybe I would have thought something like this was ridiculous before, but what the hell? I could be grateful for ridiculous, too.

"Okay, okay," Andre called. "Enough with the mushy stuff. Let's get down to brass tacks." He turned to me, placing a hand on my shoulder. "We have a bet going. Who are you and Alexis going to make Faefather and Faemother of your kids? I know that I'm a shoo-in, but some of the others disagree."

Everyone laughed.

I flicked Andre's fedora off center and patted his cheek. "All in good time, my man."

"A round of drinks for the family," Ricky called.

Hiro thumped the jukebox and "We are Family," by Sister Sledge played. She grinned, clearly pleased with herself.

Chloe returned to Riel's side behind the bar and gave him a gentle kiss. He lit up. I was glad I wasn't the only one getting a happy ending. They deserved each other.

As our friends fell into the peaceful rhythm of one another's company, I pulled Alexis into my arms. She kissed the tip of my nose.

"Are you happy, little Siren?"

"No," she replied.

I gave her a suspicious look.

A grin spread across her face. "I'm beyond happy. Happy doesn't even begin to describe how I feel." She nestled closer in my embrace. "Are you happy, grumpy dragon?"

"No," I purred in her ear.

She laughed.

"I'm yours. Eternally, wholly, and completely yours. That's way better than happy ever could be."

* * *

About the Author

Professional by day, author by night, Haven Wynne is a lover of fiction, the smell of old books, rolling library ladders, and cozy reading nooks. She believes there is nothing more magical than the chance to live a thousand lifetimes through the pages of good novels. She enjoys all things creative, deep conversations, belly laughs, and delicious food. As an introverted extrovert, she spends her time balancing soaking up the complexity of the human experience and immersing herself in fiction. Her day job as a mental health professional gives her a unique perspective on people and relationships, and she loves using that perspective in building characters you love or love to hate. When she isn't stuck between the pages of a book (writing her own or reading others), she happily resides in the suburbs of the mountainous Western United States with her husband, children, and dutiful pup.

🌐 www.havenwynne.com

♪ @havenwynneauthor